IF I FELL

A DEEP PSYCHOLOGICAL THRILLER

JOHN MANCHESTER

1

"Bob?" At first I thought it was a wrong number. Nobody had called me Bob in a long time. I was Bodine.

"Bob Hutchinson?"

"Yeah. Who's this?" The voice sounded familiar. The dying AC in my office in the theater's old projection booth cycled on with a roar. "Hold on." I could turn it off, but with this August humidity, the computers wouldn't like it. I stood and headed to the theater. Opened the door and hot, musty air blasted me in the face. Mingus lifted his furry head, raised a bleary eye, and glanced mournfully down into the dark hall. I squatted to give his ears a squeeze, but he'd already given up and collapsed onto his bed. They didn't call them dog days for nothing.

I closed the door, stepped downstairs into the dark, and sat on the bottom step. "Sorry."

"It's Buzzy."

"Well, I'll be dipped in shit. Knew I recognized your voice. It's been a while."

"Forty years, actually."

"Not exactly. Thirty-eight years, three months, and—"

Buzzy laughed. "You're still Mr. Precise."

A comfortable silence. We'd picked up right where we left off.

"Waldo's dead."

"Damn." The news kicked me out of my head, into sensations. The T-shirt, already damp against my chest in the minute I'd been down here. Light from the office streaming down through the old projection slots, glinting on the brass and gleaming on the glass of neatly lined museum cases housing my private collection.

I pulled myself back to the call. "Waldo. Oh man, that's terrible. How did you find out?"

"His wife, Jeannie, called me. It happened a few days ago."

"What happened?"

"He fell."

I gripped the phone tighter. "Fell? In the bathtub or something?"

"Off a cliff."

"No."

"Into the ocean, not..."

Into a snowbank, at the height of a blizzard? No, it was August. And it wasn't 1969. It was 2007. My lungs seized up. My mind squeezed down to a single word. The same one Buzzy had to be thinking.

Angela.

I glanced at the wall, still graced by Art Deco arabesques and sconces from when this was a working theater.

I closed my eyes and tumbled into the past. To the night Angela had gone missing, with its endless, swirling snow. A million flakes, every one a different color and size to a mind chemically blasted past the edges of the known universe.

I leapt forward a few months to that spring, the day they found Angela's body. Buzzy was in the kitchen, telling me, "We need to talk," but I was already out of there, out of that house and out of that life. I got in my car and drove away. That was the last time I saw him.

I opened my eyes, stood, and started pacing the aisle between the first two rows of display cases in my odd museum.

Buzzy asked, "You OK?" It was as if he'd heard my thoughts.

Lighten up the conversation. "How've you been all this time?"

"I've been a lot of things. Right now I'm happy to be alive. And very sad."

"Yeah." Sorrow was the right feeling, but all I had was this knot in my chest. I stared into the nearest case, at a yellowed wedding dress still in desiccated cellophane, never worn. Now *there* was sad.

"And you? How have you been?"

"Fine. Just fine. It's good to hear your voice."

"And yours."

I laughed.

"What?"

"Your voice *sounds* like mine—kind of cooled out." Except it was the other way around. I sounded like him because I'd looked up to him from the moment we met and wanted to be like him.

"Hey, we all kind of got cooled out that year."

It wasn't just his voice I'd been carrying all these years. I'd been looking up to him all this time. Still was. "Where you living?"

"I'm still in sleepy old Middleburg. Never managed to leave the nest. But Waldo was living his dream. San Francisco. Remember how he was always talking about it?" Buzzy paused. "There's a service out there tomorrow. I know it's short notice, but I had trouble finding you. Maybe I'll see you there?"

"Maybe. I have to see what I've got going on—"

"Sure."

"But this has been good." Really good.

"It has." And Buzzy didn't lie about stuff like that.

"Have you talked to Rick?"

"Email. I got his from the alumni office. They didn't have a thing on you."

"Figures. I was only there the one year. So how'd you find me?"

"I didn't think of it until this morning. Google, of course." He clicked off. What the hell. Google? No "of course" about it.

***

I scrambled upstairs into the relative cool of the office. Mingus got up and stared at me—*what's wrong?* I raced to the computer, Googled "Bodine Hutchinson."

I'm not one of those people who obsessively search for themselves online. In fact, I'd only done it once, a couple years ago. And come up with the same single hit as now. My name was buried in a blog post about bands of the early '70s. A crummy posed photo of The Nightcrawlers, listing Ray on guitar, Frank on drums, Bassman on bass, and "keyboardist and lead singer Bodine Hutchinson." There was a scanned article about us from some long-defunct rock mag, hardly *Rolling Stone*, the writing somehow breathless and bored silly at the same time. Ancient history.

Buzzy hadn't gotten my phone number from that. I tapped my forehead. He didn't know me as Bodine. I tried "Bob Hutchinson." There were a mess of them. "Robert Hutchinson." Robert the attorney. Robert the woodworker. Some LinkedIn Robert. And fourth down the results, me.

What the fucking hell.

It was a website, a cheap-shit thing with cheesy retro '50s fonts. Stock cartoon figures of a grinning guy and gal from the same era, their thumbs up. Happy customers.

Pesky computer problems? Just call Bodine.

A list of my clients. The legal ones and a few of the others. Neither of which anyone in the world should know about.

Robert "Bodine" Hutchinson. Hudson, NY. Computer expert.

How did they know I was Robert? Or Bodine, for that matter? How did they get my phone number? How did they have any of it?

I'd been living for years under the radar. No phone listing. No Facebook. No nothing. My mailing address was a PO box. The only souls that even knew I was in Hudson were my buddy Ray and a few ex-girlfriends. Maintaining a low profile wasn't really about the fact that I'm not always quite on the right side of the law. It's just my nature. Probably some dark psychological explanation. I never bothered with such stuff.

But this website had me freaked. As if I were suddenly parading down the middle of Warren Street—Hudson's Main—without a stitch of clothing. Worse. On the inconceivable occasion that I found myself naked in public, I'd survive it.

No guarantee I'd survive this.

I stood and went over to the theater's old pump organ, sat, and silently fingered the keys, as I do when I'm thinking hard.

It couldn't have come from one of my corporate clients. They knew me only as "Bodine." They didn't have my phone number, just a deeply secure email address. They came to me via word of mouth as their last option, with security issues so embarrassing that they were as interested as I was in keeping things quiet.

But that was just the legit side of my business. Between paying gigs I played digital Robin Hood. I went after asshole companies that willfully spewed poison into the atmosphere, and people's bodies and minds. I slipped into their financial accounts and silently bled them, so little they wouldn't notice on a daily basis. Diverted the proceeds into anonymous donations to the good guys. Green energy, prison reform. I wasn't fooling myself. It was just a drop in the bucket. But it was my drop.

I was well aware of the dangers of do-gooding. So I abided strictly by two rules: Never take a dime for myself, and never brag about it.

I didn't worry about getting caught. None of my targets had the technical IQ to ever know anyone had been pilfering, let alone that it was me.

But it was too easy, and I got bored. I started going after black-hat hackers. Somebody had to. Neither the cops nor even the FBI had the chops to stop them. Messing with cyber crooks was dangerous. These guys knew their stuff. Piss some of them off and they might steal my identity, a mega hassle. Piss off others, and I could end up floating in the Hudson River, an arm in Poughkeepsie and my head under the Tappan Zee Bridge. But I wasn't worried. I was very good. And very careful.

Until Brickman.

This had to be him. My eyes darted around, like he was looking in the window, lurking in the corner.

No time for him now. If I was going to this funeral, I had to get moving. I went online and booked the only affordable flight that would get me there on time. It left at six a.m.

Mingus raised an eyelid a crack and went back to sleep. It was hard to know what made dogs so tired when they slept all day. The vet calls him a "large tan hound." He eats, poops, lumbers around for a few minutes, then crashes. But he should never be mistaken for dumb. He knew I was just headed to Ray's.

I walked through the theater to the only currently usable door to the place, the old emergency exit. Headed to Warren Street, where the only reminder there'd ever been a working theater here was a scar where the marquee had hung above the now-chained public doors.

I walked up Warren, away from the river, past a dozen dusty antiques shops and newer art galleries. It was almost seven in the evening, but the sun was still fully cranked, beating buzz rolls on my head. It had been a brutal summer. With Hudson so close to the river, the air was positively gummy, as if the hot, thirsty sky had sucked up half the river. At the bodega I bought a six-pack of Ray's new favorite beer, Magic Hat, and carried it to his place.

His house was a tall, thin Victorian. The name of his art gallery, Ray of Darkness, was painted in gothic script on the picture window. I averted my eyes from whatever monstrosity was displayed there that week. I opened the door, jangling the discordant bells. Ray was seated behind his desk at his laptop.

He was tall and skinny, like his house. Scuffed leather jacket, ragged salt-and-pepper hair, leaning toward the salt. Between his messy looks and his mess of a life, he didn't make much sense until you saw him pick up a guitar. Like a magic wand, it transformed him into a confident master, a rock star whose incandescent solos had him owning whatever room he was in—whether a concert hall or this weird gallery.

But these days he wrote, working on some vague book project—but mostly he blogged. Before that it was art. I couldn't help thinking, what a waste of those hands.

Ray looked at me and raised his eyebrows. "What's up?"

I rarely visited him. He often came to the theater with his latest life conundrum, or when I got lucky, with his guitar.

"How's the writing going?"

He scowled and slammed his laptop shut. Smiled. "Already better. Actually, I was reading right-wing blogs. Useless fuckwits."

As I'd feared, *fuckwits* was Ray's new word of the month. Though I supposed it was a little easier on the ear than last month's *shitwad*.

"Torturing yourself, as usual," I said.

"Not as bad as writing. Hey, this is an essential part of my work."

Was it? I supposed if you blogged it might be. You'd think with the thirty-eight years I'd known him I'd be used to how loud he was. Not shouting loud, but wearing his heart on his sleeve loud. And on his pant cuffs, and on a lanyard around his neck.

He smiled at the beer. "What's that for? Aside from drinking."

"Down payment on a favor."

He grabbed the six-pack and headed toward the stairs. I took the laptop from his desk and followed at my measured pace, threading my way through the thicket of sculptures, doing my best to ignore them. I have boring taste in art—bright colors and pleasing shapes. Though I know Ray is talented, his "sculptures" seem closer to horror movie props than museum pieces.

Ray clanked up the Art Nouveau spiral staircase. Ten years ago—when he and his ex, Liz, had moved in—*it* had been pleasing, a thicket of metal greenery. Now it was a mass of rust.

When I reached him in the kitchen he'd already opened one of the beers, probably not his first of the evening. He handed me one. We stood leaning against countertops.

He said, "What's this favor?"

"Can you come feed Mingus for a few days?"

"Of course. I like your dog. Where you going?"

"Funeral."

"A musician?"

I shook my head.

"Oh no, not one of your exes?"

"No. One of the Four Brothers."

"Four Brothers? Remind me."

"At Middleburg College, back the year you and I met, I was living with three friends—Buzzy, Waldo, and Rick—in this decommissioned frat house. Theta Epsilon Phi Foe Fum. Gamma Lamma ding-dong or whatever."

"I remember. Big ugly old thing."

I nodded. "You were there a couple of times. When we moved in, the place was abandoned. It was totally trashed. Street people crashing there, using the furniture for firewood, pissing in the fireplaces. We kicked them out, cleaned the place up, more or less, and called it home."

Ray said, "*I* was a street person. Didn't go to no fancy-pants college."

"You were a *musician.*"

"Hey, at least I played the guitar, not some wussy keyboard."

"Touché. The Four Brothers was our joke. We weren't related by blood. We were way too hip to ever dream of joining a fraternity. But we *were* brothers in The Movement."

I paused, and Ray must have sensed something because he stopped pacing.

"Waldo just died."

"Oh, man. Sorry to hear that."

"Thanks. You remember that blizzard in February of '69, the year we met?"

"I don't know. All I remember is freezing my ass off in the place I was crashing that winter."

"It snowed for a hundred hours straight. Major disaster, power lines down, roads a mess. So we decided to do our part to help out."

Ray raised a hand. "What, you went out shoveling?"

"No, we all dropped a megadose of acid."

Ray laughed. "On the theory that you'd make the snow just go away, same as those freaks trying to levitate the Pentagon that time."

Now I laughed. "No. Our theory was that we just wouldn't care." I turned serious. "The acid was only the beginning. Even though it was coming down like a bastard, and we hadn't even heard a plow come by in hours, the cops somehow got up to campus and busted the four of us. Hauled us to the station. I suppose it was a blessing that we were past peaking. Except we were still whacked. Jail isn't what old Tim Leary would call an ideal 'set and setting.'"

"Middleburg cops. Useless fuckwits, in the vernacular." His vernacular. "How come I never heard about that bust? It's not like Middleburg was some teeming metropolis. And the grapevine was always humming with shit like that."

"That's the thing. There were never any charges. They simply let us walk. And Rick was a dope dealer."

"That doesn't make sense."

"No. We figured they'd screwed up the search warrant or something. Even so, the whole thing was weird, even for a majorly weird time. Which is why it took us a few days to realize the most important thing: that someone had gone missing that weekend." Her name had gone unspoken in the conversation with Buzzy. It stuck in my throat now. "Angela."

"I don't remember her."

"Waldo had a thing with her, but she...dumped him for another guy, around Thanksgiving. We hadn't seen her much until that night. She was there at some point during the trip—" I winced.

My tale was winding Ray up, had him pacing from one end of the kitchen to the other. I leaned back against the marble counter.

"Anyway, a week or so later it became clear that she was *gone*. There was a rumor that after the blizzard she'd had it with winter and split for California. It made sense. Folks were dropping out of school right and left. But it soured the atmosphere in the house. After that weekend we all stopped tripping. Months passed and we'd almost forgotten about Angela." Some of us, that is. "You remember Garnet Hill?"

"I heard about it."

"On the edge of campus, the steep side with a cliff facing west. It was a thing that year, getting high there, rooting around for garnets in the rocks, waiting for the sunset. By late spring the snow had melted, except for a deep pile at the foot of the cliff. With the warm days it had been steadily shrinking. First really fine day some poor kid went up there, got baked, and happened to look down. There was Angela's face, sticking out of the snow."

"Oh, man. She fell?"

"Yeah. They didn't think she suffered too long. Still."

"I can't believe you never told me about this."

"It's not something I like to remember."

"Hmm. What was she doing up there in the middle of a blizzard?"

"That hill was sacred to us pagan acid-gobblers. We could see someone getting high and going there to enhance their trip. What's spooky is that Waldo died...the same way," I explained.

Ray stopped pacing and looked at me. "If you consider water the same as snow. And if you ignore that it happened three thousand miles away, and forty years later. What it is, is a nasty coincidence."

"Yeah."

"You never told me about the Four Brothers, either."

I sighed and sat at the kitchen table. Ray slid into a chair across from me. "That Angela business was like our Altamont. The end of the dream. The one where we dropped acid and saw God and vowed to change the world."

"I had the same dream. Woke up on the road in a rock-and-roll band. Come to think of it, one of those guys looked a lot like you. Only a lot younger."

We laughed. He was always ragging on me for looking younger than my age.

"That was a different dream. A good one too, while it lasted."

"Sounds like you brothers were just an earlier incarnation of our band. Four guys out for a good time, deluded into thinking they were after something greater."

"I've never thought of it that way, but yeah. Except for Buzzy. He was a year older. Colonizing the old frat house was his idea. He lured us out of the dorms with the promise that 'Everything will be possible, man!' What was probable, of course, was a lot of drugs and, with luck, a few women. Except Buzzy was a truly spiritual cat. Already looking past psychedelics to Eastern religion. He had this crack in his smile, like he was in on some cosmic joke, and a gleam in his eyes, like he was looking out beyond the farthest horizon to the wonders of another world."

"What about the guy who died?"

Waldo. I tried to picture him, but the fact of my looking away every time I saw him in those last months before I split had somehow erased his features, leaving only vague dark hair and a scowl. "Science was his thing. Biology? *Micro*biology. Old Waldo really *cared* about those germs, or whatever they were. He certainly spent enough time at the lab. Might have won the Nobel Prize by now."

"Not that you'd ever know." Ray frowned. I didn't follow the news, politics, or sports.

"Once Waldo sunk his teeth into something he just couldn't let it go. After Angela left him, we all knew she was never coming back. But he kept working it like it was one of his experiments, and if he just kept at it, it would finally come out right. And maybe it would have, but he never had the chance."

"The fourth brother?"

"Fucking Rick. A 'legend in his own time.' The most amazing hair on campus. Light brown afro, bigger than a basketball, exploding from his head, defying gravity. It hid his face, except for the squinty eyes and monster grin."

"Yeah, man, hair was a path to fame in those days."

I laughed. "He was peaking on mescaline one night and got down on all fours and ate with the dog. Barked at the poor thing, which hid behind the couch for the next week. Rick had crazy ideas about health. He read somewhere that it was essential to cook and eat outside, like our ancestors. That winter he crouched out in the snow cooking kielbasas on a hibachi when it was ten degrees below. Scarfed 'em down half-cooked and got an epic case of the runs. Which he thought was hilarious."

Ray cocked an eye. "He doesn't sound exactly your style."

"He was our dope dealer."

"Ah." He nodded his head, as if that explained everything. Which maybe it did. "How did Buzzy find you?"

I opened Ray's computer, showed him the website.

His mouth fell open and he slammed a hand against his head. "What happened to Bodine, Man of Mystery, with no known address? Who sneaks in the shadows? You that hard up for work?"

"No."

"And speaking of not your style, pardon me, but these graphics are butt ugly."

"I didn't design it."

"I hope not." Ray was scrolling down, looking at my client list. "These are big names! I had no idea."

I put a hand over the screen to block his view. He raised his hands in surrender. "Sorry. But what the hell is going on?"

I stood, looked away from him. "I've got some ideas." One, actually. "But I've got to get home, pack—"

"Pack what?" He got up and faced me. "Bodine, you need to tell me what's going on."

Part of never bragging about my Robin Hood business was never telling anyone. Because once a guy started blabbing, who wasn't going to take a little pride in his work? But damned if I didn't owe him some kind of explanation. This was a fucked-up scene to have me violating one of my rules.

"OK. You've heard of ransomware?"

"Maybe."

"Certain asshole coders use it to 'brick' people's computers, encrypting them remotely over the net such that without the password key they're useless. In theory, you pay the ransom and get a key, but more often than not they make off with the money and the computer's still a brick."

"That sounds like a major piss off. What's that got to do with your fake website?"

"I, uh, came across one of these gentlemen. I call him 'Brickman.' I found him *bragging* about it on an online forum. He said, 'I haven't had so much fun since I was boinking my little cousin. I'd do it for free, but a dude's got to make his nut.'"

Ray blinked. "That's some evil shit. So?"

"So I did something about it."

"Really. What?"

What to tell him? But he was getting there by himself.

"You hacked him!"

"You know I don't like that term. But yeah." Ray might not know about my sideline, but I'd dropped hints. You couldn't not brag about everything.

"I carved down through the layers of Brickman's bogus accounts. He's got more handles than the devil himself. But I discovered his real identity. And the crucial thing—what he wants. He's in the market for a young Asian wife. I set a honey trap, impersonating a Korean girl. Downloaded a picture from the net and Photoshopped it to unrecognizable. Sent him a sweet love letter. Brickman got back to me in three minutes, dying to meet. Which revealed his IP address and location: Cambridge, Mass."

"Harvard?"

"MIT."

"Of course. So what did you do?"

"I wasn't schlepping up to Cambridge to stalk him."

Ray smiled. "No, that's not you."

"A little research revealed that, like any profitable online scam, the Russian Mafia was on this bricking business like white on Anglo-Saxons. If they caught wind of some wimpy American geek—an ex-MIT geek—poaching on their turf, he'd soon be a very unhappy geek.

"Except there was no way I could in good conscience sic those boys on Brickman and live with it." I didn't have to tell Ray why. I might not believe in God, but I believed no one should play him. I'd long ago vowed to never do violence to another person. I'd stuck to pacifism all these years, though it was sometimes inconvenient.

"What to do? I wasn't getting him killed—or worse. But I had to stop him. I looked up notorious Russian mobsters. Vasily Chernoskylachenko, aka Vasily Chernobyl. Terrifying-looking guy—hold on." I got on Ray's computer again and found the photo of him. Pasty vodka-pickled cheeks, capital offense stare, and bull's neck with prison tats crawling up it.

Ray said, "Yow!"

"I attached this picture in an email to Brickman, saying, 'We know your ransom business. Know who you are, and where you live. Here is deal. You retire from bricking business in next five minutes, or Mr. Chernobyl will come visiting.'"

"And it worked."

"I thought it did. Like that he disappeared from his favorite forums."

"So he put up this fake website? Why?"

"It's his revenge."

"What are you going to do now?"

"I don't know. Right now I'm going to a funeral."

We stood. Ray looked at my cowboy boots, jeans, the black embroidered shirt, straight, straight blond hair in its neat ponytail, with an amused grin. "You going like that?"

"How else?" I didn't own a suit.

"Where is this funeral?"

"San Francisco."

"If you have to go to a funeral, there are worse places."

Back home, I heated up some leftover chicken and rice for dinner. I felt bad leaving Mingus, so I gave him an extra dollop of wet food. He looked at it, then me, evoking a sharp pang of guilt. He knew I was leaving and was milking it for all it was worth. I gave him some of my chicken and a big hug.

It was ten, and I had to get up at four-thirty, but I headed into the office. I couldn't sleep until I got at least a start on Brickman. As I typed and thought and sat at the organ and played silently and thought some more, I realized I could be up all night and miss my flight and not get anywhere.

Brickman had turned invisible. I had his computer's IP address, only it was offline. Without that, or him on the forums, I had nothing aside from a physical address. I wasn't going to Cambridge, and definitely not hiring a private eye.

It was ironic. For years I'd been using the Internet to sneak into various company computers, disguised as their IT guy, or as a piece of boring maintenance software. And I was always secure in my anonymity. And here I was chasing a ghost.

I'd been so pumped when I finally outed Brickman. The sin of pride. But my worst mistake had been acting from anger. His bragging about his crimes had outraged me, convincing me to take him on as the latest conquest in my digital Robin Hood act. I lost my cool. Emotions should never rule in business. My anger had blinded me to the truth: he was very good.

Too good. As I'd been playing him, he was playing me.

It had been a long, strange day, and I was plain out of juice. Brickman was the kind of problem that required reinventing wheels and seeing things from a new perspective. Which required fresh energy. A night's sleep—or at least part of one.

The last thing I did was to unplug the router, killing the Internet on all my computers. However he'd found me, he wasn't sneaking back in that way while I was gone. And now I was invisible to him. But as I lay in bed hoping for ten or twenty winks, I couldn't help the irrational thought: he sees me.

2.

Takeoff was delayed, so we got to San Francisco forty-five minutes late. There was still time to get to the cemetery. Until the traffic on Route 101 stopped dead.

No amount of anger was going to move that pickup truck in front of me a single millimeter. I started counting breaths and smiled. That was one of the things Buzzy had taught me.

Two hundred and thirty-four breaths later, traffic resumed, as mysteriously as it had stopped—no sign of an accident.

I gunned the rental car. I was going to be late. I hate being late.

I saw tombstones, then a sign for the Italian cemetery. I turned and drove uphill past a long line of cars. There was clearly a funeral. But could this be Waldo's? There must be at least a hundred people. Maybe he *had* won the Nobel Prize. I parked in front of the first car, near the top of the hill.

I trotted downhill, past a series of bizarre constructions. The most prominent was trying for some serious postmodern statement. It looked like a giant origami bird folded from particleboard. A moment later I realized it was a cross. The same old wine in a strange new bottle.

I pulled the church door open and organ notes dribbled out some limp confection. I suppressed a laugh—it was my instrument, but not my kind of music. I snuck into one of the last folding chairs in the back. The organ stopped and a middle-aged guy grabbed a mic and started larding on the platitudes. *Pillar of the community. Tireless servant.* I shook my head as I remembered how Waldo despised this sort of thing. Whoever he'd become, it couldn't be the man being described.

A priest took over and in a honeyed voice phoned in a threadbare eulogy, with such little enthusiasm that it was clear he'd never met Waldo, didn't know a thing about him.

Whatever had happened to Waldo, he couldn't have found religion, certainly not this brand. He deserved better than this. I got up and slipped out the door.

I wandered the cemetery looking for the grave. Billows of icy fog blasted off the Pacific, creeping up the steep hill, fingering the gravestones. It parted in places, revealing glimpses of mausoleums and firs. The photographs of the dead on the older tombstones were quintessentially Italian. Sad men with mustaches, in their only formal wear, topcoats and hats. Proud, long-nosed women in black dresses.

I was shivering. Not from being on this B horror movie set, with the mist and the dead staring dolefully at me from their pictures, but because I was freezing my ass off. What kind of summer was this? I'd left my denim jacket in the backpack in the rental, thinking it wasn't formal enough, but now I wished I'd worn it.

A fresh pile of dirt lay next to a hole. It must be the spot. I peered into the hole. It was deep. Which made it real. Whatever remained of Waldo was going down there. And staying.

I became aware of the knot in my chest that had been there since hearing Waldo's news. I should have been feeling something, but all I had was a tangle of thoughts. I should forgive him, because what had come between us hadn't been his fault. He hadn't even known about it. We'd missed a lot of good times together, before and after Angela. I'd never even said good-bye to him that last day. I mouthed the word now, evoking a memory: climbing down Garnet Hill in the dusk. Rushing ahead of Waldo to avoid him, but then he loomed over me.

"Bob, man, got a minute?"

Uh-oh.

At the bottom of the hill we sat under a tree. The ground was cold. But it would be. It had to have been after Thanksgiving.

"Angela's been stepping out on me."

"Why do you think that?"

"I just know. She won't look at me. It's tearing me up."

"Aw, man, I'm sorry. But you know what they say—so many fish in the—"

"She's *fucking some other guy*! But I'm not going to let her go. I can't."

Standing in the cemetery now, I *still* didn't feel a thing.

A humming sound, and I turned. The hearse was coming. I moved away from the grave and paced, trying to get warm.

The mourners arrived, led by the priest and a woman in black pants and a gray jacket. No veil. She must be Waldo's widow. She had full, shoulder-length chestnut hair and a sweet, round face.

I glanced at the rest of the crowd, at least a hundred people. What was with all the suits? The mystery of Waldo deepened. Yeah, a lot had changed in forty years. But whatever life Waldo had lived, it was hard to imagine it ending with all these suits.

I stood at the back of the gathering as the priest wrapped up with a graveside prayer. Thankfully, short.

People tossed clods in the grave, starting with the woman in the gray jacket. To my surprise, I found myself pressing forward through the crowd, grabbing a cold clump of dirt, and throwing it onto the silver coffin. I was last. It barely made a sound.

I looked up from the grave. Buzzy! His head was shaved smooth, his face rutted from some serious miles, but there was no mistaking that grin. He wore some kind of organic outfit that looked like it had been not sewn but harvested from the floor of some forest.

I stepped toward him, and he glided up to me riding an inch of air like he'd always done. He gave me a fat hug. I wasn't a touchy-feely guy but did my best to reciprocate.

He seemed shorter than I remembered. Had he shrunk with age, or simply grown in my imagination? Without hair, his ears were more prominent. A diamond stud glittered in the right one.

We walked toward the line of cars.

"Bob—uh, Bodine! Right?" He said the name like he was tasting it, then smiled and nodded. "Bodine works."

I said, "So. What—"

"Have I been doing the last forty years? Long story. Too long."

Though there were a million words to say, we lapsed into that comfortable silence. It was good to just have him walking beside me. As we reached the cars he said, "I don't know what it is about funerals. They always make me hungry. Fortunately, there's a reception." He pointed up the hill.

The hall was mobbed. At the bar I eyed the wine. After last night, half a glass and I might fall over. I got a soda water and so did Buzzy. I made a plate of cold cuts and Buzzy got hummus and pitas. We found a relatively quiet corner of the room.

We tapped plastic glasses together and smiled.

I said, "What do you do?"

"Man, we wouldn't even think of asking that question back then."

"Why would we when all we did was the same thing: sex, drugs and rock and roll?" As I said "sex" I flinched, wondering if this was still an awkward subject for my old friend.

He parked his plate and glass on a table. He slowly swept the fingers of both hands along the sides of his shaven head in a gesture I remembered well, combing a phantom head of wild hair. He caught my expression and laughed. "Old habits die hard. I'm a Buddhist."

"Ah. Is it a good living?"

"No!" He laughed. "I'm also a therapist. And you?"

"Computers." My gaze flicked away for a second. I'd been a very hip guy when he knew me, on my way to being a rock star. Though I knew he wouldn't care, I felt a little ashamed to admit the mundane place where I'd landed.

"Forty years." He spoke with feeling, giving every year its due. But he was also seamlessly changing the subject, undoubtedly perceiving my discomfort with that sixth sense of his. The old connection between us that had come to life the moment I heard him on the phone was deepening.

I said, "You know, I never saw Waldo, or the rest of you guys, after that spring."

He nodded slowly. "That was a rough time. But I've missed you."

I bit my lip.

He said, "Waldo and I stayed in touch. Emails mostly. Sometimes we talked. He hinted his marriage wasn't the greatest."

"Really." I glanced around the room after the widow but didn't see her.

"Actually, we had quite a bit of back and forth in the last year."

"How come?"

He shook his head. "That's too complicated to get into right now."

A strong hand gripped my arm. I turned. Rick? Where was his hair? Then I got it. Time had cruelly shrunk that famous Afro—once one of the seven wonders of the hip world—leaving only a short mat of gray fuzz. If anything, he was skinnier, with the stringy look of someone who ran a hundred miles a week. His face still wasn't handsome, but its old dope-den pallor was hidden beneath a tanned, polished surface. And what the hell was *he* doing in a suit, Italian by the look? But I was thinking of the old Rick. This one seemed quite comfortable in it.

I looked at Rick and pointed to Buzzy. "Hey, you know who this is?"

Rick said, "We talked before," but they weren't looking at each other.

Some vibe was going on there. They hadn't been each other's favorites, but still.

Buzzy said, "Listen, Middleburg's probably just an hour or so from Hudson. We should get together." He handed me a card and gave me that big-eyed thousand-watt grin. Despite myself, I reached out to touch his arm. He squeezed my hand and was gone.

What Rick had lost in locks and pounds he'd apparently gained in teeth. Somewhere along the line, his old peace-and-love smile had metastasized into a world-class shit-eating grin.

He seized my hand with both of his, like a TV preacher, gripping hard. "Bob!"

I did my best to smile. "Rick."

"Richard."

Oh, we're Richard now? I was about to tell him I was Bodine now, but he was tugging at my ponytail, hard enough to hurt. "I see you haven't changed a bit."

I couldn't say the same for him. He steered me out into the crowd, like it made him more comfortable. Or maybe he wanted an audience. It was hard to hear.

He said, "What's keeping you busy?"

"Computers."

He scowled. "Bah. You were in a *band.* I never figured you for a nerd."

I let it go. He'd always been a bit of a wiseass. "And you?"

"I run the largest organic food supplement company in the country." He launched into a sales pitch, painting the contrast between the evil Big Pharma hawking its harsh chemicals, and his outfit, EdenTree, nice *people* gently plucking herbs from the good earth.

The spiel was decent. My head started nodding along. But then I remembered him down in the basement of the Four Brothers house, extolling the virtues of Michoacán grass, which he'd happened to sell, over shitty homegrown. And it came to me. He *hadn't* really changed. Just become more Rick. Once a snake oil salesman, always one. With a crucial difference. The dope he had sold was good. From what I'd heard about food supplements, they were one of the biggest scams going.

"Half the stars in Hollywood are alive thanks to me." He mentioned some names, none of which rang more than a faint bell. I nodded.

"We're starting to make remarkable inroads with terminal cancer."

Sure.

He gave me a long look over—searching for flaws, signs of incipient gout or cancer, no doubt. Whatever the damage, Rick had just the thing.

One thing that surely wasn't good for my health was this conversation. Five minutes and my insides had curdled. I was getting ready to make an excuse and move on when he brushed his fingers down my cheek. I flinched and stepped back.

He said, "Your skin—" He shook his head. "You've got some major deficiencies. But tell you what. You come down to my place, I'll gift you with a free body scan and consultation."

"I just might take you up on that." Enough was enough. "It's been solid, man."

He didn't even give me my exit. I was preparing to move away when he looked across the room, burst into his mega-grin, and marched off. Somebody more important to work.

What had we ever seen in him? I felt like I'd just lost a second brother. But forget Rick—and Buzzy. We were here for *Waldo*. Who had he become, before he died?

I approached a series of oversized photos of my dead friend displayed on easels in a corner of the room and my blurred memory zoomed into focus. The only feature I'd remembered—his dark hair—had long ago gone gray, but otherwise Waldo hadn't changed much. The bushy beard he'd worn was trimmed to an Abe Lincoln but his skin was still dark and rough. His eyes still burned from dark circles, offset by a curled lip that said he didn't take his badass self too seriously. But other people, he took very seriously. Angela, for example.

The woman from the gravesite came up to me.

"I'm Jeannie." I caught a trace of a California drawl. Her big open eyes opened wider, kindling a smile that spread to her full lips and out into the room, saying *Welcome to California, God's Country*. I saw an endless expanse of gold and green hills marching off to heaven.

I'd been preparing an appropriately sad, concerned face, but it fell away as I lit up with my own smile. I reached to cover it, but she said, "Goddamn. Such a relief to see someone smiling. Never seen so much fake solemnity in my life!"

"Bodine."

"Oh. I thought you were Bob?"

"I was."

We checked each other out. I don't know what she saw, but she was looking even better than she had a moment ago.

She said, "My, you don't look old enough—"

I laughed. "Yeah, I've been told that."

I could seem twenty years younger from across a room. More like ten close up.

I said, "Clean living." And LSD once a year.

"Really," she said mockingly. She extended her hand, reconsidered. Gave me a short but real hug. Her jacket was sewn in intricate layers of different shades of gray. Despite the color, up close it didn't fit the sad occasion, or the suits around us. I cocked an eyebrow at it.

She said, "I know. I made it. I'm a clothing designer."

"It's beautiful. Also a relief from all this. I'm sorry about your husband. But I'm glad we met."

Her eyes flitted away, and I remembered what Buzzy had said about her marriage. Maybe it wasn't so simple a loss. "Thank you. Nice meeting you, too."

I began to move away into the crowd, but she squeezed my arm and stopped me. "Are you busy after this?"

"No. My flight isn't until tomorrow."

"Can you come up to my house? I have something for you."

3.

I followed her Prius north into the city and onto a quiet street. I found a parking space a few cars past hers.

She opened the door to a small blue Spanish-style house. It was the first chance I'd had to see her hands. They were covered with green-and-purple spots.

She caught me staring and laughed. "No, I don't have some horrible disease! It's dye from my work. Indelible, as you can see."

But I wasn't thinking of diseases. I was thinking how nice those hands looked, despite the stains. Long, competent fingers. I imagined they were soft, too. I followed her into the kitchen.

I sniffed the air and glanced at an ashtray on the table with a pipe in it.

She said, "Medical marijuana."

"What for?"

"Anxiety."

"You don't seem too anxious to me."

She snorted. "I'm not, long as I keep taking my medicine. I've been smoking on and off ever since back in the day. Now I'm legal! It's been more off in recent years. Waldo didn't approve. Now I can smoke as much as I want—" She turned serious. "I'd rather have him back."

"Of course."

"Want a hit?"

"Thanks, I'll pass."

"Coffee?"

"Please."

I sat at the table. She ground beans, turned on the machine, and fired up the pipe and took a long drag as the coffee brewed. She closed her eyes, opened them, then gave a knowing smile. A sweet, pungent stink hit my nose. "Powerful shit?"

She turned up the smile and raised a finger. "One hit is all it takes."

I gazed out the window to a deck with a sliver of blue between rooftops. The Pacific Ocean. "Nice view." I raised my eyebrows a millimeter.

"We bought this really early, back in the late seventies, for a song."

"It's worth a hit song by now, I imagine."

"Well, I'm going to have to sell it. I need the money. Once it started really appreciating in value, Waldo felt guilty living here."

"Why?"

She snorted. "White radical guilt."

A silence. I looked around. A nice mixture of modern granite countertops and sturdy cabinets, maybe from the '40s. It felt comfortable. Lived and cooked in.

I asked, "Why the Italian cemetery?"

"Waldo was Italian-American."

"Huh. But his name—"

"Caron was Anglicized from Coronati."

"I thought Waldo came from Walter. That's not Italian."

"Not Walter. *Aldo.* Waldo's grandfather came here from Italy around the turn of the last century. He was a communist and got deported during the Red Scare."

She handed me a mug of coffee and sat with her own. She took a tiny sip and sighed, a woman who enjoyed her physical pleasures. "Waldo grew up hearing of Nonno back in Sicily. His father insisted he stay away from politics, get a good education, become something harmless."

"Like a microbiologist."

"Right. But Waldo had this romantic picture of the grandfather he never knew. He believed a terrible injustice was the reason he didn't know him. When he heard how the police murdered Black Panther Fred Hampton in his sleep, he lost it. It triggered those old feelings. He gave up science and became a radical."

"He was still a radical?"

"As much as anyone is these days. I'm surprised you never heard of him. Maybe he was just famous out here. He was…a lawyer."

I couldn't help it. I laughed. She glared at me.

I said, "I'm sorry. It's just that back then—"

"I know. Lawyers were the enemy. Some still are. Not Waldo. He did tons of pro bono stuff, was always standing up for the little guy. Couldn't rest until he took down every scumbag."

"He *was* a scrapper."

"He mentioned you every once in a while. Come to think of it, in the last week."

"Really. What did he say?"

She sighed again. "I was listening with half an ear. You know how it is with old marrieds. He said something about you guys, the sixties. A part of him was stuck back then. Back when things were black and white, when people put their money where their mouths were, before they just put it in their pockets and forgot about all the injustice. I think you guys symbolized that time for him. What did he say? Something like, 'That Bob. Bet he's not sucking up to some corporation.'"

"Right." I looked away. Though I'm strictly in business for myself, I take money from some pretty big companies. I glanced back. There was no sign that she'd noticed my discomfort. She seemed suddenly far away.

"A part of me is stuck back there, too." She bit her lip. "The problem is it's a different part."

"What do you mean?"

"He was so handsome, which was enough, at least to begin with." She laughed deep in her throat. "But he was *so good*. How could I not fall for him? Everybody was talking back then about changing the world, but Waldo was hell-bent on doing it. And he did. I supported him best as I could, but I wasn't good like him. I just wanted to be a happy hippie. Get high, make love, hang loose. Make beautiful things."

I nodded to her jacket. "Which you do. You're changing the world, too—"

"Thanks, but no. Waldo was too nice to ever say anything, but he had to have thought my dressmaking utterly frivolous. He never really let up on changing the world. How could he, when somebody somewhere was still suffering?" She took a long, deep breath. "None of that matters now. I miss him."

If I hadn't been staring at her I would have missed it. The little shake of her head and her eyes squeezing shut for just a moment in which the devastation she'd been hiding so well ran across her face.

She said, "Sorry."

"Hey." She was keeping her grief from me—from everyone—out of kindness, not wanting to burden anyone. "You have something for me?"

"Yes." She stood and moved to the door, then stopped. "Will you do me a favor first? Can you spare an hour?"

"Sure. What?"

"This is a little weird. I want you to come with me to where he died. I haven't had the courage to go there myself."

"Where is it?"

"Lands End."

I felt a chill. *Waldo's* end. "What's that?"

"These fabulous cliffs over the Pacific with a path on top."

I followed her to the front hall. She opened the closet door and a second later a whine came from downstairs.

"Your dog?"

Jeannie frowned. "*Waldo's* dog, Eldridge. She's inconsolable without her daddy. I'd love to comfort her, but I'm allergic. She has her own room in the basement. I just shove her food in there and let her out in the backyard. She still makes me sneeze."

"Eldridge?"

"Eldridge Cleaver, the Black Panther who wrote *Soul on Ice.*"

I laughed. "Funny name for a girl. But I should talk. I named my dog Mingus."

She smiled. "You were a musician, weren't you?"

"I admit it. But don't tell anyone."

"What do you mean? I love music!"

She disappeared in the hall closet and returned wearing a stylish dark-green windbreaker. She handed me a gray cable-knit sweater. Ratty, but it looked warm.

"I can't wear that if it's Waldo's."

"Hey, he doesn't need it anymore. You will."

We went out to her car. She said, "I can drive. I'm used to driving a little high."

"Let me."

"OK." She sounded relieved.

She directed me up some hilly streets. It wasn't far. I caught her scent. Nothing as obvious as perfume. Floral. Nice. We parked and got out. The air was cold, but somewhere between the cemetery and there, the sky had turned immaculate, except for a curtain of fog that hung far offshore. We followed a trail past sprays of wildflowers, orange and gold and an outlandish cotton-candy pink. "What are those?"

"Resurrection lilies."

And I was back at the cemetery staring down into that dark hole. *Sorry, Waldo, don't think you're coming back anytime soon.*

The path climbed steadily until we were high above the ocean, which hid behind a stand of ghostly Monterey pines. The wind had stripped their trunks bare, polishing them to a gleaming silver and bending them toward land.

I said, "This would be perfect if it wasn't for that wind. Does it ever stop?"

"No. It's freezing here all summer! But that old sun's always out there with its eternal smiley come-on, and I'm still a sucker for it. Still a darned flower child. You'd think I'd learn."

We came to a break in the trees, and there was the ocean hundreds of feet below. I moved to the other side of her, the land side.

A plaintive note sounded, round and mellow, so perfectly in tune with this place that until now it had been inaudible.

"That a foghorn?"

"You bet. The currents below are treacherous. They sunk hundreds of ships. But this is too beautiful a place for dying." She winced. "I never came here with Waldo. He jogged here. Every single morning, rain or shine. He wore exactly the same clothes, left at the same hour. Probably ran in his own footsteps. Came home at eight thirty on the dime, ate the same oat bran, went to work. He was like that about everything. I had a sad joke with myself. 'Where's Waldo?' That was the thing. You always knew exactly where he was, every minute of the day."

"He was like that back then, too."

She shook her head slowly. "I never know where I'm going to be one moment to the next."

"You guys were really different."

"No shit. Opposites attract, I suppose, but there's a limit."

"Did you fight?"

"He'd get started, but I would never play. It drove him nuts. He *loved* conflict, loved the good fight. The bad fight. Any fight. Maybe if I'd taken him on…" She raised a couple of limp fists and stuck her lower lip out.

I said, "I know. Back then we were into all that 'smile on your brother' stuff, but then one night I got into a chess game with him. I had him down two, then three pieces. I chased him all over the board, but he just would not let me beat him. Around four a.m. I was crashing out, finally just said fuck it. I let him win."

Jeannie laughed ruefully. "That was him. We were all right until we tried to have kids. It wasn't happening, and, irony of ironies, that old biologist refused to have us go for tests to see why."

"What about adopting?"

"I wanted to, but he refused. After we gave up there was a kind of pall over the house. He threw himself into work with even more of a vengeance. I tried to do that with my clothing business, but I didn't have his workaholic gene. So I…at first it was just sneaking out now and then, getting high. Playing. But then there was a guy. And then another one. I didn't care about any of them."

She stopped and looked me in the eye, as if to convince me, and herself, that what she was about to say was true. "I still loved him. Just not that way anymore. Shit, I'm going to miss him."

"I'm sure. I will, too." Which felt like a lie. She wasn't the only one with complicated feelings toward Waldo.

The path had leveled off. She pointed. It took me a moment to realize what I was seeing:

the Golden Gate Bridge.

"He didn't seem himself in his last week. I asked him and he said nothing was wrong. I was terrified that he'd somehow found me out. He was certainly competitive about *that*. You must remember that girl in college, what was her name?"

"Angela."

She didn't seem to pick up on my strangled tone of voice.

"Right. I don't think he ever got over her. I asked him one time what she was like, and he got this dreamy, childlike look, completely unlike him. Then he moaned, 'She dumped me,' like it was the worst thing that had ever happened to him. Sometimes I think she got the best part of him. The fun part. And for them to die the same way...I keep thinking it's some kind of karma, or curse."

I managed to keep my eyes from rolling. "Where did it happen?"

"No way to be absolutely sure. It was early on a rainy morning. It almost never rains here in the summer, but this was an exception. Tourists don't get up early, and the locals don't like walking in the rain. So no one saw him fall." She pointed north, up the coast to a mass of rock jutting into the ocean, maybe fifty feet tall and wide. "That's the obvious place. Lands End Point. He'd been missing a few days when somebody spotted his body in the water not far from there. Can't be sure, though, because of those crazy currents."

A few people stood atop the cliff. It looked vertical from here.

She said, "There are steps. We can walk down to it."

A twinge of...nausea. It had been a long time since I'd felt that.

We entered a narrow alley between bushes that finally blocked the wind. It was immediately hot. I caught a whiff of flowers, and a moment later a familiar scent. Something that didn't belong here, except it was already gone and I was frustrated that though it lingered in my nostrils I couldn't put a name to it. A single crow complained somewhere above.

We reached a set of wooden steps that wound steeply down toward the ocean.

She said, "Those lead to Lands End Point. A few months ago, he started coming home for breakfast exactly twelve minutes late. I asked him about it, and he said he'd added some steps to his run. He was trying to lose weight. I'm thinking he started running down these steps, around this path that makes a loop on the point, then back up."

I followed her down. At the bottom of the steps she threaded a narrow sand path through low evergreens. The trees to our right ended, opening up the view. I looked up to the brilliant sky then down toward the water. And the edge.

This wasn't an official path like the one above, which had a guardrail and was plastered with signs: "Warning! People and dogs have died falling from these cliffs." There was no sign here, and no guardrail. Just the path, two feet wide, with a wall of foliage to my left and the edge to the right. Surf pounded below.

I stopped. She continued on, skirting a tree branch that leaned out toward the water, ending just inches from the edge. The path narrowed to less than a foot, and a narrow, funky pipe emerged from the ground, snaking down the middle of it. Drainage, to keep the cliff from eroding further. It didn't seem to be doing much of a job. She danced over it like it wasn't there, like there was no forty-foot fall to the ocean, a fall her husband had taken not a week ago.

Or maybe that was just my perception. I wasn't doing any dancing. My breath caught in my throat. A motor spun in my head, slowly tilting the scene on a sickening axis, turning my stomach. I forced my feet forward, locking my eyes straight ahead. I reached the branch and stopped again in the face of a dilemma. My feet weren't going to follow in her steps past that branch. Right next to the edge. In order to avoid it, I needed to crouch down, crabwalk, or even crawl under it to stay a few feet from the edge. But I didn't want her to see me doing it.

She was still walking, not looking back. I scrambled onto all fours and got past the branch. I stood and pressed my back into the trees away from the cliff and inched forward. I stopped for a third time before that pipe. There was no way I was getting past it without tripping.

The surf below crashed like mallets on a cymbal. The sound rushed up, injecting my legs with rubber, grabbing my eyes and pulling them down. Mercifully, I couldn't see the bottom. The cliff must overhang. But it was a long way down.

What I could see was roiling white water, and above it that offshore fog like a malevolent tongue sneaking in to feast on the land. I pictured it licking a chunk of green rock from beneath my feet. It tossed up a gust of wind, and the scene was spinning again like a room after a night of vodka shots.

I stumbled back from the edge and fell on my ass, sharp pine branches biting into it. I shut my eyes and forced a couple deep breaths.

I opened them. Jeannie was standing with her back to me, twenty feet away. She turned, frowning, saying something, but I couldn't hear it over the roaring surf. She ran toward me.

She stood over me and said, "Are you OK?" But her words were empty, and she wasn't quite looking at me.

"Just a little dizzy. Jet lag," I said, but she was already heading back up the path.

She climbed the steps ahead of me. I gripped the rail tightly. As the distance between the cliff and me widened, I came back to myself. When we reached the top, I said, "I didn't hear what you said out on the cliff."

She stopped walking, took my arm, and looked right at me. "Waldo didn't slip. He would never have run out there."

"Why?"

"I always suspected that he was afraid of heights. He never admitted it to me—you know how macho he was—but he was always making excuses for why he wouldn't go up Coit Tower, or even drive down crazy Lombard Street. But when I saw that cliff, I knew. He'd never be able to go there. It's really exposed."

No shit. I shuddered. "If he didn't slip—"

"Somebody pushed him."

31

I restrained myself from rolling my eyes. "Who? And why?"

"I have no idea. But he crossed some powerful, nasty folks in his time."

We drove back to her house in silence. I liked Jeannie, but was questioning her judgment. She was a grief-stricken widow who'd come stoned to the place her husband died. First it was karma that killed him. Then it was some conspiracy. She'd been married to Waldo forever, and it was only now that she knew he was afraid of heights?

When we got to her house, I asked, "You have something for me?"

"I almost forgot. It's in Waldo's office in the basement."

I followed her as she tiptoed downstairs, whispering, "This used to be the garage. I don't want to get Eldridge going."

But the dog must have heard us because she started whining from behind a door.

I said, "Hey, let me meet her."

"Sure. I'll stay here."

The windowless storage room smelled like dog. She was little, gray, and fuzzy. She made a beeline for me and frantically licked my hand.

"Take it easy!" She was starved for affection. I gave her a solid round of petting then made for the door. I winced as I closed it in the dog's face.

Jeannie stood biting her lip. "I've tried to find her a new home, but nobody wants an old dog." She shook her head. "That thing I've got for you is on the table." She pointed across the room to a plain trestle table. We walked over.

An ancient desktop computer sat on it. No Ethernet cables led from it, just a power cord. Probably too old for Wi-Fi. Nobody has a computer without Internet anymore. It was the last thing in the world I needed.

"Not that old computer. This is what I want you to have."

I turned to Jeannie. She was holding an old wooden box that she must have picked up from the other end of the table.

The box was a foot by a foot and a half, almost a foot deep. Chestnut colored, rough hewn but varnished, with an ornate metal clasp.

"I know this. We kept—"

"Your stash in there. I know, Waldo told me."

"We kept it…" In the basement. A swarm of memory fragments welled up—a faceless smile, fingers passing a joint, hyena laughter, and a blaze of righteous electric guitar. I wrenched myself back to the present and looked at her. "What's in there now?"

"Old stuff from the sixties. Junk, if you ask me. But I can't really see throwing it out or giving it away."

Too much Waldo to keep around?

"It's his piece of the sixties. That was really your time with him, not mine. I told you he was thinking about those times recently. For years I remember this box sitting on a shelf. After he died, I found it here—open." She handed it to me.

"Thank you."

"Hey, thank *you*. One less hassle to deal with."

I followed her upstairs, carrying the box.

We stood in the doorway, not quite looking at each other, tension between us tuning up like a new piano string.

Finally, she broke the silence. "Thanks for coming to the funeral. And out to Lands End."

"No problem."

There was an awkward moment as she leaned in to hug me, but the box was in the way. She gave a little laugh, then got serious. "I'll call you, let you know what the police say."

"Do that."

She gripped the backs of my hands and a zing shot through my body. Her hands were very soft.

***

I drove downtown to my hotel. It was funny, Jeannie looked nothing like Angela, but both of them were into supernatural stuff. Curses and karma. Astrology, probably. None of which I'd ever bought. Still, she'd sparked something in me.

From what she'd told me, Waldo and I had more in common than I'd realized at the time. We were both exact guys, liked things just so. And once we got after something, nothing could stop us.

That spark with Jeannie had gone in two directions. Was that why she'd invited me there? Maybe her request for me to find out what happened to Waldo was just an excuse…

The hotel was nice but expensive. I was on the seventeenth floor. As I stepped out of the elevator, I glanced down at the crack between the elevator doors and the floor and flinched. Afraid of heights? Until today I hadn't been afraid of anything. Even after that terrible acid trip during the blizzard, I'd gotten back on the crazy horse that had thrown me. I still tripped once a year. More than I could say for anyone else my age. Sure, if some guy jumped from an alley and stuck a gun in my face, I'd freak. But that was pure animal stuff. This heights thing…

In the room, I checked my cell phone. A message from a number I didn't recognize: "This is Ruth Nethercutt of Rhinebeck. I'm such a dummy. I keep hitting the key, but my computer won't start. I'm here at my friend Nancy's. She got on the Google. The web thingy says 'Call Bodine,' so here I am."

I groaned and deleted the message. I'd started getting business from the fake website. Fucking Brickman.

What to do? I could email him, back down from my threat, but that might just egg him on. At least he hadn't bricked *my* computer in revenge. Yet.

Did he understand what a blow he'd landed on me, outing me like that? Would that satisfy him? Doubtful. I could take down the website. But he could just put up another one. It would be better to just ignore him. Not rise to the bait. Maybe he'd get bored and move on.

It wasn't just him breaching my well-constructed privacy that burned. He'd beat me in my strongest suit: coding.

I hit my laptop, aware that it didn't have the power of my rig at home. But it told the same dumb story as last night—Brickman was offline, off all his favorite forums. But I was off, too. The two hours of sleep were catching up with me. I lay down, shut my eyes, and tried for a catnap. But I kept seeing the ugly home page of my fake website. There was something about it that I was missing.

I changed the interior subject. Buzzy and Waldo had been in touch.

"That's too complicated to get into right now." What did Buzzy mean? And that weird vibe between him and Rick….

I was dozing when the missing thing arrived, jolting me awake. The Bodine website was the one link I still had to Brickman. It might have some of his digital fingerprints.

I made instant coffee in the room, got the website up, and dug into its back end. It was hosted by a company I knew that had tens of thousands of sites. And crack security, a big part of the reason they were doing so well. Their guys were almost as good as me.

Given a few days back home, I might be able to get to Brickman's account. But what was it going to tell me? What I already knew—his name and where he lived. I could hack into MIT's computers, get his student records, find out where he came from. What was that going to do? I wasn't going after his family like some thug. I laughed. MIT's computers might not be so easy.

I was wondering what to do about dinner when Buzzy called and solved the problem.

He said, "I wasn't sure if you were staying tonight. If you're not busy there's a nice Thai place down in the Ferry Building."

"Great. I'm staying just up the street from there."

"Seven?"

"Six thirty? It's the middle of the night back home, and I'm fucking starved."

He laughed. "Six thirty it is."

4.

I carried Waldo's box to the restaurant. San Francisco seemed a lot more prosperous than I remembered. I was a part of a mob that seemed to be descending on the Embarcadero with dinner in mind.

Going to see a shrink! I laughed to myself. I'd never been within a mile of a therapist's office. I was a little nervous. Long before his current profession, Buzzy had had that knack for looking right inside you.

I was early, as usual—the funeral being an exception. Buzzy had booked us a table at a large window overlooking the bay.

There was no fog this time of day. I put the box on the bench next to me, took off my coat, and covered it. I wanted to show it to Buzzy, but first we had some catching up to do.

Buzzy floated into the restaurant on the nose of six thirty. He saw me and grinned. He sat gracefully and carefully unwrapped his napkin from the silverware and placed it on his lap. I studied him, trying to understand how anyone could be so meticulous without a hint of uptightness.

I said, "How are you liking San Francisco, despite the occasion?"

"How are *you* liking it?"

I gave him a look.

Buzzy burst out laughing. "I'm sorry. It was a joke. We shrinks always answer a question with a question. I like it fine."

"I'm a little surprised. You never got out of old Middleburg."

"I *did* get out. Out of the closet." He laughed. "At which point I suppose I should have moved here, gotten a place in the Castro…"

He tossed off his admission of being gay so easily, like what he'd done was no different than replacing an uncomfortable pair of shoes. And now he as easily changed the subject.

He said, "I can't quite picture you programming computers. You were quite the musician."

"Hey, I just traded keyboards. How'd you get to be a therapist? Always somehow pictured you wandering India barefoot in long robes."

"I did go to India after college. Barefoot. I didn't get enlightened. And got sick of walking in elephant shit."

The waiter came. Wherever he came from, it wasn't Thailand. We both ordered pad Thai. Mine with chicken, his with tofu.

He turned serious. "I don't know if you remember my parents?"

"A little. Kind of straight."

"Kind of. Ha. They weren't bad people, but they were rigid. Narrow-minded. I came out to them in the early seventies. That was a big mistake. They put me into aversion therapy."

"What's that?"

"It was the rage back then in psychology. It's not a great dinner topic. They gave me emetics, made me puke as I watched gay porn."

"Jesus!"

"Worse. They hooked my dick up to electrodes and shocked me. It didn't work."

"Unbelievable."

"That's why I became a shrink. To work within the system, as we used to say. And therapists have changed their tunes. I like to think I've been part of that. Funny, I was in touch with Waldo just this summer on that very subject."

"They're still doing it?"

"Not the violent stuff. They toned it down, in theory. Now it's 'reparative' or 'conversion' therapy. It's practiced by renegade shrinks in loose collusion with Christian extremists. The methods may seem mild in comparison, but the results are still horrible."

"It doesn't work?"

"No. And worse, it encourages the tendency some gays have to hate themselves. There have been scores of suicides as a result."

"Evil bastards."

"You know how California is at the forefront of American society?"

"I've heard that."

"Therapists out here have been moving to get the legislature to ban those reparative scams, at least for minors. Seeing as Waldo was this prominent left-wing activist lawyer, I figured he might be able to help. And he was definitely interested. It's a pity he won't be involved. We could have used him."

The food came. Sweet and hot, the noodles nice and gummy. Buzzy caught me looking askance at his tofu.

"Yeah, I've been eating it for years, but it still tastes like rhinoceros snot."

"Vegetarianism go with that?" I pointed at his shaved head.

"Afraid so."

We finished eating. I asked, "Is Buddhism the real deal?"

"It is for me."

"So now we are three."

He nodded.

"It's terrible to say, but I'd rather have lost Rick than Waldo."

"You aren't the only one thinking that. Seeing him at the funeral tested every ounce of compassion I have."

"I got a vibe between you two."

"He figured out I was gay. And had a definite problem with it."

"You know, I've been thinking, maybe he wasn't that great to begin with. What did we see in him, aside from his hair?"

"Let's see…he had great dope."

"Bingo."

I looked out the window. The bay was calm. The sun had set as we'd talked. Lights on the Bay Bridge reflected on the water.

I said, "Great food and a great view."

Buzzy nodded.

"Waldo's widow, Jeannie, said he was worried about something in his last weeks. How'd he seem to you?"

"Fine. But that was back in the spring. After we got going on this gay conversion thing, it was all emails. Which don't tell you much. I think we last spoke around June."

"You remember Waldo being…afraid of heights?"

"No."

"Me neither. Jeanne took me to where he must have fallen—this hairy cliff—then told me how she'd always suspected him of being afraid of heights, but now she knew."

"A cliff like that, it could have been her own fear talking."

"Right. And she was stoned. She thinks someone pushed him. Killed him."

He raised an eyebrow, didn't seem shocked at the idea. "Waldo tangled with some bad people. And he never let anything go. What do you think?"

"It seems over the top. Before that, Jeannie had another idea. She was talking about Angela falling and karma. Which I don't believe in, not like that. Except…Waldo had been thinking about those times. That, of course, means Angela. And Jeannie was cheating on him. If he found out she was doing him wrong, the same as Angela, and he was on a cliff like she was…"

"Maybe he jumped."

"Yeah. But you think he could have killed himself? You're the professional."

Buzzy sighed, closed his eyes. "I could see it. Waldo was loyal. Loyal to his friends, and loyal to ideas, even when the going got tough. *Especially* when the going got tough. It made him a great activist."

"But Jeannie said they were having trouble for a long time."

"Trouble isn't the same as finding out your wife has been fucking another guy. Not if you're Waldo."

"But if he was afraid of heights, could he have jumped?"

Buzzy was silent. "That's a tough question."

I ordered coffee. Buzzy had herb tea. I unveiled the box and put it on the table.

He stared at it for a moment, then raised his eyebrows at me. "Is that what I think it is?"

"None other. Waldo kept it. Jeannie gave it to me."

"Hold on. How could Waldo have it? The cops must have taken it that night, given what was in it. What kind of bust was that where they left the dope? And what kind of cops?"

"A strange bust. And Middleburg cops." But the box was another thing about our arrests that didn't add up.

I opened the box and plucked out a packet of Mysore Sugandhi Dhoop incense. I sniffed. No fragrance, just a whiff of mildew.

Buzzy came up with a wrinkled copy of the *Berkeley Barb* with some shirtless freak gaping madly on the cover. He opened it but the pages crumbled in his fingers. He laughed. "This is how my family opened presents at Christmas. Your turn."

I got a cocktail napkin with some words scribbled on it. I handed it to Buzzy with a grin.

"Janis Joplin's signature?"

"Yep. It's wild like her."

He took out a pair of pants and handed them to me. Homemade bell-bottoms—jeans with slits in the ends sewn with patches of faded paisley cloth. I stopped.

Shit. I remembered these. Waldo striding out from his room with a big grin, pointing to the cuffs. "Angela *sewed* these for me, man!" Jeannie was right. Waldo never did get over Angela. And Jeannie never quite got over him not getting over her. No wonder she wanted to get rid of the box. Even after all this time, I recognized the cloth. Before it was a patch it was part of Angela's favorite skirt.

For once, Buzzy mistook my vibe. "Taking a sudden interest in fashion? I saw you with Jeannie. Maybe it's her you're taking an interest in."

"Hey. She just lost her husband." Buzzy and his damned intuition.

We were getting to the bottom of the box. I picked up a fragment of newspaper and showed it to Buzzy, frowning. A couple of short-haired men in suits, smiling for the camera. In their forties.

He raised his eyebrows. "Who are these guys? Professors from the college?"

"I don't know." I put it aside and removed the next thing in the box: an eight-by-ten black-and-white print.

Buzzy looked at me and smiled. "Hey, I think I took this."

"That's right, you always had a camera strung around your neck."

A crowd of long-hairs stood outside in fall coats, watching something slightly to the right of the camera.

I said, "A football game?"

"Our team must have been losing badly, because they look bummed."

Not a football game. "What's that expression on their faces? It's one I haven't seen in a long time." I noticed the black bands on their arms, which were linked so tightly that the crowd almost seemed like one being, and I heard the soundtrack. Not rah-rah, but *Hell no, we won't go!* "A demonstration against the war."

"Of course. I don't remember that particular one, but I took a lot of pictures at them."

"I wasn't there. I never demonstrated."

"You sure? I could swear…"

There were more photos at the bottom of the box. I took them out. The next one looked like it was from another demonstration, or maybe the same one. Buzzy pointed to Waldo.

God, hair so long, so young. So serious. So alive. Next to him, of course, stood Angela.

I squeezed my eyes shut, but she was still standing there. Looking at me. I opened my eyes and averted them from the picture.

If Buzzy noticed, he didn't say anything. He pointed to Rick, whose fist was raised, his mouth open. "He really enjoyed those things."

The next photo had a couple sitting on the grass, holding hands, beaming at each other with the look of that time: *All you need is love! We can change the world!* What were they doing now? Accountants, dentists. If they were lucky, praying the world would stay just as it was, so they could collect their retirement.

There was a photo of the Four Brothers house, with its overblown Victorian splendor. And the four of us standing at the top of the steps of the stern, ivied administration building, stark naked. Grin, grin, grin, grin. Even Waldo. I laughed. "I totally forgot this. You didn't take this one."

Buzzy put his hands over his eyes. "Jesus. Reminds me of the crap those conversion assholes showed me."

The last picture was of Garnet Hill. It took me a second to figure that out, because it was taken from an impossible angle, from which I'd never seen it. Rick, famous hair and a fake sneer, brandished a hash pipe like a rapier. I was next to him, yard long hair flying in the breeze, no ponytail back then, with a sly smile of self-satisfaction—*This is our hill, our time, our world.*

We stood in three-quarter profile, faces glowing in the dying sun. I looked down. Our feet were inches from the edge, a yawning space to our left. My fingers clenched the picture. I certainly hadn't had a problem with heights then.

I said, "You took this? Where were you?"

He grinned. "See that tree branch? I was out at the end of it, hanging right over the edge. I was lucky it didn't break."

"Jesus." Buzzy *really* wasn't afraid of heights.

Waldo was behind Rick and me, his back to a tree. Doing his best to smile, but it came out all crooked. Was he avoiding me? No. Because he *hadn't known.* But maybe he had, on some animal level. I was sure avoiding him by that point.

I glanced at Buzzy. He seemed to be seeing something in the picture, too, though it had to be different than what I saw, because he hadn't known, either…

He said, "Waldo *was* afraid of heights. See how he's glued to that tree? Now I remember how we were coming off the hill one evening when he said, 'I can't do that anymore. Maybe straight. But once I'm high, I just keep thinking about that drop.'"

"Jeannie was right."

Silence. Buzzy finally said, "I have it. It isn't a matter of psychology. It's *physics.*"

"Huh?"

"Waldo's fear has him plastered to that tree. That fear comes from deep in his crocodile brain. I can't imagine anything in him strong enough to overcome it, to move his body forward, let alone over the edge. Somebody with that fear would choose any other method to kill themselves. Somebody pushing him is another matter. Trick him into being close enough to the edge, all it would take is a shove."

"So someone killed him."

"Sorry to say, it looks that way."

We sat in uncomfortable silence. Buzzy finally picked up his phone and started taking pictures of the photos he'd taken. "I might as well have copies of my old work."

***

I stared at the box and thought of Waldo, in his own box, at the bottom of that hole, probably filled in by now. And me standing there looking in. Not feeling a thing.

Buzzy was done taking pictures. I looked him in the eye. "You of all people know that I'm not the most open person when it comes to matters of the...heart." This was tough. "But lately I've been feeling like an emotional cripple. Like a jazzer trying to play rock and roll. I know all the chords, the theory, but can't for the life of me make the music."

"You've been feeling this since when?"

"Ever since things...ended with my last girlfriend. I've felt off." I only realized it as I said it. "You introduced me to the idea of living in the present moment. For which I'll always be grateful. And I've been doing my best. You think I'm also using it as a way to escape my past?"

He smiled. "I was nineteen when I told you to 'Be here now.' Since then I've discovered that life is more...complicated. Why do you think I'm a shrink? Some folks have to deal with the past before they can get to the present. I've thought a lot about the sixties. It was a complicated time. Neither as wonderful as we told each other it was, nor as terrible as so many people think now. But one lasting gift from those crazy times was the revelation we all had—that you can change. Be different than your parents. Become more the person you want to be."

And now he turned on his thousand-watt beatific smile. It was so intense, so *real*, that I wanted to look away. But I forced myself to keep looking him in the eye, even as I squirmed inside. He said, "You've realized you want to change. That's nine-tenths of the job. Now you just have to do it."

The way Buzzy put things like that, it always sounded simple.

I said, "You remember when I left the Four Brothers house?"

"Of course."

"You said, 'We need to talk…'"

"And you walked out. But you're talking now."

I laughed. "A little bit, and a lot late, but yeah. My leaving was…a mistake. One of the first things I learned in computer coding was that if you make a little error early in a project it can come back to haunt you. Months later your little flaw has grown, metastasized, and now it's derailing the whole program. Maybe leaving you guys was that kind of mistake. We had this good thing, and we were after great things, and at the first bump in the road I chickened out."

"You ended up taking another path. And you're wondering what you lost doing it."

"Something like that."

"We *were* after great things. The kind of things that would take generations to achieve. And you were, what, eighteen?"

"Impatient."

"Like everyone that age. But that's not why you left. You're no quitter. No, it's related to what we were talking about a moment ago. Your heart. You couldn't talk to me because what you felt was overwhelming. Why Angela's death hit you so hard, I didn't know. Though I had my suspicions. You got away from those feelings before you drowned. And the only way you knew to do it was to walk away."

"Leaving so much behind."

"You weren't alone. We all should have been freaked out by the enormous discrepancy between all that those times called us to do and our puny capacity to do it. Hey, you survived. A lot of people didn't. They died—from drugs or becoming their parents. Maybe you're finally ready to…deal."

"Finally's the word, all right."

"Well, I'm beat. It's late back home."

"Me, too. It's great to see you."

"You, too. Hopefully next time won't be in forty years."

"It won't. I promise."

As we were leaving, he said, "You remember a Sharon from back then?"

"Sharon." It rang a faint bell. "Maybe."

"She ended up teaching at the college. Women's studies. I barely knew her when we were students, but we've become pretty good friends. She's been coming to my meditation group." He laughed. "I thought of it because I'll bet her office is in the new Center for Feminist Research."

"Yeah?"

"Which is in the renovated Four Brothers house."

"Oh."

"With that stuff you're dealing with? My door's always open."

He left with a little wave. I stood there for a minute, smiling. Buzzy was still the same essentially happy person. He exuded a quiet joy, and it was contagious.

***

The next morning, I was on 101 headed south, ten minutes from the airport when my phone rang. It was illegal to talk on a cell while driving there, but I picked up. Almost nobody ever called me, and now the thing was ringing off the hook. Another customer?

It was Jeannie. "I'm sorry to bother you, but someone broke into my place."

"When?"

"Last night. They did it while I was out to dinner. I called Buzzy to get your number, but his phone was off. He finally called me back this morning and gave it to me."

Why call me? "Do you want me to come there?"

"Would you? I know we just met, but…"

"My flight, uh, isn't for a while. I'll be there as soon as I can."

I turned around and headed back to San Francisco. Got off the highway and called to cancel my flight.

She was standing at the open door when I got there. The door was flanked by glass panels. The left one was smashed. I walked up the steps and she hugged me. She led me to a small office and pointed to the empty desktop. "That's where I keep my laptop. But that's all that's missing." She opened the desk drawer and pulled out a fistful of cash. "This is in case there's an earthquake. Why didn't they take it?"

The drawer seemed an obvious place to look.

In the bedroom, she pointed to an array of necklaces on a stand. "Those aren't the Crown Jewels, but they've got to be worth something."

Back in the kitchen we sat.

I asked, "What about the dog?"

"She must have howled, but the neighbors didn't notice with her in the basement. The cops came."

"And?"

"And nothing. They said there's been a rash of break-ins, stealing computers is run of the mill, I was lucky not to have a big TV or that would be gone, too. Said they'd send a car around."

"They could be right…"

She looked at me hard. "They were after *Waldo's* laptop. They must have thought mine was his. He didn't have one."

"How do you know that's what they were after?"

"I don't *know*. But nobody's broken into this house in the whole time we've lived here. Don't you think it's strange that it would happen right after they killed Waldo?"

"Mm." I thought all of it was strange.

"Another thing I didn't tell you when you were here before. Since Waldo died, I've seen this car at the end of my street with a guy just sitting in it."

"What kind of car?"

"Brown. I don't know cars."

"Maybe that was who broke in, and he was casing your house."

"But why mine?"

I didn't have an answer.

She looked at me. "I'm really scared. That's why I called you."

"You think they might come back."

"For me."

"Call the police. Not the ones who came here, but the ones who handle homicides."

"They won't do anything, either."

"You got someplace you can go?"

She nodded. "My sister's down in Santa Cruz. I'll call her." She leaned over, took my hands, and gripped them hard. "You have to find out who killed him."

I sucked in a breath and glanced over at the ashtray with the dope pipe. Was she smoking too much? Or was this grief? Because she was kind of…volatile. "Me? I'm no detective. And I live on the East Coast…"

"You're a computer genius, right? That's what Buzzy told me."

"He   did?"

"So it doesn't matter where you are. You were Waldo's friend. And nobody else is going to help me."

I sighed. "OK. I'll see what I can do."

"Thank you." She stood and got the ashtray with the pipe and a baggie of dope. She sat and fired it up. "You want a hit?"

I was tempted. "Not sure that's a good idea. I do, we might…"

"End up in bed. You're right. The timing's not super." She was looking away from me. At an old picture of her and Waldo sitting on the counter. Both smiling.

"That dope does smell good. Rain check?"

She glanced at me and smiled.

I kissed her on the cheek and left.

I felt bad about leaving. And bad for her, worrying like that, and being a little crazy. And bad for myself. I was a man of my word. What had I just agreed to?

Maybe I wasn't a total lost cause when it came to this heart stuff. I seemed to be feeling a lot of things all of a sudden.

5.

The only flight I could get was the red-eye. Seven the next morning, I was heading up the Taconic to Hudson. I got a call from a number I didn't recognize. I let it go to voice mail, then listened. A man with a crusty voice: "I bought a device that was supposed to transfer all my old LPs to digital, but I can't get it to work. I called the company that made it and this gentleman in India said he would help, but..."

I thought of calling him. But he sounded long-winded and I didn't have good news for him. I deleted the message. Keep doing that and eventually the word should get around about my supposed computer service being a dud. Though with the Internet, who knew.

I'd gotten four hours of sleep the night before last, and an hour at best last night on the plane. But as I drove to Hudson I was jazzed. Coming home to Mingus and my computers. To rustling up some grub the way I liked it. To my bed. And to my collection in the glass and brass cases in the theater, my little private museum.

Only Ray and my exes had ever seen it. It had started innocently enough, the week I moved to Hudson. In the back of the theater I found old chandeliers, a row of shabby red velvet seats, and a roll of matching curtains. I looked around the theater and imagined teenagers in those seats pretending to thrill to black-and-white Barrymores, stealing a kiss and maybe more. All dead and forgotten.

I was tidying them up, lining them up in a row as I decided how to get rid of them, when Ray showed up with a cow pelvis and...a stack of nuns' gravestones. Wooden sticks with plain boards on top, like signs, two sisters' names painted on either side. Did the nuns share a grave, too? Those gravestones were so sad, a distillation of sorrow, like some great spare tragic melody. Come to think of it, the cow bone was sad too, if you were the cow...

I set the items Ray had brought in a new row parallel to the first. And my museum was born. I looked for things to add, things signifying someone's loss. A person I'd never met, who the world had forgotten. That forgetting seemed wrong to me. I couldn't give them back what they'd lost any more than I could their lives. But I could honor what they'd been deprived of.

As my collection grew, Ray would come see it. Sometimes he'd bring candidates for inclusion. One day he asked, "You don't know any of these people?"

"That's kind of the idea."

"What idea?"

"Nothing."

"It's interesting that in all the time I've know you I've never seen a single photo or keepsake of anyone from your past. No exes, no family members. You don't even have pictures of our old band."

"Nope. And?"

He just smiled. Another time he said, "You know, this is...art."

"We might have played music together, but you're the artist. It's just a hobby."

Ray was trying to read some murky psychological shit into what I was doing, like he does twenty times a day with himself. He does more than enough navel-gazing for the both of us. Just a hobby.

***

My hobby was relaxing, as any hobby should be. Detailed, meticulous work without the consequences of work. Comforting and not without feeling. My anonymous donors spoke to me through their relics, like old actors on the vanished screen in this theater. Their whispers touched me gently, like the faint odor seeping from the cases, sweet and rotten like Madeira wine.

Like everything in my life, my collection was meticulously ordered.

Everything was in the right category and abided by two rules: it symbolized loss, and its origin was anonymous.

Every item was subject to my rigorous curatorial eye. Sad junk didn't cut it. Everything needed to pack enough sorrowful punch.

***

Now I was ten minutes from town. I looked in the rearview, eyed Waldo's box sitting on the backseat, and frowned. Did it belong in my collection? A box of '60s memorabilia certainly hit the theme of loss. What was the counterculture, if not a maw of vanished hope? But Waldo's box broke the second rule. He was not an anonymous donor. Neither was Angela, with her swatch of cloth. Just as Waldo's death had disrupted my comfortable life, the box was messing with my museum.

Some of the stuff in it really belonged in the collection, so I would let rule two slide. But there was another problem. The box was its own set of stuff but at the same time contained discrete items that could be split up.

I'd spent so many hours arranging, dusting, polishing the glass and brass, that I could see it as clearly as if I was there, pacing the aisles.

Down the first row.

Case one. *Rejections and Regrets*: letters of dismissal, notices of dishonorable discharge or eviction, letters of commitment, telegrams beginning, "We regret to inform you…" Death certificates. Nothing of Waldo's belonged there.

Two. *Wasted Creations*: a stack of manuscripts, "NO" scribbled in red pen, the effluence from the slush piles of long-shuttered publishers. Demo tapes on reel-to-reel and cassette that never made the cut.

Three. *Lost Love*: a sheaf of Dear John letters, an abandoned wedding dress. A wheel of birth control pills never opened. The pants Angela sewed could go there… No. Too complicated.

Row two.

Dead Eyes: antique viewing devices—old eyeglasses, monocles, spyglasses, a Victorian microscope, opera glasses, movie camera lenses.

Missed Highs: empty booze bottles and drug vials. Unused tickets to the Beatles at Shea Stadium. A perfect place for the Janis Joplin napkin.

I was coming down the last row in my head as I drove up the hill into town, passing the state prison on my right. I still didn't have a place for the box itself, which was annoying.

I turned onto Warren Street. Eight thirty in the morning and the town was still fast asleep. I turned on Fourth Street. Pulled into the dirt backyard behind the theater.

The door was wide open. I leaped from the car, ran toward the door. Slowed down. It was just Ray, come to feed Mingus. The dog barreled out, barking his head off. He jumped on me. I crouched and hugged him as he slobbered my face. I stood and walked inside. "Ray?"

The door to the office was open, too. The lights in the theater were on. Why? "Ray!"

I looked at the cases. Everything seemed to be there…but why was everything glittering? I was seriously sleep deprived, but not to the point of hallucinating.

Broken glass. I rushed past the cases. Someone had smashed every one.

Brickman?

I looked more carefully. Something was missing. The nuns' gravestones. And my collection had a new member, in the last case of the fourth row. A rock, about the size of a baseball. A message?

I reached for it. Stopped. Fingerprints.

But who was I fooling? I wasn't calling the cops. And tell them what? That a guy I'd illegally hacked was fucking with me? I stayed as far away from cops as I could.

With trepidation, I climbed into the office. The AC was roaring, but it was still hot as hell in here with the door open.

My computers were still unplugged. They hadn't been messed with in any obvious way.

I thought of the break-in at Jeannie's and checked the back door. It seemed intact. It didn't have a dead bolt. Whoever did it must have picked the lock.

I made coffee and called Ray.

He said, "Hey, where are you?"

"Home."

"Welcome back to Hudson."

"Somebody broke into my place."

"What? I was just there last night, feeding your dog."

"When?"

"Around seven. I was about to come over."

"Glad you weren't here when he came."

"Who?"

"Brickman, maybe."

"I'll be right over."

When he arrived, he surveyed the damage then stood shaking his head.

"You must have really pissed Brickman off."

"That's if it's him."

"Who else? This is not random vandalism. It's targeting you."

"I know, but he didn't touch my computers upstairs."

"Does he have to, with the internet?"

"Right. Of course not. Which is the weird thing. Brickman doesn't do bad shit in the real world, as far as I know. Neither do the other guys who might have a grudge against me. And he's in Boston. Much easier to fuck with me from there than drive all the way down here. And why did he take the nun's gravestones?"

"I don't know. But it's a shame. They were my favorite part of your collection."

"They *would* be your favorite." Ray of Darkness.

"You think he's done?"

"That's the question."

"Did he come to trash your place? Or…"

"Did he come for me? No telling."

"At least Mingus is safe. And you weren't here when he came. You're not calling the police."

I scoffed.

We went to the kitchen and I made coffee.

Ray said, "I know you're a dyed-in-the-wool pacifist. And I respect that. But I don't want you to end up a dead one. This guy is violent. You need to protect yourself."

"I'm there. How?"

"I know you won't go for a gun. And I don't know what use a knife would do you if you don't know how to use it. Go up to Walmart and get some pepper spray."

"All right, if it makes you feel better. But I've got another idea. A steel door. And surveillance cameras."

Ray nodded. "I'm glad you're taking this seriously. How was the funeral?"

"Cold."

"Huh?"

"Fog. Welcome after summer here. I saw the other two brothers. Buzzy's bald and great as ever. Rick turned into a dick. But the big news is that it looks like Waldo was murdered."

"What?"

I explained what Jeannie and Buzzy thought. I told him about the break-in at Jeannie's.

He said, "There's another weird coincidence for you."

"Somebody breaks in here like they did in San Francisco."

"And Waldo falls like that chick did here."

I snorted. "Get this. Jeannie wants me to find out who killed him."

"And how exactly are you going to do that?"

"You have any ideas, please let me know. Waldo's widow gave me something. It's going in my museum, but you might appreciate a preview. In fact, I know you will. It's in the car."

We brought our coffees up to the office. I got the box and brought it in. Mingus saw it and got up from his bed and sniffed at it. I placed it on my desk.

I rummaged around in it, pulled out the Janis Joplin napkin, and handed it to Ray. He cradled it like a holy relic.

I showed him the pictures, pointing out the other brothers, but not Angela.

He looked at the demonstration picture. "I could swear I was there."

I scanned the crowd. "Yeah? So where are you?"

Ray shook his head. "Must have been some other time. All those demonstrations were the same."

I came on the picture torn from the newspaper.

Ray picked it up. "This doesn't look right."

"What do you mean?" I'd just glanced at it with Buzzy. Now I gave it a longer look. Two very white guys stood in suits. The one on the left was impossibly handsome, not a hair out of place, beaming for the camera with an acre of gleaming teeth. The other guy was whispering in his ear. He was a little taller with hair that was short even by today's standards, practically a military buzz cut, except for the bald line, which extended well up his scalp. Both seemed well fed, immaculately groomed.

Ray said, "I don't know."

"It's just some professors from the college or something…" But something was off about it.

"Wait…I *know* this guy." He pointed to the man on the left.

"Who is it?"

"I've seen him online. Somebody famous."

"Really? There was nobody famous in Middleburg back then. Not that us lowlifes would have known if there were."

We both laughed.

Ray asked, "Mind if I take it?"

"No."

"Better yet, let me scan it. I'm going to post it on my blog, see if anyone knows this guy."

***

I made my living installing and maintaining cyber security systems. Now I needed a physical one. Provided I forked over an arm and a leg, or two, the best local security company told me they could get me fixed up by dinnertime. We'd see about that.

But a guy showed up in less than an hour. He was thin. Quiet and contained, kind of like me. The company's website advertised locksmith services. I said, "Before you get started on that door…what do you know about lock picking?"

A lot, judging from the way the corner of his mouth turned up and the dance he did with his eyes. Which wasn't surprising, given that guys who did it for a living on one side of the law often came from the other side. Another thing we had roughly in common. I smiled back, and he gave a little nod: takes one to know one.

He said, "What do you got?"

I showed him the back door. "Somebody broke in, which is why you're here. How good were they?" I'd looked and hadn't seen any signs that the lock was tampered with.

He leaned over and studied the lock. "This is the work of a pro. They've been doing it for a long time. Otherwise you'd see scratches around the hole. They went right in and popped it."

"Thanks."

He installed a solid steel door with a keyless lock and two dead bolts, and a camera outside, above the door. We walked around the house and I showed him the windows.

"Those I can't do today. You need bars. But they're also high enough that they'd need a ladder to get in. It's not likely someone would use one right here in town."

He pointed to the old bulkhead, which was closed with a padlock and painted shut. "I'd recommend replacing that with steel. Or you can put another solid door inside at the top of the basement steps. I don't do that work, though." He gave me the name of someone who did.

I said, "In the meantime, what if someone breaks in?"

"I can put a camera inside with a motion sensor. It sees something, it'll send an alert to your phone or computer and you can see what's going on."

I nodded. "What about my dog?"

"He'll trigger it, so it should go where he doesn't."

I thought. "You can put in in my theater, at the top of the stairs."

Inside, the guy peered in the first case, raised his eyebrows.

I didn't say anything.

He installed the camera at the top of the stairs.

"Give me your email, and I'll send you instructions for the cameras. You can access them remotely with a computer or phone. See what's going on from wherever you are, in real time. They record as well."

My email address. I sighed. "You give this to anyone…"

"I understand. Trust me."

Apparently, he believed there was honor among thieves. I wasn't sure, but I needed this remote access. I gave him my email. He handed me a clicker for the door. "Don't let the battery in this thing run down. Or you'll be seriously locked out."

He left. I headed up into my office and cranked on the AC with the wishful thought that a few days' rest had cured it. No such luck. The air blowing from it was warm, sick smelling. It roared and clanked like a machine shop on amphetamines.

I shut it off and got a fan from the closet. I took my shirt off, plugged my computers back in, and fired them up. Ran diagnostics. I spent an hour running tests for viruses, Trojan horses, malware. No spyware, no nothing. So whoever it was had just come into the theater. Maybe Mingus had chased him away.

Brickman's online avatar was an anonymous male silhouette. I'd conjured a picture of him—a pasty, sweaty kid with smeared glasses in a hoodie. A stereotype, and I should have known better, because we were essentially in the same business. But once I saw him that way I couldn't unsee him. And though I wasn't sure he was the person who'd broken into my place, I was picturing Brickman doing it. It was easier than imagining some phantom.

I hit his favorite forums, where he'd posted daily. There was still nothing since I sent my threatening email. Which, if he hadn't put up my fake website, might have been a good sign—that he'd gotten my message. What it meant now, I didn't know.

I needed to take another look at the Bodine website. I popped my name into Google, but all that came up was what had come up two years ago: that old music site. That couldn't be right. But it was.

The site was *gone.* Not just that, but the sites that had been growing links to it like malignant tendrils had been scrubbed of the links. I sensed a little pinch at the top of my gut. Brickman had gone dark on his forums. Now this. I imagined a tidal wave approaching, sucking a million tons of water into itself, leaving the ocean floor bare for a beat before it came thundering in. Brickman hiding before he attacked.

But attacked how? My computers were clean. I knew a dirty one when I saw one. My livelihood depended on it.

***

Late afternoon, I was scrounging in the kitchen for something to eat. Mingus was whining, which he didn't usually do, and prancing back and forth in the direction of the bedroom.

I said, "It isn't nearly time for bed." But I headed to the bedroom along with him, where he started barking. I smelled a faint odor and noticed a big dark patch on the duvet. I raced to the bed and the smell got stronger.

Urine. I glanced at Mingus then away guiltily. He was allowed on the bed and he was a good dog. He might have been upset about my leaving him, but he'd never act out like that. That was cat business. Except I didn't have one.

Whoever had broken in had pissed on my bed. I tore the bedclothes off and tossed them down into the basement. I was reluctant to return to the bedroom, feeling it was defiled, but damned if I was sleeping on the couch because of some asshole.

I went in and sat on the bed and tried to put this latest outrage together with what I knew about Brickman. I pushed away the geek stereotype and imagined him doing these things. He was obviously angry, but the bed thing might be something else. Marking territory, like a dog? Claiming his fucked-up corner of the Internet? But then there was what he stole. The guy was angry, but also weird. None of which got me anywhere.

I was putting clean sheets on the bed when I saw Laurel's crumpled-up note under it. I went still, eyeing it warily. Like it was a tarantula about to pounce.

I recalled getting it. I'd come home from the store. Her car was gone, and I figured she'd left for work early. The note was on the bed. *Our* bed, then. It had hit me hard. I told myself it was because I really hadn't seen it coming.

I'd crushed it in my fist and stalked through the house with a garbage bag, throwing in the shampoo she'd forgotten, the soy milk, old running shoes.

Getting rid of every trace of her. Except this note.

An old litany played in my head. *It's just that time again. Wintertime. Relationships are as predictable as the seasons. Bright green spring and a nice hot summer. Mellow fall. But at the first sign of frost…it's time to end it.*

I was just a little off my game and had let Laurel get the jump on me. If I'd pulled the plug first, I'd have been fine.

I'd be fine anyway. Sure, there'd be some weeks where I slept later and was off my feed. But a new Laurel would come soon enough. One always did.

There had been a lot of Laurels, and the rap I told myself was well rehearsed. Except this time I didn't quite buy it.

Which was perhaps why I'd neglected to toss the note. Now I uncrumpled it and read it again.

B-

I totally get it that you aren't into making a "commitment." You made it crystal clear on day one what the rules were, and I'm cool with that.

But.

But I need a little more than I'm getting.

More than flowers and chocolates and even a hard dick.

I don't care that your music sucks. Not everybody can be an artist in this world.

I don't care that for all your macho bullshit you're just a geek like the rest of us.

But.

A girl needs more.

A girl needs more than somebody she can beat at Need for Speed.

Maybe just a smidge of interest in who I am. I told you about my life's passion, gravity waves. You were like, "Sounds complicated." You never asked me about it once after that. Yeah, it is *complicated. But I LOVE it.*

What is hard to believe is I bet you're still telling yourself you're God's gift.

Coming up a little short here, fella.

I know I must sound pissed off, but what I really am is sad. The day we met you were like, "Go with the flow, see where it takes us." It's carrying me the fuck out of this house, out of your life.

Maybe someday you'll know what you missed here.

I'm not holding my breath.

L

P.S. I'm gonna miss your cooking.

I stood there, still. It was like some hatch flew open in the floor, and I teetered at the edge, staring into an abyss. Just icy blackness below going down and down forever. Blackness and agony beat in my chest. The feeling was unbearable. But I forced myself to linger as long as I could stand it. Like there might be something down there aside from agony.

There was. I felt a trembling, then my eyes bugged out as an inconceivable, unprecedented thought blazed through my mind.

What if Laurel was right? I shook my head, like I could shake it away. And the feeling began to seep away. But the thought remained.

With all my previous lovers, it had always been their fault. Too spaced out, too loud. Too nice. And worst of all, too needy. Which was what I'd told myself was the deal with Laurel when I first read her note. Now I wasn't sure.

What if I hadn't ended it in time because I didn't want it to end? What if in the back of mind there'd been the hope that this one might go the distance?

These thoughts were foreign, those of some other man. I'm well aware that in the realm of emotional intelligence, I'm no genius. But my occasional flashes of intuition, or whatever you call that mysterious sense, I trust like the sun coming up.

For decades I'd been sliding across the smooth, hard surface of my days, telling myself life was fine. I kept telling myself that even after Laurel's departure. But reading her note again had punched a ragged hole in that surface.

And it wasn't the first. The first hole had been the news of Waldo, with its echoes of Angela. Then came finding Brickman's fake website. Then the acrophobia. And the break-in.

I couldn't see what was coming—I don't believe in crystal balls or investment predications or any of that delusional crap. But I was certain that my smooth ride was over.

At least I had Buzzy. If things got too rough? *My door's always open.*

I was about to toss the note in a trash can when I stopped. I carried it down to my collection. Well aware of the theatrical nature of my act—hey, it was an old theater! —I walked to the case containing *Lost Love.* I pushed the wedding dress over, making a space, careful not to get cut on the broken glass. I laid Laurel's letter down, smoothing it as best as I could. So much for rule number two, though I'd been about to break it anyway.

I got Waldo's box and set it at the bottom of the stairs. I'd figure out which case it belonged in tomorrow. Enough decisions for one day.

6.

The next morning, I was in the office coding when Ray called. He sounded pumped. "I found the guy in the picture."

"And it's…"

"Let me come over."

"OK."

I went down and unlocked the new door.

He looked it up and down. "Your new door is…solid, man."

"No shit. Fort Knox in here."

We went up to the office and Ray pulled the scan of the newspaper fragment from his pocket and laid it on my desk. We leaned over and looked at it. He pointed to the man on the left. "This is the governor of California."

I said, "I thought Reagan was governor back then."

"No, the *current* governor. That's what looked off about this picture. It's not from the sixties. It's recent."

As soon as he said it, I saw. Something about the hairstyles, their suits, was contemporary.

Ray said, "I put it up on my blog and a few hours later got a comment identifying him. Then I found this actual picture on another blog, in a gallery of rising right-wing stars. He's the real deal, coming up fast. Wants to do a Reagan, be the next president."

"Then what was it doing in the box with all that old stuff?"

"That's the question."

I sat as Ray went over to the old projection window and peered down into the darkened theater, like the answer was there.

I said, "Maybe Waldo just threw it in there."

Ray frowned. "It was on top when you opened the box?"

"No, it was near the bottom. On top of the other photos."

"So he didn't just throw it in."

"I guess not. I didn't tell you, Waldo was a prominent left-wing lawyer, heavy into social justice."

"And this Governor Nichols is a right-wing cat. You thinking they tussled at some point?"

"It's a big state, but could be."

"Then why wasn't the picture in his office?"

"I don't know. Buzzy told me he was in touch with Waldo recently about some gay-rights bill in California."

"Now *there's* grounds for a tussle."

"I suppose." I walked over and picked up the picture. The header was cut off. I showed it to Ray. "I wonder where it's from?"

"I can poke around more online and see."

"I'm going to send Buzzy this picture, see if he knows why Waldo had it."

"Good idea. I'd like to meet this Buzzy sometime." He moved toward the door.

"Hold on. How about this week? We can go up, maybe take him out to lunch."

"And I haven't seen old Middleburg in forever. Sure."

"I'll let you know when he's available."

"Well *I* am, every day. As you know."

Ray left. I called Buzzy and arranged lunch for Friday.

I said, "It looks like I'll see you before another forty years."

"I'm glad. Middleburg's got a Thai joint now. It's not quite up to that place in San Fran, though."

"It'll be fine. Ray's dying to meet you. Oh, and I've got a picture I'd like to email you."

***

Over the next few days, I did my best to reestablish the comfortable routines of my life. I started a new paid coding job. I called the bulkhead guy and made an appointment for the next week. The new door and surveillance cameras had me feeling safe, but also disconcerted, like I was hiding in my own house. Despite the essential defensive nature of my business, and despite my nonviolence, I was a proactive guy. Problems needed to be faced, not run away from. But facing Brickman—if that was even who I was dealing with— meant going up to Boston. Armed. And confronting him. I wasn't doing that.

I didn't like waiting for a next move, either. But there wasn't one, and the whole business began to fade. Maybe Brickman had gotten his revenge on me and moved on.

Laurel was receding, too. When she'd first left, I dreaded taking Mingus out, because the sight of her empty parking space out back had threatened to put me on the edge again over that deep, dark place. Now it just evoked a momentary pang.

I hit my coding job hard, working into the evenings, catching up for the time I was in California.

***

Wednesday afternoon after lunch, I called Jeannie. It was eleven in the morning out there. She should be up. I sat at the organ.

I asked, "How are you holding up?"

"Still shaky. But a little better."

"Good. You talk to the police?"

"I did. They were no help. They think Lands End Point is where Waldo fell, but all they found was a million footprints. And his…body didn't show any evidence of 'foul play.' The guy I talked to sounded bored. He asked me if I had any reason for thinking someone killed him. I told him it was just a feeling and he laughed."

"Sorry."

I told her about the picture of Governor Nichols.

"That shitbird! Waldo hated him. You think the governor of California killed my husband?"

"Whoa. That's a stretch. You think he had a reason to?"

"I don't know. I stopped following the details of Waldo's cases a long time ago. They bummed me out. What you need to do is talk to that woman in his law office. Kaylee. She'll know."

I called the law office. Kaylee was out to lunch. I left a message and got back to work.

I had a light dinner, put in another hour at the computer, then took the dog out. The streetlights were just coming on. Muggy as it had been all summer, it hadn't rained in weeks. The yard was getting a little ripe with Mingus's shit.

I remembered my phone and turned it on. A message from Buzzy.

"Bodine, call me." Not "Will you call me when you get the chance?" but a command. Did he sound upset? It was hard to tell with a guy as cooled out as him.

I called him and got voice mail. *This* was the cooled-out Buzzy: "I'm very sorry not to be available…" Something was going on with him. I tried him again before going to bed. But I was seeing him in two days. Whatever it was, after forty years it would keep.

***

Ray and I took my Mustang up to Middleburg. We followed the Taconic through woods and open fields. The trees and grass looked tired of the heat. At least the AC in my car worked.

We reminisced about the first days of our band, that summer after I dropped out of college. As we approached Middleburg, I said, "I haven't been back since that spring."

"I didn't stick around for much longer myself."

Once we entered town, Ray took in the spiffed-up main street and said, "Aw, man, the fuckwits ruined it."

"It was a dump."

"At least it was an *honest* dump. This is the Disneyland version of what a small town is supposed to look like."

"I can't argue."

We were meeting Buzzy at the Thai restaurant at noon. I'd timed things so I'd be early as always. We walked the main street, then stepped into the restaurant as the bells at the Middleburg chapel rang twelve. I told the waiter we were waiting for a third person.

Ray said, "I hope this is better than the restaurants in Middleburg back in the day."

"I don't remember there being any."

"You've blocked it out. There was that grinder joint…"

"Ugh. I have blocked it out."

We ran out of food talk. Ray drummed his fingers on the table, and I set my phone down as a clock and watched the minutes change.

At ten past I felt a tightness in my solar plexus. The odor of Thai suddenly seemed greasy and too sweet.

At quarter past, Ray said, "Is this like him, being late?"

"No." Buzzy wasn't compulsively early like me. He'd been exactly on time to dinner. Which fit right in with the care he took with every detail of life. I called him, got voice mail. Left a message. "Uh, Buzzy. Did I get the wrong restaurant? There another Thai place in town?" There couldn't be. Middleburg was too small.

Ray said, "So he just forgot."

"That's less likely than him being late." I told him about Buzzy's phone message.

"You worried?"

I shook my head. But I was. At twelve thirty, I called him again but didn't leave a message. I said, "Let's see if we can find his office." Though it meant nothing, the act of leaving the restaurant felt like a serious step.

While we were waiting in the restaurant the day had turned muggy. We crossed to the shady side of the street and stood in front of a drugstore. I got my phone out and thought.

Ray said, "What are you doing?"

"Trying to remember his name. His real name."

Ray laughed. "Fucking hippies."

It was the same as a town, somewhere here in western Massachusetts… I opened Google Maps and started browsing around the area. "Got it." I pointed to the map. "Stockbridge."

"That his first name? No wonder he's Buzzy."

"Very funny. Last. And I still don't remember the first."

I called directory assistance, asked for a Stockbridge psychologist. I said to Ray, "Bingo. Eldon Stockbridge. His office is right around the corner."

"I guess he's not too worried about psycho patients coming after him, listing himself like that."

We walked upstairs into a large colonial house broken into offices. His door was locked.

Ray asked, "You know where he lives?"

"No." I recalled our dinner in San Francisco. He'd asked if I remembered someone.... "Buzzy mentioned a friend, someone named Sharon, and I think I know where her office is."

We walked to the other side of campus in silence. I recognized the ivied buildings but felt nothing aside from the sun beating on my head. I was grateful when we reached the shelter of a tree-lined street. If memory served, we were almost there.

But when we turned the corner at the end of the street, the Four Brothers house was gone. Its replacement was bigger, an eye-crippling mishmash of architectural styles. I said, "What the fuck. It's gone."

"No shit."

"We joked about how that Victorian heap was a monstrosity, but it was freaking Versailles next to this sorry thing. Except..." The entrance was familiar. "Hold on. That door used to be blue...but that's the same Gothic frame. And I remember those windows."

Ray snorted. "I suppose they think this is an improvement."

"More like the bad taste monster gobbled it up."

Ray read the sign in front of the building aloud: "Susan B. Anthony Center for Interdisciplinary Feminist Research."

I raised an eyebrow.

He said, "I guess it's the sisters' turn now."

I walked in, Ray behind me. I didn't quite expect the old sprung furniture and everything with a layer of grime. But I didn't recognize a thing. They'd moved the walls around, which gleamed with fresh paint. The foyer looked downright elegant. An Audre Lorde poster hung on the wall, captioned "Women are powerful and dangerous." No shit.

My eyes drifted down toward the basement. It had been cool, damp, light filtering in through a dingy casement window… Probably spiffed up like the rest of this place. We weren't going down there today, anyway.

The receptionist, a pretty woman in her late twenties, was reading something, nodding her head. She gazed up, startled, yanked out her earbuds, and asked, "May I help you?"

She fumbled to turn off her music, but I caught it: The Beatles. "We're looking for a professor, Sharon…"

"Wilson. Right upstairs. Wait." She looked us both over quickly. "Let me call up. What should I say you want to see her about?"

"Just let me talk to her."

She called, handed me the phone. I leaned over her desk.

"Sharon Wilson."

I felt a little prickle at the back of my neck. Her voice was nice, low and musical, like the woody bottom range of a clarinet. And something about it…

"Uh, this is Bodine. I'm a friend of Buzzy's. He mentioned you."

"Buzzy! How is he? I've been a little out of touch, up to my nose in this research project."

"He was fine last time I saw him. At a funeral."

"He told me he was going."

"My friend and I were supposed to have lunch with him today. He never showed up."

"Huh." She sounded distracted. "Bodine? That's an odd name. I don't think I've ever heard it before. But your voice sounds familiar."

So it wasn't just me. I said, "Could my friend and I come up and see you for a minute?"

"OK. But just a minute. I'm really busy."

I said to the receptionist, "She'll see us."

She pointed. "Upstairs, down the hall on the left."

As we climbed, Ray said, "This is not how I remember it. It's too straight."

"They gave it a complete redo."

I knocked on Sharon's door.

"Come in."

Unfiltered by the phone, her voice almost conjured a face, and then there it was as she turned in her chair and stood. There were crow's feet around her eyes, but they still sparkled. She had the same straight black hair, though shorter. The same noble, deeply intelligent face, and the same flawless skin…

I'd been wrong. I *was* going down to that basement again, in a manner of speaking.

The fingertips of my right hand tingled with a sense memory of that skin. The room shimmered as I tried to bridge forty years and a hundred feet, connecting the woman before me with the one who'd lain with me on what we called, with college hippie ironic conceit, the Free Love Couch. She'd worn no linen jacket, wool pants or earrings then. Just a T-shirt, then no shirt…

The two Sharons split apart, one flying away downstairs and into the maw of time, the other still standing there, looking at me with a hint of amusement in her smile. A little eye roll and she looked away.

She shook my hand, almost formally, then shook Ray's hand. He introduced himself.

She glanced back at me. "Bob."

"Uh, yeah. Sharon."

We burst into laughter.

She looked me up and down. "You've barely aged."

"You're looking fine yourself." I wasn't lying.

Ray asked, "You two know each other?" Neither of us said anything. He said, "You know Bodine used to live right in this building back when he was in college."

She nodded, holding onto that smile like it might get away from her. "Yes, I'm aware of that."

That couch might as well have been sitting right between us, the fat-assed elephant in the room.

She sat and folded her hands in her lap. They showed the wear and tear even a cushy academic life wrought after forty years. They were worn but nice. No ring.

I said, "Two days ago Buzzy left a message. He sounded, I don't know, worried? I haven't been able to reach him since."

"Worried? I can't picture Buzzy worrying about anything." But her forehead creased. "He stood you up for lunch? That's not like him."

"Nope. You know where he lives? We could go check. Maybe he's sick."

"I'd go there with you, but I'm on a deadline with a paper." She gave me his address.

I said, "He live alone?"

She laughed. "Yes. You know he's gay?"

"Yeah."

"He hasn't found Mr. Right yet. Although I must say, not for lack of trying. Maybe you haven't heard from him because he got lucky, forgot to call you." But her forehead was still scrunched up.

"Right."

"Well, uh, it's been good to see you…. Again." She blinked a couple of times.

Fuck, it was, I wanted to stay.

She stood and turned to Ray. "It's very nice to meet you." She turned to me. "You call me, tell me soon as you find Buzzy."

"I will."

Ray walked out in the hall. She whispered to me, "You still have long hair."

"And you still…have a nice smile." Which turned the nice up even higher.

***

Ray and I drove to Buzzy's house, past quiet tree-lined streets.

He said, "Man, she may be a hard-core feminist, but in my book she's happening. How'd you know each other?"

"She was here that year at Middleburg."

He gave me a look but dropped it.

The house was a nice compact Arts and Crafts job. A car sat in the driveway.

Ray said, "He's here."

A flood of relief. "Let's hope."

I rang the front doorbell. It chimed faintly somewhere inside. We waited. I rang again. Pounded on the door. The door was locked. We walked to the back. The door there was locked, too.

I said, "It doesn't look like he's here."

"Maybe he just stepped out."

I felt along the top of the back door for a hidden key, then under a cinder block next to the stoop. I got the key and opened the door. We walked into the kitchen and small living room with Tibetan thangka paintings on the walls, then upstairs where there were two bedrooms and a bath. The beds were made, everything was clean and neat. In the master hung a mandala and a painting of fierce demons.

Ray said, "He has good taste in art."

The places of people who lived alone often felt empty, sad. Not this house. It felt warm.

We went back downstairs. Mail was piled at the bottom of the front door. Shit.

I asked, "Where's his computer?"

"Maybe he has a laptop with him."

"But he should have some kind of office."

We found it, hidden around a corner off the kitchen.

There was still no computer. A set of keys hung on the wall over the desk. I took them and said, "Maybe one of these is for his office downtown."

We drove there. One of the keys worked. The inside was decked out in the same earth tones Buzzy had worn, with a serene Buddha and a wall fountain burbling away. There was a couch. Of course! It was a shrink's office.

I headed right for the desktop computer and poked around. It took me all of a minute to get into his email: his password was "buzzy6." *They never learn.*

Ray asked, "Anything there?"

I frowned. "A notice about a therapist's conference. Buddhist stuff. The last outgoing email is Tuesday, the day before he left his message. Something about a sitting."

I scrolled back in time. "But maybe that doesn't mean anything. He's not much of an emailer. Here's a long one to Waldo."

I started reading. "There's nothing there." I poked around some more. "His computer's pretty clean. No spyware. There are lots of appointments on his calendar. He must have a lot of clients."

Ray pointed to a phone with a blinking light. "Messages."

"Let's check them." I punched some keys and came up with the incoming messages.

"Hi. It's three twenty and you're not here…" A woman, sounding pissed off. "Where are you? I'm waiting…" A man. "I waited a half hour and I'm going now. Are you OK?" Another woman. She sounded concerned. There were more.

Ray's face mirrored my growing concern as I listened.

I said, "This is bad."

"Maybe it's time to call the police."

"Maybe." But not me. Not with the illicit part of my business. And certainly not the *Middleburg* police. They were the ones who'd busted me. Never mind that it was years ago.

Ray didn't know the details of my business, but he knew enough to understand. He said, "I'll call them if you want."

"Hang tight for a moment. I'm going to try Sharon."

I sat on the couch and called.

"Sharon."

"You again," she said. "You don't call me for forty years. Now I hear from you twice in one day."

This was one of those times when my perpetually cooled-out voice fails at the basic job of communication. As upset as I was about Buzzy, the way I'd said her name she hadn't caught it. Much as I wanted to flirt with her, now was not the time. "We didn't find Buzzy at his house or office. Does he have a laptop?"

"I don't know." She'd gotten the message. Her voice tightened up.

"There's a car in his driveway. An Audi. And mail stacked inside the front door."

"So he met someone, has been shacking up. Hey, love is blind."

"I listened to his messages at the office. He missed a bunch of appointments."

"Oh." A long sigh, in which I could hear the hope leaking out of her. "He would never miss a single appointment without giving people notice. How many did he miss?"

"A bunch." The message light blinking on his phone was getting to me, like it was speaking in some kind of fucked up Morse code: *He's gone.*

I asked, "Would you call the police?"

"Why don't you?"

"Um, I'm not from around here. I don't want to explain about Waldo and the whole funeral business. They might get confused."

"OK, I'll do it."

"And would you mind checking the local papers over the next few days, let me know if there's any news of him?"

"News?" She stopped. "What do you think happened to him?" Her voice rose in pitch.

"I'm sure he's fine." But I wasn't.

7.

We got in the car. I didn't start it.

Ray said, "What do you think is going on?"

I shook my head. I thought about the basement. Not Sharon and me down there, but the night of the blizzard.

I said, "How'd you like to take a little trip down one of the darker corners of memory lane?"

Ray grinned. "You need to ask?"

We walked over to the Feminist Research building. Though it was only a handful of blocks, the merciless sun had me overheated by the time we arrived.

Inside it was cooler. The receptionist smiled. "She's still here. But I don't know if..."

I said, "We're not here to bother her. Uh, I lived here once, a long time ago. The late sixties."

She brightened up. "Oh, I *love* the sixties!"

I smiled and pointed at her iPod. "Still the Beatles?"

"How did you know? I love them."

Ray leaned over her desk and said, "Bodine is a musician, used to be in a band."

Bodine said, "With him. He's a pretty amazing guitar player."

"You guys were in a band...in the sixties?" She looked troubled. Some kind of rock-and-roll myth stood before her, but it just looked like a couple of old farts. It was all I had to butter her up with.

I said, "Do you know when this house was renovated?"

"I didn't know it was. Before my time."

I said, "You ever been down in the basement?"

"No."

I asked, "Mind if we take a peek?"

She said, "I don't know. I think it's locked." She frowned, then sighed. "I don't see any harm in your looking. And I'm kind of curious myself." She disappeared into a coat closet. She emerged with a big ring of keys. We followed her down a maze of corridors. Not a single old wall remained. It was good she was leading.

The door was new, a hefty steel job. A sibling to my new one at home.

I gave a mock graveyard laugh. "They wanted to make sure nobody goes down there."

Ray said, "Or comes up."

I said, "Ooga booga."

She raised her eyebrows, then unlocked the door, glanced down the dark stairs, and fumbled for a light switch. There was a click but nothing came on. "Seems to be broken. You really want to see it?"

I nodded, took out my phone and turned on the light. It was small but bright. "You coming?"

She stepped back. "I think I'll stay here."

Ray and I started down. I whispered, "Her eyes are bigger than her stomach."

"Switch that phone for a torch and you're like Virgil leading Dante into hell."

I laughed. There was a weird echo.

Halfway down the stairs, I said, "Oh God, it smells the same. Minus the incense and dope smoke."

It didn't just smell the same. It was clear that the renovation had stopped at the top of the stairs. As I swept the light around the room, I saw that it was just as we'd left it thirty-nine years ago. In the center of the room sat a cable-spool table with a tin ashtray still set in the hole in the middle. A cheap Oriental rug with stains from spilled wine covered part of the stone floor. That night when the cops had come, they'd hauled me out of here barefoot, and the stones were cold underfoot.

I said, "We called this Dope Central." It was the first of three small adjoining rooms squeezed into the north side of the cavernous basement. Nine-tenths of the basement was on the other side of a wall, a vast low space stuffed with the abandoned belongings of generations of frat boys, a great furnace, and a coal room.

There was no door on the entrance to the second room. We walked in. Its light was out, too. I said, "They must have disconnected them. This was the Music Room. Smoke yourself into the mood, stagger in here, and dig the finest collection of records…"

I pointed to a couple of moldy couch pillows against the wall. "That's what passed for chairs. We just sat against the wall."

Ray winced and held his lower back.

"We were young."

"But didn't care. Because you were high. And because of the music."

"Jeez, Ray, it's almost like you were here."

"I was, just on the other side of town. Listening to Hendrix. Dylan. Jefferson Airplane." He evoked the names with a reverent tone.

But I was training the light on the wreckage in the corner, a tangle of wires, metal and wood, remembering something. "Iron Butterfly."

"No. You didn't listen to that shit."

"Not until that night. Rick insisted." I sang a snippet of "In-A-Gadda-Da-Vida."

Ray lunged over and mocked slapping a hand over my mouth.

"Sorry. Remember, that night we were tripping our brains out. Rick insisted, *begged* us to let him play that miserable song. Like his life depended on it."

"That fucking mindless guitar riff, over and over for seventeen minutes. It's musical Sisyphus."

And it was repeating right now, drilling a hole in my brain. A malignant earworm.

He said, "It's bad enough when you're straight. I can't imagine it on acid."

"Like eternity in hell. Everyone else had the sense to split."

"Why did you stay?"

"I didn't want to leave Rick down here alone. I was afraid for him. He just kept staring at the album cover. Soon as the song was over, he played it again. And again."

We'd been down there long enough now that the basement's chill had gotten to me. My sweaty shirt was wicking my body heat out into the room. I'd just had a vivid memory of the worst night of my life, and its soundtrack was playing in my head, yet I felt nothing aside from the sensation of shrinking into myself. Though maybe it was just the chilly air.

I said, "When it started playing the fourth time, I knew I wasn't going to last the song without slipping into psychosis—or worse. I was heading for the door when Rick shouted, 'It's coming!' I asked, 'What's coming?' Rick was staring at the speakers. He said, 'The Iron Butterfly.'"

Ray burst out laughing. I joined him, then turned serious. "Under any other circumstance it would be been the punch line of a bad psychedelic joke. Not that night. Because I could easily picture some great metal insect flying right out of the speakers, iron wings clanking, bearing down on us. Rick gave a howl and launched himself at my stereo, kicking the shit out of it. He tore the speakers right from their cabinets, ripped the guts out of the turntable."

I'd had enough of the Music Room. The third room had a door, which was stuck. I had to get my shoulder into it before it opened with a hellacious creak.

Ray laughed. "You got the ghost of Vincent Price in there?"

"This was…the Rabbit Hole." I winced with embarrassment.

"Where I'm assuming you guys fucked like bunnies. Don't let those feminist scholars upstairs know that."

One of them already did. "That's not the worst. We had this funky thing we called the Free Love Couch."

"You guys were into some lame shit. Makes me glad I never went to college."

As I stepped inside, the familiar and not unpleasing odor gave way to something more pungent. But my light had already zeroed in on its source.

The Free Love Couch was a mess, gray stuffing leaking from rents in the cushions, the upholstery stiff and matted like the skin of an animal carcass. I lifted the lantern to the wall above it, anticipating the sight of the great mural the four of us had painted together one brain-blasted night, in Day-Glo red, blue, yellow, and purple. Interlocked paisleys, nesting an ankh, a peace sign, other esoteric icons, surrounding the centerpiece: the words *Free Love* in high psychedelic ballooning script.

I blinked rapidly. Except for the *e* and one side of the *v*, and a pitiful yin/yang symbol, our work had been obliterated by glistening blooms of black-and-green mold.

My mouth turned down. "I was looking forward to showing you this gem of authentic psychedelic art. It was ugly, but not this kind of ugly."

I remembered what had happened in here just as clearly as that scene in the Music Room. But I made a conscious effort to shut the memory off. That shrinking into myself had continued, because now it felt like there wasn't enough room inside. And I was shivering.

Ray must have noticed. "It's cold down here. You had enough?"

"Yes."

It was even hotter outside than before. But I stood for a moment, eyes closed, drinking in the sun I'd spent most of the last month avoiding. It felt good, until I remembered Buzzy.

We drove back to Hudson.

Ray said, "What do you think happened to Buzzy?"

I shook my head. We were silent most of the way home.

I finally spoke. "LSD is some strange stuff."

Ray laughed. "I noticed."

"No, I mean that trip was thirty years ago, and I remember details like they happened ten minutes ago. At the same time, I don't remember the important part at all."

"The profound implications everything seemed to have. The cosmic meaning. The *feeling* of it."

"Exactly." But I did feel something—that sensation of being wound tight into myself.

"Probably just as well. That doesn't sound like the kind of trip you'd want to flash back on."

***

Back home I cranked up the video game console and sat on the couch. I hadn't played since Laurel left. I'd forgotten that *Need for Speed* was in the console. It came up on the screen, along with a distinct memory of Laurel beside me, jerking her head in time with the score like she did when she was ahead.

It was time for a new game. I ejected it and without thinking fired up *Resident Evil 4*. It involved chasing horrible undead creatures through a dingy underworld.

I thought of that basement and smiled. At least there were no zombies down there.

I went to bed. I was halfway asleep when the memory leapt from its vault. It was fresh and potent, undiluted by previous recollection.

It was the night of the blizzard sometime after Rick destroyed my stereo. I was lying in the Rabbit Hole, the air tracing dank fingertips down my cheeks, the reek of stale incense having me breathing from my mouth, candlelight flickering spookily on the walls. Lying on the Free Love Couch on top of a girl trying to attend to what we were doing. But my senses betrayed me, running away out into the room. Trying to escape, because this wasn't lovemaking but *screwing*. As the word appeared in my addled brain, it seemed literal, our movements a mechanical performance, a scene in some terminally depressing existential drama.

Who was she? Her name, face and body have been erased from memory. My body did its thing, but with no pleasure. There was no pleasure to be had that night on that drug. I looked up at one point at the mural above the wall, its colors roiling like a tornado in a Technicolor cesspool, and heard it mocking me—*Free love! Get what you pay for, asshole.*

I was trying to work my way to climax so it would be over, when a sudden roaring stopped me cold. A monster, coming to get us! *The Iron Butterfly*. Because those sounded like giant metal wings…

"What the hell is that?" She sounded terrified too.

A click and the sound stopped. I said, "Don't worry. It's just the furnace coming on in the other part of the basement." A sound that until that night had always been masked by incessant, loud rock and roll. Which, thanks to Rick, was no more. The furnace had killed the mood, such as it had been.

Which was a blessing. I started to get off her, but she said, "Don't. I'm afraid."

A new sound came. A huffing, rhythmic movement of air. I flinched, imagining a great duct sprouting from the furnace like an elephant's trunk, breathing, the furnace a sentient humanoid with crimson glaring eyes and...

As if my thought had flown from my brain into hers and from her mouth, she asked, "What is *that*?"

It *was* breathing, with a whistle on one of the cycles—in or out? I couldn't tell. A dying animal, trapped in the wall. Amplified by the drug into a monster.

I relaxed a hair. "It's just a—"

"I'm out of here!" She'd had enough fun for one night. I got off of her and she grabbed clothes and stumbled away upstairs. I couldn't blame her.

I lay back on the couch and pulled a blanket over me. Had that animal been there all winter? Was there a family in there, and did they bite? But the sound had stopped. There was just a periodic roaring, the storm raging outside, but somehow more benign than the furnace or that breathing.

The candle guttered out, but faint light seeped from the Music Room. I wasn't aware of just how much I had invested in it until *it* went out.

Pitch black exploded into a roiling kaleidoscope of demonic colors. The sounds crescendoed, the mishmash of sensations threatening to suck me into oblivion.

A crumb of logic told me the snow must have brought down a power line. Except I knew better. It was that *thing* on the other side of the wall. Coming to get me.

It was no longer making the sound. Which meant it had somehow slipped into the Music Room, had gotten the light off, and was sneaking up on me.

I fumbled around in the dark for matches and got the candle lit. It flickered before me, the only light in the world, keeping the darkness at bay. And that creature. It wasn't after me. There'd been a power outage.

I wasn't going upstairs. It was dark up there, and for all I knew the blackness had devoured my friends, the college. The whole world.

And then came a sound that dwarfed the others. Genghis Khan's army thundering down the stairs, shouting "Police!" and sounding my doom. There seemed to be at least fifty of them.

***

Back in Hudson, I was wide, wide awake. I suppose I should thank those police. If they hadn't come, I might still be there, lying on that couch, long ago starved to death, a skeleton. Now It was dark, but mercifully faint streetlights shone in the window. I listened for sounds on the other side of the wall behind the bed, in the theater. I had my new door and surveillance cameras. And nothing to fear. Just sad, dead things in their cases, and sad dead memories of the worst acid trip of my life. And the worst sex.

Still, I listened, on hyper alert. It was hours before I slept.

***

I got up the next morning, my head fuzzy from lack of sleep.

Coffee.

Buzzy. I hacked into his Gmail account again, remotely. Having his credentials, it was no harder than sitting in his office. I read his emails to Waldo. There was nothing personal, just strategizing on that gay conversion bill. His trash was filled with spam.

In the drafts folder I found an email, with two photos attached, addressed to me. He hadn't sent it. It said, "Let's talk." He'd written it around the time he left me that message. It looked like Buzzy had thought it was sent, but it had hung up because the files were too big. A common layman's mistake.

I opened the first picture. It was the newspaper fragment with the governor and the other guy. The second picture was one of the demonstration ones that he'd scanned at dinner in San Francisco. I got the originals and laid them side by side on my desk. I stared back and forth between them, looking for something…I got it. After dinner at the Ferry Building, I'd taken the newspaper clipping from the box, but Buzzy and I had ignored it when we saw the next picture. The demonstration one. The pictures had been *together* in the box, just as they were in this email.

I called Ray. "I've got something I want you to see."

"I'll be right over."

Ray arrived five minutes later. I let him in and we went up into the office. I showed him the email and the pictures.

He said, "These are connected."

"The obvious thing is that Governor Nichols was at Middleburg and was at that demonstration. You being the visual guy, and having that imagination of yours, I figured you might be able to subtract forty years and find him."

Ray studied the old picture for minutes. He closed his eyes and rubbed his forehead. Looked again.

"Is Waldo in here?"

I pointed.

"Who's that hot chick next to him? It's not…"

I nodded. "Angela."

"Oh. You didn't tell me."

"What?"

"That she was so beautiful."

I looked away. "Hey, we need to find the governor. You know, even though you and I were freaks, and I should know half of them, there's something about these guys. They all look the same."

"They do. It's all the hair."

Ray pointed to a tall figure in the demonstration picture, his face turned to half profile. "Who's this? He *isn't* the same as the other guys. Is he looking at Angela?"

I said, "Wouldn't be the first."

I hadn't seen him because I was looking at people I knew. Ray didn't know any of them, so he'd noticed the guy. I said, "He is different. But how?"

"See what he's wearing? That's a *blazer*. And if I'm not mistaken, those are penny loafers."

The hair and beards drew the eye so that it was easy to ignore clothes. "You're right. Every other guy is wearing army boots, T-shirts, denim jackets, and fatigues."

"You recognize him?"

"Not from this angle. You?"

"I didn't know any of the college kids, aside from you."

I stared at the blazer. "This group of preppy guys used to hang out at a table in the dining hall. We used to rag on them as 'Plastic Hippies'—they'd grown their hair, smoked some dope, but when they graduated, they were going to work at daddy's firm. They dressed like us. Except a couple of them wore the preppie stuff. They all wore preppie grins, like they owned the world and didn't give a shit what anyone thought about them."

"Entitled."

"Exactly."

"I thought you went to prep school."

"Until my father yanked me out. But I was never entitled like that."

I put my finger on the preppie guy in the old picture. "You think this might be the governor?"

"No. Even factoring a forty-year difference, that cannot be the same cat. Unless he got a serious nose job."

"You're right." My mouth turned down. We stared in silence.

"Why didn't Buzzy say more in his email?"

"I don't know. If it was complicated, it would be easier on the phone. So Nichols wasn't there. What if the connection is the day—that event, not the people?"

"You mean Nichols had something to do with the demonstration."

"But wasn't in the picture."

"What's Nichols's first name?"

"Mark."

I shook my head. "I don't remember him. But it's not an uncommon name."

My gaze slid back to Angela. A shame it was just black and white and I couldn't see the extraordinary color of her hair. A shame...

I forced myself to look away. There were other women in the picture.

Like that tall handsome one, her face more sad than angry, clutching a heavy coat closed against the cold.

A smile crept across my face. I pointed to her.

Ray said, "Sharon. I'm not blind."

"I'm going to call her, see what she remembers."

I got my phone out and walked down to the theater.

"Bob. Any news on Buzzy?" she asked as soon as she answered.

"No. I was going to ask you the same thing. I found an old picture of an antiwar demonstration in the fall of sixty-eight. You're in it. Do you remember anything about that day?"

She snorted. "Are you kidding? It was a million years ago, and I went to a lot of those."

"You remember a student from back then named Mark Nichols? Strikingly handsome guy."

"Not offhand. But I'm busy right now. I'll think on it. Does this have something to do with Buzzy?"

"I don't know."

I went back into the office. "She doesn't remember…" I looked at Ray. He was practically jumping up and down. I walked over. He thumped a finger on the guy in the newspaper clipping standing next to the governor, then on the guy in the blazer in the old picture.

"Grow the hair back, use some wrinkle remover, and you've got the same guy."

"The other guy." Just as I'd been looking at people I knew in the other picture, in this one I'd focused on the governor.

"That's the same smirk. Like he owns the world."

"Isn't that the way all politicians look?" But now I was seeing it.

"This is the same guy. I'm going to post both these pictures on my blog, see what comes back."

I took a Sharpie and drew circles around the mystery man in each photo, with a question mark, and copied them. I handed him a set. He left and I went back to work.

Ray called an hour later. "I've got something. I'll be right over."

He came in and up to the office. I said, "That was fast."

"Internet, man."

"Barking up my tree, are you?"

He cast a baleful eye on my computers. "Wouldn't dream of it. But this commenter sent me a link to an article on Governor Nichols from the *Sacramento Bee* that appeared a couple of weeks ago."

I sat at the computer and found it on Google: "Time for Another California Governor to Score the White House?"

I started to read then shook my head. "You know I cannot abide this political stuff. You give me the meat of it."

I stood and Ray sat at the computer and scanned the article. "OK. So this Nichols cat is hosting a full smorgasbord of the usual right-wing red meat: he's going to cut taxes, then cut them again, lock up the criminals and throw away the key. Build a fence between here and Mexico a mile high and shove all the gays back in the closet."

He pulled up a photo spread. The governor was in every picture, smiling with enough wattage to illuminate all of Sacramento at midnight. It had to hurt to smile so much. He pressed the flesh, every inch of which was lily white. Here he was standing at a podium, the smile gone, shaking his fist, delivering a barn burner.

Ray pointed. *The picture.* It felt a little tingle. I moved closer to the screen and read the caption: "Governor Nichols hears from a close advisor."

I asked, "What's the date?"

"August tenth."

"A couple of weeks ago. Scroll through the rest of those pictures." When he was done, I said, "Interesting. Everyone in these pictures has a name. Except for this advisor guy."

"Maybe the photographer just didn't get it."

"Hm. The governor must have a website."

Ray got up and gestured to the computer. "Your turn."

I sat, found the website, and scrolled through a series of headshots on the photo page.

"They all went to the same school—Academy of the Blinding Smile." Which was a cousin to Rick's shit-eating grin.

Ray stabbed a finger at a picture. "There! That's our guy. George Bowman, campaign analysis coordinator. Which is what, exactly?"

"Got me. I'm going to Google him." It was a common name. I scrolled through the list. A Zen master living in Kentucky. An American pioneer, Indian fighter, who died in 1768. A bluesman. The only George Bowman in government was some county commissioner in the middle of the country.

Ray said, "Nothing?"

"Oh, we have something alright. A negative. This guy works for the governor of California and there's nothing on him aside from that picture. Which is a little weird. I'm going to try People Search." A few minutes later I shook my head. "There's nobody here of the right age living in California."

"Which means what?"

"That he's keeping a low profile."

He laughed. "Like you."

Until Brickman put up that website. "The question is—why?"

8.

I got back to work. But work wasn't happening. As often happened when I was stuck, my fingers tapped out chords on the front of the keyboard, practicing music out of old habit. But there were no chords for George Bowman. I called Sharon again.

"What now?" She sounded busy.

"A favor?"

She groaned. "What is it? I told you, I've got this paper..."

"Can you get the old yearbooks at the library—I'm thinking seventy through around seventy-three—and look for a student named George Bowman?"

"I thought you were looking for...hold on." I heard the shuffling of paper. "Mark Nichols."

"It's a long story."

"Which I don't have time for right now."

"Got it. But you might remember this guy. Even though he had long hair like the rest of us, he wore preppie duds. Loafers, a blazer."

"Doesn't ring a bell...I can't promise anything, but I'll try with the yearbooks."

"Thanks. And one more thing—if you find him, can you scan me his picture?"

"Are you sure you don't need me to do anything else? Steal you a copy of the Magna Carta?"

"Hey, I owe you."

She laughed. "I've heard that one before."

She hung up.

***

Sharon didn't call the rest of the day. When I didn't hear from her by ten the next morning, I figured she was too busy to do my legwork. I folded my set of the pictures in a pocket and headed to Middleburg.

I fixed my ponytail extra tight so the wind wouldn't bother it and drove up with the windows down. The morning air rushing in was almost cool. By the time I reached the college the air was steaming.

I parked and walked to the administration building. The campus was deserted and somnolent. I rounded the corner and saw the stairs beneath the entrance: the stage for the naked portrait of the brothers. I smiled and looked up at the building. The place seemed impregnable behind its ivied stone walls. It was hard to believe student radicals had once barricaded themselves inside. Kids today were probably too occupied by their cell phones to bother occupying a building.

I pulled the heavy brass door open and entered a cool, dim foyer. The woman slouched behind the desk was a little older than me. She didn't return my smile. She must be having a bad day.

"I'm looking for an old friend. Do you have the enrollment files?"

"Those are confidential."

"I'm an alumnus."

She shook her head. "I'm sorry." But her eyes flicked down for a moment. To the basement. I went outside and around the back of the building and found a narrow stairway leading down a floor. The door at the bottom was unlocked. A corridor led to a vast room filled with filing cabinets, the air thick with the odor of rotting papers. It was very still, like no one came down here. I hoped.

I searched the freshman class rolls, starting with the class of '69 and ending several years later. I found three Bowmans, none of them George. Could George be a nickname, or middle name? It seemed unlikely. Still, I wrote down the Bowmans on a slip of paper. The mold in the air was getting to my nose. It was itching like crazy. I suppressed a sneeze, not wanting to alert bad day lady above. I vastly preferred modern-day hacking in the comfort of my office. It was easier on the nose and the nerves.

I slunk out and headed to the library. I told the young guy at the desk, "Hey, I'm an alum. Can I see the old yearbooks?"

He rolled his eyes and pointed.

You, too, will be old someday...

I got the scrap of paper out where I'd written down the Bowmans and searched for them in the relevant yearbooks. There was a Fred—skinny, majored in physics. He was all wrong. Charles L. Bowman was wrong, too, and should have a *G* for a middle initial. James T. wasn't there. He must have dropped out.

There was no George Bowman. Did George drop out, like James T. and me? It wasn't the kind of thing those preppie kids did, but in that crazy time, who knew? He couldn't have been a street person like Ray, not in that getup. Maybe he wasn't a Middleburg student at all, but went to another college. Or no college. People came from all over for those demonstrations.

It was almost lunchtime.

I walked over to the old Four Brothers building through the midday swelter. There was no good way to do it. Too slow and the agony was prolonged. Too fast and the exercise had me overheated.

***

Inside, the secretary was on the phone. I gave her a little wave and we exchanged smiles. I headed upstairs. I was almost feeling at home here again.

Sharon was at her desk, her back turned to me. I knocked at the open door, but she was still startled when she turned and saw me.

She smiled. "You are one persistent devil. I'd almost think you were after me. Again."

"I was at the library."

"Oh. Doing what you asked me to do. Sorry."

"It wouldn't have mattered. I didn't find hide nor hair of George Bowman."

"Actually, I was about to call you. I remembered something. I think."

"Tell me over lunch."

"Lunch won't take care of this." She pointed at the stack of folders on her desk.

"You've got to eat."

"I get my head buried in these projects and forget to. OK. But let's make it a good one. Marcel's Bistro is the best in town. It's pricy, though."

"Hey, it isn't 1969 anymore."

We walked to the restaurant in silence. I glanced at her. She was as fine-looking as back then. Just different. More handsome than cute. She wore the miles on her like a patina, like she'd traveled them with grace.

As if she could hear my thoughts, she broke into the most extraordinary smile. Warm and alive. If anything, it was enhanced by the hint of sadness in her eyes. I smiled back and gave her a quick hug. "It's good to see you again."

She nodded but looked away.

***

The restaurant was hushed with tasteful lighting and white tablecloths. A guy seated us at one in the middle. A college kid in a waiter's getup strode up, trying his best to look like a snotty French waiter. He still looked like a kid. A nice kid.

He handed a menu and wine list to Sharon, who glanced at it then passed it to me. I don't usually drink with lunch, but frankly I was a little nervous. I recognized the name St.-Émilion. I didn't know diddly about wine, but I'd heard somewhere it was good. I realized I had no idea how to pronounce it, so I pointed. The kid mangled it: "The Saynt Emilyon, sir?"

I laughed. Sharon scowled at me. When the waiter left, she said, "He's just a poor kid doing his job. And how's *your* French?"

"Sorry. That was mean. And you nailed me on my French. Exactly what does feminist research entail? Is it like science?"

"Yes, Bob. We catch guys like you, set them loose in a giant maze like rats, poke them with sharp instruments..." She reached out and tapped my wrist with a long fingernail.

Hearing "Bob" grated on me. "Would you call me Bodine?"

"Bodine. That's an odd name. But sure. How'd you get it?"

"That summer, after I left college, I was living with a bunch of musicians. I don't remember who started it, but the name stuck. It was a hippie thing, taking a new name to symbolize the new person you'd become, at least in theory. I embraced Bodine. Bob was that kid who went to college because his parents insisted. Bodine was free! Free of parents, the confines of uptight society." And free of that dark winter—and Angela...

She laughed. "Those were crazy times. I did crazy stuff, too."

"Like?"

She just smiled. The waiter returned. I ordered the steak frites.

Sharon said, "What the hell," and ordered the steak tartare.

I raised an eyebrow.

She said, "If I didn't eat meat we wouldn't be here. The French aren't big on vegetarian options."

"No, it's just..." *That it's raw.*

The corner of her mouth turned up, but she didn't say anything.

The waiter was leaving when she said, "Get me a glass of that same wine?"

I tried to remember just what had happened with her.

As though she could read my thoughts, she laughed and asked, "You don't remember, do you? You got me really stoned. Then *plied* me with wine. Cheap wine—Almaden, I think. A seduction technique that is highly frowned on today. In fact..."

"Whoa." I raised my hands defensively. "That was forty years ago!"

"I know. And if memory serves..." She smiled and looked away.

The waiter brought the wine and handed me a glass to taste. I pretended to know what I was doing, gave it a sniff and sipped.

She laughed. "That's it! See how easy it is?"

She'd caught me faking the wine ritual, but I didn't mind. I nodded to the waiter, who left. I said, "That's not Almaden."

"I hope not." She took a sip of hers. "No kidding. Yum."

The waiter arrived with our food. He set before her the biggest pile of raw hamburger I'd ever seen.

I took a bite of my steak. I said, "I generally go for hamburgers, but this is good."

"So's this. A bite?"

"No, thanks."

We ate in silence. She ate every morsel and drank her wine with obvious pleasure.

I said, "Hungry work, feminist research."

"I haven't eaten anything this good in too long."

She put her plate aside. She said, "So, I remembered someone called George. I never knew his last name. I don't remember what he looked like."

"I have a picture."

I fished the picture of the demonstration from my pocket and unfolded it on the table.

She pointed to herself in the picture and smiled ruefully. "That's me! How could I be so young?"

"Yeah, you looked so…"

She shut me up with a glare that said *do not go there.* I pointed at the circled figure.

She said, "I think that's him."

"How did you know him?"

"He dated my roommate."

"Oh come on, nobody *dated* back then."

"OK, he was *having sex* with my roommate. But never at our place. I saw them around campus together a few times."

"He was a student at Middleburg?"

"He must have been. Though you know how loose things were back then."

"Could he have been visiting from another college?"

She paused. "No. He didn't just dress preppie. He was a member of the preppie fraternity, whose name I can't remember."

I asked, "Who was your roommate?" But I was wondering—if George was a student, why wasn't he in the college records?

She looked away. "The girl who died."

My breath caught. "No."

"Yes, that one. Angela."

What were the odds? Actually, they weren't impossible. The school had just gone coed and there were only twenty or so girls that year. But maybe it had nothing to do with odds. I said, "I bet I met you through her, when she was hanging with Waldo. What do you remember of the weekend she disappeared?"

She shook her head. "Nothing."

"Come on, there was this giant snowstorm."

"I wasn't there. I was at Wesleyan." She looked uncomfortable, then laughed. "With some guy. It was nothing worth remembering. With the snow, I didn't make it back until almost a week later. I didn't hear she was missing until then."

It was a shame she hadn't been there. If so, she might remember something. The waiter came by and we ordered coffee and I asked for the check.

When it came, I grabbed it and she put a hand on mine. She gave me half that great smile and said, "No." She took out her credit card and we split it.

We walked back toward her office. She was silent, like something was bugging her. She bit her lip like she was deciding something. She nodded and pointed to a bench. We sat in the shade of a big tree. There was a slight breeze, but it was still stifling.

She said, "I promised Angela."

"Angela? Promised what?"

"That I wouldn't tell."

"Angela's been dead almost forty years."

"I know. But a promise is a promise. Except you bringing up George..." Sharon's face got solemn. "Angela was *pregnant* when she died."

I didn't react outside. But inside I felt a tremor.

"Angela said, 'I'm not letting George know I'm telling you this.'"

"Why not?"

"I had this feeling she was afraid of him."

"Afraid?" Another little shake inside.

"There's something else. He wanted her to have an abortion. Insisted on it."

A third jolt, and this one widened my eyes and kicked my pulse up. "An illegal abortion."

"That's the only kind they had back then. It wasn't legal in Massachusetts until 1973."

"How far along was she?"

"I don't know. She wasn't showing yet."

Lunch took a wrong turn. "Whose baby was it?"

Sharon shook her head.

A squirrel raced across a wilted expanse of lawn and flew up a tree. It made me feel even hotter seeing him.

I said, "If George thought it was Waldo's, maybe that's why he wanted her to have the abortion."

"Maybe. But he really didn't want her having that baby. I guess she didn't know what she wanted to do, so she kept postponing the decision. Those last weeks I was really worried about her. She was getting crazy. I tried to talk to her about the baby, but she just walked away. Lord knows I couldn't see her as a mother. But Angela was mule-headed. Like a two-year-old. Tell her to do something and she'd do the opposite."

No shit. Had I ever seen George with Angela? I remembered seeing her a few times with some guy, but it was from far away.

A second squirrel went up the same tree and chased the first to the end of a branch where it leaped to another tree. The second squirrel retreated. Probably too hot.

Sharon turned to me. "I can't believe I broke my promise."

"She's gone, been gone forever." But her face was racked with guilt, or maybe grief. I needed to do something to make her feel better. "Here's something I've never told a soul about, much worse than that. Something I did. That year we had a Thanksgiving bash at the Four Brothers house. After a long, wild dinner, Angela came to my room, grinning like the cat that ate the canary. She said she had a present for me. Cocaine. I'd never snorted it before. It's not hard to learn. And then…she crawled into my bed. I've always wondered if that was what broke her and Waldo up. He was one of my best friends."

She took my hand. "Hey. We all made mistakes back then. And Angela plus cocaine? Not many guys could have resisted that! She was one toasty item. I'll admit, I got a little jealous sometimes seeing all you guys slobbering over her. Another thing that might make you feel better. She got the coke from George. Which means she was already seeing him then. She was already leaving Waldo."

"How do you know that's where she got it?"

"She told me. George was one of those preppy guys who had the money for it. I don't remember any other cocaine that early. A few years later…"

"That's true. What else do you remember about George?"

"Aside from those ridiculous clothes? We never spoke that I recall. But I didn't like him. He was superficially charming, I suppose, but underneath was this major air of entitlement. I think Angela loved his cocaine more than she loved him."

"It makes sense. He doesn't sound like her kind of guy. She wasn't doing coke after she found out she was pregnant?"

"I'm afraid she was. Nobody knew about that stuff back then." Not that it mattered anymore. She squeezed my hand. "You've been carrying that scene at Thanksgiving around for all these years."

I had been, and with her words, her touch, I could feel its grip loosening on me. My mouth popped open and out came another secret. "Angela was my first."

She snorted. "You were a *virgin* right before we met?" She shook her head. "You're one fast learner. You must have been busy that winter…not that I was any saint."

I laughed. "I'm not talking about Thanksgiving. I knew her before college."

"Oh." A silence. "But she was with Waldo. What happened with you and her?"

I froze, outside and in. And I was standing at that edge, with a cold wind blowing from far below. I pulled back, got suddenly fascinated by some maintenance men unloading something from a truck across the lawn. What had happened with Angela? "I don't remember." And I wasn't exactly lying.

"Everyone remembers their first. And how it ended."

"Not me. I remember *meeting* her…July of sixty-seven, the Summer of Love."

"That's cute."

I nodded. "We were at this left-wing camp, you know, folk guitars and pottery and commies coming to lecture us. The camp was called Allyn's Rock, after this giant stone towering over everything. It was maybe fifty feet tall. We considered it sacred. The whole camp climbed up there Sunday nights and meditated. Which later led to my friendship with Buzzy. That's just one of the ways that camp influenced me. Though at the time, of course, Angela overrode everything else."

I took a deep breath. "When she came to my room, it was the first time I'd talked to her since camp. I was so happy. Hey, it's Thanksgiving! An hour later I was living a horror movie. She got out of bed, leaned over my desk, and was sucking up line after line of that shit. Saying crazy stuff. It was terrible. My first love...r was a junkie. I never did coke again. And I felt bad, because I'd been the one to turn her on to pot."

"There's a big difference between pot and coke."

"Yeah, well, I was really pissed off after. She ruined my relationship with Waldo. And for what?"

"And then she died." Tears leaked down her face. She pulled herself together. "You know, it makes sense that coke was her drug of choice."

"Why?"

"She was always into power. All that occult nonsense. Tarot, astrology. She fancied herself quite the little sorceress. It was annoying."

"Amen. But she had plenty of power, at least with us guys. You said it yourself."

"Maybe she had it before the drugs. I think she was losing it there at the end. Maybe she just had a drug problem. We'll never know. You know, my problem with all that occult mumbo jumbo is that it's trying to quantify what's essentially mysterious. I believe there might be something behind this mundane world. But I respect it too much to think it would wake up to anything as dumb as tarot cards."

I nodded, then laughed. "I'm with you. That's why I still...drop acid once a year." I instantly regretted the admission.

But she smiled. "Hey, it's nothing to be ashamed of. I've read about the recent research with psychedelic drugs. Very impressive, if you know what you're doing."

"I like to think I do. I go up in the Adirondacks, by myself."

"Buddhism's working for me."

We sat silently. Comfortably, at least for my part.

The guys loading the truck were done. They got in and drove away. She took it as a cue. "Argh. That freaking paper is calling. I'd rather hang out here, even if it is hot as the freaking Sahara Desert."

We returned to her office building and stood facing each other outside the door.

I asked, "You seeing anyone now?"

She winced, which could mean a lot of things. Yes, and she wished she weren't. No, and she wasn't about to start. Or something else entirely. A hint of that sorrow I'd seen before came into her eyes, and she looked away. She looked back at me and I felt a zing it in my gut—she'd come to some decision.

"Slow. You need to go really slow." She looked dead serious.

"Sure. Whatever you need."

She smiled and the darkness lifted. "That was a nice lunch." Her eyes drifted to the house and down. "I seem to remember a guy I went down into the basement here with one time. Young guy. Cute."

We both laughed. I kissed her cheek and left.

***

Back at the library, the kid behind the desk pecked away at his phone. I asked where I could find old pictures from the 1960s. He was ready to hit me with some snark—*Try medieval history*—but I shot him down with a glare.

He said, "Special Collections."

Things must have been slow in Special Collections. The thin woman in her forties seemed glad to see me, to see anybody, and hustled right off, returning with a thin folder and an apologetic expression. She said, "I was sure we had more."

I sat at a table and looked through it. Shots of the football team. I didn't recognize any of them, hadn't even been to a game. I'm not into sports.

Professors in caps and gowns at graduation. Frat boys, at the frats that were still in business. Just a handful of pictures of hippie freaks. Three were prints of Buzzy's, the same ones as in the box. He hadn't known he was being a historian when he took them.

There was another picture of a crowd at a demonstration. Mostly the same people as in the other one, so it must be the same one. Except in this one, instead of leaden faces, there were smiles, and a couple of the chicks had their arms up. Dancing?

To music. And it came to me. I *had* gone to one demonstration. I hadn't demonstrated, exactly, because I was in the band. It was my very first gig with Ray. The first of hundreds. The occasion was some big political deal, which I couldn't remember. I hadn't even known it clearly at the time. Something about The War.

We weren't in the pictures because we were onstage. All I could remember was how cold I'd been. I hadn't been wearing my winter coat—how would that look onstage? —just a long-sleeved purple shirt. As the political guy ranted on, I hunched over the keyboard with hands up my sleeves, wondering how I was going to get them to work when it came time to play.

Now the lady came in clutching a handful of VHS tapes, with a triumphant grin. "I found videos!"

"They didn't have video back then."

"I know." Dummy. "Videos of *movies.*" She punched on a VCR, handed me a clicker, and left.

I looked at the labels on the tapes. One read "Demonstration."

It must have been a big deal, because someone had filmed it, back in the days long before phones when film was expensive.

The visual quality was horrendous, the image jerking around in black and white. At first, we weren't there. Just my Hammond organ and Ray's Telecaster leaning against an amp. A political guy stood ranting into a mic, his words too distorted to make out, his finger stabbing down to accent his points. I fast-forwarded. There was Ray, strutting his stuff, and me behind the organ. The audio was a dull roar. I could barely discern a beat.

The camera panned the crowd, dancers waving their arms like they did back then, laughing, somebody passing a joint, which was blatant and dangerous then. The motion stirred something in me. It was like Buzzy's black-and-white stills were *moving*, bringing the past to life. Giving me a taste of the way it had felt, before all the bad stuff happened. Before Thanksgiving. Before the snowstorm.

The camera slowed in its panning, then stopped. And there she was. I sucked in a breath and groaned. She was standing next to Waldo in a peasant dress that glittered with little circles of mirror. She wasn't dancing, exactly, just nodding her head to the beat. Grinning at the camera. Or not quite at the camera.

She was grinning *at me*. I shook my head. Was I making it up? Maybe. But that was just like her, to ignore me those first months, to get with Waldo, then sneak in that smile when Waldo wasn't looking. And he wasn't. He was making a point of staring away from the stage, serious, like this was no time to party. Just like *him*.

Angela's head bobbed up and down in time with the music, and now she raised her forearms, made fists and pumped them, alternating left and right, in a parody of some dance of the time.

Angela's ghost. And now it was like those hands reached into my chest, tugging, trying to drag me back. Back to Thanksgiving. And back to before...

I rewound the tape and played it again from the band part, filming with my phone. Ray would want to see this. When it got to Angela, I looked away so I didn't have to see her again.

I left without telling the Special Collections lady, went back and asked the poor kid if they had local newspapers from the '60s. He said, "It's all on microfilm." *Papyrus, dude.*

The microfilm was tucked in a dusty corner at the end of the stacks. As I worked the machine, I found myself agreeing with the kid. Microfilm was an ancient pain in the ass. The filing system made no sense. How did people ever live without computers? When I finally located the reel with the *Middleburg Sentinel* for that 1969, I had to crank the little dial until my fingers cramped.

Finally: "Missing Student Found in Snowdrift."

The article was short. A quote from a coroner: "Injuries consistent with an accident," i.e., falling off a cliff. And, "The body was well preserved." A fat lot of good that did her. But it was lucky for the coroner. It was good to know that if you died in a snowstorm you wouldn't rot.

While I was at it, I cranked back to winter, looking for our bust. The snowstorm got nice headlines. There was nothing the day after. Or after that. I scrolled forward a week. Nothing.

This was the kind of paper that diligently reported every cat up a tree, every little old lady who heard a noise—look, right here was an earth-shattering item about a guy whose mailbox had gotten clipped by the snowplow and complained to the police. The charges being dropped was one thing. But no police report in the paper?

I'd been about to bring up George not being in the college records when Sharon dropped the bomb of Angela on me. Why was I thinking of him, now? Because he and the police report had something in common—when it came to records, they were both missing.

9.

It was five. Time to head home. Instead I walked across campus to Garnet Hill. I started climbing, just as Angela had the night of the storm. The snow was eventually a record, almost three feet. But when she'd gotten there it had to be already at least a foot and drifting heavily.

Now, I wasn't a quarter of the way up and my shirt was glued to my chest in the damp heat. But between the snow and wind she must have been cold. And it would have been slippery. Did she cradle her belly, protecting the life inside? How could she see? The lights of campus wouldn't make it here through the swirling snow. She must have had a light. A candle was her style, but it would have blown right out. So, she'd had a flashlight.

Peaking on that acid, the white must have turned every color of the rainbow and then some. It certainly had for me that night. I tried to imagine what she could have been thinking, but there was just a blank. What had she worn? I'd seen her earlier that night, leaning over Waldo upstairs in the house. I hadn't known it was the last time I'd see her, of course. She had on that favorite jacket—the brocaded one. And a parka? But my mind was drifting from that night. Her clothes...

It made sense that Waldo had married a clothing designer. In a time when the height of fashion was jeans and a work shirt, Angela prided herself on her wardrobe. That jacket. Linen blouses and crazy socks in pink and green. And the ultimate hippie accessory: a purple velvet pouch she'd embroidered with arcane symbols. It was nothing so mundane as a pocketbook.

As I climbed Garnet Hill, I slipped back to before college, to a night at camp, when we'd climbed up that rock…

We'd met on the lawn after dinner. She sat facing me, inches away, with what I already knew as her solemn sorceress look. She pulled something wrapped in a silk handkerchief from the pouch, then like a magician teased from it a dog-eared copy of the *I Ching*, and a sheaf of yarrow sticks, tied with a red ribbon.

She cast the *I Ching*, murmuring strange words. When she was done, she placed it lovingly back in the pouch and took out the tarot, unveiled it from a lace napkin, and started laying the cards on the grass. Her portentous tone and the slow, deliberate movements of her fingers had me virtually hypnotized. Her words were mumbo jumbo, but my body got the message. Blood thrummed in my temples and my belly, my body humming in a crescendo of anticipation.

She stood from the lawn and brushed off her skirt—a long peasant thing like she always wore. Like the one she made Waldo's bell-bottoms with. I followed her into the trees and up the rock. It wasn't as high as Garnet Hill, but that climb seemed to take an hour, because I knew what waited on top. Knew what, but not what it would be like, having never done it before.

Now, I was so enthralled by the memory that the top of the hill came as a shock. I was only a yard from the edge. My stomach lurched and I staggered back against a tree. My shirt was soaked, my face on fire. I bit my lip in dismay. This fear of heights was not a momentary thing. But I was safe against this tree. Like Waldo had been in that photo.

I closed my eyes and was back at camp. When we reached the top of the rock, we sat facing each other. She had that solemn look. I was afraid she'd go for the pouch again. But she took my hands and finally smiled. She stood and took her skirt off, as slowly and deliberately as she'd cast her spells.

I drifted forward a couple of weeks, to the last night of camp. Our last night. Which I'd never been able to remember.

Now a sliver came back to me. We'd climbed the rock, just like that first time. And…

I was at the edge of that abyss inside, the unbearable place.

I opened my eyes. Even imagining her death was preferable to that feeling.

Her last night, she'd walked to this edge. I needed to see what she'd seen. There wasn't a hint of breeze now, but I conjured the sound of howling wind and swirls of snow blowing against my cheeks. I pushed away from the trunk and took half a step. My stomach turned over. But I took another half step. I tried again to penetrate her mind that night. Was it *Oh wow, I see God!* Then another half step and *Oh shit...* as she slipped? Or had she clutched her swollen belly, her child, telling her *I'm sorry, but this is for the best...?*

My head shook violently. She couldn't have thought that, or anything like it. Angela would never have jumped. She might have OD'd maybe. But she hated physical pain. I took another quarter of a step, noticing how the rock here slanted down, which was why she'd slipped...

A sweet, nasty stench yanked me back into the present. It must be coming from below. A dead animal.

I peered down. The tops of trees, their leaves limp... Something was poking from under a bush. Dark red, like a big hunk of spoiled meat. That was the source of the smell. I didn't see clothing.

I wanted to look away but forced myself to study it. It was too big to be a dog. A deer? No.

A *human* body. Another jumper. Right where Angela's body must have appeared in the snow.

Buzzy.

No, no. Buzzy would never jump. But I was wincing and digging my fingernails into my palms.

I should go down and see. But I had no idea how to get down there, and the woods looked thick. And I really didn't want to see.

I raced down the hill. I needed to call the police. But not on my cell, where they could trace it. I found a pay phone at the college library, called, and told the person who answered what I'd seen. I hung up before they asked for my name.

I drove home. I'd had more than enough for one day. I did my best to change the channel. I stuffed in earbuds. Our old drummer, Frank, had made me a playlist for my iPod featuring some classical stuff he thought I might like. And classical was really changing the channel.

I let my hands go loose on the wheel, took a big breath, and expanded my vision to take in late-summer green. I tunneled into the present moment driving between Middleburg and Hudson. And into the music. Some big choral thing, Handel? It might be Bach. It was intense enough.

But the music didn't stop my thoughts.

I'd wondered with Sharon who had gotten Angela pregnant: Waldo or George? But, of course, it could have been me after that coked up Thanksgiving. Jeannie and Waldo hadn't been able to have kids, and if that was because of Waldo, my being the father was that much more likely.

I felt a plummeting sensation. I'd never had kids. Then again, neither had Angela.

The image of that body at the foot of the cliff returned. If Angela had seen it, she would have gotten her pouch out, started working her divining tools. Because she'd be certain it was some kind of sign.

It wasn't a sign. Garnet Hill had the only cliff I knew of around Middleburg. If you wanted to jump, it was the place to do it.

Weird. I'd just spent the past couple of hours snooping around being…a detective. Though I'd really been doing it ever since I heard about Waldo. It wasn't something I'd ever imagined. Then again, it wasn't that different than coding: you stumble on a problem, turn over every stone searching for clues as to how to fix it. It was a process I enjoyed.

The news of Angela's pregnancy and George's reaction to it was taking my thoughts in a nasty direction. But maybe that was just those elusive feelings of mine manifesting. When it came to all this stuff Ray didn't have any of my baggage. I needed his take. I called him.

He said, "Your lucky night. I'm just about done cooking dinner, and there's enough for you."

***

It was almost seven when I reached Ray's. "Smells good," I said when he let me in. Beef, onions, some spice I couldn't put a name on. Lunch with Sharon seemed a long time ago.

We clanked up the spiral stairs to the kitchen. It would be nice to eat someone else's cooking for a change. Ray was working on a beer and got me one. He leaned against the fridge and I sat at the table.

I filled him in on my trip, leaving my relationship with Angela out. It wasn't the time. But I did tell him about the gruesome discovery on Garnet Hill.

He said, "You really know how to party. A body?"

"Let's not talk about that. Don't want to spoil dinner."

He said, "Angela was *pregnant*. And hanging with this George character, who wanted her to have an abortion."

"Aside from the picture and video, there's no trace of him at the college. It's like he never enrolled, never existed."

He gave dinner a stir. I set the table as I talked. "Hey, you were right about being at that demonstration. That was our first gig."

"Told you."

"There's a video. I've got it on my phone."

"Uh-oh."

We watched.

Ray said, "Good thing the sound's so bad."

"We kind of sucked."

"Yeah. At least we were young when we did."

"I'm still glad you talked me into it. You gotta start somewhere."

"Tall oaks from teeny acorns."

I had an idea but wanted to see what Ray thought first. "Aside from the video, what do you see?"

He sat down and closed his eyes for a solid minute. He opened them. "I see George. His picture in Waldo's box. And his fat preppie ass in Angela's bed. And then I *don't* see him, in the college records. Those things are somehow related…" He got still. He stared into space blinking his eyes, then looked at me. "Here's what I'm thinking: Waldo didn't fall. Neither did Angela. George *pushed* them. And he's somehow covering it up."

I nodded. "That's where I was going, too. The question is, why?"

"Dinner's done. Let me think while we eat."

It was good. When we finished, I said, "You ever get sick of writing, you can become a chef."

"It's got to pay better than writing. OK. We need to start with Angela. Why would George…kill her?"

The word *kill* hung in the air like an obscenity. I felt a humming in my forearms and my lips tightened. *What if George killed Angela?* Violence wasn't my scene. But here it was. "Got me." I was already talking louder, rougher.

Ray didn't seem to notice. He said, "We have to assume it was because she was pregnant. Why was George insistent on her having an abortion?"

"Any of a number of reasons. A preppy boy like that probably had conservative parents. If he knocked up some chick, they might pull the purse strings—which if you remember back then could mean a quick trip to Vietnam."

"But how about this? George might have had a problem if his old lady was carrying someone else's child, like Waldo's."

I squeezed my eyes closed for a second. *Or mine.* "Yeah, that's what I told Sharon."

"Very effective. Get rid of the baby and mother in one shot."

"Then why kill Waldo forty years later?"

"The obvious thing would be that Waldo found out George killed Angela and threatened to go to the police."

"How could he find out?"

Ray said, "George told someone, and they told Waldo? But maybe Waldo discovered something else about George's past. Like the fact that he was supplying Angela with coke. That wouldn't go over too well today with conservative voters. Except…George W. Bush had that skeleton, too, and it didn't touch him."

"I have to take your word for it. You know I don't follow that stuff."

"Waldo had that picture of the demonstration. George is into politics now. Maybe he was during college, too. Radical stuff."

"And at the same time considering a political future? Planning to hide his dirty laundry?"

"Not if he was like us. We never considered the consequences of ten minutes from now, let alone in forty years. Then again, we weren't college Republicans, like Lee Atwater and Karl Rove."

"I've heard the names."

"They were already practicing their dirty tricks back then. So yeah, he might have been planning ahead. Hold on. Wasn't abortion illegal back then?"

"That's what Sharon said."

"Strong-arming someone into an illegal one would definitely not fly with those voters. To them, abortion is murder anyway."

"Murder. What if Waldo knew back then George was trying to make her have an abortion?"

"Knew how?" Ray got another beer and offered me one. I shook my head. I was having enough trouble trying to figure this all out.

I said, "The night of the storm, Angela was talking to Waldo. He looked really upset.

I assumed it was just seeing her, but maybe she was telling him she was pregnant, and about George pressuring her into an abortion. After Waldo finds out she's dead, he tries to forget about it, because there's nothing he can do."

"Then what?"

"He sees that picture in the newspaper, recognizes George from college, puts it together with the one in the box."

"And the picture dredges up this thing from the past. But how does George find out Waldo's done it?"

"If George is hiding things, he's worried about somebody finding out. So he sets up a Google trap."

Ray said, "How's that work?"

"There's a website that lets you set up a personal profile under your name. They code it so that when someone searches for you that profile comes up high in the search results. Click on the profile and the website sends you an email with the IP address of the searcher's computer. From that, you can find out who's searching."

"George finds out Waldo's looking into him, fears the worst, and kills him. What are you going to do about it?"

"I don't know."

Ray asked, "Coffee?"

"No, it'll just keep me awake. I found out another thing. There was definitely something hinky about that bust. It never made it into the police log in the newspaper. Which got me remembering that night."

"What, you remember? It was forty years ago, and you were spaced out on a huge load of acid..."

"I remember *because* of the acid, trust me. When those cops stormed into the basement to get me, they were pumped, like they'd just nailed Al Capone. They'd been champing at the bit to get at us college kids all year, what with our drugs and fornicating.

"They were practically singing as they hauled me to my feet, snapped the cuffs on behind me, and manhandled me upstairs. They dragged me out in the snow into the back of a patrol car and some guy was hissing about me going up for life. They tossed me into a cell that reeked of stale vomit for a long night in hell. Still tripping, no less.

"But the next morning...they looked like someone had snatched the prize right from under their noses. As I sauntered out, I turned to flash a grin at one of those assholes. He said, 'Lucky this time, ya freak. Next time you won't...' His buddy grabbed his arm and shut him up."

Ray said, "What did he mean? You wouldn't what?"

"Walk."

"Huh. I don't know where that fits into our theory."

"It doesn't, except for the fact that when I went looking, both George and the police report were missing."

"Come on. You spend the day going through old records, you'll find all kinds of things missing. A miracle you found anything at all after all that time."

I opened the computer and idly Googled George Bowman again. This time I searched past the first page of results. Around page four all the first-hit guys started repeating—the Zen guy, the bluesman, the real estate guy. But on the top of page five, I hit a new one: "Svengali to a Rising Star?"

This blogger has been chasing down our illustrious governor since he was a lowly congressman. Now that he's become White House material,

I've got company. Everyone wants to know what he eats and if that wife is as hot in person as in the pictures. And what's he going to do as president? But what I want to know right now is, who's this guy next to the governor?

There was the picture from the newspaper.

Ray said, "It's the same one. Weird."

"Not if it's the only one of them together."

I asked some other staff members about him. Once I filtered the backbiting and envy out of what they said, it became clear—this guy is the governor's right-hand man. I asked one guy why he isn't in more pictures. Is he shy or something? He said, No, he just liked to keep a low profile.

He and Nichols apparently go way back. Which is also interesting. Because when I asked the staffer who'd been around the governor the longest—at least ten years—he didn't know the first thing about Bowman's past. Not even what part of the country he comes from, let alone where he went to college or who he might have worked for before. When I asked him if he thought that was strange, he said, "I never asked." But once I brought it up, he also sounded surprised that Bowman hadn't volunteered anything.

I finally called Bowman. He agreed to ten minutes on the phone. I must hand it to him, he possesses the politician's knack—he said a lot of nice words but managed to avoid answering every single one of my questions. Fair enough. This is politics we're talking here. But what I want to know is, what is a guy like that doing in that game if he doesn't want notoriety?

I said, "George is like a ghost. There's no record of him at the college. And why is this article so far down in the Google results? It was published in the past year. It should be on the first page." I poked around in the back end of the blog. It was after nine. A half hour ago I was tired, but now I was wide awake. "I'll be damned. Somebody *reverse engineered* the SEO on that blog."

"English please?"

"Google has this set of algorithms for listing search results. Websites try to game that system using SEO—search engine optimization. You jimmy the code on the back end of the site so that it ranks higher on Google. Google discourages that with a set of rules. They catch you breaking them and they demote your site out to search result Siberia.

"What happened here is something I've never seen before. This blog breaks every one of Google's rules. Which is why they're down on page five."

"This blogger is a cyber putz—so what?"

I said, "No, you don't get it. This isn't the product of a technical black thumb. Deliberately breaking the rules like that is tricky to do. It's a *hack*."

"He hacked his own blog so no one would read it? What's the point in writing then?"

"No, somebody else hacked it."

"Wouldn't the blogger know?"

"Not if he wasn't a geek. And that guy sounded more like a political junkie."

"Someone deliberately buried this article on Google."

"Right."

"When?"

"Very recently."

"You think Waldo saw the article?"

"Not just that. I'll bet his seeing it was what triggered them burying it. And everything else."

We sat in silence. I said, "It's a neat theory—George doing all this stuff. And it's interesting that we both came up with it independently. But it's bad science. We just took our theory and glued a couple of facts and a load of speculation to it. We have no actual evidence that George Bowman killed anybody."

Ray said, "But he *is* hiding something and is still missing from the college records."

"Which could mean anything."

"What about that body?"

Buzzy. I'd kept the thought at arm's length, though it was taking a lot of energy. "I can't talk about it now."

Ray nodded, then sighed. "I'm beat. And I didn't run all over Middleburg all day."

"I'll head home. Thanks for dinner."

It had almost cooled off outside. I went inside my place. Mingus's dinner was late. He gobbled it down, but when I took him out, he was acting strangely insecure. He was sucking up to me to be petted. I reached down and noticed that my hand was knotted in a tight fist. I knew my dog was smart. He was sensitive, too. He knew I wasn't myself.

What if George had killed Angela? That meant that he'd murdered my first love. And maybe my child. I grabbed a rake that was standing against the fence and had a vivid fantasy of beating this guy I'd never met, breaking every bone in his body. I forced myself to drop the rake.

I was a pacifist. It wasn't the thought that counted, but action. I wasn't going to kill George. But I sure wanted to.

10.

The next morning was a Saturday. I rose early and started cleaning the glass from the museum cases. It was a chore, because I had to wear thick gloves to keep from cutting myself. When I was done vacuuming, I called around to find a glazier.

I got the pants Angela had sewn for Waldo and the Janis napkin from Waldo's box and put them where they belonged in the museum.

I was thinking about where the box itself should go when my phone rang.

Sharon was so upset that I didn't recognize her voice at first.

"They found a body. They want me to come identify it. It might be Buzzy."

It was like seeing the bright flash of a big explosion, too early to hear it or feel it, but any second... "Shit."

"They found it at the foot of...Garnet Hill."

But I already knew that. I'd known the moment I figured out that body couldn't be some animal. I couldn't speak. I rocketed back in time, to the moment when I'd heard about Angela's body emerging from the snow. And it had felt the same—like I'd been punched in the heart. Like *I* was falling.

My eyes bugged as I pictured that body from yesterday, clear as if it was in front of me. I'd notified the police about it, and... I got my tongue working. "Maybe it isn't Buzzy." I saw that hunk of rotting meat under the bush. Breakfast rose in my throat.

"They said the head was shaved."

Fuck. But she was losing it, I could hear it in her voice. Somebody had to keep it together. "When are you going…" To the morgue.

"They said I could come at my convenience. I was about to leave."

"Wait for me. I'm coming with you."

"Thank you. I'll be at my office."

"I'll be there in an hour. In the meantime, don't tell the police anything about me."

"What?"

"About my looking into George Bowman. It will just confuse them. If they ask, tell them I'm just an old friend of his."

"Whatever."

***

I raced up to Middleburg. I remembered that the Taconic Parkway was one big speed trap and slowed to five miles over the limit. I didn't want to have to explain to some cop how I was racing to the morgue.

Sharon was out front of the Four Brothers house. I got out of the car and she hugged me and burst into tears. I bit my lip. It always made me squirm when women cried. But I did my best to hug her back. We got in my car and she gave me directions to the morgue, a couple of towns over in the county seat.

She said, "Buzzy doesn't have any living relatives. They called me because I called to report him missing."

We drove over in heavy silence. We walked into the end of a dilapidated wing of a hospital. A youngish attendant and younger cop greeted us. A Middleburg cop. I reminded myself that he couldn't have been born when they busted us.

The cop nodded toward me and said to Sharon, "Who's this?"

"Just a friend, came for support."

She filled out a bunch of paperwork and the attendant ushered us into a small room. I was breathing high in my chest as we entered. I was relieved that there was just a faint antiseptic smell. The attendant pulled the sheet from the head of the body lying on the table, and for an instant I was really relieved. That…thing at the base of the cliff had been reddish-brown. This was white.

But Sharon gasped and clutched my hand, saying in a strangled tone, "It's him."

It was. Relief collapsed. That was his shaved head with its noble features. There was a narrow gash in the side of his head. I hadn't recognized him at first because they'd cleaned him up.

And because *he* wasn't here. His features had always been peaceful like this. But they weren't showing a deep calm with its core of energy and resilience. This was the calm of a desert on the moon.

We drove away.

She said, "Most people die, and you have to lie a little bit. You know—they were good parents and hard workers and loved the Red Sox, but they were also a pain in the ass a lot of the time. This is different. He didn't have a mean bone in his body. He got dealt a hand right from the bottom of the deck and look what he did. He made the world a better place. Made the people around him better. Made *me* better. I'm going to miss him so much…"

She was openly weeping. It twisted something up inside me. "Me, too. I was just getting to know him again." Her words, my words, were the right ones. But my tongue felt like wood. I felt her getting hotter, melting under this thing. And I was going cold. I hated it, but I couldn't stop it.

I said, "What do you think happened to him?"

"Happened? He's *dead*."

"I mean, this is crazy. Him falling right where Angela did, and right after Waldo fell. And I didn't tell you—this George Bowman might have *pushed* them."

"I don't give a fuck about George Bowman, or what he did. I don't need your speculation. What I need right now is a friend."

"I'm sorry. It's the only way I know to deal with this."

"It's a pretty lame way. What are you feeling?"

"I told you. I miss him, too."

"It doesn't sound like it."

Silence. I retreated from Sharon, from the gruesome images and flurry of conjectures to the sensation of hands on the wheel, trees rushing by the car.

After ten minutes she spoke. "I'm sorry for snapping at you. I'm upset.

And I'm sure you are, too." Liar. "So what is this about George?"

I told her what Ray and I had found out. "And I'm thinking he may have had something to do with Buzzy, too."

She said, "You may not acknowledge it, but you've just had a couple of bad shocks. Grief can cloud thinking. And when it comes to this theory, it sounds like you and your friend ran pretty far with not very much. But if you think there's something to it, it's a job for the police. We should drive there right now."

"No. A murder forty years ago and another across the country? What are the Middleburg cops going to do with that? If they don't just think I'm crazy."

"What's with you and the police? You ask me to call them. Then you don't want me telling about you. Are you some kind of criminal?"

"I have some history with the Middleburg cops. And there are aspects of my computer work which…skate around the edges of the law." *But it's for good causes…*

"Oh." She sounded disappointed. "Whatever it is, I don't want to know about it."

"Sure."

We were silent. She said, "Maybe you have a point about not going to the police with this. But you need to find out what's going on."

"That's what I'm doing." What I promised Jeannie I'd do. Though there was a lot more to find out about now.

We didn't speak for a half hour, until we got back to Middleburg.

I was turning to the Four Brothers house when she told me to take a right. We entered a similar neighborhood to Buzzy's, with nice little old houses.

"Park here."

I looked at her and raised my eyebrows.

"My place."

***

She didn't show me her house. Didn't offer me a cup of coffee. Just took my hand and led me upstairs to her bedroom. She stood, hugging herself. "One thing. Promise me you won't compare then with now."

"I wouldn't dream of it." A lie, but I was sure going to try.

I did a decent job. She was a big help, distracting me from everything but the most basic thoughts.

Afterward, she said, "I'm sorry, I don't think I have any Almaden wine. But I've got a decent cabernet…"

"Hey. You need to promise me, too. No comparing then with now."

"Fair enough."

"Except…that was better."

She laughed and I joined her. She said, "Definitely," and kissed me.

"I've got one question. How could it have just been the one time?"

"The foolishness of youth."

She got the wine.

I said, "What happened to taking it slow?"

She laughed. "Right! I don't know. Our friend died. You showed up for me. And I remembered just why I went in that basement with you. Maybe that wasn't what I meant about slow, anyway."

"What?"

She clutched my hand in both of hers and pressed it to her heart. I left it there for a minute, then gently as I could pulled my hand from hers and moved an inch away in the bed.

She said, "Sorry." She got up, threw on a robe, and stood with her back to me by the window. After a minute she came over and sat on the edge of the bed and took my hands. "No, I'm not sorry. I think I…want something. I've got no idea what you want, or *if* you want. But it kind of doesn't matter."

She'd laid down the gauntlet. This woman meant business. A week ago, and any other woman, I would have been headed for the door. But her sheer ingenuousness—the fact that she wasn't running any game on me, was really just laying down what she felt—kept me there. At least for another half an hour.

It was late afternoon, and I really had to go.

She must have sensed it, because she backed right off the heavy vibe. "Tthanks for coming up, coming to see him. And…all." She walked me to my car.

115

She stopped and stared me in the eye. "Did George kill Buzzy?"

I threw up my hands. That was the question. I didn't have an answer.

I could already taste the rush of relief that would come in a moment with escaping, but something rose up and forced me to look at her.

She looked right back and for an instant I imagined I could see inside her, eyes windows to the soul and all that...

She nodded, squeezed my hand, and headed back into her house.

I called Ray and told him about Buzzy. Not Sharon.

He said, "Ah, man. I'm sorry. Come here."

***

As I drove home, the effect of the happy hormones generated in Sharon's bed wore off. I got my iPod out, tried music, but it didn't seem right.

Buzzy. His dead face appeared. Like someone hit the dimmer on the sun, the hills and fields were suddenly bleached of color. I pushed the image away.

Sharon. The first truly aggressive woman I'd known since...Angela. But Angela was all physical come-on. What Sharon was after was far more dangerous. She was the definition of complicated. A little spiky on the surface. Warm and sweet beneath that. But I sensed if you really went deep with her, you'd hit a core of solid diamond. She was one tough woman. And then there was that touch of sadness. Would she ever let me really see that? Did I want to see it? I wanted to turn the car around and go back to her house, finish that bottle of wine, take her out to dinner. And I wanted to keep driving away and not stop until I was on the other side of the world.

Buzzy. Sharon. But all I felt was a hard pain in my gut that grew as I drove.

At Ray's we stood in the art gallery. He said, "I'm really sorry about your friend."

"Thanks. Too bad you never got to meet him."

"Now we know whether your two friends falling was a coincidence or not. Three is..."

"Three is what? Why would George push Buzzy from the same spot as Angela? It's like pointing a neon finger at himself."

"But who's going to see that finger after all that time, aside from you? Maybe

116

he just gets off on pushing people from cliffs. Or maybe Buzzy jumped."

I groaned. "That's impossible. You didn't know him."

"OK, so he slipped. Maybe he liked the place, went to smoke a little weed for old times' sake…"

I wanted to smack him. "Ray. He was a *Buddhist.* I don't think he'd done drugs in years. He spoke, moved, did everything with great care. He did not slip."

"What if George *wants* to get caught?"

"What, he's been guilty about Angela for all these years, which makes him kill Waldo? Which makes him guiltier, so he kills Buzzy? But does it in such a way that he gets caught?" I snorted. "That's nonsense."

"Yeah. That is one tangled-up explanation."

I sat on the windowsill. "Leaving Waldo aside for the moment, the trigger for what happened to Buzzy was those pictures. He put them together, tried to tell me, and within a day or so was killed."

"And whoever did it found out he put them together. How?"

"The same way as me. They hacked into his email. They could have gotten the address from Waldo's emails."

Ray sat at his desk. "What if this has nothing to do with Angela, with the past? What if it's all contemporary politics—that gay conversion bill Buzzy and Waldo were working on? Nichols is by definition on the other side of it. George is his bagman, or whatever. He kills them, and though Waldo looks suspicious, Buzzy cancels that out, because it's just too crazy."

"What, all this just to stop some legislation? That's some serious hardball. And if it starts to unravel, they're fucked."

He looked at me hard. "Which leaves you as a serious loose end."

"Yeah." His words crystallized the uneasy feeling that had been nibbling around the edges of my horror at Buzzy's death.

He looked at me. "I said a minute ago, you'd be the only one to see the connection. Maybe Buzzy is a message to you. A warning."

I sighed. "Now you're making sense. Unfortunately. Two of the Four Brothers are dead. I've got the odds of a coin toss. The next body is either Rick's…or mine."

The hard place in my stomach had turned to nausea. Despite the heat, my hands and feet were clammy. And some force pushed me down into the chair, like it didn't want me to move. I shook it off and stood. "I need to do something."

"You do. And you have two choices. Either run away from him or take him on. Fight or flight. You've never struck me as a runner, but with you being a pacifist, fighting's going to be tough. Like you've got both hands tied behind your back. But I'm with you."

"I know. And I appreciate it." My fingernails were digging into my palms. I couldn't fight. I had to. It was a mind fuck.

***

Back home I frowned at the museum cases. They looked wrong. Not the missing glass. I'd get that fixed. It wasn't Laurel's letter, either. I'd find a new lover. I might have one already, or even two if you counted Jeannie…

It was Buzzy. I thought of getting one of the photos he'd taken from the box, giving it a special place. But Buzzy was way too big to fit in here.

We need to talk. It was never going to happen, now.

I made a sandwich and ate half. I hit the couch, fired up *Resident Evil* and dutifully mowed down zombies until bedtime. I was *cold*, which was weird. It was still in the seventies outside.

When I got in bed, I was still cold and now my body was filled with weird energy. I was antsy. I took a long, hot shower but still wasn't sleepy. I lay there for a long time.

I stumbled from bed, the sun glaring in at the bottom of the window blind. I was wrung out, my eyes sandy from lack of sleep. Last night's antsiness had settled in my legs. Four Brothers. Two down. Lose a coin toss and I was next. Maybe Ray was wrong. Maybe I *was* a runner. My legs propelled me out of the house, toward Ray's, into a morning that was gearing up for another merciless day in the steam bath. As I panted up the incline of the street, the oxygen hitting my brain sliced two clear images through the fog—that awful red thing at the foot of the cliff, and Buzzy's serene face at the morgue.

Ray came to the door, looked me over and shook his head. "Let's pour some coffee in you, see if we can fix it."

We went up to the kitchen and Ray got the espresso machine hissing.

I said, "Buzzy's face in the morgue was so serene. He was a cooled-out guy, but he *felt* stuff. Somebody pushes him off a cliff, and he's, what, meditating? Or did they do something to his face at the morgue?"

"Let's look on the Internet." Ray sat at the table with his laptop and searched. "Muscles relax in death. So that could be it."

"OK. But here's another thing. When I saw…Buzzy's body at Garnet Hill, he was naked. George, or whoever, made him take his clothes off on top of the hill before pushing him? I can't picture it happening, let alone imagine why they'd do it."

Grief and sorrow were still out of reach. But the impulse to go after whoever had killed my friends was right at hand. Literally in my hands, which were balled into tight fists. "George is in California."

"Is he? Buzzy died here."

"If he's not there now, he will be soon. I imagine working for the governor keeps him pretty busy."

"Which is an argument for our theory being wrong. If he's up to his ears in a high pressure job in California, how's he got the time to come east and do whatever he had to in order to kill him?"

"I hear you. Maybe George didn't kill anybody. But he's got to know something—those pictures of him were in Waldo's box. I need to find out what the hell is going on. And he's all I've got. I'm going after him."

Ray looked at me, his face still, blinking his eyes. "I'm coming with you." He stood.

"Thanks. But no. I need you to stay here and feed my dog. And…it's too dangerous." *I can't risk losing you, too.*

"You need me. I've been helping you figure out this stuff. And you don't know anything about the political side."

I took out my phone. "That's what this is for. I'll check in with you every day. Actually…I'm going to get a couple of prepaid cell phones, just to be super safe."

"What are you going to do out there? You're sworn to non-violence." He was shaking his head.

"And you? You have a secret gun collection?"

I left before he could talk me into his coming. I dropped by a convenience store near the projects down by the river and got cell phones for Ray and me.

***

Back home in the office, I booked a flight to San Francisco that evening. I hit my email, then checked the weather in San Francisco. A high of sixty-two. I was going to enjoy the cool. I called the guy who was going to put in the new bulkhead and left a message saying I had to reschedule.

I had no idea how long I'd be in California. I called my friend Spider, who lived in the Bay Area. He'd done sound for the Grateful Dead. I'd met him at a gig. The guy had good acid, the *only* acid I knew of anymore. And I admired the fact that he knew more about the arcane workings of rock-and-roll electronics than any man alive. He was always inviting me to come stay on his houseboat in Sausalito.

He was glad to hear from me but was on the road for the next month with a band. But "my place is yours." He told me where the keys were.

That reverse SEO business was bugging me. It reminded me of something. Somebody burying the blog post about George was like... No. Not like. *Un*like. The opposite.

The opposite of my fake website. The purpose of demoting the blog was to hide George from anyone searching for him. The purpose of the "Call Bodine" website was to expose me.

On a whim I typed in my name. The goddamn "Bodine" website was back up. With a new page. "Bodine's house." I clicked. There were photos of my place. My office and bedroom. My museum. The glass on the cases was intact. And my bed didn't look pissed on. Which meant he'd taken the photos before he fucked everything up.

At the bottom of the page a close-up of the nuns' gravestones. It was captioned, "Matthew 19:12—There are eunuchs who have made themselves eunuchs for the sake of the kingdom of heaven." What?

Next to Buzzy's death, to Waldo's, this was just vandalism. Still…

I called Ray. "Now please don't start working on me about coming to San Francisco. I've got a weird thing here."

"Another, you mean."

I told him about the website reappearing and the new page.

"Let me get on, take a look at it."

I waited long minutes.

He finally said, "The previous version of your site was snarky, ironic. Like the guy was tweaking you. This new stuff has an edge. And there's nothing funny about that Bible verse. Maybe this isn't Brickman."

"What—he put up this fake website for me, then someone else hacked it?"

"That is a little baroque, but it looks different. What about George?"

"How the hell would he get onto me? Brickman's got serious computer chops, and there was a connection between us, but George…"

"Doesn't it seem a little convenient, Buzzy trying to find you to tell you about Waldo, and like that he stumbles on this website?"

I groaned. "You think George put up the website, and broke into my place? And not just to fuck my stuff up."

"Maybe he came to kill you."

"I still think it's Brickman. But you be careful when you come to feed Mingus."

"I will. At least I'm not one of the Four Brothers."

I got off the phone and took out the pictures of George from my pocket and stared. I tried to picture him picking a lock. Making a website. Smashing those cases and pissing on my bed. I brought up my image of Brickman, the central casting geek in his hoodie, and tried to see him doing that stuff.

I didn't get anywhere, because I didn't know enough about either of them. California might fix that, at least when it came to George.

I dropped off my new door clicker and the burner cell phone with Ray and explained how the security system worked. The important thing was that he not trigger the camera in the theater when he came to feed Mingus. I set him up with the app on my phone so he could temporarily override the alert. I gave him a serious, "Now remember to turn it back on."

"Yes, boss."

He seemed to have accepted staying in Hudson.

***

I called Sharon. She said, "Hey. How are you?" I caught no hint of embarrassment from her after our falling into bed.

"I'm managing. You?"

"I saw my shrink. It helped. I guess I'll see you…at the funeral."

"Uh, I may not be able to make it. I'm going back to California."

"Why?"

"To look into George Bowman."

"No! I won't have you getting yourself killed."

"My being out of town is probably safer than staying here." I explained about the break-in and gave her a sanitized version of the situation with Brickman. "I need to put a stop to this, whoever's behind it. Or he'll always be out there."

"Promise you'll call me every day." Just words people say. But she sounded like she meant them. Like she actually cared. Which was suddenly making it hard to breathe. Except that I was about to have a version of exactly what I wanted. Which was to talk to her every day, while being three thousand miles away.

I relaxed. "Will do."

"And promise to *be careful.*"

"Yes," I agreed. She hung up but her words echoed in my head.

Be careful.

11.

The plane took off at a little after 7:00 p.m. I pulled up the window blind and watched like a literal hawk as houses and cars shrank into toys and the plane swung around and set off in hot pursuit of the dying sun. This view was something I'd always enjoyed about flying… I remembered my fear and my stomach did a flip. I turned from the window and closed my eyes. I used to like being high. On the rock at camp. Later doubly high on Garnet Hill, and much later in the Adirondacks. Was that spoiled now?

The flight attendant brought me a beer and a tray of cardboard chicken. I'd had some rough days, so I dozed.

I woke and stared outside. The plane was jolting around. The captain announced turbulence and turned on the seat belt sign. Which was too bad, because I had to pee.

I cranked up my iPod to distract from the urgency in my bladder. What was this—Beethoven? It felt very Old World. Out of place here on a plane, on this iPod. It didn't matter. No one could hear me listening to it.

The moment the sign went off, I got up, but a couple of other people beat me to the rear bathrooms. I headed toward the one up front. It was supposed to be for first class, but it was vacant. No one would notice. A lot of people seemed to have slept through the rough spot. One guy in a leather jacket was slouched down, almost like he was hiding…

Ray.

I leaned down to him and said, "What the *fuck* are you doing here?"

A woman sitting across the aisle with her teenage daughter turned and glared.

"Sorry," I said.

Ray said loudly, "What is that you're listening to?" pointing at my earbuds.

I whispered, "None of your damned business," yanking them out and punching the iPod off. I lit into Ray. "Nice trick, but soon as we land, I'm booking you on an all-expenses-paid trip right back the way you came. I told you, I have to do this alone."

"That's the whole problem. You *can't* do this alone."

"What about my dog?"

"Jo will feed him."

"Jo?" Ray's friend. She and I didn't get along. "What the hell does she know about dogs?"

"Don't worry. She loves them."

"But what about the security camera?" One of the bones of contention between me and Jo was the fact that she was a confirmed and proud Luddite. She didn't even own a cellphone.

"Louise is going to handle that part of it." Jo's wife.

"Bah." Maybe she could handle it. But I was going to still end up owing somebody I didn't like who didn't like me.

The plane lurched and I almost lost my footing. The seat belt sign came back on. I ignored it.

A flight attendant came by and grabbed me by the arm. "Sir, you need to get back to your seat right now and put your seat belt on. I'm not asking twice."

I gave Ray a last stern look and obeyed her. I knew Ray. He wasn't going home.

He exited the plane ahead of me. He wasn't waiting at the gate. Probably guilty. He should be.

But when I saw him by the baggage carousel, his backpack already in hand, grinning sheepishly, I felt a rush of warm feeling. I was touched that he'd bothered to come. And maybe relieved not to face George alone. I tried to glare at him but ended up laughing. I made a lousy scold.

I said, "As long as you're here, you need to make yourself useful. I can't be worrying about you every minute."

"OK."

It was almost midnight by the time we rented a car. We headed north.

Ray was excited. "Aw, man. I've been California dreamin' ever since I was last here."

"Damn it, Ray, did you sneak out here just to have a vacation? Because I've got a job to do, and not one I asked for."

"*We've* got a job to do. I know. It doesn't mean I can't enjoy the workplace."

He did a decent of job of restraining his enthusiasm until we hit the Golden Gate Bridge.

Admittedly, it was spectacular. Towers gleamed in the floodlights, soaring like cathedral pillars, the lights of the city across the bay mirrored in the water. Ray's hands gripped the dashboard like they were keeping him from flying right out through the roof of the rental car, straight up to heaven.

He rhapsodized, illustrating with his hands as he spoke. "There's no other place on earth like this. San Francisco is literally a fairy-tale town. It's like some witch and some warlock had a spell-casting contest. She says, 'What you got, big boy.' He whips his wand around and crumples the earth into these hills, then paints streets on them.

"She looks at him—'Oh yeah?' Snaps her bony fingers and spins bales of fog like cotton candy all over the hills.

"Now he's pissed, takes his wand and sketches this freaking bridge over the straits, and as an afterthought plops Alcatraz out there with a big splash."

"Great, Ray, but I'm trying to drive. I think you'll like Sausalito." From what I knew of it, it was an old fishing village turned hip enclave, with artists and musicians and the better '60s holdouts. We exited the highway and wound downhill into town. It was almost deserted this time of night but looked awfully upscale for a fishing village.

Ray asked, "This is it? I expected something a little more...funky."

As we left town, I turned toward the bay at the other end of town and parked in a little lot. We headed down a boardwalk into a whimsical Hobbitville. The way was lined with exotic plants, cacti, gnomes, and a wooden mermaid. The boats ranged from hippy-dippy huts to faux Victorian.

Ray said, "This is more like it."

I put a finger to my lips—people lived here, and they must be sleeping.

Spider's was several steps down market from the others. It was unadorned, most of the paint gone, the walls halfway to driftwood. "This funky enough for you?"

Ray nodded, pointed to the concrete hull. "How's it float?"

"I don't know, exactly. Some miracle of physics."

We threaded our way between the boat and its neighbor, down a rickety gangway. Inside, we climbed down a half flight of steps into a surprisingly spacious living room. It was most of the length of the boat and not too narrow, stuffed with Edwardian furniture and knickknacks.

Ray grinned. "Man, this is just like the cover of that old Dan Hicks record. The band is sitting on a houseboat right here in Sausalito, wearing old duds, surrounded by Victorian stuff just like this, living the hippest lives that were ever lived. Dan and His Hot Licks, and those chicks, The Lickettes...I used to stare at it for hours, wishing I could be in that picture."

"Well now you are." I saw a computer on an antique desk. "Except for that. The question is, does Spider have Wi-Fi?"

I found the router. Taped to the back was a note with the user name and password: Tibetanbook, one word.

Ray said, "As in, 'of the dead.'"

"Yep." The password was 314159.

"This is a lot more house than boat."

I nodded. Except even though I couldn't detect any movement, from the moment I'd stepped on the boat my body knew subliminally it was floating, ungrounded, the way it knew on the plane. A sensation that suited my life as of late.

I thought of staying in Spider's bedroom. No. I pointed to the two couches in the living room. "Your choice."

Ray looked at the Chinese one and headed for the mousy brown one. He stopped and returned to the first one. He said, "I'm going for Chinese."

I walked over to the other couch and smelled why. "I thought you liked funky?"

"There's nice funky. That thing smells like something died in it."

Ray *was* the guest.

***

We sat in slung-back chairs on the downstairs deck of the houseboat, digesting the fine breakfast we'd enjoyed at a Sausalito café. The sun glittered on the bay, it's heat perfectly tempered by a slight breeze.

He asked, "Remind me again why we live back east with steambath summers and ass-freezing winters?" He closed his eyes with a big grin.

"Sorry, but it's time to get to work."

I closed *my* eyes.

Ray said, "I thought we were working."

"I am. Thinking." A few minutes later, I said, "I'm going to meet with George."

"That's crazy! If he killed your friends—"

"I'll do it in public."

"How're you going to get him to show up?"

I didn't say anything, just settled into the moment. A gentle, slightly cool breeze was kicking up little waves, which patted the hull of the boat in a nice rhythm. The ghost of a foghorn sounded from across the bay. A faint fishy smell...

"Bait. What do politicians need?"

"To win elections."

"And what do they need to do that?"

"Duh. Money."

"How about I impersonate a rich donor, eager to remain anonymous? Just the kind of guy George would like to meet."

"Well, you're white enough, and you've got enough blue blood."

Ouch. "Right."

"Wait. A rich, Republican donor—with a ponytail? That's not going to work."

"His representative? Hmm. It still won't fly. Fuck, I'll get a haircut if I have to."

"You haven't had a haircut since I've known you. I don't know. What makes you think you can pull this off?"

"Hey, if a white guy like me could pull off singing Marvin Gaye and Wilson Pickett, it should be cake."

A motorboat buzzed by and messed up the tranquil scene. Gulls screeched.

Ray said, "Where's this meet supposed to take place?"

"Hold on." I went up to Spider's workshop, filled with vintage audio gear in various stages of repair. I found an ancient guidebook to the city and brought it out to Ray. I said, "You choose."

He browsed the book. "How about the Fairmont Hotel? According to this, it's the classiest joint in town, up on Nob Hill. He showed me pictures. Here's the lobby." He pointed to a photo of a lavish chamber with an Oriental vibe.

He looked my cowboy shirt and jeans over. "You need a different outfit."

"True." Jeannie designed clothes. I called her.

She said, "What, you're back in town? Why didn't you tell me? And why haven't you come see me?"

"I will. I just got here. I'm looking into Waldo. Some other…stuff has happened. But how are you?"

"I've been better. There's been this car on my street…"

Paranoia? "I thought you were headed to your sister's."

"Oh, she's too busy for me to bother her."

"I'll be by soon as I get something taken care of."

"It'll be good to see you."

"You, too. But right now, I need a new set of clothes," I explained.

"Valencia Street in the Mission. You'll find good cheap stuff."

I hung up and called the Fairmont, telling them I needed a nice quiet spot for a business meeting. They suggested the restaurant Laurel Court.

I said to Ray, "I can't be Bodine, or even Bob Hutchinson. So who am I going to be?"

"Old money, tight ass…Sumner Pearson."

"Hey. That works. Where'd you get it?"

"Some snotty kid I once knew."

I called the governor's office.

"How may I help you?" The woman had a chiming, but chilly, receptionist's voice.

I met her voice with the slightly oily tone I used to use when dealing with corporate accounting, before I did everything by email. "George Bowman, please."

There was a beat before she answered—was it the name? "And what is the nature of your call?"

"I'm representing a wealthy citizen of San Francisco, who is interested in the possibility of assisting the governor's campaign."

"I'll see if he's available." She'd warmed right up. "Who may I say who is calling?"

"Sumner Pearson."

She put me right through.

"Mr. Pearson." His voice was deep and warm. He must be eager to get his hands on the money, but he was hiding it well. But when I asked if we could meet, he was right on it.

"Name the time and place."

"Laurel Court at the Fairmont?"

"One of my favorite spots in San Francisco."

"Tomorrow at two too soon?"

"No. I'll be there. I look forward to it."

I hung up.

Ray asked, "What was he like on the phone?"

"He sounded exactly like he was supposed to. Smooth, professional. But when I dangled the bait he still bit." I asked Ray, "What are you going to do while I'm meeting George?"

"I'm coming with you."

"My faithful cavalry? OK. But you need to stay out of sight."

"This is a fancy hotel, right?"

"The fanciest."

"Oh." Ray looked down at his jeans and frayed T-shirt, his leather jacket.

"I guess I'd better get spiffed up, too."

"It wouldn't hurt to shave while you're at it."

***

Down in the Mission the next morning, Valencia Street crawled with hipsters.

Ray asked, "Are these folks descended from us, from the hippies?"

"I don't like to judge on appearances, but their look is a little studied."

Ray pointed at a shlumpy guy in a T-shirt wearing a fedora walking next to a tall, beautiful, stylishly dressed woman.

Ray asked, "What the hell is he doing with her?"

"That is a code jock who hit the jackpot in the dot-com lottery. That fellow is worth fifty million bucks if he's worth a dime. As it says in the Bible, the geek shall inherit the earth."

Ray gave me a look—*Why haven't you inherited?* But he knew the answer: That I cared little for material things, and less for visible badges of worldly achievement. It was a legacy of the '60s we shared. We'd each remained true to it in our own way.

We hit a cavernous thrift store where I found a respectable suit for less than a hundred bucks and Ray a fedora of his own. At a wig store I bought a short hair wig.

Ray asked, "Where'd you get the idea for that?"

"This drummer I used to play with. He enlisted in the National Guard to get out of going to Nam. He had hair down to his ass, which looked great onstage. He put one of these on when he attended Guard weekends and summer camp."

"Get that suit on and you'll be looking just like The Man."

"I sure hope so."

We returned to the thrift store and took turns changing in a dressing room.

When I came out, Ray said, "Perfect. I barely recognize you."

"I bet you didn't know I was a master of disguise along with all my other talents."

After Ray changed, I looked him over. "You've certainly got the private eye part down. Fedora, hungover…"

"Hey, I had all of *two* beers last night! I'm just gonna sit in the lobby and read the newspaper. I'll fit right in."

We got in the car and headed toward Nob Hill.

Ray said, "What about lunch?"

"We're running a little late. I'm not hungry. You know I never eat before a gig."

"Yeah, but you're not playing."

"Oh yes, I am. Playing George."

"Hm. I hope it's not the other way around. *I* should be the one meeting him. You don't know shit about politics. These guys speak to each other in a special code."

"Give me the five-minute primer."

I swerved to avoid a bicycle. There were almost as many of them on the streets as cars.

Ray scowled at the guy on the bike. "Those suckers are aggressive for being on two wheels. OK. You're talking to him about immigrants? They aren't 'migrant workers,' but 'illegals.' You don't talk about 'gay rights.' It's the 'homosexual agenda.' There's no harm in tossing in that old slur about 'Adam and Steve.' Oh, and this is essential. You never refer to the 'Democratic Party.' It's the 'Democrat Party.'"

"Why is that?"

"It's some kind of put-down, sleight of hand to try and cover up the 'democracy' in 'Democratic.'" He snorted. "Not that that shit has done much for them here in California. Call them what you will, those Dems have got a super majority in the state legislature."

"What about Jesus?"

"Try to stay away from religion. They've got their own separate code for that. Though I doubt it has much to do with the real Jesus."

The traffic on Market was heavy, but at least moving.

Ray asked, "Does this thing have heat? I didn't notice in the Mission because we were walking. It's really cold."

It was. I turned on the heat.

Ray had borrowed Spider's San Francisco guidebook and had his nose in it. He said, "This is the Tenderloin." Hookers stood in doorways. They must be shivering in those short skirts.

I said, "Here's one part of the city that hasn't gone all upscale."

"No kidding."

We left the Tenderloin and climbed steep California Street onto Nob Hill and into the lap of luxury. We stopped at an intersection and Ray had a tour guide moment.

He pointed across the street to our right, to a grand brownstone mansion. "That's the Pacific-Union Club, where muckamucks make their deals. Your fictitious boss would belong to it, though I don't know how you'd work that into your act. Grace Cathedral's at the end of the block." He pointed to a tall, handsome building to our right. "And that's the Fairmont."

I turned right and drove past the hotel looking for parking. Past the next cross street our street plunged downhill so that all I could see was a little patch of blue bay. Ray pointed at the elegant apartment building to the right.

He said, "I'll be damned. I know that building."

"You were here when we came out in '70?" We'd come out to San Francisco together, chasing the tail end of the hippie times.

He shook his head. "I don't think they let us riffraff up here."

"Funny, that building looks familiar to me, too."

I turned and found parking further up the hill.

"Ray, you go in first, just hang in the lobby, read the paper."

"Like Sam Spade."

"Whatever. But don't move."

"OK."

Ray got out and walked toward the hotel. I waited ten minutes then followed him. The sun gleamed on upscale row houses and the facade of Grace Cathedral, but the air was chilly.

As I went through the grand doors of the hotel a frown tugged at my lips. I ordinarily wouldn't be caught dead in a place like this. This was my father's world, gleaming brass and obsequious smiles, fine cognac and interest rate deliberations…

Spider was right about the lobby. It was a mindblower. Despite the unwelcome memory of my father, I couldn't help but be impressed by this display of lavishness—marble floor and gold columns, a riot of tropical plants, and brocaded couches with more than a hint of the Oriental.

The Fairmont might be the fanciest hotel in town, but that town was San Francisco. This was no stodgy businessman's abode, but an opium dream of some exotic palace. My father, who had the imagination of a Formica countertop, would never have stayed here.

Ray perched on a grand paisley armchair doing his best to look invisible reading the newspaper. He still looked like a character who'd strayed up from the Tenderloin. I ignored him.

I heard voices and looked for the source. What was this? The geek squad seemed to have followed us here from the Mission. Jeans, T-shirts, bad hair...name tags.

It was a computer convention. I'd come here expecting my father's world and run smack into a version of my own. The geeks *had* inherited the earth, including apparently the Fairmont. It was a shame that Ray wasted twenty bucks on his getup. He would have fit in fine dressed as he was.

12.

The entrance to Laurel Court was off the lobby opposite the doors I'd come in. The maître d', a young Asian woman, smiled warmly.

I said, "A Mr. Bowman will be joining me."

She sat me in the bar area on a comfy couch with a view of the lobby.

I ordered coffee. The room was a large oval. The ceiling was made of three domes, each nesting a chandelier. Their light glowed on curved walls with murals of the Italian countryside. At the center of the room an ornate staircase wound down to unseen wonders. Tumblers glittered and silver gleamed, tinkling like frosting on melodious waves of chatter and innocuous classical music.

I could feel all of it working hard to soothe me, but nothing was going to take the edge off George's imminent appearance. Which was good. I would need every bit of edge I had to pull this off.

I sensed an accelerated pulse in my tight lower belly. My forearms were knotted with potential energy. My offhand comment to Ray about this being a gig felt true—this was exactly how my body had acted before a big one. As I'd learned to then, I relaxed what muscles I could and sank into the other sensations, even though they weren't pleasant.

I had an eye out to the lobby. The guy in the picture appeared, looking more substantial in the flesh. The photo hadn't captured his vibe of self-possession.

He spoke to the maître d' then strode over to my table and gave my hand a good squeeze. He was impeccably groomed, with sandy hair, fine skin, and the kind of handsome face that aged well.

He was perfect, except for a bandage over the bridge of his nose.

He must have noticed I'd seen it, because he touched it, explaining, "Golf accident. Can you believe it?"

He sat and inspected his place setting with a practiced eye. He moved his fork a millimeter. He seemed very much in the moment. Not like a holy man, but a tiger. I could picture him carefully picking the lock on my door. Taking photographs. But stealing the nuns' gravestones? And pissing on my bed? Those didn't seem like his style.

But it was time to rock and roll. "Mr. Bowman. Thank you for meeting on such short notice. I imagine it's a bit warmer up in Sacramento."

He laughed. "It was a hundred and three yesterday. I appreciate your giving me the opportunity to come here and cool off. What do you think of those Giants this year?"

Giants—football? Baseball?

I shook my head. "I'm sorry, I've been so busy I've barely had a chance to keep up with the news, let alone sports."

"Doing your boss's business." He nodded.

"Business is why he is so concerned about the illegals overrunning the state."

"If you've followed the governor's work you must know that he's equally concerned. What you don't know is that he is about to unveil a new piece of legislation that will become a model for the rest of the country."

"How are you going to get it past the...Democrat majority in the legislature?" My hands clenched under the table. I'd almost slipped, saying *Democratic*.

"That's where your boss comes in. With the proper resources, we'll scare them into it."

Scare? I couldn't help looking surprised.

George saw and explained, "With enough of the right kind of ads, they won't have a choice in how they vote."

"The man I represent is especially concerned about the horror of 'gay marriage'—as if there could ever be such a thing."

"I'm so glad you brought that up. Again, I'm sure you are aware of the governor's stated positions. Here we also have a plan. The homosexual forces are strong, especially in this town. What they aren't counting on is our raising money from out of state. If we gather enough seed money here, the floodgates will open across the country from God-loving Americans. That's how it works. Trust me, I've been doing this for a long time."

Doing what, exactly? What was the status of that gay conversion therapy bill? Was it public knowledge? I wished I'd boned up on it more. But it would be great to see George's reaction to it. What the hell. "We've heard about a bill to prohibit therapies designed to reorient homosexuals."

George waited a half a beat before answering. Was he suspicious? Or did he just not have a standard response? "The so-called 'gay conversion' bill. You've done your homework. We will fight it tooth and nail. But I believe we have some time."

His voice had cooled. Whoever he thought I was, I shouldn't know about that bill. My hands curled up again.

He said, "I'm curious. Why did you ask to speak with *me?*"

My face got hot. I hoped he couldn't see. "My boss told me you were…a man we could trust. Trust to be discreet."

A pause. "I'm flattered. But perhaps now you can tell me his name?"

"I'm sorry. He insists on remaining anonymous."

A membrane descended on George's eyes, like a cat's.

He finished his coffee and gestured to mine. "Are you done? Before we get to the next part of the conversation, I suggest we find a place a little more private."

"Of course."

Bowman paid the check and led me toward a door I hadn't noticed before, at the back of the restaurant. I glanced back at the lobby but couldn't see Ray from this angle, which meant he probably couldn't see me leaving. I followed George to the right, then left, away from the lobby, down a long corridor past shops selling jewelry, flowers and vintage Cuban cigars, then into a mirrored hall. There was no way Ray could guess where we were going.

Something else bothered me as we walked. George acted like he *belonged* here. He must have been to prep school like me. Of the many things I'd felt during my time there, belonging was never one of them. I remembered guys like him, who thanks to money and blood just slid right into the scene, the same as he'd slid into his chair at Laurel Court. He acted like *he* should be governor, not skulking around behind the scenes on behalf of one. So why wasn't he?

George opened a door at the end of the mirrored hall. Cold, damp air struck my face. I saw an unexpected riot of green, yellow and red.

We were outside, in a courtyard garden. The chill in the air I'd felt walking to the hotel had been the advance party of the fog. In the short time we'd been in the restaurant it had overtaken Nob Hill. Its ragged fingers reached over the hotel roof to my left, their invisible tips brushing against my cheek. Even in my suit I had to restrain myself from clutching my sides for warmth.

"This roof garden is one of the better-kept secrets in this city," George said with a big smile.

Roof garden? What was he talking about? I glanced up at the towering stories of the hotel to our left, where the roof should be.

He swept his arm regally across the verdant scene: giant palms towering over a finely clipped lawn with circular flower arrangements, echoing the curves of Laurel Court. The door we'd entered was mirrored by one across the garden.

It took me a moment to make sense of what I saw to my right. The garden ended at a low… parapet. Which was what? Something you built at the edge of a roof, or *cliff* to keep people from falling. Falling where? I looked up. There were buildings, but they were some distance away. Which meant there was a street down there. We'd passed it right before coming up the steep hill. It was way down there.

In the second I was putting this together, George was walking across the garden, right toward that parapet.

I hesitated. I should run. But the desire to keep talking to him, to *know*, had me following him. He glanced back at me. He was still smiling, proud of his secret. Or maybe preparing to throw me off the edge. Images rocketed through my head: Angela and Buzzy off Garnet Hill, Waldo off Lands End. Or did he have a gun?

These terrible possibilities assumed that my cover was blown. And that he was a very good actor. Because he was still smiling…

I stopped, and a moment later he did, too looking back, the smile replaced by a raised eyebrow.

A couple of tourists wandered through the door across from us. He wasn't going to kill me with an audience.

I steeled myself and walked toward George on rubber legs. He continued to the edge of the garden. He rested a hand on the parapet.

Get a grip… I walked over, stood about a yard from him, and placed a hand firmly on the stone. I couldn't see what was on the other side of the parapet without leaning over, which would be obvious, not to speak of nauseating. But I felt the drop, the void sucking at me…. I reeled in my attention and divided it between George's patrician face and voice, and those tourists, making sure they didn't leave.

He looked at me, not betraying any awareness of the conniptions I'd just been going through. "What kind of contribution are you considering?"

I needed to get this done, fast, while the tourists were still moseying around the garden.

"Tell me about Angela." I took a half step back from the edge.

The cat's membrane on his eyes flicked away and then drilled into mine. "Who the hell are you?"

"Never mind. I know Angela was pregnant, and…"

George took a step toward me.

This was the moment. I jumped back from him and away from the wall. He followed me and got right in my face. But he kept his hands to himself.

The tourists seemed oblivious. I nodded toward them.

He ignored that, hissing, "Now listen very carefully. I don't know who you are…" Except as he said it, I saw recognition come across his face. "Why, if it isn't one of the Four Brothers. Degenerates, out to save the world! You think you know something? You know nothing. You have no idea what you're dealing with here."

"I'm afraid I do. A right-wing governor with ambitions—"

"You're just admitting how little you know. There are deep waters in this world, and if you're not careful, your puny ass is going to get drowned."

Deep waters. Lands End…

"You killed Waldo, didn't you?"

His gaze flicked away for an instant. He licked his lips then sighed. "If you think I had anything to do with that… I wasn't even in town. I was on vacation."

Out of the corner of my eye I saw the tourists walk to the door opposite the one we'd come out of. They hesitated, then left. Shit. We were alone.

I don't know if he saw, but as I backed away from him, he grabbed my arm.

I said, "Look, anything happens to me, I'm not alone. Other people know about you. And they're prepared to go to the media and burn you and the governor right down."

He glared at me and grabbed both my arms. My eyes flitted to the yawning space past that wall and I struggled to get away. But George was strong.

He laughed. "Oh, you think I'm going to throw you over that wall? *Hutchinson*, I know what you do for a living. I can make one call and have you arrested. And the charges aren't just going to be hacking. You—all you socialist fucks—are terrorists."

"Are you a Catholic?"

"What? No. I'm born again. What does that…"

"Then why did you take my nuns' gravestones?"

His mouth dropped open. "Did you do too much acid back then, lose your mind? Because you aren't making a bit of sense."

"What about Buzzy?"

"Buzzy? Your faggot friend? That space cadet? What about him?"

"You *pushed* him. From Garnet Hill, just like…"

George went still. "I haven't seen 'Buzzy' in forty years. Pushed him? What the heck are you talking about?"

I didn't answer. There was no question, Buzzy's death was news to him. A look flitted across his face. Fear?

He recovered and came back with a snarl. "We're done here. You go crawl back in your grubby little hole and don't come out again. Forget you ever heard of me. My buddies don't care about courts. I'll get you rendered to Uzfuckistan, see how you like breathing with a couple of lungs full of water."

"You pushed Angela, didn't you?" He squeezed his eyes shut. He opened them, sneered, and said in a mincing tone, "Even if…somebody…*pushed* Angela, how could anyone prove it after forty years, with no witnesses?"

His eyes had darted away at the word "somebody," and there was that look again: fear. Then he'd revealed that no one had witnessed it happening. How could he know that unless he was there?

And I knew then that he'd killed her.

It came from nowhere. A volcano, erupting in me. I thrust my arms up, breaking George's grip and making him leap backward. As his leg struck the parapet he let out a yell. He snaked away from it onto safe ground, stalked across the garden, and disappeared through the door opposite the one we'd come in.

I stood still. *My buddies.* What if George hadn't come alone? What if they had Ray? I ran to the door we'd come in through, and down the corridor past the shops. I ducked into a bathroom and called Ray on my cell.

"Yeah."

I was relieved to hear his voice. "Where are you?"

"Still in the lobby. Where did you go?"

"I'll tell you in a minute. Meet me at the car."

***

In the car, Ray said, "I was getting worried about you. I saw George go in, but then I looked in the restaurant and you guys were gone."

"I told you not to move!"

"I was getting this vibe."

"OK. Correctly. There's a back entrance. He took me to the garden there."

"What happened?"

I glanced around. "Not here."

"What, you think George is out there?"

"I don't know what to think."

"Well, I'm starved. Tell me over lunch. I'm sure Laurel Court has a fine…"

"No! We need to get away from here."

"Let me see what's in the guidebook." He consulted it. "How about John's Grill? It's right down the hill. Old-school San Francisco. Apparently, the food's decent."

***

We entered a dark-paneled dining room. Every inch of the wall was covered with signed pictures of celebrities. Hillary Clinton. George Lucas. The place felt comfortable, not too fancy. Safe. And warm. Even so, my body was on the verge of shivering. That damned fog.

I consulted the menu and tried to lighten up. "Well, Ray, I was going to go the usual route, but 'Man doth not live by cheeseburgers alone.'"

"Not sure about that. You're not going squishy on me, are you?"

"Maybe. I'm going for the salad with crab and avocado."

"Me, too. Suppose it won't kill me."

After we ordered, Ray went upstairs to the bathroom. Beers came and I took a large medicinal gulp. A second later I felt a little better.

When Ray returned he said, "Speaking of Sam Spade, they have the Maltese Falcon up there!"

"Huh?"

"The prop, from the movie. Which made me realize why that street by the hotel felt familiar. We weren't there in person. It's the opening shot of that Hitchcock flick, *Vertigo*."

I flinched.

"What?"

"Nothing. I haven't seen it in ages." All I remembered was a sweating Jimmy Stewart staring down into that tower, the bottom zooming up as crazy music played. What was over the edge of that parapet on the roof garden? Maybe I should have looked. Then I wouldn't be imagining it was a thousand feet down…

Ray eyed my beer, which was already half gone, and said, "It must have been bad."

"George is a nasty piece of work." I took off my coat and rolled up my sleeves. There were red marks on my upper arms where George had gripped me.

Ray said, "Damn."

"That garden hangs over a drop, and I thought for a moment…"

"That he was going to push you."

"Yeah." *Or that I was going to push him.*

"Wow."

"He had this bandage on his nose, said it was a golf accident."

"You think Waldo hit him before George pushed him?"

"Could be. As soon as I sprung the name Angela on him, he made me."

"How?"

"He must have recognized me from back in college—I don't look that different."

"But you were in disguise. And a pretty good one."

"Right."

"Did you recognize him?"

"From the newspaper, sure. Not from college. But in recognizing me, he as much as admitted that he was at Middleburg. He made a snide reference to the Four Brothers."

"How'd he know about you guys?"

I laughed. "Oh, we were famous back then. You know how they used to have 'big men on campus,' football players and such?"

"I'll have to take your word for it."

"By the time we got there it was 'big freaks on campus'—the guys with the longest hair, strongest dope. Or who played in a band. Especially guitar players."

"Now look at what I missed not going to college. So he would have known you guys."

"The secretary of the economics department, the janitors knew of us."

"Did George call you Bodine or Bob? Or Robert?"

"He called me Hutchinson."

The salads came. They were huge.

Ray started inhaling his. "There's a boatload of crab in here. And the avocado's good."

"This is where they grow them."

I wasn't sure about my appetite, but a couple of bites and I was scarfing it down, too. We finished eating in silence. Both of us got close to the bottom of the bowl. I pushed mine away and said, "George didn't just recognize me. He knows who I am. What I do for a living. And where I live. He couldn't have gotten that from remembering me back then."

"*I* don't even know what you do for a living, not exactly. Nobody knows where you live but me and your exes. It *was* George who put up that fake website and broke into your place, not Brickman."

"I don't know. He was very slick. Fastidious. I really can't see him smashing those cases, let alone pissing on my bed. I brought up the nuns' gravestones and he really didn't seem to know about it."

"Huh."

I explained George's threats about his "buddies."

"He's blowing smoke there, or something. Because that part of his story is mixed up. Having you arrested means police, FBI. Having you rendered is the CIA. Who are forbidden from operating in the United States. Not that they stick to it."

"I don't know. The CIA could explain how he cracked my identity."

"It still sounds fishy. In any case, now he knows something new about you—that you're out here in California."

"Right."

Ray glanced around the room, which was full of diners. "Do you think he had us followed here?"

"I can't see how. He really thought he was meeting with the assistant to a donor."

"So he came down from Sacramento by himself."

"I hope. I tried the old dead man's trigger ploy on him—you know, telling him I had stuff ready to drop on the media if anything happens to me. I don't, of course. Even if I did, what we've got here is at best a Mexican standoff. I can't expose him without him getting me busted for…certain things I do."

Ray seemed about to say something, but to my gratitude let it go.

The waiter came and asked about the food. We praised it. He asked us if we wanted more beer. I declined, and Ray did, too, with a sad look.

He asked, "Did he kill Waldo and Buzzy?"

"I'm not sure about Waldo. He said he was on vacation at the time. Which I can check soon as we get to a computer. But he seemed genuinely shocked by the news of Buzzy. The only thing I'm sure of is that he killed Angela. At the end he admitted it to me in so many words." The fire burst to life in me again. I hid my fists under the table.

"What?"

"Nothing. It doesn't matter. She's still dead."

But I could see Ray wasn't buying it.

"What kills me is that he was taunting me, saying nobody could prove it."

"Which means you're gonna, if it takes wrapping those famous San Francisco trolley tracks around his neck."

13.

We drove toward Sausalito in silence. A good part of me was replaying the scene in the roof garden with George. I imagined myself looking over that edge, cars way the hell down below. What if he'd had a knife or gun? What if *I* had?

Ray was talking. "…always wanted to, if I ever got back here. How about it?"

"Sorry, what have you always wanted to do?"

"Walk the bridge."

"What bridge?"

Ray snapped his fingers in front of my face. "You're a million miles away."

We came out of a tunnel.

"*That* one. The *Golden Gate*."

My gut contracted.

No. I needed to face this thing with heights. Control it. Turn around, face the monster like they say. Look it in the eye and tell it to go fuck its demon self. I should have done it before now. "Let's do it."

We parked and climbed stairs leading up to the bridge. Ray played tour guide again. "I've been reading up on this. They built it back in the thirties, which is why it's got that fine Art Deco thing happening…"

But I wasn't listening. I was preparing. Drawing my life force inside, concentrating it in my lower abdomen.

Breathing, sensing my feet on the steps. Feet knew how to walk. Lungs knew how to breathe.

This fear of heights was a phantasm, a figment of dark imagination that had no real life, no home in my body. Which I needed to stay rooted in. And then I'd conquer it.

We started across, Ray to my left, a handrail to my right. A chain-link fence was fixed to the rail, extending well over my head. My body flooded with relief, along with a twinge of disappointment—this was too easy.

Twenty feet later the fence ended. Energy streamed out from my center, pulling my muscles into tight coils as it went.

But this rail was a few inches higher than that parapet at the hotel. If I stayed half a foot away, I'd be OK.

A bike whizzed by, almost clipping Ray, who lurched into me, nearly knocking me into the rail.

The Spandexed rider whipped his head around and yelled, "Assholes!"

Ray said, "Sorry."

"Not your fault."

Ray nodded across the lanes of traffic to the other side of the bridge. "Speaking of assholes, bikers are supposed to ride over there. They must be working on it. We need to walk single file."

I got in front of Ray and walked on. In theory my path was now plenty wide. But between the bikes rocketing by to my left, like some lost leg of the Tour de France, and the railing to my right I felt like I was threading the eye of a needle of electrified steel.

As if somebody had goosed a volume knob, my ears came wide awake. That railing was *humming* like a third rail to my right. Traffic roared to my left, accented every few seconds by an even louder two-beat metallic buzz—*bzzt-bzzt!* Like aluminum insects scolding me, chewing at my nerves like a wood plane on soft pine.

I stopped and Ray caught up to me and stopped. I asked, "What the fuck is that noise?"

"Rumble strips. To slow the traffic down." He pointed to a slotted steel plate in the roadway. "Can you feel it sway?"

"It's *moving*?"

"The bridge vibrates in sine waves, like a giant guitar string. Too bad whatever sound it makes is subsonic. It would make an awesome musical instrument."

I hadn't been imagining that railing humming. And now it sounded kind of like an electric guitar in that moment before it feeds back...

"The fact that it's able to move is what keeps the bridge from falling in the wind. Or if there's an earthquake."

An earthquake. *Falling.* Wonderful. I wanted to speak but couldn't. For all this vast expanse of sky, there was barely enough air to breathe and none to spare for conversation.

I started leading Ray across the bridge again. A tourist barged by, hitting my arm. He probably couldn't see me because he had a *phone* glued to his eye, taking a picture. *That thing's for talking, fuckhead!* I looked up at his target—the first tower. It was still a hundred feet away. We were just getting started.

One of the great orange cables holding the bridge up—almost a yard in diameter—rose here at a gentle angle. As I traced it with my gaze, it curved steeper and steeper until it reached the top of the tower. Though I was down here, and the top was up there, the cable was somehow pulling me *up*, like it was connected to those coils of tension in my body, like it was part of this whole steel conspiracy of rails and bikes and rumble strips.

My eyes locked onto the peak of the tower, and a moment later the sky and bridge started wheeling around it, like I was on a merry-go-round. I forced my eyes away and down, focusing narrowly on the backs of tourists walking in front of me. The spinning in my head slowed.

Except...any one of these walkers could be George, come to knock me over the rail. The crafty devil had known the drop from the hotel garden wasn't high enough—so he'd come here. This drop must be plenty high.

Enough. It was time to get a grip on this thing. A literal grip. Look this monster in the face. I stopped, turned to the bay, placed both hands firmly on the rail, and prepared to look down. The humming of the rail translated into intense vibrations in my hands. It glued itself to my fingers, and some force *in the rail* overcame my will and angled my torso down, my eyes with it. The rail, I realized too late, was connected to that great cable above. Which had tried to haul me right up into the sky.

I fought it, making a desperate attempt to enjoy the view: container boats from China, filled with flat-screen TVs. Alcatraz. My gaze fell to the water. The air was crystal clear. It was a long, long way down. Where was that damned fog when you needed it?

I'd been wrong. The force didn't originate in the railing or in the cable. It came from below. From the bottom of the bay.

I felt an invisible line whip up from the water and *hook* me, piercing my chin, nose, and eyes. It tugged my face out and down, and with it the rest of my body.

It was fish, *fishing* me. They were down there working the crank, reeling me in. My neck arched and my hands began to lift from the rail.

But Ray was talking. "...the most beautiful bridge in the world. Ironic that it's also the most popular suicide spot. Maybe there's something in that, great heights and great depths, heaven and hell. Maybe it's the center of the universe, the nexus of life and death..."

A white-hot jolt shot through me, breaking the crazy spell, snapping the fishing line, spinning me around to face my friend. *Maybe this, Maybe that.* How the fuck could Ray be blithely philosophizing while I was freaking out? Never mind that I was doing my best to hide it. My fist flew from the rail. I turned to him, to grab him, to smash in that piehole, which spewed crap while I...

"Bodine!"

I was so worked up that I wasn't looking at him, wasn't looking at anything, really. Literally blinded by rage. Now I gazed at him. He looked scared. Like whatever he saw in my face was something he'd never seen before.

I took a slow, deep breath. "Sorry. I'm not feeling well. Something in that lunch..." It started as a lie, but as soon as I said it, I became aware of intense nausea. Though I doubted it was lunch's fault.

I turned and marched forward. Step, step, step. There were a lot of them. We crawled up and past the first tower. Months later, the second tower. As we passed the water's edge and continued another couple of hundred feet to the end of the bridge, the tension that had my whole body in knots eased a hair. I was finally walking on solid ground.

But when I saw the bathrooms I pointed and told Ray, "I'll be right back."

I raced into a stall and puked up crabmeat and avocado, a pint of beer and a gallon of bile. I hadn't vomited in decades, not since the one time I ate peyote. Puking hadn't gained any charm in the meantime.

I'd set out to face the monster—my fear of heights— and it had taken a fat bite out of me.

Worse, I'd almost *hit* Ray. I shuddered. I had reason to want to go after George. But Ray was just being himself, just talking to me.

George killed Angela. I'd wanted to throw him right over the edge. I shuddered.

I'd been committed to non-violence for so long that I took it for granted, like a little toe. But it had never really been tested. I'd seen violence. I'd played dives where the fists flew on Saturday night. On the worst night, a brawl had exploded into the parking lot and a guy was stabbed to death. But I remained safe behind my instrument.

All it had taken was George admitting to killing Angela for my nonviolence to teeter like a house of cards. Angela, and possibly my kid.

I finally came out of the bathroom and with an effort smiled at Ray.

"You OK?"

"A little sick. So much for crabmeat. Or maybe it was the avocado. I don't really want to walk back."

"No problem. I'll get the car and meet you here." He stared at me, not unsympathetically. "You look like shit."

"Good to know."

I sat on a bench, my back to the bridge. I followed my breaths, with each exhale trying to let go a bit of the tension that had my body tied in one big knot.

I had almost reached a tolerable level of relaxation when the monster pounced one last time and trotted me off into a nightmare future. How was I getting on the plane home? What about those spiral stairs at Ray's? What about…

I stopped the train of thoughts dead in its tracks. I got back to those breaths.

By the time Ray arrived, I was feeling OK. Just tired. All right, exhausted. We drove to Sausalito in silence.

***

At Spider's, I got my computer and we sat outside on the deck. The funky odor on the breeze was not unpleasant, and the temperature was perfect.

I said, "George is a talented guy. He turned on a dime from handling a smooth meet at the chichi restaurant to threatening the shit out of me. And he's a busy guy. I'm sure the governor keeps him hopping, but here he is on both coasts, killing, vandalizing, hacking."

"That one's easy. It isn't one guy doing all that stuff. He's got someone working with him. He already suggested as much when he alluded to those 'buddies' of his."

I nodded. "It's got to be someone he can trust, because this is some dirty business."

"And there's your way in. He must be communicating with said person."

"Maybe they're emailing. Getting into that is going to take a little doing. First let me see if his alibi for Waldo holds up. It shouldn't be hard to get to his schedule."

But it was. I got on the governor's website and snuck around into the back. Soon as I reached the server, a warning popped up... "Damn. I almost got caught. Nichols's system is protected by a pack of pit bulls and razor wire."

"What would happen if you got caught?"

"They'd know someone was trying to get in."

"Come on, you can crack it."

"Maybe, given a lot more time. His IT people are good. Very good. I could see that at the White House, but it seems like overkill for a governor's office. Maybe it's a right-wing thing."

"Au contraire. The Internet may turn out to be the right-wing's Achilles' heel. Silicon Valley is about ninety percent lefty libertarian. Those fuckwit wingers don't know any more about computers than they do about rap music. Their best guy probably has a Commodore 64, has been reading the instructions for years, trying to figure out how to get it out of the box."

150

"They didn't do this shit on a Commodore 64. Maybe these buddies he was bragging about are CIA."

Ray scoffed. "Maybe he knows someone there, but there's no way the governor's computer system is run by the CIA. That would be illegal as hell, and guys like Waldo would be all over it."

"I have to take your word for it. It's your area."

"Trust me, this Nichols is smart. He wouldn't risk it."

I took another crack at getting into the system. Ray said, "I'm getting my computer."

He returned a minute later. I'd never worked next to him before. He punched the keys like they were sparring partners and muttered stuff under his breath. Concentrating took extra effort. I could try to explain to him the art of key whispering, but I'd be wasting my words. When he wasn't typing he was drumming paradiddles on the plastic.

I asked him, "What are you doing?"

"Checking out my favorite blogs."

I coded a splice so that my snooping would appear to have originated from the computer of some nice guy or gal in downtown Bangkok. Even tiptoeing disguised into Nichols's system, I immediately saw signs that this gentlest of poking was being detected, that someone was staring at me, at every routine spam attack that…

Spam. I could impersonate a spammer. Those assholes pretended to be trying to sell you useless shit you didn't need, but that was just a cover for data mining, i.e., poking around, like I wanted to do. I went offline and got to work on it.

Five minutes later, Ray said, "That wheel thing's spinning, I can't get onto this site."

"Ray. I'm busy here. Just quit the browser. If that fails, restart."

Another five minutes later, he said, "This shitbox is not working!"

I went upstairs and recycled the modem. But I was just getting back into it when Ray was complaining again. "Aren't we right up the pike from Silicon Valley?"

"Yeah. I've heard about pockets of lousy Internet around here. There are so many people hitting it that it's overloaded."

"It sounds like the cobbler's kid with shit for shoes."

I said, "We can go downtown in the future, find an Internet café, but right now I want to get done with what I'm doing."

Lights came on across the bay and it got cold. We went inside and I sat on the Chinese couch and continued working. After a few minutes, Ray sighed deeply, stood, and paced. That was an interesting trick in the confines of a houseboat. I said, "Go cycle the modem again."

He went upstairs. I ignored him and burrowed into my coding. After forty-five minutes I was ready to direct a fake spam attack, ostensibly hawking no-scrip Vicodin, Valium, and Viagra from somewhere in the former Soviet Union. It was the middle of the night there, but that didn't matter. Spammers never slept.

I got a few layers into the governor's system. But nowhere useful.

Ray had given up, was sitting in a wingback chair enjoying the analog pleasures of staring out at the bay.

I said, "I'm going to dig around, see if they've been hacking my computer."

After about a half hour I closed the computer and shook my head. "Nobody's touched it. So how did George get on to me? I'm too beat to figure it out now. You hungry?"

"Nah."

"Me neither. Nothing to eat here, anyway. Beer?" I'd usually wait for him to bring it up, which he would, but now that I was done on the computer I could feel the nightmare on the bridge lurking at the back of my mind. A drink would help.

Ray went to the kitchen. He returned with a couple of glasses.

I asked, "What's that?"

"Borrowed a little of Spider's freezer candy. I hope he doesn't mind."

Freezer candy? I took a sip. Vodka.

Ray said, "Playing Sam Spade is thirsty work."

"I'm the one playing, and I don't remember him having a computer."

We drank quickly, in silence. When it came to vodka Ray was a gulper. I was a sipper. But tonight I was neck and neck with my juice-loving buddy. I tapped my empty glass.

Ray smiled and nodded. "You're finally coming around to my persuasion after all these years! Better late than never. I hate drinking alone."

I suspected that was untrue, that he liked drinking alone just fine, but said nothing.

He returned with even bigger drinks. "Now George…"

I said, "Fuck George. At least for tonight." I lay down on the couch and stared at the ceiling.

I went into the kitchen and to the freezer. Just one more. I smiled. Control hadn't gotten me over my fear of heights. But it would get me through tonight. Control meant intending to do something and then doing precisely that. I intended to pour another half glass of vodka, no more or less, and drink it down in one shot. And that was just what I did.

I went back to the couch. In the five minutes that I'd been gone it had apparently reconsidered the nature of our relationship, because when I sunk into its corner it gave me a warm hug. I returned the favor and was conked.

***

Something jolted me from a dream early the next morning. I never dreamed. The boat felt wrong. It wasn't moving. I gazed out the window at tidal mud flats. The sound or sensation of the boat coming to rest on land must have torn me from the dream.

There was a rotten taste in my mouth, but I was ravenous. Ray was still conked, so I went out to the café by myself. Chilly fog seeped onto the sidewalk from the bay. It suited my inner state.

I flashed on the dream. What was bizarre was that I somehow knew that it had been full of feeling—I'd been drowning in the stuff. Yet all I felt now was a pulse of dull dread in my temples.

I devoured the number two special: bacon, eggs over easy, toast, and hash browns, vaguely wondering how I could be so hungry.

The answer came as I paid the check. I'd lost my lunch and skipped dinner. I ordered a second coffee to go. Breakfast had chased the bad taste from my mouth, but not the residue of that dream, which covered the morning like a shroud.

***

I was walking back to the houseboat when Sharon called.

She said, "I thought we were going to talk every day." She sounded bad.

"I'm sorry. Yesterday was insane. What's wrong?"

"They postponed the funeral. Something about an autopsy."

14.

I flashed on Buzzy's body on the table, a guy with an electric saw descending on it. I felt sick. I shoved the image away, but a faint alarm rang somewhere in my brain fog.

She said, "I was looking forward to the funeral. I need to say good-bye."

"Know what you mean. Maybe I'll be back for it."

"It would be good to have you there."

I stopped at the boardwalk leading to Spider's. Leaned against the rail and looked at the bay. "I've made a little progress in figuring out what's going on." I told her about the meeting with George. "We were on this roof garden, near the edge. I was afraid he was going to throw me over."

"I told you to be careful!"

"I didn't see it coming. That's not the worst part. George pushed Angela off that cliff."

"He confessed?"

"He danced around it, but I'm sure. And I was afraid I was going to throw *him* off."

"Why's that worse? He killed your first love. "

"I know it sounds quaint, but I'm committed to non-violence. A pacifist."

"That's not quaint. Not if you're the real deal. I'm curious, how did that happen?"

A woman in her forties was coming toward me down the boardwalk, pushing a grocery cart. She must be hauling groceries to her boat. I got out of her way and walked out into the small parking lot.

I'd never told anyone. Not Buzzy, not even Angela. It was like my Robin Hood gig. My private business. But suddenly I *wanted* to tell.

"My old man was an officer in World War Two, but never saw combat. That's probably why he was such a hawk. He used to threaten me with military school if he didn't like how I set my fork on the table. When Vietnam came, he tried to get me to enlist in the army. He said he'd disown me if he ever caught me going to an antiwar demonstration."

"Your nonviolence was a reaction to his macho bullshit."

"I suppose. But the clincher came at that camp where I met Angela. These Japanese women came to speak to us. They'd been young girls in Hiroshima and gotten horrendously burned by the bomb. But they didn't have an ounce of anger toward us Americans. Just this gentle plea for peace. You could practically see this aura around them, like they were saints."

I flashed back to camp, that night. They'd finished their presentation— no PowerPoints, no visuals in those days, just words and those devastating smiles. I was headed out to find Angela when something compelled me to the front of the room, to grasp the hand of one of those women, to thank her, but she was thanking *me,* and it triggered an explosion in my chest. I stumbled out into the dark and there was Angela. "What were you doing in there?" I turned away, mumbled something and escaped to my cabin without her seeing the tears.

Now a guy got out of his car carrying a couple of bags and headed toward the boardwalk. Not everyone had a cart. What about Spider? I couldn't see him doing either.

She said, "Are you still there?"

"Yeah. Sorry. After that night I started reading, hearing stuff, you know, about Gandhi— 'An eye for an eye makes the whole world blind.' About the Quakers. But behind it was those women. Knowing that nothing could justify hurting the innocent girls they'd been."

"Hiroshima was unspeakable. But George killing Angela is…personal. Not that I think you should kill him. But wanting to is normal."

"You can't start making exceptions. All life is precious."

"Put that way it's hard to argue. A lot happened to you that summer."

No shit. "Speaking of that summer, I just dreamed about Angela. I never dream."

"Well, you obviously do. Tell me. Dreams are fun."

"What do you know about them?"

"That I've spent a fortune telling them to shrinks. Some well spent, I suppose. It's other people's dreams I like. They make me feel like I'm not so crazy. And I happen to be free right now. So shoot."

She didn't seem crazy to me at all. "This one needs a little set up…" I told her about Waldo's box, and God help me, about my museum.

She said, "Your collection is unusual. Perhaps even weird. I already feel less crazy. Any idiot could see why you do it."

"Then I'm an idiot. Tell me."

"Two good friends die. As far as I know, you don't feel much about it. Or about anything, for that matter. At the same time, you hoard these objects of complete strangers, objects imbued with sorrow. You keep them right in your house. Are you getting it yet?"

"Uh-huh." But I wasn't, not really.

"This isn't really my place. This was Buzzy's turf. But let me try. When you described your museum a minute ago, I heard *feeling*. The feeling you don't feel for people close to you…"

Really? Because I hadn't felt a thing. What she said made logical sense, like a rudimentary arithmetic problem: If A plus B equals C, then… But it didn't mean anything to me. Like I was missing an essential element in the equation. All I felt was a tightness in my chest.

She said, "So, the dream?"

"I'm in my office, kneeling in front of Waldo's box. Inside is my collection, in miniature, like one of those Victorian dollhouses in a real museum.

"Suddenly I'm inside the box, in my theater."

She laughed. She was having a good time. "Were you small, or did it get big?"

"I don't know. It isn't *Alice in Wonderland*. The thing is, everything is exactly as it should be. Except in the corner I see…the box."

"Cool! That's some serious recursiveness. Like a mirror in front of a mirror. Sorry. Go on."

"I tiptoe up to the box, suddenly scared. Because I hear something scratching inside."

"Spooky. What?"

"Wings. The wings of an angel."

She burst out laughing. "You don't need me or Sigmund effing Freud for that one! Angela."

"Yeah. She's trying to get out."

"Of her coffin. Like in that Edgar Allan Poe story. That's even spookier."

"So…"

"What's it mean? You build this collection of sad, sad things that belong to strangers. But Angela is no stranger. And come to think of it, neither is Waldo, whose box it is."

"Yeah?"

"To use a hackneyed phrase from the seventies, you are 'trying to get in touch with your feelings.' Finally. Or at least some part of you is. Better late than never. That box isn't Angela's coffin. It holds your *feelings* for her." She laughed. "Whoa, slow down, girl! You didn't ask for that."

I was squirming, rubbing my fingers together. "Oh, but I did. I told you my dream."

Enough of this stuff. I said, "Back to George. What about friends? He must have had some."

"I suppose. When I get a minute, I'll think on that. I have to go. Speaking of life being precious, you…"

"Be careful. I know."

She hung up. I stood, a fine sifting of fog brushing my cheeks, gulls wheeling overhead. I'd never been Catholic, never seen the inside of a confession booth. But here I was, blinking, like I'd just exited a dark chamber, this woman I barely knew suddenly my mother confessor hiding behind her screen, coaxing, teasing out things I'd never told a soul. They weren't sins, but it felt like it.

And the phone was an accomplice. Not having to see her, be close to her, made this process much easier. What process?

I shuddered.

***

I woke Ray coming onto the boat. He grumbled something about drinking on an empty stomach.

I remembered Jeannie and called her. She said we should come right over. When Ray was done eating, we headed into the city. The sun was brilliant, but as we approached a tunnel through a steep hill, the fog lurked above, a solid wall like the one out to sea at Lands End. Only this one was much closer.

We exited the tunnel and drove downhill. I anticipated the glorious view of San Francisco, but the mist had swallowed the city whole, along with half of the bridge.

Ray said, "See how the fog looks solid until you're in it? Then it just vanishes, like it's always keeping one step ahead of you."

"Yeah, it does lend everything an air of unreality."

"Like the whole place is on drugs. Good drugs, that is."

Fifteen minutes later, we arrived at Jeannie's. We climbed from the car into a chilly breeze.

Ray frowned and hugged himself.

I said, "There's the other side of your fog."

Jeannie greeted us with a big smile. "I asked you to look into this thing. I meant poke around a little. I didn't mean for you to come all the way back out here!"

I said, "Well, here we are. This is my friend, Ray."

She turned to him. "Waldo said something about a Ray."

I said, "Probably about his guitar playing. My buddy is some kind of genius."

"You guys had a band. I'd love to hear you play." Some ancient sorrow flitted across her face. Did she wish she'd married a musician instead of a lawyer?

I heard a howl from the basement. Eldridge.

She invited us into the kitchen and made coffee.

"What *are* you doing back here?"

There was no easy way to get into it. "Buzzy's dead."

She blinked rapidly. "What?"

"Not just that. He *fell*."

She shrunk back in her chair, her eyes wide. "Like Waldo." She narrowed her eyes at me and her voice rose. "You believe me now?"

"I'm afraid I do. Somebody killed them."

She closed her eyes. Opened them, and they flitted to the pipe in the ashtray. I couldn't blame her.

Ray didn't seem to notice, which was good. I didn't need a stoned Ray right now. He was behaving himself, sipping his coffee.

She said, "This is not my life. Someone killing my husband. Killing his friend. And it wasn't Waldo's life, either. No matter who he was hassling with."

"I hear you. It's not my life, either."

"Sorry. You just lost another friend, too. I'm scared."

"You said you saw a car on your street."

"Some guy was sitting in it. It's been there several times."

"What's he look like?" I asked.

"I don't know. I've been afraid to walk down and see."

"The car?"

"I don't know cars. It's not too big. Brown. And yes, I called the police. They said they'd send someone around, blah, blah, blah. They didn't. I called again and they made excuses about being busy with 'a domestic.'"

"We'll go check right now."

Ray and I walked down the street.

He said, "She's a dope smoker."

"Legally. She has a script from a doctor."

"Got to love California."

We were approaching the end of the street when a brown car pulled out and turned onto another street and disappeared.

I said, "So she's not seeing things."

We walked back to her house. "I think we saw it," I told her.

She said, "Damn it."

"I know you don't want to bother your sister, but you really should go see her."

"OK. What have you got?"

I told her what I knew. She'd never heard of George Bowman.

She said, "I'm sorry, I don't know anything about that political business. I don't want to know. Did you call Kaylee, like I suggested?"

Waldo's associate at the law firm. "I left a message, didn't hear back."

"She must be swamped, picking up the slack without Waldo. Let me call her."

She got her phone out and went in the living room. She came back. "She says come down anytime today. Apologizes for not returning your call."

Eldridge gave it another try. I said, "Let me go say hi, introduce her to Ray."

The dog leapt up on me with an eagerness bordering on desperation, eliciting a furious round of petting. Then she went to work on Ray.

I said, "Damn, I miss Mingus. Jo better take care of him."

We said reluctant good-byes to the dog and were headed upstairs when I remembered that old computer of Waldo's. In the kitchen I said to Jeannie, "When they ripped off your laptop, you said Waldo didn't have one. Did he use that computer downstairs?"

"Sorry, I don't know. But he did spend a lot of time down there."

"Mind if we check it out?"

"Go right ahead."

The computer was off—another sign, if I needed one, that it wasn't hooked up to the Internet. It took forever to boot up. I was about to give up when the screen flickered feebly. More waiting, then finally a desktop appeared. It didn't require a password.

There were many folders titled with proper names—probably cases. I opened a few. Each contained a single word processor file with notes in some kind of legal shorthand, or just Waldo shorthand.

I said, "With no Internet he wasn't networking with his computer downtown. Maybe he printed these things out, or just used it as a glorified notepad. Which is lucky for us. If it was George who broke into this house, he overlooked this dinosaur."

Ray pointed at the screen, at a folder titled "Gay Conversion Bill."

"Yeah, I saw that. I've just been getting the lay of the land first."

I opened the folder, then the sole file. Ray read over my shoulder. We saw a list of names. Some had question marks after them, some asterisks.

Ray asked, "You recognize any of these?"

"Not offhand."

"Dennis Meacham rings a bell."

"Hmm. Hold on. Look at the bottom of the list."

It read, *Rick?*

Ray said, "Your friend?"

"It's the only one without a last name. And what is his last name?" There were no bars on my phone down in this basement. I could wait and Google natural food supplement companies later, but wanted his name now… It came. I remembered Rick one time saying, "I may be Arlington, but I sure as shit ain't going to be buried in that cemetery…"

I said, "Richard Arlington."

I sorted the desktop folders alphabetically. "Arlington" appeared at the top.

Jeannie came downstairs and into the office.

"Find anything?"

I said, "Maybe. Do you have a blank CD?"

"I think so." She went back upstairs.

Jeannie returned and handed me a CD. I fed it into the drive, and it made a worrisome whining, followed by a crunching sound, then sat silent.

Busted. But after a minute it started whining again, and the CD showed up on the desktop. I copied files onto it and ejected it.

We went back upstairs. I said to Jeannie, "Call your sister."

"I did while you guys were downstairs. I'm leaving in an hour."

"Good."

We left. In the car, Ray said, "I like her."

"Yeah. Too bad we had to ruin her day."

"It sounds like it was mostly screwed already."

***

I put directions for the law office in my phone and set it between the seats. As I drove downtown, Ray picked it up.

"Hey, you've got your own."

"Not this model." A minute later, he said, "Stop the car."

I pulled over. He was looking at my scan of the second demonstration picture.

I said, "What with that silly video of us I forgot to show you that."

He zoomed in on a guy in the picture standing next to George. "He wasn't in the other picture."

I'd been so focused on Angela that I'd missed him. "That's not a face you easily forget." Wiry hair was kept from his eyes by a headband. He would have been a pretty boy if his features weren't slightly distorted, like his maker had gotten sloppy, slipped, and given his face a little pinch. "But that's all I remember."

"He was a dealer. I remember because a few days before that gig of ours he burned me. Sold me some 'pot' that turned out to be a bag of weeds, or oregano or some shit. I'm playing at the gig, and I look up and there he is not ten feet away, staring at me. The fucking nerve."

"Did you call him on the burn?"

"I was afraid to. There was something creepy about him. What was his nickname? Some kind of animal. Badger? No. Weasel."

"That doesn't ring a bell. But that face…I saw him around. Just one more of a hundred weirdoes."

"It was the age of the weirdo."

"I never copped from him. We got all our dope from Rick."

15.

Waldo's firm was in a large, slightly run-down Victorian off Geary. I wasn't sure we had the right office at first. Instead of the usual billable-hour bait—leather sofas and dark paneling—I was looking at drab, uncomfortable furniture from the 1970s.

Ray said, "Angela..." and I whipped my head around, "...Davis," pointing to an ancient poster on the wall of a fierce black woman with an Afro and her fist raised. Who was she? Something to do with the Black Panthers. It came together. This *was* Waldo's office. It looked like an old-school no-frills activist office because Waldo put his social justice money where his mouth was.

The receptionist, a woman our age in a T-shirt and jeans, didn't buzz Kaylee but just strolled down the hall and knocked on her door. Kaylee came out and stood outside the door.

I recognized her from the funeral. Early thirties, with sharp eyes and a handsome, very round face beneath a buzz cut. Her T-shirt and jeans were set off by a semi-respectable jacket.

I said, "Jeannie called..."

"Right."

"I'm a friend of Waldo's from college. You know, in the late sixties."

She said, "Yes, I know."

If I expected some acknowledgment of the fact that we'd been there, on the front lines—at the revolution! —all I got was a small eye roll, if that. There was something solid, implacable about her, her shoulders set like she'd been swimming upstream for a long time against some fierce opposition but wasn't about to quit.

She ushered us into her office and sat us in plain chairs. Despite the informal scene, there was a Columbia Law diploma on the wall.

She shook her head. "I don't know what we—what the world—is going to do without Waldo. He was the boss here, but you'd never know it. He pulled his weight with the rest of us, stayed up all night finding any little thing you could use to nail the bastards to the wall. And nail he did."

"I wish I'd seen more of him lately. He was a…good friend."

"I considered him a good friend, too. But you're not here to commiserate."

"No." I fished the pictures from my pocket and showed her the one from the clipping. "You know this guy?"

"Of course. Governor Nichols. Mr. 'Take California Back.' Back to the dark ages."

"What about the other guy?"

She stared. "I've never seen him before."

"It's George Bowman." I asked Ray, "What's his position with the governor, again?"

Ray said, "Campaign analysis coordinator."

She looked interested. "That's a bullshit title. Which suggests he might be up to something."

I asked, "What do you know about Waldo's dealings with the governor?"

"Oh, they had a long history, even before he got into office. I think their first run-in was over the Diablo Canyon nuke. It was in the eighties, before my time, but Waldo told me about it. They built this nuclear plant in an earthquake zone, which triggered some of the biggest protests in the antinuclear movement. Nichols was a state representative then. He tried to pass a bill making the protesting of energy businesses a special crime."

"That seems a little heavy-handed for the time. After 9/11, maybe. What about recently?"

"Earlier this year there was this anti-immigration law Nichols was pushing in the legislature. Waldo had me doing research, seeing what our options were to stop it."

A young intern popped in with a tall stack of files. Kaylee nodded to the desk, where she dumped them and left.

I asked, "Did the governor's office know you were doing that?"

"Sure."

"Any blowback from them?"

"Not to us directly. But there was some funny business with some activists we know down in Riverside. We suspected the governor might have been behind it, but there was no proof."

"What about this bill about gay conversion therapies?"

She snorted. "Good thing those assholes tend to stay away from us lesbians. I don't think we were involved with that. Yet. Then again, Waldo had this thing about never making it personal. Maybe he kept me out of the loop." She laughed. "Probably a good idea."

"Did Waldo seem different those last weeks?"

Ray had been uncharacteristically quiet, but I could feel him perk up as I got to the meat of it.

She narrowed her eyes. "He did seem a little distracted recently. Down, maybe? He usually talked a blue streak, but he was quieter. Yeah, something was bugging him."

"Any idea what?"

"No. What's with this George Bowman?"

"It's complicated. You have time to hear about it?"

"Mysterious pictures, right-wing creeps—I've always got time."

"Back when Waldo and I were in college…" I told her about Angela and Buzzy.

When I was done, she got still. Her voice took on an edge. "Let me get this straight. You think this George Bowman killed this girl back, when was it?"

"The winter of 1969."

"Then forty years later he suddenly decides to kill his old love rival Waldo. Then Buzzy. Who's Buzzy exactly?"

"A therapist. I don't know if it's relevant, but he was…gay."

"Great. Does that mean I'm next?" No one laughed.

I shook my head. "But Buzzy and Waldo emailed and phoned back and forth about that gay conversion bill. I think Buzzy was trying to get Waldo to do something."

"Listen, the governor is an asshole, no question. He twists arms and twists facts. He's a demagogue with the soul of a crocodile. But murder? That's not his style. Remember, he wants to be president."

Ray asked, "But what if Nichols put George up to it?"

She said, "And Nichols is doing the old plausible deniability."

Ray said, "Or doesn't even know about it. Maybe George has been cowboying it."

She said, "Whole lot of maybes. How did you find out about this George?"

I showed her the old demonstration picture and explained.

She said, "You know, one day, about a week before he fell, Waldo left the office in the morning. Which he never did. He always scheduled meetings for the afternoon. Morning was his closed-door brief-writing and research time. I happened to run into him on his way out, asked where he was going. He shook his head, said, 'Nowhere. I'll be back,' like I'd caught him sneaking out. He was a very straight guy. That wasn't like him."

I asked, "He had a meeting?"

"That's what I thought. I'll check his book. He didn't trust computers for scheduling."

We walked down the hall. Waldo's office was as plain as hers, the same dumpy furniture, same tall ceiling.

She said, "This feels so empty."

She meant without Waldo, and it was. I looked around for some clue as to my friend's death, or his life, but there was nothing. No mementos. Ah, but there was a computer on the desk.

We stood. She leaned over his desk and flipped pages. "There's nothing here in the morning in his last month."

She stepped away from the desk, shaking her head. "Damn. I'd love to get something on Nichols. But even if you're right that he had something to do with Waldo and Buzzy dying, you have absolutely no proof. Nichols's star is rising fast. He's golden right now. Nobody in this state would dare bring these kinds of charges against him unless they had an airtight case. And that includes our outfit. Nichols would crush us like a bug."

I said. "He's not going to crush me. Nobody even knows we're here."

"You haven't gone to the police?"

"What police? Massachusetts or California? Tell them what I just told you, they'd think I was crazy."

"You've got a point. And California cops were no friends of Waldo's. He was involved in a couple of high-profile police brutality cases." She stared into space, tapping a finger on the desk. She looked at me. "I'd like to help you. Provided my fingerprints are nowhere within a thousand miles of anything."

I said, "You can start by letting me look at Waldo's computer."

I took a step toward the desk.

She stepped in front of me. "I can't let you do that. It's full of stuff that's subject to attorney-client privilege."

"Come on. Waldo is dead."

"His clients aren't. I'll go through it, see if I find anything having to do with Nichols."

"Can I just see his Internet browsing history?"

She scowled. "I don't like this. Alright. But no funny business."

She hovered over my shoulder as I sat in Waldo's chair at the computer and opened the browser. Ray sidled over and stood at my other shoulder.

A few seconds later, I said, "He's wiped his whole search history. There's nothing there."

Ray said, "Maybe he was snooping around after George and hiding his tracks."

I said, "Unfortunately, if I'm right about that Google trap, it was too late. George was already onto him." I explained the Google trap to Kaylee.

She said, "Maybe he was just being private. He was skeptical about the whole Internet thing. He wasn't a nut about it, but he feared it was a tool for the rich and powerful."

I said, "That's a real fear." But now I *really* wanted to get into the rest of this computer. It was not going to happen with Kaylee here. Push come to shove, I could probably hack in from the Internet anyway. I stood. "You'll let me know what you find."

"Yes."

"And check out that gay conversion bill."

She nodded. "But it'll be a couple of days…"

"Soon as you can."

We exchanged cell phone numbers and Ray and I drove back to Spider's. I said, "I'm thinking about Waldo's fear of heights. I can see him running down those stairs, provided he turned right around and came back up. Maybe that day he arranged to meet George down there. It's certainly a nice remote spot. George walks him out on the path. You can't see the cliff until you're right on it. And then it was too late."

"We could go there, and you could show me. I'll put in my two cents."

No. "Yeah, maybe later."

***

Back at Spider's, we sat on the Chinese couch. I popped the CD from Jeannie's in my laptop and opened Waldo's Arlington file. It was the same as with the gay conversion bill file—a single word processor doc with just a few notes:

CEO—EdenTree Elixirs. Wikipedia. LA Times. FDA invst. Talk radio. Illeg? Nichols.

I said, "It looks like he did a bunch of research online—at the office? Then made notes at home. At some point he wiped the history on his work computer. But was that after he got afraid of George? Or was it simply a habit, like Kaylee suggested?" I selected one of the other files at random. It was named "Lomo Linda." "This is the same thing: a short set of notes. I think this is how he worked. He searched stuff at the office, taking notes, then wiped the history and entered the stuff into a non-Internet connected computer at home. Not a bad way to work if you're paranoid about the internet."

When I tried to get online, I got the wheel of death. "It's hard enough to do this without having busted intertubes. Let's go downtown, see if we can do better."

"A cyber café?"

"I was thinking of the library. A rich town like this, I bet they've got a T-1 connection. Whatever I find, I have a feeling we're going to get into your area—politics. You want to come?"

"What else do I have to do?"

Ten minutes later, we parked parallel on a very steep hill next to an orange vintage VW Bug.

I said, "You'd never see a car like that back home. The winter salt rots them."

Ray pointed at the window. "Aw, look! A dream catcher. How cute."

"Old hippies."

"Speak for yourself."

The library was new and airy. Not stodgy like the ones in the Northeast. I asked the young woman at the front desk, "How's your Wi-Fi?"

She said, "Awesome."

We sat on a couple of straight-back chairs in a corner and huddled over my computer. I went to Wikipedia and typed in *EdenTree*. A full page came up.

Ray said, "This Wi-Fi is awesome, like lightning."

We read together.

I said, "So Rick wasn't lying when I saw him at the funeral. EdenTree Elixirs *is* the biggest in that business."

Ray asked, "Did he tell you about this shit?" He pointed to the screen, at accusations of labor abuses and intimidation of workers trying to unionize.

I sighed. "No. Old power-to-the-people Rick."

"Now that he's the person with power…it's an old story."

A librarian came over, leaned down, and whispered, "This *is* a library."

I said, "Sorry."

She said, "You have your own computer. The Wi-Fi works out on the terrace. You guys can talk all you want."

"Oh. Is it on all the time?"

"Twenty-four-seven."

That was good to know.

We went out and sat at a table on the terrace. Nobody else sat there. It overlooked a lawn with a small playground to one side. A couple of little kids and their moms or nannies were there.

Ray nodded toward them. "I don't think they're working for George.

I handed the computer with the Wikipedia page to Ray. "Translate for me."

He read for a while, then said, "The FDA has been investigating complaints of contaminated ingredients and dangerous side effects. But their hands are tied because these compounds slip into a crack between the strict regulations applied to drugs and food. I've heard about how those loopholes were written into law at the behest of the companies that peddle this crap."

He read, "'EdenTree has donated generously to the campaigns of certain libertarian politicians.' Apparently, this is all legal." He kept reading. "Ah. AM talk radio. There's a link to an article in the *LA Times*."

I asked, "You mean Rush Limbaugh?"

"And a hundred other guys pushing all their right-wing jive to old white people. But the politics is just the razzle-dazzle behind which they run their grift. Sketchy advertisers fleece the poor listeners, hawking all kinds of snake oil: quick IRS fixes, guaranteed gold investments, and every kind of patent remedy, promising to cure all the ills of old age, from incontinence to impotence."

"Including Rick's food supplements."

"Exactly. Hold on. I'm reading... Bingo. EdenTree Elixirs has been paying the radio jocks millions of dollars—not to advertise its products, but to insert plugs for them right into the 'content' of the show, in between dire warnings about black helicopters and FEMA death camps. And that part is illegal. Except it's hard to prosecute."

I groaned. "*Rick.* Anything about the governor in there?"

"No. But I can tell you that the go-to guys for deregulating business are not liberal Democrats. Something else you may not know—the Republican Party in California has in recent years spun off the moderate parts, becoming this hard, little ball of extremism."

"I'll take your word for it. But that suggests Rick might know George."

"You think..."

"Rick might be part of what's been going on? What's in it for him?"

We were silent for a moment. Those kids had been whooping it up the whole time we'd talked but I'd tuned it out.

Ray said, "Maybe he was afraid Waldo would come after him for this illegal stuff with AM radio. But what does that have to do with Buzzy?"

"Nothing. Though Rick was giving him a vibe at the funeral."

"Vibe?"

"Like he doesn't like gays."

"No surprise there, given who he hangs with."

"EdenTree is in Anaheim. What's there, aside from Disneyland?"

Ray looked at me. "The biggest bunch of right-wingers in the state."

We drove back to the houseboat. Rick and EdenTree were guilty as sin, as bad as Brickman. Screwing workers, scamming poor fools. Disseminating political propaganda. Maybe Rick could be my next project. I could sneak into his books, bleed him a little, mess with his business.

No. Whatever he'd become, Rick was still one of the Four Brothers, still an old friend. I'd just taken Rick's turn to the dark side *personally*. It was the same mistake I'd made with Brickman. To the rules of my do-gooder game— Never take a dime for myself; Never tell anyone—I reluctantly added a third: Never make it personal.

Rick didn't deserve it, so EdenTree was getting a pass.

Ray slouched on the couch, his face drawn. I asked, "What's wrong?"

"Just a coffee jones."

"I could use a hit myself." Up in the kitchen I filled a pan with water, put it on the stove, and got out a filter and cups. I waited for it to boil.

I looked at the stove, the sink and refrigerator, as if searching for something. What? As I made the coffee the feeling that there was something there got stronger.

Ray appeared in the doorway. I said, "Hold your horses. It's almost boiling…"

"Amazing that a little boat like this would have a fully stocked kitchen."

"It's not. It's just…"

"It's got the essentials—beer, coffee and vodka."

Kitchen. That's what I'd been looking for. The kitchen in the Four Brothers house. I said, "Fuck. That Weasel guy? He gave us the acid that night."

"I thought you got all your drugs from Rick?"

"We did. Except that one time. I was perfectly straight, getting a peanut butter sandwich—all there was to eat. There was a knock on the kitchen door, which was strange. No one used that door. It was that guy, Weasel. He said, 'I have some amazing new product. It'll put you on Mars.' I said, 'Hey, great—but I'm a little short.' 'Have these on me. First one's free. Taste of this, and you'll be back.'"

"His head and shoulders were covered in snow. I looked out the window and for the first time noticed how it was really coming down. The wind gave a howl. I thought, maybe it's not the best time to do acid. You see how that worked out. Weasel held his hand out, with four capsules in the palm. The strange thing was, he was wearing gloves."

"It was cold out."

"When a deal goes down, money and drugs exchange hands. Bare hands. You ever try to get cash from your wallet with gloves?"

"Right. You take them off first."

"And then when I reached for the acid, he just turned his hand over and dropped it in my mine."

"Huh. You sure you didn't pay for it?"

"Absolutely."

"I don't get it. He burns me and then he *gives* you four powerful hits of acid? That doesn't compute. I don't remember him wearing gloves...though there was something creepy about him."

The water was boiling. I poured it into the filter. "Weasel was standing next to George in that picture because he was his dealer. I'll bet it's where he got all the coke he gave Angela. And...Weasel was branching out into psychedelics and expanding his turf from those preppies to us real hippies."

"College hippies."

"Whatever. He was taking a loss leader with that acid."

Ray nodded. "Too bad his product sucked, from what you've told me."

"Yeah, that was the last anyone saw of that acid. Thank God."

"How come you didn't remember this before? You seem to have pretty vivid memories of that trip. 'In-A-Gadda-Da-Vida,' those cops..."

"Because I was still straight? Maybe it's like when you're in an accident. You remember every detail of the crash, but nothing about what you were doing before."

16.

We took coffees out on the deck. It was midafternoon. I said, "I'm going to poke around and see what old Brickman is up to. See if he learned his lesson."

I got the computer and looked on Brickman's favorite forums. He was back. And more. I said, "Brickman's got a new venture. You need to look and tell me what the hell it is."

He sat up and took the computer. "Oh, man. This is worse than bricking. He's put up a revenge porn website."

"What's that?"

"About the ugliest thing on the Internet. The website posts naked pictures of a woman that they ostensibly get from pissed-off ex-boyfriends—hence the revenge. But most of the stuff is just plain stolen from phones. In some cases they Photoshop a woman's face on some other body."

"Oh Jesus."

"Most of them just do it to hurt women. But at least one shakes the victims down—they pay a fee and supposedly the pictures come down."

"It *is* worse than bricking. It's almost like he's doing it to taunt me."

"What are you going to do?"

"Something. The gloves are coming off."

"You're not…"

"I could have gotten him killed. No, I've got another idea."

I researched online. The FBI was starting to get involved with taking the creeps down. But they had to waste a lot of time just finding out who was behind the sites.

That would be a lot easier with a name and address. The FBI's online tip line required my info. So I'd put together a package and mail it to them. Give them enough to link Brickman to the revenge porn site, and for good measure throw in evidence of his bricking.

It was too bad I couldn't make a personal connection with the Bureau. If I ever got enough on George, they'd be the guys to handle it, not any local police.

Ray said, "You're not going to tell me what you're doing to him?"

"Nope. Just let it go."

"You're no fun. Hey, you still think he put up your fake website?"

"I don't know. Why don't you look, see how the style of that revenge thing fits with it?"

"I don't have to look. They don't fit at all. Apples and pomegranates."

"George doesn't fit that website, either."

"He doesn't have to, not if he got this guy who designed the governor's computer system to do it."

I nodded. "He would certainly have the chops."

Ray looked at me. "When you saw him, George knew who you were and what you do. What are the chances of two unrelated parties outing your identity in the same week, after decades with your neighbors on the block not even knowing you're there?"

"Between zilch and nada. OK. So George had some geek make that fake website."

"You said that it was the email you sent Buzzy with the pictures of George that triggered what they did to him. If so, they had your email address. You think they got into your computer through it?"

"My password is tough—using random tries it would take a computer about a hundred and eight years to crack it. Unless it's the NSA. But..." It took a while to think it through. "My place was broken into *before* I sent Buzzy that email. And the fake website was up even before that. Which means that email isn't how George got onto me." I could feel the little sense we'd made of the thing evaporate.

"You found the website after Waldo was killed, after Buzzy first called you."

"Yeah, but I don't know when it was put up. Let me check." I went into the back end of the website. It only took a minute to find the date it went up online. "Brickman's off the hook for that website. It went up on August twenty-first, before I did anything to him. The day after Waldo fell."

"That can't be coincidence."

"No."

"Waldo's death was the trigger—not for Buzzy, but for going after you."

"It must have been. Why? I'd had nothing to do with Waldo or anyone from Middleburg College in decades. But whoever set that website up has got to be in communication with George. If I could just get into his email. It's too risky through that system of theirs." It was midafternoon. I went to Google Maps, then the Best Buy website. We had just enough time.

I said, "How about we take a ride up to Sacramento?"

"Fine. Are we going to stake out George?"

"Sort of. I need something first."

We drove to the Best Buy in San Rafael. Ray waited in the car while I went in the store. I returned with a square box. "Now you drive. I'm going to put this thing together."

I sat in the backseat, where there was room. It didn't take long. I climbed over into the front seat. We passed tawny hills like lions' haunches. Enormous oil refineries. I got the satellite view up on Google Maps and identified the big mountain brooding over the whole scene. I pointed and said, "You'll be happy that big thing is Mount Diablo."

Ray grinned. "It looks more like Mars than Hell out there." He pointed at the contraption I'd just assembled. "Which that thing fits right in with."

It did look like a miniature space ship. "It's a satellite dish. We can follow George after work, see where he goes, but here's the main thing. I'm going to use it to get into his email."

"You want to drive now?"

"No, if you don't mind. I need to figure out what I'm doing." I got busy on my phone.

After fifteen minutes, Ray said, "Getting anywhere?"

"I'd be done if it wasn't written in geekese."

"Hey, you ought to be fluent."

I snorted.

The hills squashed down into farmland. The AC in the rental worked fine, but I could feel the heat radiating from the windows. An hour and a half later we approached the city.

Ray asked, "You ready with that thing?"

"I think so. But we don't need it quite yet. First, we've got to get to him. I'm hoping he eventually ends up at home, because that's where I'll get into his home network."

"This could require a little patience."

"A lot, I'm afraid. Which isn't your main suit."

"And it's yours?" Touché. I did my best to hide it, but he'd nailed me.

I directed him to the Capitol building. It had a nice spiffy white dome. I said, "George might recognize me from that meeting, even though I'm out of disguise. Did he see you in the lobby?"

"I don't think so."

"Go inside and ask somebody where the governor's staff parks."

"Won't they think I'm a terrorist, staking the place out?"

"You don't look *that* much like one… Tell them you're doing some kind of traffic study. I'm going to drive around a bit. I'll see you back here in twenty."

I looked for public garages in the neighborhood in case that's where the governor's staff parked. I found one a half block from the Capitol grounds.

Ray was back in fifteen minutes. He got in. I said, "How is Sacramento?"

"Sleepy. Because it's hot as fuck."

"At least the heat's dry."

"Yeah, so's a crematorium. I asked if there was parking under the building, had a vision of all kinds of security. The nice lady said there was, but it's only for the legislators. Governor's staff catches as catch can. She wasn't the least bit suspicious, by the way. Though I did have to go through one hell of a metal detector."

"We may be in luck. Because there's only one garage close, and street parking is only two hours."

We found a spot across the street from the garage entrance. It was quarter of five. People streamed in the garage and cars out.

Ray said, "What if we get hungry?"

"You have until five to get us something. I don't imagine the governor's top people leave before then. But if I see him…"

"Don't leave me stranded here!"

"No, we'll just have to come back tomorrow."

Ray got in the car with sandwiches at two minutes before five. We waited a half hour. The only excitement was a couple of muscle cars roaring past.

At six, Ray started eating and I joined him. We were half done when George came strolling down the street. He was wearing a suit like when I met him. He was walking fast like everyone else, eager to get home. If that was where he was headed. He disappeared into the garage.

His car appeared a few minutes later and turned on the street in the opposite direction we were pointed. I waited a beat then made a quick U-turn and got behind George before he turned.

Ray said, "Fortunately, people make a lot more U-turns here than back east. What do you know about tailing somebody?"

"Nothing besides what I've seen on TV."

We stayed a couple of cars behind George. He got on a highway headed east. The traffic was heavy, so I didn't think he'd spot us.

A half hour later we followed him onto an exit that lead to Granite Bay. I pointed to the sign and said, "Look that town up on the Internet."

A minute later, he said, "It's one of the wealthiest suburbs of Sacramento."

"The kind of place he'd live." We followed him onto a quiet street. Now I hung back, but not too far. I needed to see where he stopped. We came around a curve and I almost missed him pulling into a driveway. We passed the house, a sprawling McMansion with Spanish overtones. I said, "Stuff can't be as pricy up here as in San Fran, but that's got to be worth well over a mil."

I pulled over a block away, in front of a sign: *Neighborhood Watch. We Immediately Report All Suspicious Persons To Law Enforcement.*

Ray said, "That means we're fucked."

"Yeah. Except do you see anybody out?"

"No. And this time of day, you'd at least expect somebody to be home from work, walking their dog. Unless it's too hot."

It was still in the low nineties. "It doesn't matter if you've got a dog."

"How close do you need to get with that thing?"

I said, "A hundred feet. Which, with houses this big, means almost in front."

"We better hope that's his house and not that of a lover."

"Indeed."

I turned around in one of the drives and headed back toward George's. I parked next to a tree that partially hid us from his windows. No such luck with the neighbors. If they saw us and did their neighborhood watch duty we'd be cooked.

I got in the backseat with the dish. "If the cops come it's going to be hell explaining this thing."

Ray handed me his leather jacket, and I draped it over the dish.

"You'd better be fast."

I did my best. I opened the laptop and started tracking. Ten minutes later, I was getting a signal, when Ray said, "Shit." He started the car and pulled away. A woman was coming toward us from a couple of houses down, with her dog, a little pure breed-looking thing.

I said, "I knew our luck would run out."

Ray started the car and drove. We passed the woman and he waved. She waved back. He headed slowly to the end of the street, turned around, and stopped and waited. He said, "She's gone."

"Until she turns around."

"Maybe she's walking a loop?"

"Can't count on it...go for it."

He drove back toward George's and parked again.

I worked frantically. The problem was that the dish was too powerful. I had three Wi-Fi addresses. Which was George's?

Ray said, "She's coming back. A couple of streets away."

"One more minute..."

"She saw us. She's got her phone out, calling the cops."

"Or a friend…Done!" Ray took off and raced down the street.

"Slow the fuck down. Drive normally."

"Actually, no." He took a quick left, sped to another intersection, and turned again. "Somebody's following us."

"Huh?"

"They got off the highway right after us. And I just saw them again when I pulled out. A brown car."

"Like the one at Jeannie's."

"Yep."

He got on the highway and I scoured the rearview. "I think you lost him."

"How'd he know we were coming here? You didn't tell anyone but me. And you didn't tell me until we'd already left."

"I don't know. Maybe it's another brown car. Did you see who was driving?"

"Just that they were wearing a hat and shades. It happened too fast to get more."

"I'm going to take a look at George's emails." A few minutes later I groaned. "There are ten thousand just in the last few months. I'm going to deal with this later."

"This spy shit is exhausting. As far as that brown car goes, if it was following us, at least we know it wasn't George, because we were following him."

"Duh."

"You think it's that coding genius who's working for him?"

"It's a really different skill set."

"So he's got two people working for him."

"At least."

***

As we entered Sausalito, Ray said, "What with all the excitement we never finished our sandwiches."

Ray and I got sushi takeout, raided Spider's dwindling supply of Anchor Steam, and ate out on the deck.

I said, "Even though today might have been a waste of time, a part of me still enjoyed it."

"Really."

"I love puzzles. The harder, the better."

"It's why you're such a good coder."

"And this one's a doozy."

"It would be a lot more fun if people didn't keep getting killed."

"Of course. But sometimes I get into the challenge and forget."

"That was a full day's work. We going to walk to Reno tomorrow?"

"Today isn't done yet." It was dark and cooling fast, so we went inside. I went back to George's emails and waded through, starting at the beginning of the summer.

Ray was fading. He got another beer and lay on his couch. He said, "I'm about to check out. Got anything?"

"Nothing, but I'm only about two weeks in. So far all I've got is that 'campaign analysis coordinator' is a very boring job."

"I could have told you that. Except for the nonboring parts, of course, like killing Waldo."

If he did.

***

Ray snored. I was about to hit my couch when Kaylee called. I took the phone up to the kitchen so as to not wake Ray.

She said, "I was here until midnight last night scouring Waldo's computer. As I expected, there's a fat file on that immigration bill. But nothing I didn't already know about. Not a goddamn thing else having to do with the governor."

"The gay conversion bill?"

"Nothing."

I was just about asleep when she called back. I tiptoed up to the kitchen again. "Hey, I don't know why I didn't think of this. You asked if I knew anyone who works for fuckhead Nichols? This woman I used to go out with does some contract work in the Capitol building in Sacramento. Annie. She's a techie."

"Think she'll talk to me?"

She paused before answering. "I'll ask. Though I hope it doesn't start up some shit."

***

The next morning, my phone woke me from a dream. *Buzzy's calling! And he's going to explain this dream to me.* I was shivering, the blanket piled on the floor. Fog blew in the open window, so thick that all I saw outside was a hundred feet of dark waves. No boats, no harbor.

I whispered, "Yeah."

"Good morning, sleepyhead!" Sharon sounded full of coffee.

"Hold on a minute…" I got up, slunk toward the door, but needn't have worried about waking Ray. He was dead to the world, doing a good imitation of one of his reliquary parody art installations: "Body of St. Raymond Recumbent on a Chinese Couch."

Outside the houseboat I said, "OK." It was before seven. I turned my back to the fog blowing in.

"This morning I was walking on campus past that frat house where George lived. I remembered another guy who lived there. Angela set me up on a blind date with him. I spent the night with him. One night."

"Do you remember his name?"

"Cyrus—Cy for short. I couldn't think of it to save my life, except then I remembered that he was one of us who actually graduated. I looked in the yearbook, and there was his picture. The pompous asshole. He was not nice. He wanted me to…" Her voice trailed off.

"Sorry. His last name?"

"Wentworth."

"Thanks. I'll look him up. How's that paper of yours going?"

"I'm at the procrastinate-and-hope stage."

"What, you hope it will finish itself?"

"I wish. For better or worse there's a next stage. Terror, leading to panicked completion. I'm just not scared enough yet."

"Good luck." I huddled in the damp cold, wishing I'd put on a coat.

"Any more fun dreams?"

I laughed. "Mind reader. I had another one. In fact, you just woke me from it."

"Right. I keep forgetting about the time difference. Pony up."

"So, I'm going to visit you in your dorm room."

"Which you never did. If you had, maybe things would have gone differently…"

"Hold on. In the dream it's in the basement, down this arched stone corridor. There are no doors, just dark openings in the wall."

"That sounds like a crypt."

"It was, now that you mention it. Your room's at the end of the hall. It's like a monk's cell, with a single bed in the center. You're not there."

"And a good thing. I don't want to be in your creepy dream. I remember sleeping with guys in a single bed. Very uncomfortable. I prefer my bed."

"Me, too. Your…roommate's in your bed."

"Angela. Why am I not surprised?"

"She's lying in a filmy nightdress, on her side. She looks like a marble statue. It's freezing in there. I step toward her.

"I've wanted to…kiss her for so long. Now that she's there, I'm afraid. But I have to. I lean down and the moment my lips touch hers they go numb. Ice races into my cheeks and through my body…and then you called."

"Not a moment too soon. You'd be dead otherwise. As Angela is, need I remind you? I don't know, Bodine. I've got some ideas, but this is a job for a shrink. Have you ever seen one?"

"No!" I softened my voice. A gray cat slunk down the boardwalk, scowled at me or the fog, then leaped onto one of the boats and vanished. "Don't get me wrong. I don't have anything against them. It's just that I've always been a DIY guy. I taught myself music and every bit of coding I know. Besides, I don't exactly have time to go to a therapist right now."

Shrinks. I spaced out. I'd seen at least as many dogs as people on the boardwalk in my time here. But there was also a shitload of bicycles, chained to the sides and tops of some boats. More dogs or bikes?

"Understood. Here's my take. First of all, I'm not worried that you're a closet necrophiliac."

"That's a relief."

She laughed. "Angela's body was frozen, of course, when they found her. But dreams often speak in metaphors. You haven't told me, but something traumatic happened with Angela."

"Yeah, she died. George killed her."

"Before that. Have you ever been married?"

"What does that have to do with anything? I've had a lot of girlfriends. Have you been married?"

"Once, long ago. It ended badly."

"How?"

"Let's just say I was very young."

"And recently?"

"A few years ago, my shrink and I agreed that I should swear off relationships for a while."

"That mean sex, too?"

"Yes."

Oh. The swearing-off period was over. I paced the boardwalk to try and get warm.

She said, "That was slick, the way you changed the subject to me. But your dream. Now don't be upset. I think when it comes to relationships, you're…frozen. Stuck back with Angela."

For a moment I was at the edge of that abyss again, the terrible cold feeling coursing into me like an icy wind. I pushed it away. My fists clenched. Frozen? What the hell was she talking about?

She said, "These dreams. They mean you want to change. And that's good news."

It didn't feel like it. "You sound like Buzzy. 'Realizing you want to change is the hard part.' It's one of the last things he said to me."

Just like that, she lost it, sobbing.

I said, "I'm sorry." I felt tugging in my chest, but even now I was stone cold as in the dream. "I've told you all this stuff about myself. You never talk about yourself."

"I told you I was married. I've been spilling my guts to shrinks for years now, and frankly I'm sick of talking about myself."

"Tell me a dream?"

"Not now."

Which made me even more curious, but I let it go. "It's not true that I don't feel things. A minute ago, when you asked if I'd been married, it annoyed me."

"Not that I would have noticed. But I'm sure you get angry. It's the deep feelings that you have trouble with. Loss. And…love?"

"I love my dog."

"Your dog. My point exactly."

I was certainly feeling something right now. "I've got to go." I couldn't keep the edge from my voice. I punched the call off and stalked out into the parking lot. Sharon was opening me up, getting all inside my shit. No. It was worse. I was *asking* for it. Offering up my dreams for interpretation. She might be in that booth behind the screen, but I was the one showing up for confession. What was so frustrating was that this business, this *feeling* business, was as much a riddle as George and the murders. In both cases, the more clues I found the less I seemed to know.

17.

I shook off my thoughts, and the phone call, like a wet dog. A cold, wet dog. I was shivering. It was still early and I didn't want to wake Ray, so I headed downtown to the library.

I was planning to look further into Rick, but as I drove there something bothered me. Something to do with Sharon. Not our uncomfortable conversation. The one before. An autopsy? That had set off an alarm, and I could still feel it. The Middleburg Police Department must have computers by now. It didn't mean they knew how to use them any more than they knew how to do anything else. Getting in should be easy as slipping a knife into warm butter.

I reached the library and parked. It was still too cold to use the Wi-Fi outside. I looked up the hours online; it was opening in ten minutes. It was a long wait in which I stared at the door. A woman ambled up with keys three minutes late.

I went inside and was into the Middleburg Police system in five minutes. The report on Buzzy was a predictable tangle of police jargon. But I got the gist right away.

For the first time in a very long time I felt on the verge of losing my cool. Even with George in the roof garden, I'd maintained my calm exterior. Now my face felt on fire. Fists were curled into painful knots. I looked around at the people in the library—a mild-mannered bunch, I'm sure—and they barely seemed human. I printed out the report. I didn't want to count on flaky Wi-Fi at Spider's, so I saved the police report onto my laptop just in case and rushed back to the houseboat.

Ray sat listless on the edge of the couch, apparently having just woken.

He must have caught my vibe. He sat up straight. "What?"

"Buzzy was dead before he went off that cliff. I hacked into the police report. His body was messed up, like it would be if he fell. But there was also a gash on the back of his head, long and narrow, like it was made by something like a tire iron. I saw the edge of it when I saw his body. But neither the fall nor the wound was the cause of death."

"What was?"

I read from the report, "'Exsanguination from a puncture to the carotid artery, deliberately made with a sharp object.' Somebody stabbed him in the neck and he bled to death. Except they didn't find a trace of blood at the top of the cliff."

"He was killed somewhere else?"

"No. There were no signs of the body being dragged. They must have used a tarp or something. Here's the spookiest part. Someone *painted his body with blood*. After he was dead."

"What?"

"I wasn't totally surprised, because when I first saw his body at the foot of the cliff it was all red. They'd cleaned him up at the morgue, but I saw traces of it behind his ear..." I winced, remembering.

"One last thing. Someone pinned a note to his chest."

I read it to Ray from my laptop, "'Homoz must surely die. It is written. Vengeance is mine.' *Homos* is spelled with a *z*."

Ray asked, "How did whoever killed him know Buzzy was gay?"

"He was out of the closet, so it would have been easy. And there are the emails between Buzzy and Waldo on that anti-conversion legislation."

Ray looked at the report. "This note reminds me of something. 'Vengeance is mine.' The Bible?"

"I haven't read it, myself."

"That makes two of us. Maybe Spider has one?"

"If he's got a Bible it's the *Tibetan Book of the Dead*. It'd be easier to just Google it, even with this sucky Wi-Fi." I typed, then read. "'Romans 12:19. Vengeance is mine, sayeth the Lord. I will repay.'"

Ray asked, "What does it mean?"

I found a commentary. "It looks like the gist of it is that revenge is *God's* business, not man's."

"Huh. That's not how whoever did this interpreted it. Try, 'It is written.'"

"We've got a long-running gospel show... Hold on. The quote is from Matthew—'It is written, man shall not live by bread alone.' Damn, even I know that one. It must be one of the most popular quotes in the Bible. Maybe this has nothing to do with the Bible."

Ray said, "Wait a minute. *Homos* with a *z*."

"The damned Internet—nobody can spell for shit anymore."

I typed homoz into Google. It came back with *homozygous*.

I said, "That's a genetics term, related to alleles and diploid organisms..."

"No, it reminds me of this blog." Ray took the computer, typed, and showed me. The header read, *Brane Fartz*.

"That's cute. But just because..."

"No, there's more." He swiped a finger repeatedly on the trackpad. "The goddamn page won't scroll. The Wi-Fi's down again."

I said, "Back to the library."

When we got there, we headed for the terrace. The fog was lifting. A basketball thumped on a court behind the trees.

Ray scrolled down posts on the blog. "I swear... Wait. The comments. Here we go." He showed me:

Homoze and liebruls, hippeze and feminasties...

"Your commenter is just aping the blog name. And he's using *ze*, not *z*. Maybe they have nothing to do with each other."

Ray typed *Homoze* into Google.

The first hit was a doctor—it seemed to be an Arabic name. Second was the same comment Ray had just read. The third was a comment from another blog:

Homoze suckin hozes. KILL THEM ALL!

Ray asked, "Kill them all? That note says 'Must surely die.' That's close."

I shook my head. "Sadly, lots of people feel that way. Who made that comment?"

Ray pointed to the screen. "Levity-z."

"Sounds like some kind of stand-up-comedian-slash-rapper. Who's the user on your 'Homoze and Hippeze' comment?"

Ray checked. "The same guy. Levity-z. This comment is not from the live blog, but from somebody's cache. The bloggers of Brane Fartz police it pretty well, deleting the most offensive comments."

"Why did somebody save it?"

"Evidence, I suppose. Just in case somebody goes live with these threats."

We had company. A guy in his thirties sat at the next table and started pecking at a laptop. He looked more like an entrepreneur than a writer.

Ray scowled and said, "Now we're going to have to whisper just like inside."

I Googled around and found lists of Levity-z comments from various blogs and showed them to Ray. After a few minutes he groaned. "Okay, you can stop now."

"Do you see anything?"

"Aside from the fact that he's a rageaholic troll? Well there aren't any more gratuitous z's." He looked out at the lawn for a minute. "Oh, yeah. There's a rant about Jane Fonda."

"Old Hanoi Jane? What, they haven't given that up yet?"

"Apparently not. But maybe there's something there. I usually assume these trolls are about fifteen years old. Jane Fonda's Vietnam stuff is really old news. As is Vietnam. I don't think our guy would know about her, or more important, care unless he's our age."

I said, "Speaking of the previous century, there's this ancient bluegrass song."

"Hum me a few bars."

"I don't remember the melody. All that shit sounds the same to me. It's called 'Washed in the Blood.'"

"Everybody knows that." He sang, "Are you washed in the blood of the lamb?"

I winced. The guy next to us gave Ray a look. He got up and left. "Don't worry, it's not your singing. He probably hates bluegrass, too. So somebody covered Buzzy in blood, with a rag or something. Washed him, so to speak."

"With lamb's blood?"

"I doubt it. I'll bet it was his own. But what does that mean, 'Washed in the blood of the lamb'?" I Googled it, then shook my head. "Now I'm really confused. In the Bible it refers to being forgiven for one's sins, being washed in the blood of Christ."

"This guy killed Buzzy for being gay, but then forgave him by covering him in blood? That make sense to you?"

"Nope. What this feels like is some kind of ritual."

"None of this sounds like George. There are only twenty-six letters in the alphabet…"

"It's not the letter, but the misuse of it."

"Now he's got an army working for him? Because we've got a coding genius, our brown car operative who staked out Jeannie's and broke into her place and followed us."

"And an online loony tune of the religious persuasion. Talk about a motley crew."

I shook my head. "I think the z thing is just coincidence, but I'll indulge you and see what I can find out about Mr. Levity-z."

I poked around for ten minutes, at which point Ray said, "You still working at that?"

"This guy's hiding, but most of these trolls do these days." Given a few hours I could probably find him….

I remembered the guy Sharon told me about, Cyrus Wentworth. I walked out onto the lawn and tried calling the alumni office. Their outgoing message said they were out to lunch. I returned to Ray.

He said, "Now this is really dark, but if Rick was homophobic, and Buzzy had that note on him…"

I Googled Rick again. I searched past page one. I found something in the middle of page three. I pointed to the screen. "Rick's name is in this article about an organization called True Love Restored—TLR. Their purpose is—

get this—gay conversion therapy. They're a nonprofit. But last year they spun off a for-profit company, a chain of boot camps which will feature the therapy. The cat who wrote the article did his research." I read a little more, then looked at Ray. "Rick is…one of the investors."

"Uh-oh."

"I wonder why the company's building the majority of these camps outside of the United States."

"I've read about this. Some boot camps have gotten in trouble here when kids complain about abuse. So, do the camps try to fix things? No. They move out of the country, away from our laws. And then they do some really evil shit. Beatings. Starvation. Torture. Parents go crazy trying to bring them to justice."

"You think that's what this company's going to do?"

"It sure sounds like it. This changes the whole picture, doesn't it?"

I said, "It does. We might have a motive for Buzzy's murder. Waldo's, too. Not politics, but money. If the legislature shuts down this company, Rick's out his investment. Buzzy was talking to Waldo about helping with that bill."

"Where does George figure in this?"

"I don't know. He knew about the Four Brothers. Knew who *I* was. Maybe because he and Rick are in it together."

"Hillary Clinton's 'vast right-wing conspiracy.'"

"What's that?"

Ray laughed. "Never mind."

"But what about Angela?"

"Maybe that's unrelated. Everything doesn't have to fit all neat and clean. Did Rick strike you as a killer?"

"I don't know. He's an asshole. The only killer I've known is George."

"Who's also an asshole."

"Right. That doesn't mean Rick's a killer. There's one way to find out."

"Yeah?"

"I'm going to LA to see Rick."

"You gonna just show up? Aren't you afraid? And if he is involved in this, why the hell would he admit it?"

"That's why I'm going to just show up. I don't want to give him any warning. I'll make some hints, and the way he reacts, I'll know. I'll go to his office during working hours. He's not going to pull anything there."

"You want me to come?"

"It'll go better with Rick if it's just me." The truth was, much as I love Ray, the close quarters were wearing thin.

Ray didn't argue, just said, "Okey dokey. You flying?" Maybe he was getting tired of me.

"I don't know. It might save a few hours, but it's such a hassle. This is California, land of the automobile. I'll drive. You need a car, you can rent something."

I got in the car and circled the bay over to Oakland, then boomed down the Central Valley. If I didn't stop for lunch and didn't hit bad traffic—a huge if—I might get there before the office closed. It would be good to hit Rick at the end of the day when he was tired.

I passed modern windmills atop golden hills, their blades serenely rotating like giant robots doing tai chi. Next came orchards and green crops on either side far as I could see. I'd been hitting it hard ever since the phone call from Buzzy and welcomed this quiet time. With each mile from San Francisco, I felt lighter, as the murders and George receded from my mind. But soon my inner drama took their place. The dreams and Sharon. Those holes in me and the change they seemed to portend.

Buzzy.

I'd been avoiding thoughts of him, like he represented a real chasm I might trip into. But his loss was also plain practical. Sharon was stirring up all this...stuff. And it was Buzzy's kind of stuff. I was really ready to talk to him now.

I surfed the radio, then gave up. I tried Frank's music on the iPod, but it wasn't happening. I rode in silence.

I approached Bakersfield and the land turned brown and a foul smell seeped into the car. I stopped for gas. It was hot as fuck out there, and worse than Spider's stinky couch—the air saturated with some poison cocktail of fertilizer, ozone, and crude oil.

I was back on the highway when Sharon called. "Bodine."

"Didn't we just talk this morning?" They were angry words, but in truth the sound of her voice had already dissolved my pissiness of earlier.

"I know. It's becoming a habit. If you're busy…"

"I'm driving through the desert, counting cacti. What stage are you at with that paper?"

"It's hard to believe, but the faint light at the end of the tunnel stage. Though right now my brain's fried."

"I've got all day. Literally. I'm on my way to LA."

"You know, last time we spoke you told me how you never went to demonstrations?"

"I didn't."

"Then why do I remember you at that one, you know, where that picture was taken?"

"Oh. I was playing in the band."

"I don't remember."

"Come on, we were loud as hell. How could you forget?"

She said, "I'm sorry."

"It's just as well. We were god-awful. That was just the beginning, though. Later my band made a record then toured opening for Karl Maxwell. Before crowds of twenty thousand…"

"Oh. What do you play?" She didn't seem impressed by my rock star bragging.

"Keyboards. And I sing."

"I'm trying to picture you as a musician. I guess with the computers I see you as more of the scientist type."

"It's a long story."

"As you said, you've got all day."

"OK. We had this huge grand piano in our house, which my father forbade me to play, because it wasn't manly."

"Of course, you had to play it."

"I did. And I saw it as this great machine, like I did with computers later. I see a machine, I've got to master it. Except it wasn't so easy."

"And you taught yourself."

"If my dad caught wind of lessons, he'd break my fingers. How else was I going to learn?"

"It always amazes me, people who can do that. It took me a PhD to learn anything, and I still don't get teaching."

The cell phone network dropped us. The hills I passed were burned to a crisp and infested with mantis-like oil rigs.

She called back. I said, "Sorry. Shitty connection here in the desert. People liked my playing, but I wasn't really sure I had something until…Angela."

"Her again."

"Yeah. Hey, you wanted to hear my story."

"I do."

"At camp they had this old upright upstairs in the barn. I was wailing away on it one afternoon when she appeared, like out of nowhere."

"That sounds like her. She had a knack for drama."

"I told her I knew a song with her name on it and sang her that old B.B. King song 'Sweet Little Angel.' It was my come-on to her."

"And it worked."

"It was all I had at that point."

"Now I'm green. Angela got a lovely song, and all I got was cheap wine and that ratty couch. I wish I could hear you play."

"I'd be happy to, but this rental doesn't come with a piano."

"You can sing."

"What you want to hear?"

"You do…soul music? I know you're white, but…"

It was my lucky day. Blue-eyed soul was my bag. "You know that houseboat we're staying on, it was on one of those that Otis Reading wrote 'Dock of the Bay.'"

"Oh, God. I love that one."

I gave it a good shot. Without noticing I slowed down. A truck zoomed past and honked.

When I was done, she was silent. When she finally spoke, she was choked up. "When you told me about that museum of yours, I heard something in your voice. Now I get it. You put your feeling in your *music*."

"If you say so." I'd just been singing, the same as always. "Hey, when I get home, I'll come up, find a piano over at the college, and do it right."

"OK. But now I really have to get back to work."

As we spoke, I was looking for the moment to mention the police report on Buzzy. It didn't come.

18.

I went up and down some mountains then ran smack into rush hour, Los Angeles, California. But I made it to Rick's company by ten to five. I parked in the visitor lot of a tall building with a giant EdenTree logo out front. It was first tree I'd seen in Anaheim.

I rode the elevator up to the executive suites. The girl behind the desk, with her sparkling teeth and gleaming straight platinum hair, seemed wasted here. She belonged on TV.

"I'm here to see Mr. Arlington."

"Do you have an appointment?"

"No. I'm an old friend."

"Oh. Who should I tell him…"

"Bob Hutchinson."

She buzzed him.

Rick stepped out of his office, looking surprised.

"Bob. I didn't think you'd take me up on my offer."

"What offer?"

"The free body scan and consultation." His mouth turned down. "But I wish you'd called for an appointment. Our people are busy."

"No, that's not why I'm here. I was just in the area."

"Oh. I have a few minutes. For you."

He spared me the preacher handshake this time, instead draping an arm around my neck and ushering me into a large office. I was relieved when he let go of me and strode past a massive slate desk to the window, sweeping his arm triumphantly across the view of endless LA sprawl.

I said, "Nice," trying to sound like I wasn't biting my tongue.

He turned and gestured for me to sit on a comfortable looking chair in front of the desk. It was lower than his. As I walked to the chair, I stopped for a second to look at the only item on its gleaming surface: a family photo of a brood of Ricklettes, all blond, all smiling. There were three girls, with Rick's genes, and in one case braces, having variously compromised their mother's boringly impeccable good looks. Separating the girls were two boys, one a dead ringer for Rick back then, except for the retro crew cut. The other's hair was a few millimeters longer. Rebellion? Maybe there was hope for him.

Lose twenty-five years and the wife could be a clone of Rick's receptionist. Intuition told me that Rick had something going on with her. I said, "Nice receptionist."

"Yes." He didn't rise to the bait.

I sat and Rick sat across from me, his hands flat on the stone desk surface like he could fuse himself with its solidity. But the desk just made him look small and a little silly.

I said, "We didn't have much time at the funeral. I thought we might catch up."

He glanced away, trying to smile, but the corner of his mouth was quivering. "Catch up. Sure." Was he guilty? Remembering chowing down with the dog, zonked out of his head? Or those teenyboppers he sold dope to, some of whom he ended up with on the Free Love Couch?

"I hear you've really been getting around. You know the governor."

"It happens that I am honored to call him a friend. A fine man. And we're hoping he will make...where'd you find that out?"

"Your Wikipedia article."

Rick frowned. "So you've seen the bad stuff. It's all lies and distortion. My lawyers are looking into a libel suit."

"I don't believe everything I read on Wikipedia. But I'm wondering if you know a guy in Nichols's office. George Bowman."

"I've never heard of him." He stared at me, shaking his head rapidly. "Where are you going with this? What are you doing here?"

"Bear with me. George Bowman went to college with us."

"College? What the heck does that have to do with the governor?"

What the heck sounded odd, weak sauce coming from a mouth that had slipped a fuck or two into every sentence.

I took the photos from my pocket. They were getting tatty from use. I stood and pushed

the old demonstration one across the desk to him, leaning over and pointing to him in the picture.

He saw himself gesturing and shouting, and he winced. He frowned at my ponytail but kept his mouth shut.

I set the recent picture next to the old one and said, "George Bowman is the circled guy," watching his face as he looked. I saw definite recognition. I sat down.

"I may have seen him around. So?"

"I think he had something to do with Waldo's death."

"What? Waldo was running and slipped..."

"I'm afraid he didn't. Someone pushed him."

"No. How do you..."

"What do you know about Waldo's hassles with the governor?"

"You can't think Governor Nichols had something to do with Waldo's death? He's a good Christian. Just because he doesn't want the illegals and environmental extremists taking over..." As he got excited his voice raised in volume and pitch, the way it had when he gave me his sales pitch at the funeral. The way I imagined it had at the antiwar demonstrations. He must be missing the irony.

Christian. So that was where that heck came from. He was one too, or playing one. No swearing, no hippie dancing, no teenyboppers on the Free Love Couch... "Those things are exactly what Waldo opposed Nichols on."

He pointed to my ponytail. "You never gave it up, did you?"

"Gave up what?"

"Playing the rebel. Raising your middle finger to the *values* that made this country great. You and your famous *revolution.*" He spit out the word like it had a foul taste. "*Reveling* in...OK, I'll say it. Sin! The country's never recovered. It's been sliding down the drain ever since that time. But *we* aren't standing for it. We're taking it back."

His rant wasn't getting to me. Partly because he had me all wrong. I would wager my values were a lot more in line with his dear Jesus than his were. And his rap sounded canned. It reminded me of those blogs of Ray's. I poked him back. "This is too rich. You were a drug dealer."

He waved his hand. "That was a long time ago. I have received forgiveness. And it's not too late…"

"I'm not in the market. Sorry." It was time to stop fucking around. "What do you know about this bill to ban gay conversion therapy?"

Rick scowled. "It is never going to pass."

"Why, because Nichols and his buddies won't let it?"

"Because it's wrong."

"You saw Buzzy at the funeral. Did you know he was gay?"

Rick's eyes flicked around the room. "I, uh, I didn't want to assume anything, but…"

He was lying. "Buzzy's dead."

He sucked in a breath. "What?" He grabbed his head, the remains of that hair, and bit his lip. Whoever Rick had become, it wasn't someone who could fake that.

"He disappeared the week after the funeral. Then a week after that, his body showed up." I stood and looked down on him. "At the foot of Garnet Hill."

"What?" He shrunk from me. "He jumped?"

I didn't say anything.

"Oh my. Give me a minute."

I didn't.

I put my hands on that monster desk and leaned forward. The stone was cold. "Did you know Waldo and Buzzy were communicating about that gay conversion bill, right before they both died?"

"The governor…"

"I don't give a rat's ass about the governor right now. It's *you*. You're the one with a dog in this fight."

"What dog?"

"Your investment in True Love Restored."

"How do you know about that?"

"Come on, it's in the newspaper. You actually believe that crap, that gays 'choose a lifestyle'? Given what a burden it is for them?"

"What I believe is none of your business."

"Ah, but it is, if you're involved in *this* business."

"I just believe what's in the Bible. But..." Rick started drumming his fingers on the slate. "You can't think I killed him. Did you ever hear the expression 'love the sinner, hate the sin'?"

On the last word, his eyes flicked to the front office. To his receptionist. Bingo. He *was* banging his secretary. What kind of Christian was he? Did he just sin and expect instant forgiveness?

I started walking around the office. I picked up another family photo from the shelf.

He said, "Hey."

I said, "Love the sinner, hate the sin. You know, Rick, I can perhaps get behind you demonizing my lifestyle—which you happen to know nothing about—when you were the biggest dealer on campus and used to fuck anything that moved. But tell me. How old is Amanda, or Heather, or whatever her name is out there? Young enough to be your daughter, for sure."

Rick reached for a button to buzz her then thought twice of it. He rose, his face coloring. "We are done here. You can either leave, or I'm..."

"No. We're not." I returned to the desk and leaned toward him. "Listen to me. Buzzy didn't jump. He didn't even die from the fall. Someone killed him on top. They smeared blood all over his naked body. Pinned a homophobic note to him then threw his body over the edge. The question is, was that someone one of your investor buddies? Did you guys kill both Waldo and Buzzy to protect your interest in those camps and try to disguise it as a hate crime? Or was it you? Maybe you hate the sinner as much as the sin. Provided it's somebody else's, of course."

Rick winced as I spoke. "You have to believe me. I had nothing to do with any of this. I don't know anything about it." His voice was rising in pitch again.

Now it sounded like a whine. "And I never invested enough money to…"

"How much?"

He glared at me. "I'm not telling you that!"

I needed to dial it down if I was going to get any further. I sat. "OK. Assume I believe you. Listen, we've taken different paths. But those two guys were our friends. And whatever your political or religious beliefs, they were good guys. I'm trying to find out what's going on. And frankly, I'm worried."

"Worried?"

I didn't reply.

It took him a moment. "They're coming after you next."

"Or you."

He blanched.

I said, "Strange as it may seem, you and I are in this together."

"But what do we have in common?"

I had to hand it to him, he won question of the day. "You need to understand one thing. I'm not letting this go until I find out who's been killing my friends. And if I find out you're involved…"

"I swear, all I did was donate a little money. That's no crime. This is just terrible. What—you want to know where I was when they died? I'll prove it to you, get you my schedule…"

That part I believed. I was done. Rick offered his hand, but I left without shaking it. Even if Rick was innocent of anything to do with Buzzy and Waldo, he was still a hypocritical, sanctimonious prick. I felt like I needed to take a long shower. I was ashamed to have ever smoked Rick's dope or slept under the same roof. Ashamed to have called him a friend.

I found myself driving down a giant strip past big box stores and fast food franchises…. I hadn't eaten since morning. I found an In-N-Out and fixed that. It was only six thirty. I'd passed a few motels, but the idea of spending the evening on this soulless street was not inviting. I could wait a bit until the traffic subsided and head home. But I'd had enough driving for one day.

Our old drummer Frank lived up in North Hollywood. Google Maps told me it wasn't too far away, and on the way home, I called him and told him I was in the neighborhood.

He said, "Got a gig tonight, but you're welcome to come by. Jazz club, the Baked Potato on Cahuenga."

"Great!" Actually, jazz wasn't my thing. It would be good to see Frank again, though.

It was the tail end of rush hour. I inserted earbuds to try and distract myself from the nightmare on I-5. But even a symphony orchestra couldn't compete with the roar of ten thousand motors.

I joined Frank in some dinner before the set. He asked, "You want to sit in tonight?"

I rolled my eyes. Frank's guys were some of the top jazzers in LA, which was to say, the world. Asking me to sit in with this band was like asking some kid to pitch for a Major League ball team. If I didn't know Frank so well, I would have seen it as a dig. It was just Frank's dry wit, honed to an exquisite edge as his chief weapon in the music wars he'd been fighting since he was a skinny kid witnessing his first band argument in a basement in Queens.

"I'll just enjoy hearing you guys play."

After the set we had a drink. He said, "How's that classical playlist working for you?"

"Better than I expected. You've always had good taste."

"I tried to give you a rounded introduction. I can't believe the cat I forgot—Mozart. I've got something of his that kills. His Clarinet Concerto. One of the last things he wrote." I must have raised my eyebrows. "You think clarinets are dorky? Give it a listen, you'll change your mind. Hey, you can stay at my place tonight if you like. My couch is yours."

I laughed.

"What? My couch is very comfortable. Hey, take my bed if you want."

I laughed. "No, no. I'm sorry. It's just that I've been crashing on this real stinker up in Sausalito."

***

When I got to Frank's, I was anticipating a long night, but he smiled apologetically and said, "I'm beat. Now I know I'm getting old." He was about to head into his bedroom, when he stopped. "Oh, that Mozart I told you about?" He found the CD in the ten thousand that covered an entire wall of the apartment, popped it in the player, and handed me headphones. "Second movement."

I wasn't in the mood for Mozart. I was wide awake. Keyed up. Was it the long drive? Tangling with Rick? Being in LA, knowing there were ten million people out there?

No. It was this *feeling* business. The riddle of my heart. Buzzy would know... I'd never wanted to speak to anyone so badly.

I Googled him.

He'd certainly made his mark. He'd won awards, been featured as the speaker at a convention. And published a number of articles. One was from *The Journal of Psychospirituality*, titled "Back to the Garden."

It was a philosophical, but also highly personal, take on the sixties counterculture. In his view, the essential thing we'd shared was not politics, but an inner search. We'd all had some taste of heaven, usually through psychedelic drugs, but then fallen from grace. Some of us—him, obviously—were spending the rest of our lives working to taste it again.

He explicitly tied our fall from grace with the Biblical fall, from Eden. He ended quoting Joni Mitchell's "Woodstock," the part about us having to get back to the garden.

I'd been looking for answers in Buzzy's words. What I got was an amplification of my unsettled state. I stared out the window at the quiet residential street, my mind aswirl.

The *garden*. I pictured the garden at camp where us dutiful lefties hoed the dirt like peasants. Angela swooping in and dancing down a row of swiss chard, grinning, her long skirt flying in the breeze. Angela in my dreams, scratching her wings in the box trying to get out, and lying on the stone bed in that crypt. Angela at camp, on the rock, taking off that long skirt...

Fallen from grace. The fall. *Falling...*

Even here on the second floor of Frank's low building the fear of falling lurked in my gut.

The words in my head muted as my body drowned in unfamiliar sensations—pins and needles, blood racing to the wrong places—and I swear

I *sensed* a pristine memory dislodging in my brain. It rushed into awareness, as vivid as those dreams, only with the terrible knowledge that this was real, how it had gone down:

Waiting for Angela, the last day at camp. Earlier in the day, she said, "I'll meet you at the foot of the rock, after dinner." But it's been at least an hour since then, and night is coming. Where is she?

I'm startled by leaves rustling to my right. It's her, coming out of the woods. From the moment she appears I know something is wrong. She doesn't kiss me, doesn't touch me, and she has this funny look on her face. And clutched to her side, like a weapon, is that velvet pouch. At the sight of it something deep in me goes cold.

I follow her up the familiar path to the top of the rock. I make a half-assed attempt to embrace her, but that kind of business is clearly not in the cards.

We sit facing and she slides the Tarot deck from the pouch and hands it to me, murmuring, "Shuffle." The cards are big, awkward, but I give them a rudimentary shuffle and cut them and thrust them back at her, with a look—get on with it, we don't have much time.

But she apparently has all the time in the world. She lays them out in a cross, with the appearance of each card making little sounds of surprise in her throat. When they are complete, she looks up at me and gives me her best sorceress's leer and launches into her interpretation.

I don't pay attention to the words any more than I ever have during her incantations. They're nonsense, and even at the time I know it. But nonsense that is all tangled up in her sex magic, and as such, lulling and exciting all at the same time.

Not tonight. Darker magic is at work here. And it's scaring the hell out of me.

The cards apparently aren't doing the trick this evening, because she stuffs them back in the pouch and pulls out the I Ching.

She casts the sticks and her voice falls to a whisper, her jaw set, brow like a looming thunderstorm.

The memory was vivid to that point. But then came a gap, at the crucial point. Did we exchange last words, a final kiss? I don't think I'll ever remember. But the next part is clear again.

> *It's almost dark, and I'm alone on the rock, sitting with hands clasped around my knees. It's only the end of August, but there's a first fall chill in the air. Am I waiting? For what?*

Another gap.

> *I'm climbing down the rock, a path I know like the back of my hand, but it's night with a new moon. And it's so much harder to climb down than up. But if I fall, does it really matter?*

Now came a very long gap. Years, until this moment. A gap in which…

It all came together, as neat as a jigsaw puzzle. Buzzy would be proud of me, might even write me up in one of those journals.

That last night on the rock I'd fallen from the grace of first love. And somehow Angela dying had made me incapable of moving on, frozen inside…

Like in the dream. Sharon had been right. I'd been frozen, forever seeking Angela in a line of lovers. Trying to get back to Angela. Back to my personal garden.

I always had to be the first to leave relationships, because I was terrified of returning to that place. Up on the rock in the dark and cold. Above that abyss of terrible feeling.

Alone.

Now I was very close to something, could feel the hum of it hovering around me. But I was *still* missing a piece. The essential piece.

What did Sharon say? Something about my feelings being in my music. What CD was "Woodstock" on? I tried to make sense of Frank's enormous collection. It didn't seem alphabetical or chronological. It could take all night to find it, if he even had it.

I needed to hear some music. Anything. I popped the cart on his fancy

CD player. And there was the Mozart. What had Frank said? That it *killed*. I was ready to be slain. I donned the headphones, sat on the thick carpet with my back against the window, and hit track two on the CD.

One of my secrets, which I'd somehow managed to conceal from fans and bandmates alike throughout a long performing career, was a musical sweet tooth. I loved a good melody, and the sweeter the better. Frank must have known me better than I thought. Because here was a sweet tune, serene, warm, the notes rising in pitch. Happy. The clarinet played it, backed by some polite strings. Then the strings repeated it, staying polite.

Yet something hid behind this innocent melody and resonated with what I'd been feeling all evening. A strain of danger. The vibration of something about to happen.

I reached up to silence the player but withdrew my hand.

A second melody came, again played by the clarinet.

But this one was made of three phrases that descended through a devastating series of chord changes. The clarinet had me gripping the carpet.

Now the melody repeated, played by the strings. Oh, fuck. They'd dropped all pretense of politeness. The resin of their bows dug in and sawed away inexorably into my chest. *This* was what I was afraid of. This...feeling. The muscles in my limbs knotted up, resisting.

My brain was resisting, too, spouting words, speculating, philosophizing:

I don't know squat about classical music theory, but I know true genius at work when I hear it. Maybe it's because the poor guy was at the end of his short years. Maybe he had a premonition of what was coming.

But in this piece, Mozart nailed the emotional truth of existence.

The rising part of this piece is youth, hope, the sun at dawn. Life.

And it's followed by the inevitable falling. Old age, despair, sunset. Death. Angela falling. Waldo falling.

Buzzy.

Ray and Sharon and me, eventually. Everybody.

To my great relief, a new section played. Those treacherous strings hid behind the clarinetist as it diddled around, old Mozart giving whoever the musician was a chance to prove he could play the damned thing. I couldn't blame him—I'd heard clarinet was a bear to master.

But Mozart had been just preparing to sandbag me. Because that infernal melody returned, this time, impossibly, even sweeter and sadder.

The strings hacked at my chest. I bit my lip, contracted every muscle in my body, but the music was just too strong. And there was too much built up over way too long.

The dam broke and hot tears streamed down my cheeks, mingled with a trickle of blood from my lip.

When had I last cried like this? A long time. Maybe forever.

A glutton for punishment, I found the Joni Mitchell album and put on "Woodstock." I didn't make it through the first verse. How could she sound so fucking sad? Woodstock was supposed to be this huge party.

Sadness. Anger and fear were tough, no doubt. But sadness was the very worst.

I was done. I tiptoed into the kitchen, opened cabinets, but there was no booze. What self-respecting musician didn't at least have a bottle of gin squirreled away someplace?

I checked my phone for messages. There was one from Kaylee, "I finally heard back from Annie." Kaylee? It took me a moment to remember who she was—the lawyer who'd worked with Waldo. It took a longer moment to remember who Annie was. Kaylee's ex-girlfriend, who worked in the Capitol building, where George's office was.

And I was back fitting pieces together, George and Rick and the Governor and all the rest. I can't say I didn't welcome it after all that emotional shit.

19.

I hit the road at the tail end of the morning rush. I called and left Kaylee a message, then headed up into the barren beauty of the mountains, leaving LA behind.

I mulled Rick's possible involvement with the murders. Yesterday's meeting was too fresh. I needed it to steep, then talk it out with Ray. I came down out of the mountains into the scrublands, my breathing shallow as I anticipated the stench of Bakersfield.

Kaylee called. "It took Annie a while to get back to me because she was up to her neck—she gets wrapped up in these jobs and can't get her head out of the computer."

"I hear you." I knew all about getting your head stuck in a computer.

"I didn't tell her about your suspicions about Waldo. Just said you were a friend of his who was looking for someone who might know the governor's staff. Even asking that got her uptight."

"Uptight how?"

"I don't know. Maybe it's just our history, stuff we never worked out. Which there was no shortage of. Anyway, I don't know if she'll talk to you…but here's her number. I should warn you, Annie doesn't have the world's best people skills."

"She wouldn't be the first coder."

"She can be pretty spiky."

"Why does she work there if she's gay?"

She laughed. "The money? Annie doesn't give a rat's ass about politics.

And she does exactly as she pleases, PC be damned. She's a strange one. But I'll be damned if I don't love her. Or did."

I called Annie.

She answered on the first ring. "Yuh."

"Uh, this is Bodine. Kaylee gave me your number."

"Yeah?" Her voice was affectless aside from a hint of ice.

I tried to break it. "I'm in your line of work. Do you do hardware or software?"

"Some of both."

"Kaylee said you work in the Capitol building."

"Among other places. What d'you want?"

"Can I email you a picture?"

"Mm. You better not spam me or get me on some fucking list…"

"I'm not giving your address to anyone."

It was a trick finding the picture and emailing it while driving. But traffic wasn't too bad.

There was a silence. "Got it. Governor Nichols."

"You know the other guy?"

A pause. "Seen him around the office."

It seemed impossible, but her voice had become even more toneless.

"That guy in the picture is George Bowman. I would really appreciate anything you can tell me about him."

"Why do you want to know?"

"It's better if you don't know."

"Suit yourself. Well, I can't tell you about him. They made me sign some fucking nondisclosure thing when I went to work there."

"OK. Do you know a Richard Arlington?"

"Nope."

"Head of this food supplement company, EdenTree. You at a computer?"

She scoffed. "I was born at a computer. Hold on, I'll Google him." A minute later, she said, "Never seen him. But he looks like the rest of those assholes."

"He is. You never saw him there with George?"

She hesitated. "No. Which I shouldn't have told you."

I could feel she had something she wasn't saying. Something bigger than a fear of breaking some non-disclosure agreement. "Listen, I don't know what's going on with you, and I don't care. But I really need anything you can give me. *Anything.* Has George seemed different recently? Done anything weird?"

She laughed, a kind of strangled bark that was painful to hear. "Weird? Are these guys ever anything but?"

She definitely had something. "Is your phone safe?"

She did the horrible laugh again. "You shitting me? Somebody tries to hack us, we're going to sound like a couple of Martians. No, the question is, are *you* safe? I'm calling Kaylee."

She hung up. A few minutes later she called back. "If Kaylee says you're good people, then… But if my name comes up, I'm tracking you down and slicing your heart out and feeding it to my cat."

"No worries."

"Not for me. OK. About a month ago late at night I was in the office, rewiring some shit. Easiest to do it while they're gone. My head's stuck under the desk, about four hundred seventy-three wires hanging around my neck, when I realize I'm not alone. I hear George talking to some guy in his office." Now that she was opening up, she spoke faster, relishing her tale out of school.

"You recognize the other guy?"

"No. And I just heard him."

"How do you know George's voice?"

"I told you, I've seen him around the office…"

She was lying. Why?

She rushed on with the story. "I didn't hear them come in—I had my earbuds in—but then they started arguing."

"What were they saying?"

"I didn't catch much, just the loudest parts. George was louder. The other guy was just this rumble. George yelled something like, 'I never told you to…' Then a little later he says, 'You and I are done!' He said it at least twice. Then I heard a smack and George said, 'You fuck! I think you broke it!' A door slammed. I waited a long time and finally snuck out of there. That what you were looking for?"

"I don't know. But thanks. And if anything else weird happens there..."

"Oh, I don't think I'll know. I believe it's time I get another gig."

"Why?"

"Because I can. Seller's market in our business, if you haven't heard. And telling that sorry tale made me realize it's time. I thought I could float in and out of that scene without getting dirty, but some shit just stinks too bad. I'm done."

"I'm sorry to mess up your scene."

"Nothing to do with you. But wait." A pause. "You're a coder?"

"I am."

"Kaylee said you're an old friend of Waldo's, too."

"Yeah..."

"What am I thinking? How many Bodines can there be in the world?" She brayed the long version of her laugh. She finally found her voice. "This is some clusterfuck! Yeah, I am so out of there."

She hung up.

I'd have to discuss the overheard conversation with Ray. But Annie was definitely hiding something.

***

I was past Bakersfield, barreling down a straight road with nothing to see but toasted scrubland. I called Sharon.

She said, "Where are you?"

"Driving through the desert again."

"What's up, aside from cacti?"

"You were curious about what happened with me and Angela."

"Hey, only if you want to tell me."

This was harder than I thought. "She...dumped me."

"I can't say I'm shocked. It ended, so it's fifty-fifty that that's how it went. But I'm sorry. Knowing that, some other stuff makes sense. How's that song go? The first cut is the deepest..."

I hated Sheryl Crow. Never mind. "I had another dream."

"You have a lot of dreams for someone who never dreams. OK. Shoot."

"I'm back in my museum. In that corner, where the box was, is that couch from the basement."

"The Free Love Couch. I know you guys called it that."

"Yeah, well. A naked girl lies on it with her back to me. And I think it's Angela."

"I'm getting tired of this. You were coming to see *me* in the last dream, and there she was. Now she's naked?"

"But it wasn't her. She turned her head and it was one of those Japanese girls from Hiroshima, only her face was completely…melted off. It was horrible."

"Yikes! I'm going to have to give that one some thought. But I was thinking about something else."

"What?"

"You and I have something in common."

"Really?"

"You aren't just hiding from the police, are you?"

"Where'd that come from?"

"You like to keep a low profile."

"How could you know that?"

"I'm getting there. What was your childhood like?"

Christ on a cross. I'd never told anyone about it. And no one had ever asked.

"It was fine. As long as I kept to myself."

"Uh-huh. You were self-sufficient."

"You bet. My dad had a bit of a…what do you call it? Anger management problem. Which is probably why my mother checked out with booze and pills and finally checked into the nut hatch."

"You had to *hide* growing up. It's the only way you could survive."

"How do you know that?"

"It takes one to know one. And I have spent centuries in therapy."

"What the hell was *your* childhood like?"

"I've talked it to death. I swore I was done. But…a lot like yours. Hiding out. I still am."

"But I was a *rock star*. I performed for thousands of people. How does that fit into your theory?"

"Hey, everything doesn't have to fit. And you quit that, didn't you?"

"Yeah. And I never loved the screaming crowd aspect, though I did my job. What I loved was…"

"The music. Do you miss me?"

I paused. "Yeah."

"You have my lovely voice."

"But I don't have…"

"Mmm-hmm. There's always phone sex."

A long silence in which I counted cacti. Fourteen…

She said, "OK. So there isn't phone sex. I suppose that means we're too old…but give me your email address."

I did.

"Now I have to go. Did you get in touch with that Wentworth guy?" She sounded relieved to move on to business. I was definitely relieved.

"Damn. With all that's been going on, I forgot. I'll do it soon as I get back."

Back at the houseboat, Ray was lying on the Chinese couch. He sat up as I came in. I sat across from him on the stinky couch. "How was LA?"

"Big and ugly."

"So—Rick."

"He was small and ugly. He swears up and down he didn't kill anybody."

"What do you think?"

"He was defensive. Prickly."

"Guilty?"

"Good catch. That's what it was."

"Ah!"

"Don't get so excited. He might have been guilty for being up to his neck in this thing. But seeing me, being reminded of the past, maybe he was simply guilty for turning into such a jerk. Or maybe it was about the fact that he's a Christian family man who's banging his young secretary."

"He told you that?"

"I'm sure he wanted to, to brag about it, but no. I figured it out. But if there's anything going on with him, the key is True Love Restored. I'm going to hack into his financial records."

I brought my laptop over and sat next to Ray. As soon as I was into Rick's computer, I found QuickBooks, unprotected by any password. I shook my head. "This is too easy for somebody trying to hide something." A minute later, I said, "Damn. All he invested in that camp project was five grand. That's not nearly enough for someone well-heeled as him to kill somebody over."

"Or enough to make much profit on. Why do it?"

"Who knows? Maybe just to make his right-wing buddies happy, or maybe it was some kind of quid pro quo. I don't know squat about how these guys operate."

"You think that's why Waldo had Rick's name in that file?"

"It could be. We'll never know."

"So where are we?"

"He was genuinely shocked when I told him about Buzzy. He didn't kill him."

"Waldo?"

"He was at his *funeral*. He's a smarmy prick but he's not cold blooded. And I don't think he's a good enough liar to get involved with killing someone, then go to their funeral. He does have a thread of a soul. Probably why he was so freaked out seeing me."

"Rick's a dead end."

"I'm afraid so." The admission made me tired. And it had been a long drive.

Ray asked, "What have we got?"

I told him about the conversation with Annie. I said, "She overheard George saying, 'I think you broke it,' which could explain the bandage on his nose."

"But who was it, and what where they fighting about?"

"No telling. But I'm not surprised. I'm thinking 'campaign analysis coordinator' is a rougher job than it sounds. What's more interesting is Annie. She was withholding something from me. I basically didn't tell her anything, but it was enough that she was ready to quit her job."

"Huh."

"What else do we have?"

I sighed. "George's emails, but I'm beat." I closed my eyes and rubbed my face. I opened my eyes. "Oh, yeah. This guy Sharon knew might have known George." I looked at my phone.

It was almost five back east.

I went out on the deck and called the Middleburg alumni office. "This is Sam Smith. I'm looking for an old buddy of mine—a Cyrus Wentworth."

The woman gave me his work number, in Chicago, right away, then started in on her sales pitch. I told her I was broke, which got her off the phone. I called and left a voice mail for Wentworth. I didn't like the sound of his voice.

Inside, Ray asked pointedly, "You hungry?"

"I am, but I should get back to George's emails." Working and getting nothing done just makes me want to work harder.

"All million of them. I'll go get some sandwiches."

"Thanks."

I was just getting into August in George's emails when my email pinged. Sharon.

Bodine—

First, an apology: It's been bothering me, what I said at lunch about our night back in the day. If you "plied me" with wine, I was eminently pliable. It was fun! There, I said it.

But not as fun as in my bed, which you must admit is more comfortable (not to mention bigger and cleaner) than that old couch. And you've, uh, picked up a few tricks since then.

As I think you've gathered, I am a sensible woman. You and I are on the same page regarding Angela's mumbo-jumbo spiritual trip. But that doesn't mean I don't…believe in anything outside of this sad, mundane world.

OK, I'll come right out with it. There's something about our coming together after all that time, added to what at least for me is some Nobel Prize–level chemistry, and I think we may have something here.

My colleagues would try to take my tenure away if they caught me with the following generalization, but never mind. There are two kinds of people in the world. The kind that can't—or won't—change, and the kind that can. Not just can, but are actively striving to do it. To become a better person.

I've wasted far too much time with the first kind of man.

You're the second kind. At least you've grown into him.

My. I'd intended to write a steamy little note, in lieu of phone sex. Sorry this is so serious. But it's me.

I found it plenty sexy. And scary as fuck. She *really* meant business. What did *I* mean?

I attempted a reply. "Words fail" was as far as I got. I should call her. But not now. It was back to work.

***

Ray came back a few minutes later. I must have been smiling. He said, "You found something."

"Not yet."

"Huh. Because…" He let it go.

We ate out on the deck, then I went inside and hit George's emails again while Ray sat with his computer.

Ray said, "I've got something." I sat up and he came over with his laptop and sat next to me. I looked at his computer screen. The governor's clean-cut mug grinned from the lid of a toilet, as though the rest of him had already been flushed down the drain.

I said, "The wonders of Photoshop. That is an eyesore. Where'd you find it?"

"One of the blogs I follow." He read and then gave me the run-down. "Last month, the guv delivered a speech about packing every single 'illegal' in the state of California back to beanerville. Our diligent researchers have just discovered that a couple of said illegals have been toiling away for the guv and his lovely wife for the last five years…"

I shook my head. Blogs were a waste of time. But this immigrant worker thing sounded like something Waldo might have been involved with. I'd deal with that later, when I was sober. "What do you see in those blogs?"

"Hey, I'm studying my craft."

I rolled my eyes. Ray was a good writer, I supposed, though I didn't know any more about writing than art. But I couldn't see how this stuff would further his cause. I said, "That toilet business got old around junior high."

"I know. The writing is better."

I raised my eyebrows.

He said, "OK, I'm busted. I'm really there for the trolls in the comments. It's like staring straight into the black heart of the wingnut id."

"You always have been a horror junkie."

"Let me show you."

Five minutes and I'd had enough. "Who the hell are these people?"

"Rage addicts. Addicted to feeling it, addicted to fomenting it. What I just read you is a drop in the ocean of hate online. It would be enough to fuel a small sun if you could harness it. My question is this: on the one hand you've got thousands of nut jobs frothing at the mouth every day, demonizing the opposition, threatening to take up arms, start another civil war. It's truly frightening. On the other hand, so far it's all talk. None of these freaks has actually harmed anybody, at least physically."

"Thank God."

"One theory of mine is that the blogs soak up all the rage, give these guys an outlet that keeps them from physical violence."

"Huh. You mean like the heat sink in my computer back home that keeps the circuit boards from melting down?"

"Yeah. The thing is, the temperature just keeps rising. The claims get crazier and crazier. I worry that one day it's all going to blow, and it's going to be a lot worse than a fried computer. People are going to die."

I waved open palms at him in a calm-down gesture. "My two cents? You read it, you feed it."

"I don't know. I feel like if I don't keep tabs on it something terrible is going to happen, and I won't know."

"Look, I'll let you know when the tanks start rolling in. Explain to me again the profit path for your blog?"

Ray shook his head. "I thought for a while there was one. Goddamn Internet. Land of the free. As in free music. Free writing. Free everything."

A few minutes later Ray interrupted me again. "Hey look at this crazy thing I just found on Reddit, something about 'Through A Glass Darkly....'"

He got up and was bringing the laptop over when I raised a hand. "Enough. I'm trying to work."

I finally bagged it. I said, "At least you've got your blogs. I've got diddly-squat. I got through August. Past Waldo's death and the funeral. There isn't anything remotely suspicious. He sets up meetings, discusses the fine points of political strategy. He meets with potential donors—the real versions of what I was faking. How's he communicating with this mysterious person?"

"Persons, remember. I don't know. Dead drops in the park? Tin cans and string."

I sighed. "We're just chasing our tails."

"We need a break. How about a drive out into the great state of California?"

We got in the car.

Ray said, "Napa Valley's not far. Wine country."

I laughed. "OK. But you'll just end up smashed and I'll have to cart you home in a wheelbarrow."

"Fine. Be that way. How about a nice, healthy hike in Muir Woods?"

"You're on."

We drove over to Mill Valley and around the side of Mount Tamalpais. After the turn off for Muir Woods, the road got steep and narrow without nearly the guardrails I required to keep my lunch from grumbling. It was just another reminder that California was no place for acrophobes.

We were coming around a nasty turn with a steep drop off to the right when my phone chirped.

"Cyrus Wentworth." He sounded annoyed. "You called?"

"Hold on…"

There was a turn out ahead and I took it and parked.

"You there?" He had a short fuse.

"Sorry. I'm in the car. Uh, we went to college together. Bob Hutchinson. I don't know if you remember me, but…"

"Bob? Musician?" He'd warmed right up.

"Yes."

"Oh man, I remember a concert you did…" Now he was whispering, "Hey, you musicians… Middleburg, home of the Middleburger. Remember?"

"Uh, refresh me."

"When we used to, you know…" He made a long inhaling sound. "We'd get the munchies and go to the dining hall and get a Middleburger. Best-tasting thing in the world. Still is."

I said, "Gotta love a good burger. Ever heard of the In-N-Out?"

"I have."

Burger bonding.

"You still playing that guitar?"

"No, you're thinking of my friend Ray. Actually, I play organ."

"Oh." He sounded disappointed. "What's up?"

"I heard that this guy George lived in your frat house at college. Do you remember him?"

He laughed nervously, then whispered, "How could I forget? First nose candy I ever had. Him and that sidekick what's-his-name were into some scary shit. Why do you want to know about George? What the hell are you up to?"

"I'm…writing a little article for the alumni magazine. A 'Where are they now?' on the late sixties. I have this demonstration picture. We've tracked down most of the people in it, but not George."

He barked an ugly laugh. "Yeah, and I've got a bridge to sell you. I'd think a graduate of our prestigious alma mater could come up with a better story than that. Wait—did you even graduate?"

"No. But…"

"Can it. Why should I care what your scam is? But no more bullshit. And you have five minutes. I'm counting."

"Do you remember George's girlfriend?"

"Which one?"

"The one that fell off the cliff."

"God, how could I forget? What a loss. She was some fox."

Sharon was right. He was an asshole. "How did George take it?"

"I don't know. We weren't close. Except at parties, when he came around with that stuff. Look, why are you interested in him? Wait…" He gave a strange laugh. "This is about his dad, isn't it? You haven't turned into some kind of reporter, have you?"

"No. What dad?"

"George Senior."

"George Bowman, Senior."

"Bowman? Where'd you get that? No. George Hunter White. You've never heard of him? Whatever you're up to, you suck at it." Now he was laughing hard. "Have some fun and Google him. But watch out. You might be in for some spoooooky shit. Your five minutes is up." He hung up.

Ray asked, "What was that about?"

"This George wasn't Bowman back then. He was White."

"Huh?"

"That's why we couldn't find him at the college. He changed his name at some point. His father was George Hunter White."

"I've heard that name somewhere."

"I haven't, but the way this Wentworth was talking, I think I should have. We're going to have to take a pass on the woods. Mill Valley must have a library with computers. It's right down the road."

We were there in ten minutes.

I pointed at the redwoods surrounding the building. "We didn't miss them after all."

The first hit on Google for "George Hunter White" was Wikipedia. We read a few paragraphs and looked at each other. I'd imagined that when I finally broke this thing open, I'd get a buzz, like when I find the key to a coding problem. This was a break, all right, but it didn't feel good. It felt like stepping into some alternative reality where up was down and everything was ugly.

We left.

When we hit the street Ray asked, "The CIA?"

"Wentworth was laughing at his own weird joke, saying we were in for some 'spooky shit.' I didn't get it. He meant spooky as in *spooks*. Company men."

"What the hell have we gotten ourselves into?"

20.

We headed to Spider's to do more research. The Internet was finally working. I handed Ray the computer. "You read and tell me about it."

Ray said, "George Hunter White started out in narcotics and moved on to MK-ULTRA—the CIA's covert program of mind-control experimentation on unwitting civilians. George Senior headed up Operation Midnight Climax. He operated fake brothels in San Francisco, Marin County—right here—and in New York City, under the pseudonym Morgan Hall. Unsuspecting johns were dosed with LSD, then observed by White through one-way mirrors, from a little toilet, as they got it on with prostitutes. The johns were considered fair game because of their illegal activity, and unlikely to complain to police. It worked. The lid stayed on until they dosed an army soldier and he jumped from a window to his death. The brothels in California were closed down in the early sixties. But the one in New York operated until 1966, right after White retired."

"What was the point?"

"Initially, the MK-ULTRA plan was to weaponize LSD. But things got a little out of hand."

"This is hard to believe. You sure this isn't some elaborate hoax?"

Ray scrolled down. "It's all sourced. No, I heard about this before." He read some more, then said, "It came out in the Church hearings in the House in 1975. The Freedom of Information Act released a ton of documents in seventy-seven—the year White died. This is the kind of stuff we used to dream up when we were stoned back then—you know, all that paranoid stuff about Nixon and secret agencies. Here's where it gets really funky. All the time George Senior was running this project, he was doing acid himself."

"Really? A CIA guy?"

"Shitloads, along with his buddies at the Company. He started slipping it on his wife's friends, including one woman who was at a party at White's house with her *baby*. She went crazy and tried to sue the government. But for all the acid he dropped, gin was George Senior's drug of choice. He died of cirrhosis. No wonder he was all kinked up. Into shoe fetishes and stuff."

I gave him a skeptical look.

He said, "It's all right here."

"Sure. So the old man was getting off on watching through the one-way glass."

"It looks that way. You know how LSD has that unique property of inducing suggestibility? People get the idea that they can create their own reality. George dropped enough that he came to believe that, too. Only the reality he dreamed into being was some totalitarian hell. Look at this quote from him. 'It was fun, fun, fun. Where else could a red-blooded American lie, kill, cheat, and rape with the sanction of the all-highest?'"

"Wow. Just wow."

"Fun, fun, fun. A far cry from getting daddy's car and going to the burger joint. One last thing—though the CIA claimed they were done with the experimentation after the hearings, one agent in 1977 said it all just went underground and continued."

"What, it's still going on today?"

"It might be." He read on. "You won't believe this. Ken Kesey first got turned on to acid by MK-ULTRA.

"Ken Kesey of the Trips Festivals, which the Grateful Dead played."

"The very one. One of the founders of the psychedelic movement. Of the hippies."

"So the CIA spawned the hippies. There's a sweet irony. Or sour."

"Yeah. I feel like *I* just dropped acid. We're part of some bizarre full circle. Here we are on the houseboat of one of the Dead's guys, one of the original San Fran hippies, and without knowing it we've been chasing down the son of the guy who started it all."

"OK, Ray. Time to come down. This scene is weird enough without jumping to acidhead conclusions. We need to focus."

"Fine. But that requires coffee. Or else I need a nap."

We went up to the kitchen. He stood while I made some. Spider had an empty jar above the stove. I sniffed it; it didn't smell like dope. I put in five twenties to cover the vodka and coffee we'd been using.

We brought coffees back down to the couches.

Ray said, "George changed his name to Bowman. A bowman is a *hunter*."

"Good. I missed that. Except why leave that clue to his past?"

"Maybe he was somehow proud of his dad, didn't want to break the connection completely."

"That's psychobabble, Ray. Plus, we know nothing of his relationship with his dad. Maybe he hated him."

We sat silently for a few minutes. There was the distant buzz of a motorboat. Finally, Ray asked, "Why do you think he changed his name? You think it's because of Angela?"

"When I met with George, he didn't seem overly concerned that his role in her death might be revealed. And it does seem like a cold case if there ever was one. Maybe it's his *father* he's trying to hide."

"A career in politics would definitely be awkward with his dad's shenanigans in the closet. Maybe people wouldn't care, now. But maybe he changed his name right after that Church commission stuff came out."

"Then he starts working for Nichols, with his new identity."

"And can't let on who he is really is."

"Who his father is."

I stood and leaned against the back of the stinky couch. Ray got up and paced a short run of three steps between the walls. "That makes sense. George said he had 'buddies.' He threatened me with rendering. He wasn't bluffing. He got hooked up with the CIA through his dad."

"I don't know. They do some bad shit, no doubt. But torturing Americans, here in America?"

"That's how he knows where I live, what I do for a living. I imagine the Company has some of the best hackers in the world."

"I don't know. They're the same bozos that came up with exploding cigars with Castro. Not to speak of this MK-ULTRA nonsense. So I don't know how competent they are. Then again, they do seem to have gotten a real taste for torture recently."

"There's a warming thought. With this MK-ULTRA piece, things are making less sense than ever. I feel like we've got part of a leg and maybe a trunk, but we're not close to the whole elephant."

"So to speak—these guys being Republicans and all."

I could feel Ray trying to lighten the conversation, which had taken a dismal turn. "We're not even sure it's an elephant…" I laughed.

"What?"

"This reminds me of this speed freak from back then. A real loon, who used to sidle up to me on the street, babbling, 'It's all connected, man,' his eyes all the time spinning round like pinwheels. And I'm thinking, 'Hey, man, I am most definitely not connected to *you.*' He pointed down at a sewer cover and said, 'They're down there.' I said, 'Who?' 'The *controllers*, man. They're listening to us talk right now.' Maybe he was on to something."

"Put another way, the Four Brothers were part of some CIA plot all these years and never knew it."

We were trying to laugh it off, but there was a definite edge in the air.

Ray must have sensed it, too. He said, "You think old Spider has any weed?"

"Does the sun come up in the morning?"

"You think he'd mind if I borrowed a taste?"

"He'd be hurt if you didn't. But watch out. Whatever he's got might just take your head off."

"I'm brave. I couldn't live with myself if I came out to old Hippieville and didn't indulge at least once."

Ray went up to Spider's workshop and returned a few minutes later with bloodshot eyes.

"You survived."

"I did." He gave me the dead eye. "And you, sir, are way too straight."

"Alright. But I need to keep this clear." I tapped my head. He scoffed. "What the hell."

I went up and poured myself a large vodka. Back downstairs, we went out on the deck. It was getting close to sunset but was still warm.

I said, "So. Faking Buzzy falling. Religious rituals. The CIA dropping acid. What's that add up to?"

"Crazytown."

"Where'd you get that?"

Ray snorted. "Blogs—where else? I keep trying to fit it all together, but I can't."

"Because you're stoned."

"No, dope promotes lateral thinking." In all seriousness he said, "We need to think outside the box."

I laughed. "Rule number one of thinking outside the box is that anyone who suggests it is incapable of doing it."

"Wait. Outside the box. You put that box of Waldo's in your theater. And the nuns' gravestones were…outside of the box, so to speak."

"You're talking gibberish. And they were stolen before I put the box there."

"I'm saying that you've got *two* wacko religious things. They've got to be connected. The only thing weirder than those nuns' gravestones is stealing them. And that blood ritual stuff…"

I wasn't following him. Maybe I was using the wrong drug. I hit the vodka again, hard, and though we'd taken different rides, I sort of caught up to Ray.

I sat on the stinky couch with the computer. Ray lay full down on the Chinese couch and in minutes was snoring. So much for dope-fueled lateral thinking solving this thing.

But the nuns' gravestones… I looked at the Bodine website. It hadn't changed. I checked my email. I idly went to Rick's Facebook page.

His wife, Cindy, had posted the message "Richard has passed away." I Googled him:

Supplements CEO Found Dead

The body of EdenTree head Richard Arlington was discovered in his office this morning by cleaning staff. His body was badly beaten, and police are treating the death as suspicious. Arlington leaves his wife of twenty-five years and five children, and will be remembered…

***

"Ray." I scrambled over and shook him awake. "Rick is dead."

Ray groaned. "Huh? Give me a moment."

He sat up, scratched his head. "Don't tell me he fell."

"No. It looks like somebody beat him to death."

"That's terrible. Even if he did turn out to be an asshole, like you said."

"Yeah. And it makes even less sense than Buzzy. Rick was playing on George's team."

"When did it happen?"

"Sometime last night. Not long after I was there."

"That can't be a coincidence. You think they were trying to kill you both?"

"Or maybe trying to *frame* me. But how the hell would they know I was there? You're the only one who knew about my trip to LA."

We sat for a moment. Then Ray said, "What about the CIA?"

"I've been all over my computer. Nobody's been in there."

"You sure those boys don't have stuff you can't see?"

Was I? But Ray was moving on to something else.

He asked, "What about a physical bug? Right here on the houseboat?"

"That doesn't make sense. Because then they know I'm here. They would have killed me a week ago… Wait. Shit! When I told you I was going to LA, I was at the library…" I had a terrible vision of scores of spooks in some vast bunker, snooping on computers. Snooping on computer searches at the Sausalito Library, then figuring out we were *there*, then somehow listening in on our conversation. Which was right out of the playbook of that old speed freak guy, with his controllers in the sewers.

Ray said, "Tell me what you're thinking."

"Nope. It doesn't do to give voice to paranoia."

"How did they know you were in LA? That can't be just a coincidence."

"I don't know. The important thing is that I'm the last brother left. Which means *I'm* next. And I don't want to take you with me. You need to go home."

"I'm not abandoning you. And you need help figuring this out. We have to find the connection between the three. Thrown from a cliff. Bled to death. Beaten to death. I'm…"

"Ray, you're stoned. And I'm not in great shape."

"It's true. My brain feels like a soggy loaf of bread."

"We'll discuss it first thing tomorrow morning, sober. Then I'm putting you on a plane."

Ray ignored that.

I had one more glass of vodka.

***

My phone woke me, vibrating in my pocket. Sharon. I whispered, "Hold on a minute, I don't want to wake Ray." I stepped outside onto the boardwalk. The morning was foggy and cold. "You're getting to be a regular alarm clock."

"Sorry."

"I don't mind." I'd been looking forward to talking to her since that email, but with Rick dead it was going to be a very different conversation. She started it.

"I still haven't heard about a funeral for Buzzy. It's getting weird. How long does it take them to figure out that he fell off a cliff?"

I sighed. "I didn't want to upset you…" I told her about Buzzy's autopsy report.

"That's completely insane. What monster would do such a thing to…" She broke down into sobs.

"Yeah, it's terrible." The morning was clear and warm, a slight breeze carrying the perfume of the bright flowers that lined the boardwalk, sparkling in the sun. It was no setting for such a conversation.

"How did you find out?"

"I got into the Middleburg Police computer and found the autopsy report. Believe me, a high school kid could have done it."

"It's still illegal!"

"It was the only way I was going to find out. And I needed to know."

"This maniac was in Middleburg. And I was a good friend of Buzzy's."

"You have nothing to be afraid of. Your only connection to this thing is me. What I need you to do is go out and buy a prepaid cell phone and call me on it in the future. And you'll be fine."

"How can you know that?"

"Because this killer is on the West Coast." I told her about Rick.

"Oh no. You're next, aren't you?"

"Not if I find out who's doing this."

"You need to go to the police."

"As soon as I have something to give them, I will." *The CIA.* "Or maybe not."

"What do you mean?"

"I'll explain. I talked to Cyrus Wentworth."

"How is the old buzzard?"

"Buzzard's about it. It doesn't seem like age improved him." I told her about George Hunter White.

"OK, now you're making stuff up."

"I wish I was."

"You're afraid to go to the police because of the CIA?"

"I don't know what I am. I need to find out more. And you can help me with one thing."

"Anything."

"Look and see if George White was registered at college."

"I will. But it's making me crazy having you three thousand miles away, and there isn't a thing I can do."

"You can get that prepaid phone. And find out about George White."

"Uh, I know this is the wrong time, but did you get my email…"

"I did. You are a fabulous writer. You should have no trouble with that paper."

"It's a different subject matter, but thanks. I guess." She hung up, but her voice had already gone dead with—disappointment? *I* was disappointed in my response. But I was really not in the mood. And to respond properly, I needed…energy? Coffee? *Courage.*

Never mind that I wasn't in the mood. I needed to call her back, apologize for my robot response to her deep, heartfelt email. Try to put in words what I'd felt when I read it, because I *had* felt something....

Fuck. I couldn't call her. Not on her regular number, not with this shit going on. *You have nothing to be afraid of.* Then why did I suggest she get a burner phone? Because someone might be listening to her phone. I needed to wait for her to call me.

To my shame, part of me was relieved to be off the hook for the moment. Except I wasn't. What I wanted to talk to her about would be of no interest to whoever might be listening... Enough.

I shook my head and changed the mental subject back to George and this mess.

I tiptoed back onto the houseboat, wrapped a blanket around myself, and took my computer out on the deck. Where was George when Rick was killed? I Googled Governor Nichols. He was speaking at a campaign event in Redding on Friday afternoon when I was seeing Rick. I looked on Google Maps. Redding was far north of San Francisco. There was no way George could have reached LA in time to kill Rick.

I heard a squeak as the sliding door opened. Ray came out. I said, "You don't look too bad. Better than I feel. Maybe pot is better than booze."

"That's what the hippies said, before most of them became drunks."

"Speak for yourself."

We went out to breakfast. Ray blew like mad on his coffee, poured a little water in it, then lifted it to his mouth with both hands, like he was performing a religious rite.

I waited until he'd downed half the cup. "I'm serious about you taking the next plane home."

"And I'm serious about staying. You need me."

"When the shit comes down, I don't want you getting hit."

"And I don't want *you* getting hit. So we have, what did you call it? A Mexican standoff. Unless you plan on handcuffing me and manhandling me onto that plane..."

"You're being a total pain in the ass. But as long as you're here, you might as well lend me those cannabis-ruined brains of yours."

Having won for the moment, he brightened right up. I told him about the campaign event.

"But how do you know George was there? We don't even know what he does for Nichols."

"True. It's one thing to push somebody off a cliff in a youthful moment of panic. But painting someone in his own blood, beating someone to a pulp? Those acts are just too *crude* for the pompous asshole I met. You know, when it came down to it up on Garnet Hill that night, I bet he was looking away, and his hand just reached out when he shoved her, like it was someone else's. And by the time he slogged down through the snow, George told himself she fell, or jumped—whatever, the stoned-out bitch. And when I saw him, I swear he was surprised to hear about Buzzy…"

"You're giving me all these reasons why it couldn't be George. Why do you sound like you're arguing with yourself?"

"Damn, Ray, you are getting perceptive in your old age. It's that quote from George's father. 'Where else could a red-blooded American lie, kill, cheat, and rape with the sanction of the all-highest?'"

"Sins of the fathers?"

"Maybe it's time to reassess George. What did I see? Maybe it was a slick act. What if he inherited his dad's crazy?"

"And hides it real well?" We ate.

Ray wiped his plate with a last piece of toast. He said, "Why did they kill Rick?"

"I don't think that's the question. The question is what do Waldo, Buzzy, and Rick…and I have in common?"

"I need to hit the can."

Ray returned looking a little pale. I asked, "The bathroom's haunted?" I started in on the *Twilight Zone* theme.

Ray didn't laugh. "I was looking in the mirror, thinking about George Hunter White, and remembered this post on Reddit I was going to show you. It had a bathroom window in it."

***

Back at the houseboat, he typed at my computer then got still as he read. He handed the laptop to me gingerly, like it was hot.

THROUGH A GLASS DARKLY

We drive down to the city. He says, "I'm gonna show you something like you've never seen." We go upstairs into a hall. He opens a door and shoves me into a dark room. I say, "What are you doing?" but he just laughs. Shuts me in and locks the door. I can't see but I can tell from the stink I'm in a bathroom.

A light comes on behind a window. I press my nose to the cold glass. I'm looking into a room with just a small bed, the sheets rumpled, and a chair. A door opens and in comes a woman in a bright dress and a smile followed by a man in a suit. He's not smiling. He hands her something from his wallet.

They talk, but I can't hear through the glass. Now they're taking off their clothes. She's white as a dead fish. Her udders hang down like rotten fruit. Between her legs is the source of all wickedness. I cannot see it, but I can smell it.

They lie on the bed and PERFORM the ABOMINATION of which I have read. Its smell is upon me like poison gas, and I choke. My eyes burn from the sight, but I must not close them, must not turn away.

For I am THE WITNESS.

Ray said, "This guy talks about 'Down to the city.' One of those MK-ULTRA safe houses was in New York. When I read this thing before, I wondered, what kind of window looks on people? Not a window. A one-way mirror."

"Huh. But how do we get from some dead spook to a post on Reddit?"

"Somebody wrote it—who?"

"Oh, God. It's *George*. Junior. It was take your kid to work day. Now that is sick."

"He didn't seem to enjoy it much."

"I can't say I much blame him. Except it sounds like he has serious sex issues." I shook my head. "George got it on with Angela. Likely got her pregnant."

"Hey, issues never stop most people from doing it. Biological imperative. I wouldn't make any bets about what people get up to in their private lives."

"I suppose." I had a horrible thought. "What if his dad made him go in there with the woman and then he watched? What if he dosed junior with acid?"

"In that case, I almost feel sorry for the guy."

I glared at Ray. "Before you start getting all weepy for poor George, remember that he murdered Angela."

"Right. That safe house scene could certainly mess him up in the sex department. Or drive him completely nuts, which would explain the ritual stuff with Buzzy."

"George didn't seem the least bit crazy." But I wasn't sure anymore.

"Maybe he's one of those psychos who wears a good mask. He acts perfectly normal, like Ted Bundy."

"What's the user name on that Reddit post?"

Ray looked. "What the fuck? Levity-z. The same guy who posted those comments about gays."

What the fuck, indeed. This whole process had been crawling along, one unconnected thing after another, and suddenly it was coming together, so fast that it was like time was speeding up.

"Levity-z, the guy with the weird z's. Who's most likely the same person that pinned the note on Buzzy.

"See if he posted anything else."

Ray clicked around on Reddit. "There's just one other. It's way down the feed, probably never made it to the front page."

It was a scan of a handwritten note. Old, crinkled, and yellowed, the writing faded.

——— ———
——— ———
——— ———
——— ———
——— ———
——— ———

The Receptive Earth

The six horizontal lines with a break in the middle, followed by the words, were a symbol, which sparked faint recognition. Along with a sinking feeling. As I read on, it got worse.

> *Hey, the snow is really coming down now. Frozen tears from heaven. And I'm close, almost there.*
>
> *It's true, a million flakes and every one is different, because I can see each one in the moment before it dies, melting on my tongue. So beautiful in its brief passing. Like us.*
>
> *Look out the window now and you and I can be as one with the snow.*
>
> *It was good to see you. I'm sorry I hurt you. I was just following the flow of the great river, going with him. Only now I know it wasn't him. It was his potion, his wicked potion. The bad snow. Ask my nose. The nose knows, blood on my pillow.*
>
> *It's taken this, the good fairy's potion, to see that his was bad. And he's bad. I told you what he wants me to do. I can't do that, crush a flake before it's fallen. My flake. And yours...*
>
> *Someone's at the door...*

I knew who'd written this, and when. But as if it might prove me wrong, I grabbed the computer and Googled "Receptive earth."

I said, "It's hexagram number two from the *I Ching*. It makes sense—the earth, receiving snow. It also has to do with the primal power of yin, the female principle. Angela was into the tarot and the *I Ching*."

"She wrote this?"

"It's not just the use of the *I Ching*. She had a thing for bad poetry."

"Snowing. You think?"

"Yes. She wrote this the night of the storm. To Waldo." As I said it, I felt an old pang. She'd written to him and not me. Then came a flash of anger. You got it right, girl. Every *flake's* different. Including you, Angela.

Ray asked, "What—George stole this note from Waldo?"

"No, no, don't you see—she didn't finish it. Waldo never got it."

"George got it from Angela."

"She never finished it because she was *dead*. It was George at the door, come to take her to the cliff."

"Why would George keep it, let alone post it on the Internet forty years later?"

"The only thing I can think of is what you said before—he wants to get caught."

"If so, not too badly. My finding this was like stumbling on a needle in a field of haystacks. She was already tripping when she wrote this."

"Oh, yeah. The imagery—the good potions and bad potions. Almost there, to heaven. She was blasted."

"The bad potion was…"

"Cocaine. And the good, acid."

"'Crush a flake before it's fallen.' The abortion."

"I'm afraid so. She hears someone coming—George, right? Coming to take her to the cliff. He says, 'Come with me out into the snow. Let's go up Garnet Hill. It will be really far out!'" When I'd last climbed Garnet Hill, I'd pictured her final moments. Now as I visualized them, she wasn't alone. She and George were wading through two feet of snow, huddled against the wind. His arm was around her and her hands were at her belly. She had no idea what was going to happen. Or maybe in light of that note, she did.

I shivered. I imagined myself tearing from the Four Brothers house after them. Catching up and tackling George, yelling at Angela to run…

"Are you OK?"

"Yeah." I wasn't, not really. Angela's note had brought her closer to me than in a long time, and though I'd only imagined her final moments, they felt real.

Ray asked, "What if the murder wasn't about her pregnancy? What if it was about MK-ULTRA?"

"I don't follow."

"She was tight with George. Maybe she found out something she shouldn't have…"

"Like just the fact that it existed. Oh God. I can just see George in bed with Angela, coked up, bragging about what his dad does. Later he says, 'You're going to have this abortion. How do I know the kid's mine? How do I know you haven't been fucking every guy on campus?' Knowing Angela, she would have been ripshit. She threatens to tell us—her real friends—about MK-ULTRA. Before she can get the chance, he lucks out and this giant snowstorm arrives." Again, I was making it up, but it had the reality of an intense memory. Maybe it was intuition.

"That would be pretty ballsy of her."

"You didn't know her. She was never one to underestimate her personal power. Especially if she was coked up. The note proves that George is hiding behind Levity-z. Who else could have it? He killed all of them—Angela, Waldo and Buzzy."

"Don't forget Rick."

"And Rick."

"But you said George was in Redding the afternoon he was killed."

"So the governor has a private jet."

"But he was on vacation when Waldo died."

"Maybe he faked that on his schedule."

"What was that note doing on Reddit? And what about the CIA now?"

Ray was pissing me off. I wanted to solve this so badly that I'd become infatuated by my latest theory. I didn't need him pointing out that it was half-crazed.

21.

What about the CIA? I started imagining the Controllers again, only now with a drone a mile overhead, listening to our conversation.

As if reading my mind, Ray said, "Let's assume for the moment that the CIA is involved. On the one hand, it's a stretch, but on the other the power of their 'intelligence' could explain a lot. Like how George found you when this business started, and how they could know you were in LA. But if it was spooks that knew that, why didn't they finish the job when you were there?"

"If they knew I was there, they'd...have to know I'm *here*. They would have killed me a week ago, like I said before."

"Right."

"I swear my computer's clean, but with the CIA possibly involved, I'm going to give it a more careful look. This'll take a while."

"Fine." Ray took his computer out on the deck.

An hour later, I joined him. "It's spick and span. Unless these spooks actually wrote the original operating system code and embedded something."

"Could they do that?"

"Nobody knows what they can do, except them."

***

Ray and I walked to lunch in town. We were almost back to Spider's when my phone rang with an unfamiliar number.

"Yeah."

"It's Sharon."

I squeezed the phone, really glad to hear her voice. "Hold on one second…" I gestured for Ray to head on inside and leaned against the boardwalk rail, waiting until he was out of earshot. It was afternoon, but the fog hadn't burned off. No one was about, as usual, just a slight cool breeze tinkling a couple of pleasantly dissonant sets of wind chimes. "You got that phone. Good."

"I felt weird doing it. Isn't that what drug dealers use?" There was an edge to her voice. A cold edge.

"It is. Never mind. Uh, I'm glad you called. I would have called you, but I needed you to have the safety of that burner. I'm sorry about how our last conversation ended, I should have…"

"This isn't the time for that. I've found out some stuff."

Her voice was still cold…but she was right. This wasn't the time.

"There *was* a George White registered at the college. And he graduated. But that's it. They didn't have a file on him."

"No transcript, no grades?"

"No nothing, except on a little freshman intake list, saying he came from White Plains, New York."

Just up the river from the safe house where George Senior brought Junior. She asked, "Who took his files? And why?"

George himself? Or his dad's buddies at the CIA? And when? After the Church Committee findings? "I told you. George's father was in the CIA…"

"Oh, come on! You and that sidekick of yours—what's his name?—are on drugs!"

"Ray. No." At least *I* wasn't on drugs. *Sidekick.* "Shit. Wentworth said something about *George* having a sidekick, how they 'got up to some scary shit together.'"

"Yeah. That creep Wheezer."

"You mean Weasel."

"No, the way I remember it was *Wheezer.*"

Hippie nicknames. "Why haven't you mentioned him before?"

"I don't know. He was a creep. Not somebody I like to think about any more than the score of other loons running around back then."

I almost felt her shudder through the phone. "You sure his name was Wheezer?"

"Yes. Because of the funny thing that happened with his breathing. I heard it one time when I found him in *our room*."

"Your room with Angela."

"It was one of those deals where we each had our own room, but one door to the hall. You went through mine to get to hers. Today you'd say he'd been kind of *stalking* her. Things were way looser then. Still, she said something to me, complaining about him. Anyway, I came back from class one day, sat at my desk, and almost jumped out of my skin. The door to Angela's room was open, and he was just *standing* in there, quiet as a mouse. He'd been there when I came in, didn't say anything. He was a *literal* creep. I yelled, 'What the hell are you doing here?' 'Waiting for Angela.' 'You think Angela wants to hang out with a weirdo like you?' And I laughed. I shouldn't have, but I couldn't help it. He came toward me, and I was suddenly really scared. But then he started this strange breathing thing. I think it embarrassed him, because he left. Thank God. Anyway, that's why I'm sure his name is *Wheezer*. Because he wheezed. I think it was asthma." I heard her talking to someone. "I have to go." She hung up.

Tell Ray? No. I needed to digest this first. I walked out into the parking lot and toward town. Cars whizzed past, people came in and out of stores, but they barely registered. I walked out onto a pier, passing a restaurant. I stood at the end.

My mind became still. There was just the sound of waves gently kissing the pier and cold fog brushing my cheeks. Here it was invisible, but as I gazed out over the water, I watched it disappear under mountains of the stuff. It had swallowed the entire city except for the tip of the Transamerica Pyramid and Sutro Tower.

I stared into the fog as if I could pierce its mysteries, as if it held the answer to my burning question: where did Wheezer fit into the puzzle?

I let my eyes unfocus, gave up the struggle, and surrendered to boundless white and the damp on my cheeks.

I stared again. Though the mountains of mist remained unchanged, inside me came a little clearing. And at its center, the key.

The letter *z*. My rational brain started up again and began working it out.

I needed help. I headed back to Spider's, slowly, carefully at first, like I might lose this key. A minute later, I was running.

I burst into the door of the houseboat. "Ray!"

He was lying on the Chinese couch, glued to his laptop. He held up his hand.

I stalked over and leaned down. "Leave those blogs of yours for a minute. In fact, put that computer down and look at me."

I sat across from him on the stinky couch. "I talked to Sharon. She told me that dealer's name was Wheezer, not Weasel."

That finally launched him up to sitting. "Wheezer! Of course. Why didn't I remember that?"

"It was a long time ago. Memory lies. Weasel, Wheezer."

"So?"

"So the name Wheezer's got a *z* in it. That's the key to this whole thing."

"You care to explain?"

"I don't quite understand it yet, but here goes. You came up with the solution a while back. You said George is working with someone."

"Or ones…"

"Let's keep it simple for now. He's working with Wheezer. Sharon said Wheezer was George's sidekick back then. He still is. We thought George was some kind of bagman for the governor, but Wheezer's *George's* bagman. He does his dirty work for him. Maybe George was up north in Redding when Rick was killed in order to establish an alibi. And he went on vacation when Waldo was killed for the same reason. Meanwhile Wheezer was busy.

"The acid that night was the most powerful I've ever known. George Senior was dosing citizens, and himself, with what was undoubtedly the purest government-made product."

"You think George copped the acid you took from his *dad*?" Ray asked.

"And gave it to his buddy Wheezer, a known dealer, who gave it to us."

"But why give you the acid?"

"George was planning to kill Angela. He saw a weather report and sent

Wheezer over with free acid, figuring between it and the snow Angela's friends would be distracted while he killed her."

Ray said, "He was right."

"And if that wasn't distraction enough, after he killed Angela, he called his dad, who made the bust happen. Manipulating any local police department— let alone those Middleburg bozos—would have been child's play for George's boys. That's why the charges were dropped and didn't even make the newspaper. It was never a real arrest. Just local cops doing what the CIA told them to do. Sharon also told me George's college records were all missing."

"It seems like a lot of trouble to go to."

"To cover up a murder? And aside from the name change, it wasn't George's trouble. His dad's buddies did the work."

"How did George Senior make things happen so fast, in the middle of a snowstorm?"

"As long as the phones still worked, all it took was the right call to the Middleburg Police."

"Maybe those spooks killed Angela?"

"No. George as much as admitted to doing it. And there's that note..."

Ray leaned forward with his elbows on his knees, looked at me intently. "That explains then. What about now? What about Buzzy and Rick?"

"Wheezer killed them."

"And you know this because..."

"That's where the z comes in. We have an older guy, who's Levity-z on Reddit. Who killed Buzzy and put the note on him, spelling homoz with a z. Who writes Homoze and Hippeze with z's in the comments. Wheezer's name has a z. He's an older guy, our age. George probably put him up to it, but he killed Waldo, Buzzy and Rick."

Ray didn't look convinced. "Come on. To paraphrase Freud: sometimes a z is just a z. And Buzzy had *two* in his name. Is that why he's dead? I don't think so."

He was silent. He finally said, "I don't necessarily buy your z theory, but Wheezer working with George? It explains a lot of things. And you know the two of them are like our evil twins. Buds back in the sixties who still hang out. Twin doppelgangers."

242

"Hush." *With your nonsense.* I needed to think, because…Shit. "If *Wheezer* is Levity-z, then what about the Reddit post?"

"He could have gotten Angela's note from George's room back then."

"But George's testimony about the MK-ULTRA safehouse?"

Ray shook his head.

"I'm going on Reddit to see if I can get past the user name Levity-z." I got the laptop and typed for a while. "Damn. These Reddit folks have things sewn up tight. There's a brick wall hiding his real self."

"Let's look at those Reddit posts again."

We drive down to the city. He says, "I'm gonna show you something like you've never seen…"

Ray looked at me. "Is that the way a father speaks to a son?"

"We're talking George Hunter White, the CIA acidhead madman, so who knows." But there was something else. "The tone of this still doesn't sound like George."

"I have to take your word for that. Oh shit."

"What?"

Ray closed his eyes. He got still, as still as a Buddhist monk, stiller than I'd ever seen him. I waited.

He opened his eyes. "This isn't George talking about his father. It's *Wheezer* talking about George Junior!"

Soon as he said it, I knew it was true.

I kept silent because he was on a roll. "That explains the weird attitude toward sex. It's *Wheezer's* attitude, not George's. Also explains Buzzy at the same cliff as Angela. Maybe he does have it in for his longtime boss. Because putting that note on Reddit, it's like he's trying to burn George."

"But why is he being so subtle? Why doesn't he just go to the *New York Times*?"

"I don't know. But get this—he planned for this possibility in 1969. That's why he took Angela's unfinished note. He's been saving it all this time."

"Which means he never trusted George."

"You blame him?"

"No. But if he wants to pin Angela's murder on George, why now?"

Ray said, "Maybe he isn't trying to burn George, but it's something else."

"Huh. I need to get into Wheezer's computer. Which is going to be hard if it's part of that system at Nichols's offices. But wait. How would he feel about George knowing about those crazy blog comments?"

"Asking my political opinion? That stuff would be a huge headache for George."

"Not to speak of posting Angela's note and the safehouse account on Reddit. He wouldn't want George knowing he was Levity-z. George wouldn't think for a moment before snooping on Wheezer's computer on the system."

"So?"

"Maybe he did that stuff from another computer. A personal one. When you first found those blog comments, I dug a little to see who Levity-z was."

"So get out your power shovel."

I was five minutes in when Ray asked, "How long is this going to take?"

"As long as it does. And longer if you don't let me do it."

"We skipped dessert." He pointed toward town. I nodded and he left.

I worked. Ray returned fifteen minutes later. He could see I was entranced and handed me something chocolaty. It seemed to help the process.

And whatever he was doing now, he was being good. A half hour later, I said, "I'm inside Wheezer's computer. You're looking at his desktop."

"It's scary how you can do that."

"It is. I'm going to his web browser first and look at the history." I read. "*Sacramento Bee*—his local paper. Fox News. The Weather Channel. Google Maps. He doesn't go online much. And tends to do the same things."

I pointed to the computer screen. "He visited a Bible study site."

Ray asked, "What about those blogs he commented on? And what about Reddit?"

I searched back over the last months. "He must have deleted those items."

"Which means we have a selective history."

I clicked around. "Here's a funny thing—there are no bookmarks."

"Maybe he doesn't know how to use them."

"Everybody knows how to use them." I clicked on the email folder. A dialog came up asking for a password. "Ah. Getting touchy now."

"I'm going to get under the hood, check a few things…" I was only poking around for a few seconds when I saw some scary stuff. I shrunk back from the screen like it was radioactive. "That was close. It was the same when I tried to get into the system from the governor's office."

"This guy's got computer chops?"

"More likely it's a legacy from Nichols's system."

I was about to close the laptop when Ray pointed to the screen and asked, "What is that, 'Insurance'?"

"I don't know, car, maybe he owns a house?" I clicked on the folder and the same alert demanding a password came up as before. "Weird. Why would his insurance policies be under the same protection as his email? Now I want to get into both of them. Hold on."

I called Annie and left a message. "Call me, soon as you can."

Ray had gotten on the computer while I called. He said, "I just looked up that phrase 'through a glass darkly.' It's originally from the Bible."

"More religious stuff. Maybe that explains him stealing the nuns' gravestones."

"Who knows. Maybe he's got a collection."

I took a break and went out on the deck. The air was still cool but the fog on the bay had vanished. Fickle stuff.

***

By three I hadn't heard back from Annie. But George emailed, saying, *We need to meet.*

We went back and forth:

OK. Someplace public.

Top of Coit Tower?

I shuddered. *No.*

Crissy Field, outside The Warming Hut?

I looked it up. It was right on the bay. No cliffs. *Good.*

Now?

OK. See you there in half an hour?

I told Ray about the meeting.

He asked, "What the hell does he want?"

I shrugged.

"You want me to come as backup?"

"No. I managed him fine last time. And there's no place for him to throw me off of. We're meeting at sea level."

Rush hour had the bridge tied up coming into Marin from San Francisco. But traffic headed south was fine. I made it to Crissy Field in twenty minutes. I was early, as usual. I got out. It was clear with a strong chilly breeze from offshore. Frolicking dogs swarmed across the grass, barking up a storm at one another. Mingus would have loved it.

George was standing by the water near The Warming Hut. There were almost as many tourists as dogs. Nothing to be afraid of.

I walked up to him. He looked at my hair. "That was smart, hiding that ponytail last time." He offered a hand and I reluctantly took it. He still had the firm grip, but seemed shrunken, like the stuffing had fallen out of him. We walked a path by the edge of the bay.

I asked, "How did you get my email address?"

"The same place I found out where you live?" George raised his hands in a conciliatory gesture. "I'll explain. I want to try to work with you."

"Work with me?"

"Whatever else has happened, right now you and I have the same problem."

"Wheezer."

He paused for a beat. "You've been busy."

"Trying to stay alive."

George nodded. "My associate has gone rogue."

No shit.

"And I can't seem to find him."

"You must know where he lives."

"I don't. He's always been...secretive. Now he's really disappeared. I'm clueless with computers. You know them. You found out who he is. I need you to find him."

"Why don't you get your spook buddies to find him? Your father's friends."

His eyebrows flew up and he stopped walking. He peered at me like I was still wearing a disguise. "You've been *really* busy. Listen, that's ancient history. I don't have the remotest connection with Langley anymore."

It sounded like he was sad about it. Or was playing sad. "That stuff you told me about your buddies and rendering was all a bluff?"

"Yes."

"Who does your computers? This Wheezer?"

He scoffed and started walking again. "No. This muncher geek at the office."

"Muncher?"

"You know, carpet muncher. Dyke."

Annie. Now I knew why she'd been so cagey. Better her than the CIA. "She's the one who figured out what I do for a living! You told *her* to investigate me, not some spooks."

He nodded.

"If I'm going to help you—and I'm not saying I will—you need to start telling me the truth. Why did you kill Waldo?"

"I didn't kill him."

"You ordered Wheezer to."

George waved his hand. "No. I'll get to that."

The wind had picked up, cutting right through my jacket. I zipped it up but was still cold.

"Let me tell you the whole thing from the beginning. A while ago, Wheezer put some kind of alert thing on his computer, so that if anybody searched for my name, we'd know."

"A Google trap."

"Whatever. Your friend the lawyer came up. He was looking into me."

"Which got you thinking about Angela. Who you killed. You worried that he had put something together about that night."

"How could he do that after all that time? No, I was just worried Waldo would remember who I was and would out me to the governor. Nichols doesn't know some…things about my past."

That was what Ray and I had thought. "Aside from Angela, your name change."

He looked at me then away.

I asked, "Did you know Waldo and Buzzy were in touch before they were killed?"

"No."

He was lying. "They were talking about this gay reparative therapy thing."

"I told you before, I know about that bill. I didn't know they discussed it. All I know is that I sent Wheezer to talk to Waldo to find out what he was digging for. And…OK. I told Wheezer to back him off. But Waldo was stubborn."

Waldo was.

"So I told Wheezer to meet with him again."

"To kill him."

"No! I just told him to scare him."

"Scare him?"

"Explain to him the consequences of his actions. *Political* consequences. Wheezer told me it was an accident. They got in an argument, it was wet, and your friend slipped. But Wheezer was afraid of me. Then. Which means he could have been lying."

Damn. I was never going to know what actually happened to Waldo.

"Except…" He shook his head. "Wheezer never lied to me. He's obsessed with rules. He's a guy who does things strictly by the book." He laughed.

"What?"

"That book would be the Bible. He comes from a strict fundamentalist family. Listen, I go to church with the governor, but it's basically part of my job. Just like you lefties smoke pot and listen to NPR. Wheezer is very devout." He looked at me. "As soon as I found out Waldo was dead, I fired him."

"When was that?"

"A few days after Waldo fell. As soon as I got back from vacation." George sighed. "He got really angry. He hit me."

He gestured to his nose. The bandage was gone, but the bruises were still there, yellowing.

"Was he always violent?"

"Never before that! He was upset. You have to understand, I'm all he has. Had."

"I don't understand."

"Aside from me and his parents, he's never had any kind of relationship with anyone. Now he doesn't have a job anymore, and he's way too weird to get one. And I didn't just fire him. I *banished* him from my life. I know how he thinks. It was like casting him into the outer darkness."

Speaking of the Bible. "Then he killed Buzzy. Why?"

We'd reached the end of the path and stopped.

"I have no idea. But the fact that he pushed Buzzy off the same cliff as, um…"

You pushed Angela. I took a step toward him, felt my fists balling and coming up. He stepped back.

"…Angela, makes me thinks he's trying to link me to it."

"To frame you."

"Not exactly. I think it's more like a warning. He's been leaking stuff on the Internet, too."

I nodded. The Reddit stuff. We headed back down the path.

"I don't think he's trying to get me in trouble, so much as telling me he has power over me. I think he's trying to get me to take him back."

I said, "Buzzy was bludgeoned to death before he was pushed. And his body was washed in blood, in some kind of ritual. Does that sound like your boy?"

He looked frightened. "He's gone way too far." But he hadn't denied my suggestion.

"Farther than you think. He just killed Rick."

"What?" He shook his head. "Rick's one of *ours!* Not just a Republican. A Christian. And Wheezer is tighter with Jesus than…"

"You, for sure."

George ignored me. He said, "I can't see how Wheezer could do it." But he was looking away, like he was accepting the possibility.

I asked, "What exactly did he do for you?"

"This and that. I'm really not getting into that. But we go way back."

"Yeah, back to your dad's safe house."

"You saw the thing he posted on Reddit."

"Yeah."

"How the hell? Never mind. I thought I was doing him a favor, letting him watch. Then I was going to let him into the room. Get that weirdo's ashes hauled. About the only way it was going to happen. Instead he freaked out."

"Did you give him acid before you brought him there?"

"No! I'm not stupid. But my dad gave it to me like candy."

"Did you watch your dad from that window? Did he watch you?"

He glared at me. "Don't *you* get all judgmental on me. It was just harmless fun."

Fun, fun, fun… Rape and murder. I glared at him. "Why do you think that scene freaked Wheezer out so badly?"

"I didn't know then. I hadn't known him that long. But I got it soon enough. He won't let anybody close to him."

"He has problems with intimacy."

"No, I mean *literally*. He can't stand to touch anyone. He won't shake hands, even wearing gloves. So how could he get laid?"

Gloves. I flashed on him delivering the acid that night, how he'd kept his gloves on. "You think he's a virgin?"

He didn't answer right away. He put his hand to his mouth. "You'd assume. Except…he took me to his house once back when I was in college. There were Bibles up the wazoo. The place was spotless, so neat I was afraid to sit, afraid I'd mess up the chair. His mother was actually beautiful. But she never smiled. The creepy thing was that she hovered over him the whole time we were there. Stroking his hair, holding his arm, all the time speaking in this teeny little voice, like she was a girl herself. He just sat frozen in his chair, his face white as parchment."

"Touching him. You think…"

"I can't say it never crossed my mind." He shuddered.

Some stuff was too pervy even for one-way-glass George. "And his father?"

"He wasn't there. Wheezer never talked about him. But look, it doesn't take Sigmund Freud to know this is a kid who's afraid of *some* parent. Afraid of terrible punishment. That's why he was always terrified of me. Maybe the father was an ogre. Or it could have been the mom. She was scary enough."

"Are you afraid he's going to kill you?"

He groaned. "I hadn't quite gotten there yet. But I wouldn't put anything past him at this point. And you know, I think he might be following me. He's good at that—it's one of the…"

Things he used to do for you.

"I think he might have followed me to the Fairmont when you and I met." George said.

Shit. "What about today, here?"

His gaze darted around. So did mine. There were just people with dogs, and a harmless-looking jogger.

George said, "This is a very public place."

But he didn't sound totally convinced.

I said, "Well, I'm worried about him killing *me.* I'm the last of the Four Brothers. Why would he be killing us? And why has he left me for last?"

"I have no idea." He stopped and turned to me. We were almost back to The Warming Hut. "But here's what has to happen. You need to find him."

"Wait. Why do you need me, if you've got Annie?"

"That's the thing. She hasn't been returning my calls. I think she's gotten cold feet."

So she had quit.

I said, "Now this is very important. Did you turn the stuff she found out about me over to Wheezer?"

"No." But his gaze slid to the side.

"You're lying."

"I didn't give him that."

Maybe not. But he'd done something he wasn't owning up to.

George said, "Neither of us can go to the police."

True. "What would your dad do?"

Despite the situation, George laughed. "Oh, the old man had twenty-seven ways to Sunday to take care of some little dipshit like Wheezer. But I don't have his resources. You find him for me, and I'll take care of him."

"I find him, then you'll take care of him? Like you did Angela?"

George tried for a fierce look and failed. "Just let it go. That's ancient history. What I do with Wheezer is none of your business."

No way was I finding Wheezer for George. But I needed to keep him on the hook. "I'll think on it."

22.

Back at the houseboat, Ray and I sat on the deck with beers. Warm, clear, nice breeze coming off the bay. I told him about the meeting.

He said, "At least he has a plan. We find Wheezer, he kills him, and we go home."

"Ray!"

"Joke."

I glared at him. "You know what was odd? George gave me an in-depth psychological analysis of Wheezer. It seemed a trifle touchy-feely for a right-wing political operative."

"Hey, consider his dad—the psych in PSYOPS."

"Right." I told him about Wheezer's touch phobia.

Ray got the computer and brought it out, typed and read. "The no-touch thing's got a really sexy name—aphenphosmphobia. So much as put a finger on somebody with it and they go into a full-scale panic attack. It's no little nervous tic. Then add in what George suggested about his mother. This guy has serious problems."

"Yeah, but he's also, what do you call it? Functional. Which is *our* problem. Hold on. Rick was beaten to death. How could Wheezer do that if he can't touch anyone?"

"That's easy. He used a baseball bat. Isn't that the usual way? Plus, didn't he use a tire iron or something on Buzzy? What did the article on Rick say?"

"'Beaten'? 'Battered'? If he used a weapon, wouldn't it be 'bludgeoned'? I'm going to try to sneak into the Anaheim Police file." I took the laptop from Ray.

It took me ten minutes. I said, "As I suspected, this was a lot harder than the Middleburg Police site. He was found faceup on the floor of his receptionist's office. There were bruises all over the front of his body. They're assuming they were caused by *fists*. Weird."

"What, he just lay there while Wheezer hit him?"

"Hold on. There was a big bruise on the back of his head."

"Ah. Maybe another tire iron. He knocked him out first."

"I was at that office. He could have hidden to the side of the door, sandbagged Rick when he came out. Rick fell on his back."

"But why not kill him with the tire iron? Why not just shoot him?"

"It would have been easier to shoot Buzzy, too. And a gun really takes care of the no-touching thing. There's got to be some reason for all this.... elaborate stuff."

I read on. "Ah. Rick had a note pinned to him, too. Look at this."

Adultererz zhall zurely die. Vengeance iz mine. It iz written.

"It ends like the one on Buzzy. Except..."

"It's got a lot of *z*'s."

"A shit ton."

"'Adultererz.' Rick was stepping out on his wife with his secretary. But how would Wheezer know?"

"Hacked into Rick's email and found some love notes?"

"This fucking guy is everywhere."

Ray turned in his chair and looked at me. "I know you don't want to hear this, but maybe it's time to go to the cops."

Sharon, now Ray. I looked away but considered it. Just because my instinct was to stay away from them didn't mean it wasn't the thing to do. The answer was still no. "That just got even harder, with this MK-ULTRA business. They'll think we're conspiracy nuts. And we still don't have a shred of proof of anything."

"OK. But in the meantime, we've got to do something. Speaking of Wheezer being everywhere, we never figured out how he knew you were in LA."

"If he did."

"Come on, he killed Rick right after you left."

"Yeah. I guess I'm in a little bit of denial because it was such a close call. Hold on." I went back into Wheezer's computer, into a folder called "tools." A PDF, "Quantum Security Systems Products" caught my eye, seeing as to how security was my gig. I opened it. I felt a spark of excitement. "Look at this. Among other things, they sell GPS trackers. They claim to be 'impossible to detect.'"

"What are they for?"

"Putting on someone's car."

"That's easier than breaking into the houseboat. When did he get this?"

I looked at the creation date on the document, then shook my head. "He downloaded it last year. He couldn't know we were coming here."

"Then why was he looking for a tracking device?"

"Maybe he wasn't. They sell all kinds of other shit, too. And even if that's what he got, it's just part of his job, doing George's dirty work. But let's go check the car."

Ray followed me out into the parking lot to the rental car. I lay down on the pavement, scooted under, and started feeling around. I found the tracker in the right rear wheel well. Damn.

I got up. Ray said, "Find anything?"

I nodded.

"Show me."

"I left it on the car so he doesn't know we found it." I barked a mirthless laugh. "All this time I've been looking at whoever's doing this through my own narrow eyes—assuming he's doing everything like I would, with a computer. I couldn't understand why he didn't even *try* to hack into my laptop.

"But Wheezer's old, like us. He's old school. He knows about following someone with a car. Or putting a tracking device on it. They've been around forever. For all we know, he's watching us now with *binoculars*." I looked around. He wouldn't be on another boat. That would be too much hassle. The parking lot ended opposite the boardwalk at a windowless warehouse.

There was nowhere for him to hide. Still.

When we got back to Spider's, I Googled GPS trackers. I said, "There are two types. The passive type you retrieve gives you a log of where the car went. The active one sends out a signal every five seconds, which you can pick up on a computer, or a phone if you're on the move yourself. That's how he tracked me to LA, to Rick's. I'm sure glad I stayed at Frank's. I was going to go to a motel…it would have been the perfect place to ambush me."

"So he knows we're *here*."

"Yeah."

"Why hasn't he come after you?"

I thought. "Because it's too public here. And if he saw me, I was with you."

"So we're safe."

"No, staying here now would be pushing our luck. It's time to find a new home. You rented another car while I was in LA?"

"I did. And with all the excitement I forgot to return it."

"Good." I got a grocery bag from the kitchen. "Put in a change of clothes and I'll do the same. We leave the car with the bug here and take yours. He won't know we moved."

"Where are we going?"

"To a cheap motel."

"Tell you what. In case he's watching right now, I'll get the other car. You walk to the café with that bag and I'll meet you there."

We walked outside. Strong cooking smells wafted from a neighboring boat. Ray said, "I've never seen them, but whoever they are, they sure can cook."

"We'll eat soon as we're settled."

Just walking to the café I was hunched down, my eyes darting around like pinballs. I must look like a cartoon character, but I wasn't laughing. Being exposed on the Internet was bad enough. The idea that some psycho creep might be watching the real me was terrible.

When Ray got there, I checked the underside of his car. I got in and said, "No bug."

We found a motel next to Route 101. The traffic was loud outside. It was tolerable inside the room. Ray said, "It's clean, anyway."

"Depending on your standards."

Ray pulled the curtain open to the view of the parking lot and the back of a Home Depot. "I'm going to miss the view."

I wrinkled my nose. "I wonder when the EPA's going to get around to investigating whatever they soak the carpets with in these joints." I sniffed the bed. "Then again, this is Chanel Number 99 next to that stinky couch. The Wi-Fi better work."

"About that food?"

I was suddenly ravenous. In all the excitement we'd skipped lunch. The room came with the stack of takeout menus. We agreed on Chinese. Ray was studying the menu when Annie finally returned my call.

"You called?" She sounded as warm and fuzzy as before.

"Hold on…"

I said to Ray, "You mind getting food again?"

"Nope."

"I'll have the orange beef."

I didn't have to ask him to get beer. He left.

I said to Annie, "I just saw George again. I think you know him a little better than you let on."

"So? He's got a fat mouth."

"You worked for him, doing their computer security."

"Bet your ass. I gave them Fort Knox."

"He asked for that?"

She snorted. "No. A matter of professional pride."

"Which apparently involved hacking into my personal details."

She groaned. "That's what I get for trusting a Nazi. He said nobody would ever know. I didn't know who you were when he asked me to look into you. Doesn't matter, anyway. I quit working for him right after I talked to you."

"I'm curious, how did you get onto me?"

"You're old, right? Came up in this stuff with some ancient language like BASIC? You snooze, you lose in this business. It ain't for geezers. Let's just say there are things about the cloud you don't understand."

I suddenly pictured the cloud as a noisome patch of that San Francisco fog. What the hell hid inside there? Nothing good. Despite all that concerned me, her words burned. Because it was undoubtedly true. I felt like that scholar way back who'd known everything there was to be known. Computers had once been more or less like that, but who could know everything about the Internet?

"What about that blog about George?" I couldn't help a little rancor from slipping into my voice. "You dicked with the SEO, buried it on Google."

She laughed that awful laugh. "I'm proud of that shit!"

"But you're done working there. What are you doing now?"

"That's your fucking business exactly why?"

I needed to get through to her, if that was possible. "Because...now listen carefully. That guy you told me George was arguing with? His name is *Wheezer*. He killed Kaylee's boss, Waldo, and two other people. Friends of mine. And he..."

"You're fucking with my head. You making this up to get back at me, because I hacked your scene?"

"Believe me, it's all real. You still didn't answer the question of how you got onto me."

She scoffed. "George told me to find these guys who were at some college back in the dark ages. You were a little harder to find than the others, because you never graduated and your first name had changed. And I suppose you were more or less hiding. Until I plucked you out of your little hole."

She was enjoying herself. "I popped 'Hutchinson organ player' in my buddy Google, found an article on your 'band,' though with a fossil like you I can't imagine you made what I'd consider music. Ran the dates and I had the right geological era."

"But how did you find out I code, where I live, my fucking phone number?"

"Believe it or not, you and I travel in some of the same circles. And you do have a bit of a rep, if that makes you feel any better. So I know this twerp who worked on something with you. He fed me the 'I could tell you but then I'd have to kill you' line—as if *that* wasn't old when I was a kid—but then I brought up a very embarrassing piece of personal information. Opened him up like a can of pickled kale."

Damn. I knew who she was talking about. I'd been safe as long as: a. no one had a reason to out me, and b. they didn't know one of a few colleagues in the business who knew me.

George had the reason, and he knew Annie, with her macho geek motivations. "You put up that fake website on me."

"My bad. My very very bad! You have to admit it was hilarious."

"I don't have to admit anything. You have no idea how it fucked me up."

"You left yourself wide open. Being one of us, you should know better. Can't stand the heat, get the fuck out of the kitchen."

I didn't have time for one-up games. "Those friends of mine from George's college? They've all died recently. Look up their obituaries. Aldo Caron in the *San Francisco Chronicle*. Richard Arlington in the *Anaheim Register*. Eldon Stockbridge, *Middleburg Sentinel*."

"Okaaay."

I heard her typing.

After a few minutes she said. "Weird. They have some disease?"

"They were murdered by Wheezer. And Stockbridge? You might know him as Buzzy. Buzzy Six." His email address.

"Oh." Her voice took on a semblance of human feeling.

So she'd hacked Buzzy's email. "Oh yes. This Wheezer maniac painted him in his own blood and pinned a homophobic screed to him. And Wheezer never would have known about him if you hadn't hacked his emails to Waldo."

I was laying the guilt trip on a little heavy, but I had to get her to help me.

She said, "I just got George into their accounts. I didn't read the emails." A strangled sound came through the phone as she gave up. "OK, OK, OK. I'm your slave."

"I need you to get me into this Wheezer's email. He has—or had—an account in the system you built. I'm into his laptop, but the mail is still locked up. And this folder, 'Insurance.' Do you know anything about that?"

"No. But I know how he locked it. I showed George this very simple thing, a black box you drag stuff into, and it's tight as a snail's asshole. He must have showed this guy."

"How come I couldn't find it?"

"It's in a special folder buried deep in some obscure application folder with the sexy name 'Xp734.' No reason anyone would look at it. You need the same sixteen-character password to get in, same as with his email and the insurance file."

She gave it to me, and I wrote it down.

She said, "Give me the IP address of Wheezer's computer."

"Why not." I gave it to her. "I *did* get into George's email."

"No, you didn't."

"Sure did. But didn't find what I was looking for."

She sputtered. "That's his *personal* account, which he set up himself, believe it or not. He's a moron with computers. I set up another account for him, for sensitive stuff… Fuck."

"What's the problem?"

"George had emails with me."

"I need to get in."

"Ah, fuck it to hell. I already told you the worst stuff."

She gave me the keys to George's secret email.

She said, "You done?"

"For now."

"Oh, here's a little icing for your cake. I was poking around in this Wheezer's computer as we spoke. You know he has a blog called 'Judgment Dayz'?"

"No."

"He hid it. Spelled with a 'z.' Weird. And…look at this. Some of it is published on the web. But you might want to look in the drafts folder, too. You'll find them in that black box."

She hung up. Now that I was done playing cool with her, I felt the burn. She'd gotten over on me as a coder. Was still doing it right while we were on the phone. How could I have missed Wheezer's blog? Soon as I was done with this thing, I needed to bone up. The cyber world wasn't waiting for me to catch up.

Ray arrived with the food. We inhaled it, then began working on the six-pack of Anchor Steam Ray had bought. I told him about the conversation with Annie. We sat side by side on one of the beds. He surfed his laptop while I dug into the small pile of George's emails from the black box.

I groaned. "This may be a secret account, but he's still being cagey as hell." I showed Ray a couple of typical ones:

1/14 G to W: Are we good to go?
W: Consider it done.

1/27 G to W: Any luck?
W: Still working on it. Soon.

3/4 G to W: Let me know after Thursday. Easy does it. But not too easy.

Ray said, "*W* is Wheezer."

"Yeah, but what are they doing?" I kept reading. "Hold on." I showed him one:

5/14 G to W: Rockin n rollin in San Berdoo! That's my kind of ugly.
W to G: Just the appetizer.
G to W: Can't wait.

I asked, "San Berdoo?"

"San Bernardino. Near LA. I know that from some song."

I Googled the town and date, but I had no idea what I was looking for. "Wheezer was doing something for George here. Something bad. I'm going to call Kaylee."

She picked right up. She said, "San Bernardino, late May? Hold on while I Google something." A minute later she asked, "The fourteenth?"

"Yeah."

"OK. This is kind of inside baseball, but in my world it was a big deal. An article was published that day about a local immigration activist, supposedly describing the smoking gun in a scandal he's involved with. I was suspicious, because the author is super right wing. The whole deal smells. This activist guy, Gonzalez, has been a thorn in Governor Nichols's side. Gonzalez is a hero from the Gulf War and rising fast. Here's where it gets interesting. He keeps getting accused of stuff. He's at a protest earlier in the year and some anti-protester says Gonzalez punched him. But it's not on camera. Then details from his messy divorce are leaked and exaggerated by certain bloggers. But the 'smoking gun' was a bunch of Gonzalez's emails involving some sex ring. He swears on a stack of Bibles he never sent them, and this guy is a serious Christian. But it doesn't matter. Because since then he's really lost credibility, especially with women."

I asked, "You think somebody's been setting him up?"

"I know it. There are too many coincidences. But whoever's been doing it is good. There's no evidence."

"Was that protest on a Thursday in March?"

"How did you know?"

"I may have the evidence you need." I told her about George's emails.

"But how did you get them?"

"Well…" I gave her a vague explanation.

"I can't use them in court. But at least I know now exactly who's been doing it. Thanks."

I told Ray what she'd said. He said, "This is classic rat-fucking. It started with Nixon's dirty tricks. So that's what Wheezer's been doing for George."

I scrolled to the emails from the summer, before Waldo died.

8/12 G to W and A: Headed out to vacation. But still on the job.

Ray said, "So George wasn't lying about being on vacation. *A*? Annie?"

"It could be." I read forward, then looked at Ray. "I think we just caught a break. Before his vacation I'll bet he was saving the explicit orders for in-person meets. But once he was gone, he had to tell his people what to do via email."

8/15 A to G: Someone has been searching for your name online. Aldo Caron.

Ray said, "Who's that?"

"Waldo. That's his real name. Long story. And A *is* Annie. She set up that Google trap. That's how she knew Waldo was looking."

8/16 G to W: The attorney Caron, in San Francisco, is looking into me. You might remember him from college. Go see that commie piece of shit and find out why.

I said, "A few hours later that day, we've got this."

G to A: Can you get into Caron's computer?
A: LOL. Does he have one? If so, I'm in there.
G: I need his emails for recent months.
G to W: Look through these emails.

I said, "There's an attachment, a zip file…" I opened it. A stack of emails. "These are Waldo's."

"Buzzy's in there."

"That's how they got to him."

G to W: Pay Counselor Caron a visit.
8/18 W: I met with Caron. He wouldn't tell me anything.
G: He's playing the tough guy. You know how to soften him up.

Ray said, "Kill him?"

"I don't think so. George said he wanted Wheezer to scare him."

8/19 G to W: How did the meet go?

I said, "That's the day Waldo was killed."

Wheezer hadn't replied right away. Instead, there was an email from George to Annie.

> *8/19 G to A: That Hutchinson? I want you to make a website for him,*
> *like he's looking for computer business. Then manipulate the SEO so it*
> *ranks high.*
> *A: Fun times!*

My eyes bugged. "That lying sack of shit! He acted all innocent about the nuns' gravestones. The website was *his* idea. He's got serious acting chops. Why lie about that?"

"Maybe he ordered it made but never looked at it. The pictures of the gravestones didn't go up until later when you got broken into."

I scoffed.

Ray said, "Yeah, he must have seen it."

"If he lied about the website, what else is he lying about? About Wheezer going rogue? Is he somehow setting me up?"

23

8/20 G: Your email broken or something? HOW DID THAT MEET GO???
    8/21 W: I'm sorry. My email was down. It's fixed. And so is that
    problem. I'll fill you in when you get back tomorrow.

I said, "Wheezer was afraid to let him know he'd killed Waldo, at least in an email."

8/22 G to W: My office, tonight, 10.
    8/23 G: You know that you broke my fucking nose? OK. Let me explain
    how it's going to be from here on in. I don't want to see you. I don't want
    to know you're alive. If I even hear from a friend of a friend of a friend
    that he heard you fart down in Tijuana, I'm sending my father's old pals
    after you. They've got some new toys. Ever think about what it's like to
    drown? That can be arranged. Do that for a few weeks then they'll ship
    you to Egypt. How about picking your nose without your fingernails? Oh.
    And I have it on good authority that those sand nigger spooks don't abide
    by our rules regarding pleasure on the job. Let me put it in plain Englaise:
    they're gonna fuck you til their cocks come out of your nose.

Ray said, "Nice. You think he meant it?"

"He told me all that CIA stuff was a bluff. My guess is he's still bluffing. It gives me the creeps anyway. But he wasn't lying about the break with Wheezer."

"I understand George's interest in Waldo, then maybe Buzzy, who he might have thought was plotting against him with that gay conversion thing. Why the interest in you?"

"That's one of the pieces that's still missing. But I can see it. Waldo leads to Buzzy, and George gets paranoid. He remembers the Four Brothers and sends Annie to check into me."

"And you asking around about Angela could spell trouble."

"Another loose end to tie up," I said.

***

I opened Wheezer's "Insurance" folder.

Inside I found the "Through a Glass Darkly" post from Reddit, Angela's note, and a third document:

The Night of the Storm

George hands me six hits of acid. He says, "A gift for Angela and the Four Brothers."

"That's five. The last one?"

"Use your imagination. Make sure Angela stays in her room."

I go to Angela's room and give her the drug. As I'm leaving, she says, "Where are you going?"

"The Four Brothers' house."

"I'm coming!"

"No! George said…"

"Who cares about George?" And THE WHORE puts her painted face in mine so I can smell her breath. She laughs at me, saying, "I'm going to kiss you, boy, if you don't let me come!"

I shove her away and slam the door in her face. I go and deliver the capsules. When I come out, she's there, in the snow, waiting for me! This time she does kiss me, before I can get away. I run to my apartment and thank the Lord she doesn't follow. The snow's getting very deep. I eat the last capsule.

I was on the verge of shivering, a combination of the reading material and the cool breeze coming in the window. I closed it and opened another beer. Ray followed me. I was actually ahead of him.

I said, "It just like Angela to tease someone like that, pretending to come on to Wheezer. And Sharon said he was *stalking* her."

Ray got up and paced.

I said, "What's the matter?"

"Hold on…fuck! What if *Wheezer* killed Angela? He thinks she's coming on to him and he's attracted. At the same time, he's calling her a whore. This is classic psycho sex killer stuff. He wants her, doesn't want her, the conflict's killing him, so he solves it by killing her."

"I told you, I'm sure George did it. And that sounds like psychobabble."

We went back to reading.

Then I descended into the darkness, into the pit of hell.

Ray said, "Looks like he had as bad a trip as you did."

George comes to my apartment. He says, "You have to get to Angela's room right away, clean everything up. There's a bust coming."

"What about here? And your place?"

"Don't worry. Nobody will bother us. My father…" He gives me a look—Big George is going to fix it. "Take some of her clothes—a suitcase if you find one. Make it look like she just left. And next week, when people start wondering where she is? Say you heard she was sick of the cold and left for California."

I said, "Wheezer started that rumor. Who would have believed that weirdo?"

"It doesn't matter with rumors. Once they start, they have a life of their own."

Up in Angela's room I clean up her drug mess. There's white powder

everywhere. Filthy clothes that stink of her. I stop breathing and my
skin crawls as I stuff them in a suitcase and slam it closed.
I take her note.

Now I was shivering. As I read this alternate account of the worst night of my life, I was falling back through the years, and the past was coming alive.

Ray didn't notice. He said, "You can nix my theory about Wheezer killing her."

I nodded. "George killed her and made Wheezer cover it up. Which sealed their working relationship. They had the goods on each other."

"But George's was the greater crime. I know we were talking about someone framing George for Buzzy. But Wheezer setting up the frame thirty-nine years ago? That's way too much of a stretch."

I got into Wheezer's email account and read. "Damn. This is the other end of the same stuff that was in George's folder. There's nothing new. George is the only guy he emailed with."

"Which tends to confirm what George told me, that he's all Wheezer had."

"Let's look at his blog."

I opened it. Garish primary colors and mismatched fonts leapt from the page.

Ray winced. "Ugly website design is one of the telltales that you're on an extreme site."

"You said my site was ugly."

"Not nearly this bad. Plus, Annie was doing that as a joke."

JUDGMENT DAYZ

It led with a quote:

"Liberals are like Slinkies: good for nothing, but you smile as you push
them down the stairs."

I said, "Cute. A lot of low-hanging *s*'s in this motto. I wonder why he didn't turn any of them into *z*'s like the name?"

"He didn't want to misquote whatever genius came up with it?"

I scrolled down to the bottom of the blogroll. "The earliest post is from late spring."

"WHAT IS RIGHTEOUSNESS?"

Righteousness is the quality that God DEMANDS of us if we are to meet Him in heaven.

I read on, shaking my head. "This is some snoozy shit. He quotes scripture then explains, like he's some kind of theologian. But this one's a little zingy: 'The right is righteous, just as the left is sinister, the path of the serpent, of evil.'"

I read a few more posts then skipped to a few weeks before Waldo died. There was a piece cross-posted from another blog:

"PUTTING SODOMITES TO THE SWORD"
By The Reverend Roger Hall

The Bible says:

Lev. 20:13—**If a man also lie with mankind, as he lieth with a woman, both of them have committed an abomination: they shall surely be put to death; their blood shall be upon them.**

God's word is clear. The homosexual is to be killed. But who is to do God's work?

The civil authority, the magistrate, who

Rom. 13:4

beareth not the sword in vain: for he is the minister of God, a revenger to execute wrath upon him that doeth evil.

America is a Christian nation. Every official must act in accordance with the word of God, and put the sodomites to the sword.

Rev. 21:8—**But as for the cowardly, the faithless, the detestable, as for murderers, the sexually immoral, sorcerers, idolators, and**

all liars, their portion will be in the lake that burns with fire and sulfur, which is the second death.

The post ended with a picture of faceless people staggering through a lake of fire. I winced at the literalness of the image.

Ray said, "I dig it when Hieronymus Bosch does hell. But he had talent. This is just awful. But what do you expect—that last quote is from Revelations, last refuge of the religious nutcase."

Reverend Hall's post was followed by Wheezer's commentary:

READ YOUR BIBLE!

Finally, someone has the courage to speak the truth.
Their blood shall be upon them.
If the magistrate in a nation under God refuses to follow HIS word, then does he not sin himself? Who will put him *to the sword? STAND AND BE COUNTED, PEOPLE!*
READ YOUR BIBLE and ACT IN RIGHTEOUSNESS!!!

The words were just letters on a screen, but they seemed palpable. Because... I said, "He read this stuff. Believed it. And acted on it. 'Their blood...'"

"The blood of the homosexuals. Wheezer put Buzzy's blood on him. 'Washed' him in it. That Lev. 20:13 quote is from Leviticus. It's the most popular one in the Bible among homophobes. They use it to justify their hatred. What they conveniently leave out is that Leviticus applies the death penalty to a raft of heterosexual sins. Not to speak of shellfish eating and wearing different fabrics at the same time. Wheezer was plenty primed by the time he got to Buzzy."

I focused on the faint sound of the cars rushing by on 101 outside of the room. Because I felt myself being sucked into the computer screen, into arguing with these lunatics. "So it's just a bunch of ancient hooey."

"Not if you believe in it. And let's unpack what Wheezer's actually saying.

If the authorities won't do the holy killing prescribed in the Bible, then *they* need to be killed. He's advocating sedition—armed revolt against the government."

I said, "With swords? Good luck with that against the US Army. Shit. Buzzy bled out from that wound in his neck. You think Wheezer used a sword?"

"I wouldn't put it past him."

I said, "Where's the printout of that first Reddit post?" I found the page. "He uses that same word here: abomination. What about this user name, Levity-z?"

"It's no joke after all. *Levit* is the beginning of Leviticus. And then he added that weird *z* of his."

"He's a religious fanatic."

"I think you're giving religion a bad name here. I suspect he's no more of a Christian than you or me."

"Or George."

"He's just cherry-picking the Bible to support his madness."

Someone walked by the door of our room and we both tensed.

Ray said, "You think that was old Leviticus, come to get us?"

I didn't laugh.

"No. It was Wheezer."

Ray didn't laugh.

We opened the last beers.

Ray asked, "Should I get more?"

"Not yet."

I scrolled to an article cross-posted from another blog, from the beginning of August:

The Culture War
By Michael Waters

American society is rapidly approaching a state of decay from which there can be no healing. Millions of babies murdered in the womb.

Unwed mothers living on the tax dollars of the righteous. Rampant drug abuse and sexual perversion of every flavor. "Moral relativism" and "tolerance" taught as gospel in major universities. The flaunting of all forms of authority. What do all these evils have in common?

The same roots—in the leftist "revolution" of the 1960s. Counterculture "Hippies," treasonous "antiwar" activists, and Marxist professors are the roots of today's evil, roots that have snaked deep into the very soil and bedrock of our culture. Is it any wonder that now our great institutions are crumbling, their pillars thundering to the ground? Pillars that the Lord God gave us—Faith and Obedience and Knowledge of Sin.

Before that black decade children respected and obeyed their parents, teachers, ministers, and coaches. Women worshipped their husbands as God intended, and all worshipped Him. Advertisements of the time show everyone smiling, and one wonders, Could anyone be that happy? But of course they were.

You look at the advertisements of today and all you see are piercings and tattoos on sluts, faggots, and drug addicts. Our once Shining City on a Hill is rapidly becoming a stinking ruin.

Ray said, "Those happy-go-lucky fifties! Before sex, drugs, and rock and roll."

"Because, as everyone knows, we invented sex."

"The fifties, when everyone was hardworking and good."

"And white and straight."

"And drank buckets of good old American gin—like George Hunter White."

"But Wheezer was a drug dealer."

"He got born again—as a wingnut. Not the first one. Look at Rick."

"Right."

"Blame it on the hippies. In fact, left-wing blogs satirize this meme with the acronym DFH, short for 'Dirty Fucking Hippies.'"

"Wasn't that Nixon's ploy, blaming the hippies?"

"It's an oldie but goodie. Reagan used it before he was president, when he was governor of California. What's amazing is that they're still working it, long after the last hippie hung up his tie-dyed shirt. Except for you and me, of course."

"Speak for yourself."

Ray eyed my ponytail and smiled.

Now I was really shivering, even with my jacket. And it wasn't the past or religious nuts doing it. I asked, "You cold?"

"You bet. Some summer they've got here."

I got up and found the heat. I turned it on but nothing happened.

We read Wheezer's commentary:

> *Mr. Waters describes the problem quite well. But where are his solutions? He speaks of the "Culture War"—well, where is his regiment? When is he mustering to battle? And what are his weapons? Words. Did we vanquish the Godless Germans and Japanese with words? No. WE KILLED THEM. With guns and nuclear weapons. Man, woman, and child.*
>
> *If you're not part of the solution, then you're part of the problem. Stand up and be counted.*

Ray said, "He ripped off that solution line from the Black Panthers."

"Good. They can sue him."

> *Mr. Waters speaks of the "roots of decay." The poisonous roots that are the roots of SATAN. Like THE SERPENT, they wind down into a time of darkness, like THE FALL before it: the 1960s. I WITNESSED those roots when they were but slender tendrils. I SHOULD HAVE CUT THEM THEN. Instead I watched them grow there under the earth, even as the hair grew long on all the heads of the wicked ones.*
>
> *Instead I WASTED my time with him. He smote the whore Angela for her wickedness and thus I believed him to be righteous, and followed him and did his bidding, even when it broke the COMMANDMENTS.*

He said, "The slow way is best. We will fight with votes. And words"
But his words were just more babble from Babylon, as of old: "Where the
rubber meets the road. Thinking outside of the box. Hitting the ground
running. Drilling down." And always, "At the end of the day."

Ray said, "I've got to say, I'm with him on that corprospeak. Guy starts
spouting that shit, I know he's either lying or a moron."

At the end of the day.
    Just words, because what has HE done?
    Only BETRAYED me, HIS FAITHFUL SERVANT, and CAST
ME OUT.
    It IS the end of the day. Night approaches with the thundering of
hoofs and unsheathing of zwords.
    Who will stand with GOD in the night of his vengeance? Who will
BE HIS VENGEANCE?
    It is the end of the day. Those that have only spoken will be counted
among mine enemyz.
    War is fought by GENERALS. A GENERAL needz an ARMY.
    When people see the proof of my works, they will come and join,
and vengeance WILL BE MINE.

Ray said, "When are these commentaries from?"

"The article was at the beginning of the month. They aren't dated, but the
last one has to be after the fight with George."

"He posted that 'Culture Wars' piece. He was thinking about it when he
killed Waldo. Then he started adding to it."

He looked at me. "I don't know exactly where we're getting, but we're
almost there."

"I'm afraid so."

"You notice we're seeing more and more z's?"

I nodded. "And his tone seems to be shifting. He's pissed off in the earlier
stuff. But this…"

"He's decompensating."

"Huh?"

"Psychobabble for coming unglued. Taking a one-way trip to Crazytown."

"Psychos are your department. Give me the tour."

"First of all, he's essentially narcissistic. And I don't mean your garden-variety self-centeredness. He not only sees himself as the center of the universe, but really as the only person in it."

"But what about George?"

"Wheezer doesn't see himself as separate from George. George is an extension of him, and at the same time a means to important ends, like money and a sense of purpose in life."

"So when George cut him off…"

"It upset the delicate balance he'd been maintaining his whole life. He lost his job, his money. His only human contact. And his purpose."

"Except he seems to have found a new one. Killing. Why doesn't he kill George?"

"Maybe because he's still enmeshed with him. Still sees him as a part of himself. I think leaking that Reddit stuff, his blog isn't him trying to frame George, but trying to get George back."

We read on.

The Great City of RIGHTEOUS MEN stood on its hill. And in that dark time from the zwamp crawled a stinking legion, bearing potionz and trickzter smilz and a clatter like the gnashing of Zatan's teeth, their "rock" muzic, with their "danzing," like the writhing of zerpentz.

The ARMY OF ZATAN INCARNATE: HOMOZ and LEZBEENZ and FEMINAZTIES, LIEBRULZ and COMMIEZ, TREEHUGGERZ, HUMANITIEZ, and RELATIVITYZ.

Every one of them will fall under the zword.

MY ZWORD.

But not until I have CUT THE ROOTZ OF EVIL.

Ray said, "You were right about this *z* business."

"Yeah, but what does it mean?"

"I don't know. He's always talking about what he smells—Angela's 'whore's breath.' How he could smell the real prostitute in his MK-ULTRA safehouse post *through glass*? Which seems impossible. Maybe he has a heightened sense of smell. But maybe he's imagining odors for some reason."

"Nasal hallucinations. I never had those on acid."

"Which I'm sure is a good thing. I'm going to take a leap here. The smell thing is connected to this *z* business. They're both signs of brain damage. Like he's got this kink in his head."

"From what?"

"George's coke, the Company's acid? Or when he was young. A parent could have bashed him in the head. It tends to scramble the brains."

I wished we had more beer.

Matthew
Mark
Luke
John

Air
Water
Earth
Fire

Winter
Zpring
Zummer
Fall

North
Zouth
Eazt
Wezt

Heartz

Zpadez

Diamondz

Clubz

Four

Fore

For

4

4

4

4

4

Z

Z

Z

Z

Zzzz

Zzzz

Zzzz

Zzzz

Zzzz Zzzz Zzzz Zzzz

Zzzz Zzzz Zzzz Zzzz

Zzzz Zzzz Zzzz Zzzz

Zzzz Zzzz Zzzz Zzzz

S iz the zerpent.

S iz curvez.

S is zin.

Curvez r hipz & breaztz r roots of ZIN.

Straighten out all the curvez.

Ray said, "Wow. This stuff is so whacked it's making *me* feel a little crazy."

"I can relate. He seems to have added fours to the *z*'s."

"*Magical* fours."

"What do you mean?"

"I don't know, exactly. It's like he thinks 4's and z's have some kind of supernatural power."

"Why?"

"Why does a rabid dog bite who he bites? I don't know. Four. As in Four Brothers. Ah, man. Is that why he's killing you guys?"

"He didn't mention me in that list. But it could be. At least you have an answer to your question about Internet crazies. You wanted to know if it was all talk? This guy's a lot more than talk. And we'll never know, but it could be all that online bile set him off."

"I don't know about you, but without more beer I'm about to call it a night."

"When I was down in LA I found this article Buzzy wrote about your favorite subject, the sixties."

"Let me see it."

I Googled it and he read. He said, "Man, I wish I'd gotten to know the guy."

"I wish you had, too. I wish *I* had."

"Interesting that he saw that time as the beginning of a road to salvation. And whatever fuckwit Wheezer was quoting saw it as the path to hell."

"Exactly. You know me. I've always steered a thousand miles away from politics of any kind. Whenever I see extremes, I tend to assume the truth must be somewhere in the middle. But this is different. I've actually got a dog in this fight. Buzzy was right. Wheezer is wrong. He thinks he's on the side of the angels. But he's the devil in this. And not just him."

Ray smiled. "You dip into Spider's acid stash before we split? Because this doesn't sound like you. But I like it."

I hit the latest article on Wheezer's blog: "Worzhipping Falze Godz." I gave up after a few paragraphs. "We're out of beer. And I am sick to death of religious diatribes, and sick of z's."

"Speaking of z's, I'm going to crash."

24.

The next morning, we went out to breakfast in Mill Valley. It was after ten on a weekday and the place was crowded.

Ray said, "Either we're seeing a lot of power breakfasts or people up here don't work."

"They don't seem to in the city, either."

"*We're* working. What's the next step?"

"We smoke Wheezer out."

"Huh?"

"I set up a meeting with him, he shows…"

"Whoa. You want to meet that guy? He's like the plague."

"I'm talking in public. And getting Kaylee involved. Hey, maybe I meet him, you find his car and stick a bug on it."

"He'll find it. He's a pro. Even if he doesn't, then what?"

"All right. I'll email him. Put out a feeler."

"Even that…"

***

Back at the motel, I got on the computer to email Wheezer and found one from George.

> *We need to meet again. How about the Sutro Baths, around 7 this evening. Got a dinner at the Cliff House.*

I showed it to Ray.

He asked, "What's he want now?"

"No idea. But this is my chance to confront him on that fake website, find out why he's lying. Have you heard of the Sutro Baths?"

"No."

"You look them up. I'll call Jeannie. She must know."

She said, "Hey. I was just thinking about you." She sounded happy to hear from me.

"And me of you." Though it was not why I'd called. "Have you seen that brown car?"

"No. But I just got back from Santa Cruz. Which did me a world of good."

"I'm glad to hear it."

"Are you getting anywhere with…"

"Yes. We've learned a lot. And may be about to learn more. This George I told you about wants to meet me at the Sutro Baths. What can you tell me about them?"

"They're right on the water, next to the Cliff House restaurant. They used to have swimming races there. I've seen photos, guys in those silly one-piece suits. It's a ruin now. It burned down in the sixties."

"Does anybody go there?"

"Tourists. And everybody goes there to watch the sunset. You and I were already there, almost. The Baths share a parking lot with Lands End."

I got off the phone. "That's weird. The Sutro Baths are near where Waldo died."

Ray shook his head and frowned. He pointed to a picture of the Baths on the computer. "Does that look safe to you?"

It looked like a ruin, like Jeannie said. Just a big funky pool next to the ocean. It was deserted in the photo. "Jeannie says the place is crowded around sunset. It doesn't seem dangerous, just sad. I'd put it in my museum, if I could move it." I scrolled to a picture of the ancient swimmers in those suits. "All these guys are long gone, and…"

Ray had been shaking his head and now interrupted me. "I don't like this."

I looked up. Morning sun streamed in the window. I took the computer and typed. "Sunset tonight's right around seven, when we're meeting."

Ray said, "I'm coming."

***

We got to the parking lot at around 6:30. I recognized it from when I was there with Jeannie.

We got out of the car and stood in the parking lot. I pointed to the path to the north of the parking lot. "That's where Waldo ran mornings."

Ray said, "Why is George meeting you here?"

"He's not exactly meeting me at Lands End. The place Waldo died is about a half mile up the coast…"

"I'm not buying it. George is playing you. He's been lying to you all along. He killed Waldo, or at least set him up, and he's doing the same with you."

"I admit, it's a little spooky. But if George was going to try something, why would he choose this place and tip me off?"

Ray shook his head.

"Hold on." I called Jeannie.

"Hi again."

"To somebody from out of town, say Sacramento, how well known are the Cliff House and the Sutro Baths?"

"The restaurant's famous. The Baths are fairly well known, too."

"If somebody came from Sacramento for a business dinner, would they eat at the Cliff House?"

"Happens every day of the week, I'd imagine."

"Would they know that Lands End is right next door?"

"I doubt it. That's more of a well-kept local secret."

"Thanks." I hung up. I told Ray what Jeannie said, then added, "I don't believe in coincidences, but this is one. There's no reason George should know Lands End is here."

"OK. But I'm staying close."

"Not too close. I don't want to chase him away."

As we walked toward the ocean, Ray said, "That fog is intense. Unless it burns off in the next few minutes, there isn't going to be any sunset."

We headed down a steep path. Rows of waves marched in from under thick fog, then disappeared under a wall at the shoreline, spewing licks of froth skyward. The ruins appeared: a large rectangular pool half full of water, surrounded by jagged clumps of wind-eaten concrete. The only swimmers were a flock of ducks. Dark cliffs loomed over the pool to either side, the higher one to our left capped by the Cliff House and the one to the right topped by a stone wall.

I swept my arm across the view. "It's like an amphitheater with the stage down there where the ocean is, backed by a curtain of fog."

Ray asked, "You're getting poetic in your old age! It does have a vibe, like one of those gloomy Romantic period paintings. David Caspar Friedrich, or…"

I help up a hand. "This is no time for an art history lesson." I pointed to a half dozen young people hanging around the edges of the pool, laughing and smoking. "There are people."

A minute later, the sun appeared, a cold silver disc. I said, "And there's the sun."

A minute after that, it vanished in the swirling mist. Ray said, "And there it went."

I glanced to the right into the fog, up the invisible coastline. *Where Waldo fell.* And I was back on the edge of that cliff with Jeannie… No. I was standing here on a flat rock about ten feet above sea level. I couldn't be spooking myself out.

I said, "I'm meeting him alone."

"I know. Where should I wait?"

I nodded to a path that led up to the northern promontory. "Up there. Stand back a few feet from that wall and no one will know you're there. Any trouble, I'll yell."

"It's a strange world where you get to trusting George Bowman."

"White. George White."

Ray nodded. He pointed to a black opening at the base of the northern cliff to our right. "That a cave?"

"Or a tunnel."

"You better hope so. Otherwise there might be a dragon."

The joke was weak, but I was reassured that Ray had made it. The place was definitely affecting my mood. Ray headed off up the path.

I waited by the pool. It got darker. It was impossible to tell if it was dusk or thickening fog. The ocean was now fully shrouded, just a roar behind the amphitheater curtain. The fog painted icy tears on my cheeks. I shivered.

I became aware of sounds that had been working on me subliminally.

Foghorns, each sounding its own lugubrious tone.

A quartet.

The four horns of the apocalypse. Ha.

Four. I flashed on Wheezer's nutball 4s…

I was sliding down inside, into some dismal place. I shook my head and opened my eyes wide. I'd been spending too much time with Ray, getting infected with his "poetry." Or maybe it was something in the water around here. The ocean, making everyone weird. I imagined mythological Sirens, lounging out there on that rock. My exes, my old flames, singing, Angela conducting, high on a rock like back then, sitting cross-legged on a ledge above the others, setting the beat for those waves with a fist full of yarrow stalks…

Where the fuck was George? I got my cell out. It was ten past seven. Time crawled at a time like this. He was just a little late.

A new darkness stole over the scene. Something told me this was the real deal this time, sundown. Minus the sun. An arsenal of lights winked on up at the Cliff House, doing their best to penetrate the mist and gloom. Down here they only made the scene that much drearier. The wind tore another hole in the fog and for a few moments a three-quarter moon appeared before the fog swallowed it.

Without a sunset, most of the kids had drifted away. A few lingered on the far side of the pool, indistinct. I heard an occasional burst of laughter— or was that the gulls?

A voice from the hill above, and I looked. George? No. A second voice joined the first. Both were loud and loaded. They must be strays from the Cliff House bar.

"She says, 'Whatya got, big boy?' and I say, 'An IPO,' and she says, 'The fuck is that?' and I say…"

Dot-com drunks. I'd thought that was all over.

They neared the bottom of the stairs and one of them saw me and let out a yell. "Scared me, dude. What're you doing down here?"

I scowled at him. He gave his buddy a frightened look and they weaved back up toward the bar.

OK. It was almost 7:30, and really dark. Time to bag it. Get Ray. Hit the Cliff House bar ourselves.

My back was to the tunnel opening. A voice rumbled from it, "Hutchinson," and I jumped.

George? It didn't sound like him. I whipped around to face the figure standing in the entrance. He hid in the shadows of the overhanging cliff, but I caught a black watch cap on his head. Something George would never wear. He inched closer and into the dim light from the Cliff House.

It took me a moment to recognize him. Time had treated him cruelly and had etched his face with deep fissures, erasing all but traces of the pretty boy. And the years had enhanced the distortion of his features. I looked into his eyes and forgot all that. They were dead and cold, with no sign of anyone in there.

I yelled, "Wheezer!" and took off for the stairs. I heard an answering yell from above—Ray!—and felt an excruciating pain at the back of my head….

***

I came to, more or less. It was pitch black. Something was wrong with my head. The back of it throbbed with sharp pain, but that wasn't all that was wrong. Despite not being able to see a damned thing, my vision was out of whack. My heart pounded hot blood to the back of my skull, but my thoughts, which should have been racing, revolved in lazy loops, like an old vinyl record at half speed. I started drifting out of consciousness.

I shook my head, dispelling a little of the brain fog, but it spiked the pain and I let out a groan. But now I knew that I was lying on my back with something cold and damp below me. And that I couldn't see because it was dark.

Wheezer's voice of a minute ago—or was it an hour?—came back to me, saying my name, Hutchinson. He sounded like he'd been gargling with kerosene.

The foghorns were oddly muffled, but still blew that Frisco quartet. Where was Ray? Up top. Up on the rock, up on the roof. *When this old world starts a-getting me down...*

I wised up half a notch. *Sand.* I was lying on wet sand. And it wasn't totally dark. I saw a

dim light. *The light at the end of the tunnel.*

Careful, there was a wicked *weasel* in this hole. Nasty fuckers, weasels, with sharp little teeth.

Not weasel. Wheezer. I'd yelled his name, and bam! I was lying here in the dark, a hole in my head, arms and legs full of Jell-O.

I crawled toward the light and reached the end of the tunnel. A chain strung across the opening, with a metal sign: End of Trail, which I could barely read, what with the letters squiggling about.

End of trail. I took it personally: a message from Wheezer. End of the line, bro.

I had to get the brain working. I shook my head. The pain flared hot and bright, but more of the fog cleared.

I'd seen him standing in a dark opening. Except...there was no chain across it. I turned around. Ah. A tiny, dim semi-oval of light. This tunnel had two ends. And this was the other one.

The back of my head. I'd been running from Wheezer...and he'd *hit* me. The same as he did Rick.

I scrambled up onto all fours, grabbed the chain and hauled myself upright. I kept ahold of the chain because my legs were rubber. I peered out into the night. There was a beach maybe ten feet below me, the ocean to my left and a cliff to my right. Ahead loomed a jumble of rocks, another cliff. Up the coast past it was Lands End.

Waldo...

I turned and staggered toward the light at the other end of the tunnel. Sand squished underfoot. I was pretty much myself again. Which was good, except that now there was nothing between me and the agony at the back of my head. *Keep moving.*

I heard a sound and stopped cold. Silence. I waited.

"Hutchinson!" The same sound came, louder, a skittering like a scorpion crossing the desert…

I reversed direction and crept toward the chain, staying to the side out of the dim light.

Wheezer hopefully couldn't see me. The sound behind me stopped. I reached the chain. The beach was only ten feet below, but my stomach still clenched at the thought of descending to it.

Fuck it. I willed my legs over the chain, pushed off with my feet, and landed on them, smashing my nose onto hard sand.

A new pain trumped the one at the back of my head, but a moment later the throbbing was back. Waves crashed to my left. The cliff to my right was sheer. The one in front of me didn't seem to be.

I dashed twenty feet across the beach to it and saw a rough path that wound steeply up a slot in the jumble of rocks. I ascended quickly, but the path was narrow enough that I felt safe. If I slipped, I could jam myself into the walls before falling. At the rate I was climbing, I should soon be on top, where I could find Ray.

Hope.

There was faint crashing, which got louder as I emerged a moment later from the slot. I was not on top, but on a ledge with the edge of the sheer cliff at my feet. The ocean raged far below, buried in fog which was slapping me cold in the face.

I turned and looked up at a rock incline of about eighty degrees, its top also hidden by fog. I was going up. At that thought, my pulse started ticking in my neck like a crazy clock.

I forced my arm to reach up for a nub of rock, a handhold. It locked up, refusing. A battle of wills ensued between me and the fear. With a painful, almost audible crunch of bone, I won, a shaking hand reaching up and gripping a knob of rock. It was hard and cold.

I pulled myself up a few inches. But now it was my foot that mutinied.

Make it move. More bone grinding against bone. I got a foot onto something and rose another six inches. Rinse and repeat. As I rose, I became more exposed to the icy fog blowing in from the ocean. It sprayed the raw back of my head with searing pain. Behind it, I sensed a vast emptiness.

The mental fog blew into my head again. Those clever fish from the Golden Gate Bridge were at it again, casting up from the bottom of the sea and onto the cliff, hooking my shirt collar, my sleeves. They snared my eyes, tugging at my head, turning it, even as I told myself, *Don't look down!* But I did.

Mercifully, there was no ocean, just blank, cold white with invisible crashing behind it. It was rhythmic, like the pulse slamming in my neck, like the seasons. Those waves were the sound of wicked time itself, beating its inexorable way to the final chord. It wouldn't be long now. A gust of wind unveiled the moon and the tips of waves lashing the bottom of the cliff a mile below. A moment later, moon and waves were swallowed in white, but now there was no denying just how high I was.

I turned my face back to the cliff. In my moment away from it, my legs had become sluggish. Now they surrendered to paralysis, starting with my feet. The sensation rose to my hips and past. It hit my diaphragm, and my breath escaped to the top of the lungs, rasping, sour as it blew back to me from the rock in front of my face.

I willed my left leg to climb. It refused, but then with a jerk moved on its own, trembling, then jacking up and down. I'd heard about this from a rock climber. *Sewing machine leg*, he called it, barking a derisive laugh at all the weenie climbers out there before going on to brag about scaling El Cap in Yosemite. Arrogant prick.

Now the right leg joined the left in the sewing machine business, jacking up and down in tandem. If they didn't stop, they were going to jack me right out into space.

Angela's face appeared in my mind—long curls, a wicked smile playing at the corners of her mouth like she was about to say something smart. How could she smile at a moment like this? Childish, but she couldn't help it, she'd never grown up. Now her face was melting, morphing into that of one of the

Japanese girls who had stared into the devil's sun and been burned.

Buzzy's voice, soft and calm even in this moment, mouthed a word: *compassion.* Compassion for poor girls and silly Angela, and for myself, stuck halfway up this miserable cliff running from a madman.

A flame burst in my chest, burning with pity and sorrow. At its white-hot center was a hard kernel of desire to live. The feeling spread from my chest and surged out into my arms and down into my legs. It propelled me, clawing, scrambling, practically *flying* up the rock, accompanied by a roar that drowned out the waves. My scream.

I reached the top of the cliff and dove forward, flopping down onto flat rock. The relief was almost unbearable. I'd stopped screaming. The rock muffled the waves. Louder were my legs beating a tattoo on the rock.

25.

I pushed up and rolled into a sitting position. Wheezer sat facing me, cross-legged, maybe eight feet away. I flashed on one of the Tibetan demons in Buzzy's Thangka paintings. Wheezer seemed no more real, no more probable to be sitting there. And he was as still as a Buddha, not acknowledging my presence with so much as a glance.

Where were we? Not quite at the top of the cliff. We sat on a truncated spire of rock, roughly square, roughly ten feet to a side. I'd just ascended the side facing the ocean. The other three sides ended in darkness. More cliffs.

How the fuck had he gotten up here? There must be another way up. Or else he could fly....

I stared at him. In my peripheral vision I caught scraps of mist skittering across the moon. Its light flickered on Wheezer, herky-jerky like an old-time movie. It was lighter up here than in the tunnel. I could see now that he wore a black quilted bodysuit, and black leather gloves. A good choice if you didn't want to be touched.

I glanced behind at the edge, little more than a foot away. I scooted in, but not too far. I didn't want to get any closer to him than I had to.

What had someone once told me? It's a lot easier climbing up than down. They were right. You can see handholds coming up. You can't with footholds, going down. A plain case of bad design. Why don't we have a set of eyes on our ankles? People weren't made for climbing, period. Climbing is monkey business. But down was the only way from here.

I was spacing out again. I yanked myself back and my whole body knotted up as I anticipated Wheezer rushing me, shoving me off the cliff. But he just sat there.

I calculated. Wheezer suffered a couple of handicaps: his phobia of touch and, if he got stressed enough, an attack of asthma, or whatever it was. But what was I thinking? I wasn't *fighting* him. I wasn't a fighter.

Then how was I getting off this cliff alive?

"Hutchinson." His lips barely moved.

I pointed up the coast. "Why did you kill Waldo?"

"I did not…George sent me to tell Caron to stop digging into the past. I talked to Caron once, but he ignored me. George sent me again, said to put a scare in him. I needed to get him alone. He was cagey after that first time, refused to meet. I found out where he ran, followed him, saw that he went down these steps.

"But Lands End is popular. Then I saw a weather report. Rain. I went down before he came, stood at the bottom.

"I just wanted to talk. But when he saw me, he turned and ran onto a path that leads to the cliff."

"You followed him. And then you pushed him."

Wheezer shook his head violently. "No. I reached for his arm and…he fell. I feared that I had sinned, for 'thou shalt not kill.' But then I knew. It was the *Lord's* hand that cast him into the waters. The Lord's hand that brought the rain that day in summer, when it never rains. It all turned out to be a great blessing." His voice changed as he spoke. Before that it had been a strangled approximation of human speech— like someone had tried to teach him how it was done, but he'd never really gotten the hang of it. Despite its rasp, his voice was flat, like he really wasn't talking to you, but was talking to himself. But now it had assumed a slight singsong. Though it was no tune you'd choose to listen to.

"A blessing? My friend drowning?" Killing someone, then fingering God for the deed. Didn't that qualify as blasphemy?

"It was a blessing because I saw it was part of His plan. It showed me the way."

He fumbled in one of the pockets of the voluminous suit and my body sprung up into a crouch.

What he pulled out was not a weapon, but a book. He began reading: "'If a man also lie with mankind, as he lieth with a woman, both of them have committed an abomination…'"

Not a book, but *the* book. A Bible.

Leviticus.

I sat back down.

As he read from the Bible, the singsong found a rhythmic groove. A preacher's cadence. He must have spent a lot of time in church as a kid. I'd never spent a minute in church. The absurd combination of prissy intonation and nails-on-blackboard delivery should have had me laughing. To my horror, something primordial in me was responding. My head was nodding along, despite it kicking up the pain at the back of my skull, despite everything that was sane. *He was good at this.*

Wheezer placed the Bible lovingly down on the rock, just like a pastor preparing to add his personal two cents.

"The first brother God struck down, showing me the way. The second was homosexual. I punished him according to the verse, 'His blood shall be upon him.' The third I stoned, as it is written. 'And the man that committeth adultery with another man's wife shall surely be put to death.'"

Wheezer had beaten Rick to death. Not touching him with his fist but with a stone.

I said, "This isn't my line, but the way I understand it is you don't get to go casting stones unless *you're* without sin. You watched through that window. Watched and got off on it. *You* are the sinner."

Wheezer's head whipped from side to side in a tiny quivering arc, like a hummingbird. But he didn't raise his voice. "You understand nothing. I am God's witness. I never touch evil."

"You took the nuns' gravestones, didn't you?"

"*You* committed sacrilege."

"And you blessed them? Is that why you pissed on my bed? You were praying?"

He ignored me. Though maybe he had considered it prayer. After all, I fornicated in that bed. Sinned. Being around him was making me think like him.

He lifted his Bible, fondling its spine with gloved hands—like the flesh he could never touch—and thumbed it to a page. He read: "'Woe to those who call evil good, and good evil; Who put darkness for light, and light for darkness; Who put bitter for sweet, and sweet for bitter.'" He looked up and bored his eyes into mine. "Free love. Free love is not free. It is not love, but hatred. It is enslavement to Satan. And it corrupts the very earth on which it is made. Unstopped, it will corrupt the whole world."

"Free love? What's that got to do with anything? Free love is ancient history."

"It is written. Written on the wall."

The wall? In the Rabbit Hole, under that couch....

"You were in that basement?" He could have easily been. Half the freaks in Middleburg had made it down there at one point or another.

"A banner of heresy, under the earth, where the roots of evil grow."

He was really losing me. "What roots?" But then I remembered that thing he posted on his blog, something about the counterculture being the roots of today's evil.

He didn't seem to be listening. "You opened the door to abomination. It's late, but I'm closing it."

"Abomination? You mean sex." *The Reddit post about the safehouse. The stuff George implied about his mother.* I ran with it by instinct. "You saw that john and the hooker getting it on through that window and it set you right off, didn't it? It drove you right round the bend. You never did get laid, did you? Never have..."

As I spoke, I became aware of a sound. At first, I couldn't discern its source. A huffing, whistling...coming from Wheezer. It was getting louder.

I'd heard this sound before. Once before. *The sound of a dying animal.* I flashed back to the basement the night of the storm, after Rick smashed the stereo, after the monster furnace shut down when I was lying on top of that girl. Wheezer had *been there.*

But where? Not in the Rabbit Hole. In the Music Room? But the girl had gone through there after she left me. It was the only way out. And the sound seemed to come from the walls. I'd assumed because of the acid...

Now Wheezer choked out words. "I watched those roots writhing in sin, like serpents, heard their wicked cries, smelled the stench of Eve's evil..."

Roots? My body and that of the girl, making love, screwing, what have you. Beneath the mural we'd painted on the wall that said Free Love. *It is written. Written on the wall...*

He must have concocted the smell part, as in the safehouse, but he'd seen. From where? "You saw me that night, didn't you? The night of the snow? You love to watch, don't you?" And I got it. "Not just that night. You were down there *before*. It was a habit."

It hit me in a rush, like thoughts on an acid trip. That night, Angela had come on to Wheezer. It turned him on, so he'd snuck down to the basement like he'd done before, hoping there'd be some action. What had he said in his writings? He'd "descended into hell." Not figurative hell, but the literal basement, with its den of iniquity, its Free Love Couch.

He's seen me and that girl, but I'd also been there once with *Sharon.* That thought was the most horrifying. I curled my lip and started to rise again. I stopped, but my mind followed through, sprinting across the rock, hitting him like a football player. Jumping back so I wouldn't go over, too.

I'd stopped myself because I'd vowed to never strike another man.

"...one by one I pull them from the ground and cut them away." He returned from his trance, boring his gaze into mine again. "You're the last."

The Four Brothers.

The literal roots of evil. The roots that nut was spouting about on Wheezer's blog. Who embodied the counterculture in Wheezer's scene back then more than me and my friends?

Wheezer's rasping crescendo was winding up, cranking itself up toward some explosion.

Here was the dreaded moment behind all the old arguments about nonviolence, waged in dorm rooms and vans on the way to gigs, me implacably on the side of peace. The moment where the killer comes at you with a gun, knife, or just bare hands. Do you kill, or get killed? I'd never had to face it. Sure, I'd known anger. But it was mastery of that lower nature that made you a man. That made you human. My hands clenched, not in rage, but in the effort to suppress it.

You don't fight. You run.

But there was nowhere to run to. There were cliffs on every side. I wondered again, how had he gotten up here? I glanced around but didn't see a way.

The pacifist arguments were losing ground as terrible forces massed in my body. Rage and terror, sides of the same coin, and the coin was flipping in me, faster and faster. Hot and cold. Fire coursed into my hands. *Beat the motherfucker into jelly, shove him in the ocean.* Yet my body shivered, so weak I thought I'd keel over.

Gandhi's words playing on my lips— "An eye for an eye makes the whole world blind." Eloquent words, but tiny against the torrent within.

Wheezer's hand disappeared into the pocket of that bodysuit. He didn't have a second Bible. Nor a knife or gun. He held in his palm a rock, about baseball size. Like the one he'd left in my museum. It had been a warning....

He bolted toward me like he was pumped on angel dust, ready to root lampposts from the ground and toss cars across the street.

He wasn't going to push me off the edge. He was going to *stone* me. Smash that rock into my face until it was pulp.

I wasn't fighting. And wasn't going to take flight, unless I sprouted wings. There was only one other choice.

I froze.

In the instant before Wheezer reached me he slowed and hesitated for a moment. *He's afraid to touch me.* I rolled onto my side, glimpsing the edge of the cliff inches from my face. Wheezer pounced on me, crushing my hip into the rock and shoving me onto my back. His deafening breath was hot in my face. It smelled like the devil's shit. *He ought to floss more.*

The proximity to another body seemed to have infused his limbs with crazy energy, like we were magnets of opposing poles. He twitched and shook, pinning me to the rock. My arms were free. I grabbed folds of his body suit but it was useless as trying to pull down the side of a mountain.

Wheezer lifted the rock and brought it down toward my face. I whipped my head to the side, and the rock struck the ground with a hollow *tock* and sprung from his fingers. I couldn't see where it had gone. Over the edge?

He rose up and lunged down. Something pressed hard into the sides of my neck. I glanced down. He'd crossed his arms and was pressing his forearms into the sides of my neck, trying to strangle me. Even with the gloves he couldn't get himself to do it with his hands. I could still breathe but I was getting dizzy. He was cutting off the blood to my brain.

I jolted my head up, and his arms lost their grip.

I twisted my hips, trying to knock him off. He slammed his legs onto mine. He got his forearms onto my neck again, but I flailed my head from side to side and broke their vice grip.

I wrapped both legs around one of Wheezer's and tried to use it as leverage to knock him off.

No dice. One of his arms snaked to the side, grabbing at the rock, but it skittered away.

This spire of rock wasn't entirely flat, after all. From the corner of an eye I could see it sloping toward the ocean. And our struggle was inching us in that direction.

All the time he was on me, his breath rattled away, each exhale putrid. My breathing slipped into sync with his so I didn't have to smell it. Like a Tantric exercise I knew, and to my horror, it did make us more intimate.

Wheezer laddered himself up on me. This time, when his forearms came down, they had the added weight of his upper torso. The dizziness was immediate.

My arms were still free but useless. Maybe not. *See what happens if I touch his bare flesh.* I snaked a hand in and *touched* his cheek with my fingers. A light caress, but his whole body recoiled from mine, like he'd been branded with a hot poker. I easily shoved him off, possessed by my own crazy energy.

He landed on his back, just inches from the edge. I crouched on the rock. He didn't move. My little touch had kicked his asthma up to a final gear. He croaked in a rapid rhythm, like rusty hinges, like that Latin percussion instrument, the ratchet. And I heard all the sounds—the moaning foghorns, rustling waves, Wheezer's ratchet and the screeling gulls. They were all out of rhythm with each other. Where was Angela and her yarrow sticks when you needed her to conduct?

I shook my head. This was no time for music. This was time for business. One more push and he'd go over the edge. And I'd have payback for Waldo and Buzzy. Even for Rick.

No. I needed to control the beast within. There had to be another way. *Motherfucker.*

I had my body under control but not my tongue. "You're no virgin. You *fucked* your mama." This was not me but some snarling creature. "I never got to the incest part, but I can't imagine old Leviticus took too kindly to mama diddling. What did I say about casting the first stone?"

He stopped breathing, and for an instant it was quiet again, just that high foghorn singing its descant, and now the contrabass starting to boom…

He sprang up at me with terrible speed, and a gargling roar issued from my mouth. He hit me hard, knocking me toward the opposite edge. I reached for his chest and grabbed the padding to keep from going over. But it was too late. I was over the edge and pulling Wheezer after me.

For an instant I was sliding down a steep slope, scraping against the rock with a terrible rasp.

I lost my grip on him and wheeled into space. Flying. Every child's dream.

It was overrated.

In the last instant before hitting the water, some wise voice told me to point my toes and take a deep breath. I sliced through the surface and plunged down. It was shockingly cold. I flailed my arms. I had no sense at all what was up or down. The wise voice said, *Stop struggling. Let the air in your lungs take you to the surface.*

My head emerged into the night. A wave smashed into my face and I caught a lungful of water. I coughed, gagged, puked up saltwater. I glimpsed waves crashing into rocks and swam away, out into the ocean. Those rocks were a good way to die. Where was the beach? All I saw was rocks.

I felt a hand tug on my collar. Wheezer! I reached for his head to push it down. He flailed around and I went under. I surfaced.

"Bodine!"

Ray. Gratitude burst in my chest, then I was back in the freezing ocean, trying to keep my head above water. Ray still gripped my collar.

I didn't feel the current, but it had to be strong because the black mass of cliffs was rushing by as it dragged us north, up Lands End.

There came the whine of a motorboat, followed by a light emerging from the mist. Somebody yelled. There was a splash and Ray let go of my collar and swam away. He launched himself onto something and paddled to me. He was on a surfboard.

I grabbed the side of it, and a big wave came, and I lost hold and went under. I came up sputtering. Ray thrust a rope into my hand, and I yanked myself up onto a side of the thing.

A surfboard. It beat the hell out of my poor excuse for swimming. We clung to the sides, riding the board, though not as the Surf God intended. What did he expect? We were East Coast boys.

The boat had been puttering around. Now it sped off.

Ray said, "Fuck! We could be out here all night."

Like that, I was violently shivering. The current brought us close to a rock sticking out from the water. We paddled clear.

Lights appeared above the black mass of cliff, a minute later illuminating a figure in a wet suit rappelling down. He launched off his rope and crashed into the sea.

This guy could really swim. He reached us in no time.

"Just hang on." He towed us out to sea, past the current, then in to a beach. Just before he pulled us from the water, I reached down to my pocket with numb fingers and dumped my wallet.

***

A crowd of firemen surrounded us, draped us with blankets.

Ray beamed at our wet-suited savior. "Thanks, man!"

He didn't return the smile. "Just doing my job. You need to talk to him."

He pointed to an older man, obviously the head honcho. He was talking with one of the younger men. He finally came over to us.

"Tell me what happened." He spoke professionally, but I imagined his thoughts added, *You bozos.* The guy sounded weary, like he did this a couple of times a week. Maybe he did.

I gave Ray a look—*Lie your ass off.*

He said, "We were walking on the cliffs above, when my friend here slipped."

"Trespassing, you mean, in the protected zone. You can't read a sign?"

"I'm sorry, we just wanted to get a better view of the moon."

One of the other men laughed. "There's a new one!"

The head guy ignored him. "Did one of you call?"

Ray said, "No."

The chief said, "Why did you jump in?"

Ray said, "I thought I could save him."

"The police are going to ticket you for this. Where are you men from?"

"Um…New York."

"Let me see some identification."

Ray produced a license from his soaked wallet.

The guy stared at it like it might contain clues as to why people did such stupid things.

He turned to me. "Yours?"

I fumbled in my pants. "I must have lost it in the water. Now how will I get home? I have a meeting…"

"Do you guys have a car?"

"In the lot."

He inspected the back of my head. "That looks nasty. Did you get that falling in?"

"Must have."

He looked at me for a moment, skeptical, but then sighed and said, "You should go to the emergency room, have that checked out. You're lucky to be alive." *Morons. Lying morons.*

We escaped and staggered to the lot. I'd dumped my wallet but still had the keys. We got in the car and I started it up.

I said, "Wait a minute, then I'll blast the heat." My shivering had stopped while we'd talked to the rescue guy. Now it returned with a vengeance. "That water was fucking cold."

"Yeah, but I'm not shivering like you. You sure we shouldn't go to the hospital? You might have a concussion."

I remembered how messed up I'd been after coming to in that cave, my thoughts all screwy. I probably did have a concussion. "I don't care. The only medicine I need is what they call a 'stiff drink.'"

"If you ever stop shaking, we can maybe still get one over at that restaurant there."

"The Cliff House."

"Yeah, and I guess I'm buying. What happened to your wallet?"

"I dumped it."

"Why?"

"Wheezer washes up, I don't want anyone connecting me with this scene."

"What if they contact me?"

"We'll cross that bridge if we get to it."

The Cliff House was a five-minute walk away. As we got out of the car, Ray asked, "You think they let drowned rats in that joint?"

"Oh, I imagine we're not the first to show up after a little swim. This *is* San Francisco."

"But your head…"

I plucked Ray's fedora from the backseat and gingerly put it on.

26.

The tall bright-eyed female receptionist looked us up and down—*some party you came from*—and still gave us a hundred-watt California Girl smile. "Just in time for last call."

She led us to a table overlooking the ocean.

I asked her, "Do you mind if we sit away from the window?"

Ray asked, "Had enough of the old Pacific for tonight?"

I nodded.

Ray ordered an Absolut martini, dry, straight up with olives.

I said, "Same thing." When the waiter left, I said, "I've never actually had one of those before."

"Uh, I've had…a few."

I laughed.

"If they know how to make them it's not a lot different than what we get out of Spider's freezer. You know—the old 'wave the vermouth bottle near the glass.' The olives can be our dinner."

The waiter brought the drinks, which were filled almost to the brim.

Ray grinned at his. "Days like today—not that I've ever seen one just like today—I wish they had a little diving board attached to the rim. Bounce, bounce, and you're in."

I rolled my eyes at the ocean. "Ray."

"Sorry. Well maybe not today. I can't imagine what it was like for you going off that cliff into the water."

I looked away. I squeezed my eyes shut, but then I was falling again, through the fog… I opened them and took a big gulp of the drink. Within seconds the nightmare of the cave, the cliff, and falling receded.

Ray pointed to his glass. "This drink looks half-empty. Sadly, with the shape of the glass, it's more like two-thirds."

When had Ray become an alcoholic? Was I headed there, too? Never mind. The guy had just saved my life.

I said, "We'll live. What happened to you out there?"

"I stood up on that cliff, biting my nails, getting cold. I was about to come down and get you when those drunks arrived."

"Right."

"When I heard you yell, I ran down there, and some guy was hauling a body into the tunnel."

"Me."

"That's what I figured. He must have heard me yell, because he came right back out and chased me. I ran up the path to the top. Man, I was winded. I reached the car, got in, but didn't see him. I figured he'd gone back after you."

"I was out cold. He must have."

"I raced back to that cave and turned on the flash app on my cell. There was nobody inside. I came out the other side and heard voices up on top. I looked for a way to climb up, but there didn't seem any obvious way."

"It's a good thing you didn't." *The way up was rough.*

"That guy wasn't George. He was *Wheezer.*"

He didn't seem surprised. "I told you it was a bad idea meeting George here. He came here to kill you?"

"Yes."

"And you got him instead."

Had I? Was that what had happened?

"Anyway, next thing, you guys come tumbling down. Like Jack and Jill."

"You saw both of us fall?"

"I guess. It was just a blur. It was dark."

"Did you hear a splash? Or two splashes?"

"I don't know. It all happened very fast. He must have drowned. I don't think anyone could have survived those breakers against the cliffs."

"You and I did."

"That was different."

"Yeah, because you...saved me."

"Not me. Frogman. I called 911 and reported 'men in the water.'"

"Me and Wheezer. But when they arrived it was you and me."

"Right. And they must assume someone else called."

"Unless they trace your call."

"I have a burner, remember?"

"Right." I was still a little slow.

We stood to leave. Neither of us were touchy-feely guys. But he'd just saved my life. I hesitated for a moment, then gave him a reasonably big hug, though it caused a shudder. "Thanks, man."

"For what?"

"Jumping in the water."

"Hey, anytime." He turned and started walking before the moment got any more awkward.

We drove towards Marin. Ray asked, "With Wheezer gone, you think we can go back to Spider's?"

"Sure."

***

When we approached the Golden Gate Bridge, it was shrouded in fog.

Ray said, "What exactly were Wheezer's reasons for going after you guys?"

"He saw us as the literal 'roots of evil,' which he got from that blog post by that guy. The rest of it, though, is your territory. Shrinkology."

"Here's how I see it. He's brought up to be strictly religious. Old Testament style, I suspect, with a vengeful God breathing down his neck, looking for the slightest sin. He's already steeped in shame and guilt when his mother starts banging him, giving him a case of world-class inner conflict when it comes to sex. An existential conflict—so strong that it threatens to stop his breathing."

"The asthma."

"Right. Which is maybe connected with his nasal hallucinations, as you so ripely put it. What's one of the feelings associated with smell? Disgust. And this is a guy who feels seriously unclean. And no filthier than when it comes to sex. He more or less avoids the issue, until George takes him to that safe house. The conflict comes to a head as he stares through that window at the thing he desires and hates. It shakes a major screw loose. He reenacts that scene in the basement, watching you hippies get it on. And now added to his conflict is resentment, because he doesn't go to a fancy college like you guys, like his friend George. And he'll never get to enjoy sex, which his body still naturally craves. He attaches his resentment to the Four Brothers.

"Add in the catalyst of potent LSD the night of the storm and another screw comes loose. He projects all the horror of his world onto you, that basement, a whole erotic scene he can never be part of. His understanding lies dormant in him all those years. Then he stumbles on these wingnuts online telling him the counterculture ruined everything, and he conflates that with his original resentment against the Four Brothers.

"He kills Waldo—intentionally or not. We'll never know. Unlike George, he takes his religion seriously. And he's done a major no no, breaking one of his God's commandments.

"George firing him severed his last thread of connection to the human race. But I think it was his guilt over Waldo that finally knocked the last screw out of him. He's no psychopath. He has a conscience, granted that it's all mixed up with his wackadoodle religion. His breaking of the commandment against killing is unbearable."

"Unbearable, without the intercession of magic."

"Magic?"

"Magical thinking." I told him more of what Wheezer had said on the cliff. "If Waldo's falling was part of God's plan, and God wants all the Brothers dead, then all Wheezer needs to do is oblige and he's off the hook."

"God as the fall guy. Literally, in the case of Waldo and Buzzy."

"And if he kills you guys, cuts out those 'roots of evil,' he'll finally feel better. And this guy is really hurting."

"Do God a solid and God will heal him."

"And make him finally feel clean. Which he is now. Washed in the waters of the great ocean." I shuddered. *I'd killed a man.* The Bible might not be my book, but I had my own set of commandments.

***

The effects of the martini had worn off. I sat on the couch with a blanket around me but couldn't get warm.

Ray asked, "You alright?"

"Just cold."

"You need another touch of Russian medicine?"

"No, I'm good." I wasn't good.

"Well, I'm going to drink to good riddance to bad trash."

"Don't say that. He was human. I feel terrible about it."

"What? He was trying to kill you. It was poetic justice—he went in the sea not a half mile from where he sent Waldo."

"No! If I believe anything in this life, it's that every life is precious, and there's never an excuse for..." I couldn't go on, because none of my philosophy mattered any more than excuses did. No thoughts, no words could ever change what I'd done, could bring Wheezer back to life.

Ray crashed on his couch. Sleep was a long time coming for me.

***

I woke to the gentle rocking of the boat, morning sun gleaming on a patch of floorboards. *I'm alive!* A second later came the thought, *I killed a man.*

Ray stirred then sat up. "Man, I am starved."

"We skipped dinner."

We had breakfast back at our café.

He asked, "Time for us to saddle up and go home?" He sounded sad.

"I suppose so."

"I don't know. It's pretty nice out here with Wheezer out of the picture."

"I have to get home to my dog."

"Yeah, time to get back to my life too, I suppose."

"My credit card went in the drink with my wallet—you mind booking something for tomorrow? I'll pay you back."

"Sure. But you don't have an ID."

I waved my hand—*I've got it covered.*

Ray raised an eyebrow.

What *was* I going to do? I'd figure something out. But it was going to take cash. Ray agreed to lend me some. We went to a couple of ATMs and he handed me five hundred dollars.

"I've got one question. How did Wheezer get into George's email and invite me to the Sutro Baths?"

"I don't know. Why does it matter? He's dead."

It didn't matter, but having spoken it bugged me.

We walked back to the houseboat. I said to Ray, "Have to make a few calls." I stayed outside while he went in.

I called Annie.

She asked, "How's it going with that Wheezer fuck?"

"Uh…fine. Listen. I've been checking my computer regularly and he wasn't hacking me. I've been assuming he's old school and doesn't have great computer chops. But then he somehow hacked into George's email and impersonated him."

She laughed. "That George is a dodo. He hands his passwords out like candy."

"Did you deal with George in person?"

"No. Not if I could help it."

"And you never met Wheezer."

"I told you."

I got it. "Wheezer has been pretending he was George for a while. George told you to look into Waldo, but after that, with Buzzy and Rick, it was Wheezer telling you. And you thought it was George. Wheezer ordered you to put up that website on me, which was why George didn't know about it."

"Email sucks. Even when you know you're dealing with the real person, it's impossible to read what they're saying."

Especially if you are somewhere on the Asperger's spectrum.

I said, "Speaking of email, you hacked into Buzzy's. And I assume Rick's."

"Yeah?"

"Now this is really important. I don't know how you could, but did you get into mine?"

She laughed. "You aren't a complete loss. I gave up after a couple of hours. Now if I had a week… Are we good now?"

"Yeah."

I hung up. What else had Wheezer done impersonating George? It didn't matter, because he was dead.

I called Sharon. I dialed her regular number.

She said, "Why are you calling me on this number?"

"It's over."

"They busted George?"

"No, it's way more complicated. It wasn't George. It was that Wheezer guy." I told her what happened up on the cliff.

"Oh my God! Are you alright?"

"A bump on the head. I'll be fine."

"Whew. I'm so relieved. For you. For me, too, I'll admit. I've been scared."

"You're safe. We're all safe." A tattooed twentysomething whizzed by on a skateboard. Headed to work? I smiled and waved at him.

It was time to take my medicine. "Uh, I wanted to talk about how I responded to your email."

"You sure?" Her voice had taken on that cold edge.

"Yes. I was touched by what you wrote—who wouldn't be? But coming out and admitting it was just too hard. I needed some time, or I don't know what…"

"You think writing that, making myself so vulnerable, was easy for me? You're not the only one with issues here. And when it comes to that stuff— which is the *really* hard stuff—you have to promise you're going to meet me half way. Three-quarters, in fact."

Could I really promise that? Did I want to? I needed to answer before I dug myself deeper. "You have my word."

"You may be safe physically, but nobody goes through something like that without serious emotional repercussions."

I sighed. "I'm not sure I wasn't culpable in this guy's death."

"He was trying to kill you!"

"Yeah, but that's no excuse. I could have walked away."

"What, from on top of some rock?"

"I guess not. I could have done something."

"You're being too hard on yourself. Listen, I really respect your nonviolence. It's a marvelous ideal—for an ideal world, where everything's clean and black and white. The real world, unfortunately, is messy and gray. And that's the one we get to live in. I've been thinking about that dream of yours, where Angela turns into the Japanese victim of Hiroshima.

And...maybe this will make you feel better. I think you off-loaded your feelings for Angela—the good and bad—onto those anonymous girls. The same as you'd do later with that museum of yours. Because to feel that stuff with Angela was just too much."

"What's that got to do with killing someone?" My face was hot. A woman walked past on her way to the parking lot, a yoga mat strapped to her back. Early class. She glared at me. It must be my bad vibe.

"This is a bit of a stretch, but I'm thinking that while you see your pacifism as a deeply held belief..."

"It's not pacifism. That implies passivity. It's nonviolence I believe in. Which means the hardest kind of action, going against your animal impulses."

"Whatever it is, I'm wondering if it's really about those feelings you can't feel. Which means you're off the hook for killing him."

"Thanks. I've gotta go."

I punched the call off. Stalked down to the end of the boardwalk. I was dimly aware that she'd been trying to make me feel better. I felt worse. And the ugly thing was that she might just be right.

But enough was enough with this touchy-feely stuff. I couldn't do it anymore. It was good I hadn't brought up her email. It hadn't been the time before. The way I was feeling, there'd never be a time.

***

The next morning, we sat in back on the terrace. He sucked the last from a second cup of coffee then said, "We should get going. You never know with the traffic here."

"I'm not coming. I couldn't get an ID in time." I hadn't actually tried yet.

"I *thought* it wouldn't be so easy." He glanced around at the diners sucking down the fine food and soaking up the California sun. "I'm gonna miss this scene. Aside from George and Wheezer."

"I'm glad you insisted on coming."

"Anytime. A little excitement never hurt anybody."

"When it didn't kill them. Can you spell Jo with the dog?"

"Sure. Which car should I take?"

We still had the two. "It doesn't matter."

"I'll take the first one we rented."

Ray left. Where was I going to get an ID for the plane? Not Jeannie. Kaylee? No. She was on the other side of the law. Annie. I called her. She said, "I...heard of this guy in Chinatown."

She gave me his number. She said, "Now you and I are really good. In fact, I'd say you're starting to owe me..."

"I wouldn't go that far."

27.

The soonest the ID guy could see me was eight the next morning. Since I was still here....

Should I call first? No. Just show up. I left Spider's and headed for the City. There wasn't a wisp of fog today. Just brilliant blue sky, dark blue water and the handsomest bridge in the world. I was going to miss it.

I rang the bell. Jeannie opened the door. Her eyebrows rose a little. But she didn't seem entirely shocked to see me. "You still out here?"

I patted my arms and chest. "I think it's me."

"Come on in." She led me to the kitchen.

Eldridge whined downstairs.

She said, "She likes you."

"The feeling's mutual. You know what? I could take her. My dog Mingus is a guy. Is she spayed?"

"Yes."

"Then they should get along fine."

"She'd like that."

I appreciated that she didn't concoct some fake argument, just accepted my offer.

She did give me a fake pout. "You just came for my dog."

I rummaged around in a pocket. "Damn. I was sure that rain check was in this coat."

She grinned, then got serious. "You've been out here a long time. Are you...getting anywhere?"

"It's done."

She said, "I don't want to know about it. Would you like a glass of wine?"

Technically, the rain check was for her dope. "I would."

"White or red?"

"Red, I suppose."

When she returned with glasses of wine she said, "Jesus, what did you do to the back of your head?"

"Nothing."

She gave me a skeptical look but dropped it.

I eyed the glass of wine. "Uh. Before I get into that, my laptop's in the car..."

"It's going to get stolen in about two minutes if it isn't already."

I went out and got it. I hadn't told her my suitcase was locked in the trunk. I'd left Sausalito pretty sure that I'd be staying over here and wasn't coming back. Back in the house I asked, "You mind if I plug this in? And I should check my email."

"Long as you don't spend an hour on it."

"I'll just be a second."

She pointed to a table by the window. I plugged in, opened the computer and email. There was nothing I had to deal with today. And nothing from Sharon...

I sat and had a sip. I said, "I don't usually drink wine, but I could drink more of this."

"It's hard to argue with California cabernets. Expensive habit. Then again, so is weed."

"Speaking of which..."

She didn't say anything, just curled one side of her mouth with an eye roll.

She got up and brought over the ashtray with the pipe and dope. She pulled a lighter from her pants, set the pipe gently in my mouth and fired it up.

I did acid once a year but couldn't remember the last time I'd smoked dope. One hit and the high was instantaneous and utterly familiar.

Her cell phone chirped. She snagged it from the counter. She listened, her face darkening. "A free cruise? With my husband? He just *died*. Don't you check these things? Don't you fucking call here again."

She slammed the phone on the counter, sat, and buried her head in her hands.

"That wasn't me. That poor fucker's just doing his job with a starving family in Bangladesh, and here I am biting his head off. But me and Waldo on a cruise? That's the last thing…"

"Hey, I hate those asshole telemarketers."

"It's not the telemarketers. It's grief. I thought grief was about being sad, but what I feel is crazy. Everything upsets me. Ordinarily I just hang up on those calls, but now they make me want to scream. And my guilt about Eldridge is getting to be like an obsession. I'm really glad you're going to take her. And I'm glad you're here."

"Me, too. It'll get better."

She took my hand. Hers was warm. The sun was about to set, streaming in the window, painting her face with oranges and reds. There were lines in it I hadn't seen before, but I didn't care. I cared that her sunny smile had returned, at least for a moment.

I'd long enjoyed hiding out in my theater, pretending to be some kind of man of mystery. But there was nothing truly mysterious about me.

Women were the mysteries. And no more so than in this moment on the verge. Not that sex ever did anything other than create the momentary illusion of revelation.

She leaned over, cradled the sides of my head, carefully avoiding its sore back, and placed her lips on mine. I'd forgotten how marijuana socked you right into your senses, all your troubles, the whole world collapsing into the present—just warm and moist and the urge rising to open my mouth, open myself to her.

I was smack in the present moment, when the thought barged in—What would it be like to get high and do this with…Sharon?

My mouth stayed closed and she gracefully leaned away. "It's Waldo, isn't it? You think it's too soon."

"Yes. I'm sorry." But it wasn't Waldo and it wasn't too soon. It was

Sharon. *Maybe you'll pony up another rain check, for this....* No.

I was in this moment now, and it was awkward, as such moments are. More dope? But I didn't want to get high and run.

She said, "I understand. But I really like just having you here." *And I don't want to be alone.* "Would you stay the night?"

"Of course." Now it was time for more weed.

***

We lay in her bedroom, clothes on, over the covers. I alternated views of the sliver of ocean from her window, the moon spilling silver on the wave tips, and Jeannie's serene face on my shoulder, eyes closed, with the hint of a contented smile. Would these sights be better if I had another hit? But for that to happen I'd have to get up. I was tired and it was a long way into the kitchen. At the same time, something nagged at the back of my mind. Something very out of keeping with this relaxed, prone scene. I was about to finally rise and get some smoke to chase it away when her eyes opened.

She said, "I was enjoying you watching me pretend to sleep."

"You were doing a pretty good job pretending."

We talked music. Our taste was about ninety percent aligned, a big relief from trying to explain to Laurel why the Dead Kennedys basically sucked. I became aware of the cultural DNA we shared. Her touchstones were mine.

Music. *Mozart.* That thing at the back of my mind returned, nagging, stronger now.

Like she'd read my mind, she asked, "What are you thinking?"

I'd spilled a lot to Sharon. I'd hoped—and feared— I'd spill a lot more before my boneheaded reaction to her email, before things cooled off. But even in that last conversation she'd still been analyzing my dreams, though it had gotten a bit clinical.

I'd sworn off the touchy-feely stuff, but now the impulse was here again. Blame it on the marijuana.

I said, "I haven't told anybody else this. But recently, since Waldo died, I've been getting this weird thing with heights. You know, like he had. What do they call it? Acrophobia. And I think it might be connected with this stuff from my past, that girl Waldo knew, Angela…"

If I hadn't been so wrapped up in what was spewing from my mouth, I would have noticed sooner that she was asleep. The real thing this time, with gentle snoring.

I was awake. After all the nights floating on the houseboat, the bed felt weird. It was too still, too concrete. The last of the THC was gone from my bloodstream, leaving me clear.

It was just as well that'd she'd nodded off to my soliloquy. It had been wrong to try to open up to her. She had enough drama in her life without mine. I was new at this, didn't understand that you couldn't just go laying this stuff on any woman, even one as nice as Jeannie.

And though there was nothing wrong with her, she was wrong for me. She was too damned easy going. Too nice.

A brand-new feeling sprang up in me. It was so unfamiliar that it took a moment to get it.

I *wanted* something. With a passion I hadn't felt in a long time.

What Jeannie wanted was some fun, a warm body in the dark—to get laid. Exactly what I'd wanted when I showed up here. There wasn't a thing wrong with that.

But now I wanted more. It was ironic. All those years, all those women had wanted something from me. Occasionally they were explicit—like Laurel with her devastating note—but usually it was just this subtle feeling I picked up on. *What* they wanted I could never figure out.

Now I knew. It was below my ribs, in the very spot that yawned in the terrible moments recently that I'd stood at the edge of that precipice inside.

And now came the real shock. It wasn't just *something* I wanted. It was someone. With a name.

Sharon. She'd meant business, at least until I'd blown it. I really hoped she still did. This business of hers still scared me, but there was a process going on here, something deep and inexorable, and if I could just give in to it…

I was making it too complicated. I just wanted to see her again. With that thought, I drifted off with a smile.

***

I woke to the smell of marijuana smoke and vague sounds from the kitchen. It was still dark.

Another hit? No. I just wanted to go back to sleep. The clock said two. I was drifting away when some sense had me opening my eyes, but I was more than half asleep. An apparition appeared silently in the unfamiliar doorway, and I started and rose up in the bed.

It was just Jeannie in the doorway, lit by the moon. She said, "I'm sorry to scare you like that. But your computer's making this funny noise."

Now I was wide awake. "Noise?"

"Pinging sound."

Wheezer.... I leapt from bed, but by the time I hit my feet I'd calmed down. I'd been leaving my computer open with energy saving off so that I'd get an alert if anyone broke into my place. Wheezer was dead. I said, "It's just my computer."

"Could you make it stop?"

"Of course."

I threw on pants and padded into the kitchen. Jeannie was standing next to my computer. I leaned over it and navigated to the app, about to shut it down.

"What was that?"

"Have a look." I clicked on the camera feed.

She leaned over my shoulder and asked, "That looks like an old theater."

"It is."

She shook her head, confused.

"That's where I live." I turned up the sound on the computer. I heard distant barking. It got louder. Why? If Jo was there, Mingus should be eating...and last time she'd left the back door open. Good that she'd closed it.

Jeannie asked, "What is this, some kind of YouTube? I don't understand."

"Hold on." A moment later, I said, "Fuck me."

I zoomed in on the ceiling of the theater. A filament of...

She asked, "Is that smoke?"

I pulled my cell from my pants and punched in Ray's number. He'd be asleep at this hour. It was a good thing the guy still didn't know about turning his ringer off at night.

He asked, "What?"

"My theater's on fire. Call the fire department. Call them and call me right back."

Jeannie said, "This is freaking me the fuck out."

"That makes two of us. I should have explained before. The guy who was doing all this stuff...fell into the ocean. Only..."

Ray called back. "Hear the sirens? I'm heading over."

I did hear sirens through his phone. I said, "Don't go near there! He could have seen you with me, and if he recognizes you..."

"Wheezer?"

"Who else?"

"What about Mingus?"

Oh, shit. "Stay away."

A figure appeared in the theater, coming down the stairs from the office. Why from there? And the barking had stopped. Where was Mingus?

The video froze.

"What the hell?" I frantically punched keys. There was nothing wrong with the computer. It was the goddamn San Francisco Internet. I turned to Jeannie and said, "My house is on fire. And I just saw a ghost."

I was clean! I hadn't killed anybody.

I must have smiled, because she said, "This is good news?"

"No." I lost my smile. Wheezer was in Hudson, trying to kill me.

She asked, "What do you mean, ghost?"

"The guy who did all this stuff fell in the ocean, and I thought he was dead, but..." The video started up again. Museum cases were on fire, smoke billowing up toward the ceiling, which was invisible under it. Part of the wall over by my bedroom crashed down. The screen went black. Not the Internet going down, but the camera failing in the fire. *Mingus...* I reached for the screen, like I could touch him.

I moved closer, tried to block her from seeing, but she leaned over my shoulder and saw.

She opened her mouth, but nothing came out. She backed away from me slowly and finally spoke. "I told you before. This is not my life." She gestured to the computer. "And that shit is *really* not my life."

I said, "I'm going back east," but she was leaving the room.

I went on the computer and used the credit from my cancelled reservation to book something at ten in the morning. It was only two thirty. I had time to kill before heading for Chinatown to get my new ID.

Jeannie appeared in the door. "What did you say?"

"I'm going home, this morning. And I'm taking the dog. Do you have a crate?"

"She doesn't need one. She fits right under the seat in a Sherpa pack. I'll get you that and her leash."

She frowned at my computer. "You don't think…"

"You have nothing to worry about. That fire and that guy are on the east coast. It has nothing to do with you."

"But it started with Waldo…" I tried to explain, but she was fairly wrecked. Each twist in this twisty story made her eyes a little wider. She finally held up a hand—*enough*—and hit the weed again. The couple of hits I'd had had been plenty, but she was sucking it down like tobacco.

She yawned and said, "I'm going back to bed." She wasn't inviting me to join her. She stood, hesitating for a moment, then gave me a sisterly hug. "If you're gone before I wake… You take good care."

I thought of Sharon—*You be careful!* I gave Jeannie what I imagined was a complicated smile.

She floated to the bedroom and closed the door like she was shutting out the world. I couldn't blame her.

I looked for news of the fire on the computer but there was nothing. I could hack into the fire department's computers…it didn't matter. And I was beat.

Ray called. "I went by the fire."

"I told you not to go there!"

"Don't worry. There were a hundred people there. I was looking for Mingus."

"And…"

"I'm sorry. No sign of him. And your place was really blazing."

Mingus was smart. He would have gotten out of there. But if he hadn't…

"Can you come get me at the airport?"

"Sure."

I lay on the living room couch and tried to get back to sleep but I was too wired. I gave up and went downstairs and got acquainted with my new dog. Which was likely my only dog now…

I drove to Chinatown and locked Eldridge in the car with the windows cracked. I met the ID guy at his apartment. It looked more Danish modern than Chinese, but he looked Chinese, though his English was perfect. He said, "I told you on the phone, the rush job is extra. How big a rush are you in?"

"A half hour?"

"That's extra extra."

"I've only got…four hundred and fifty." I was saving a little cash just in case.

He nodded, waving his hand. He asked, "You need anything else?"

"Like what?"

"A gun?"

Did I look that desperate? "No." I thought. "But I could use a haircut."

He grinned.

"What, you do hair, too?"

He shook his head and walked in the other room with his phone to his ear. A few minutes later a woman came in. She didn't look Chinese. Aside from her cheeks and chin, every visible inch of her was brightly tattooed. She kissed him and got to work.

She freed my ponytail from its tie. "It's been a while."

About ten years. Ah, well.

She was done in ten minutes. He snapped a photo and inside of twenty-five minutes I had my new ID in hand. It didn't look like me. Neither did I.

I called Sharon on her regular number and left a message. "You need to call me as soon as you get this." I was worried about her. Really worried. *Wheezer was back east.*

But he didn't know about her. How could he? I'd emailed her, but Annie had sworn my email hadn't been hacked.

I drove to the airport. I felt bad for exposing Jeannie to more of this nightmare. And damned if she hadn't *saved my life.* Because if I'd gone back east with Ray, I'd have been home when Wheezer came. The second friend to save my life in as many days. It was a good thing I didn't believe in karma or I'd be footing some bill.

I got to SFO with a half hour to spare. I paid for the animal surcharge and got coffee.

In the departure lounge I hacked into the Hudson Fire Department computer and skimmed a report on the fire:

> *Though there is no record of any individual living on the premises, one witness claimed an acquaintance lives there. It will be a few days before inspectors can determine if there are any remains in the ashes…*

Ray had done a good job witnessing.

Waiting had always been tough for me. Right now, I was so impatient that I couldn't even count ten breaths without the questions barging in: How did Wheezer survive? Where is he now? What about Mingus? Was Ray safe? And what if Wheezer *hadn't* survived, and George had sent someone else after me, or that it might even be Brickman?

And *Sharon?* I called her again. She picked up.

I said, "I left you a message. Why didn't you call back?"

"I haven't checked my messages. What's the matter?"

"Wheezer's alive."

"What do you mean? I thought he fell in the ocean."

"He got out somehow. He came east and burned down my house."

"Oh, no. Why?"

"He must have thought I was there. I had a flight booked home with Ray. But I decided to stay a little longer…"

"What are you going to do now?"

"I'm flying back in a few minutes. I'll figure it out when I get home."

Though I no longer had one. "Here's the thing—you need to watch out."

"Why?"

A good question. "I don't know. He can't know about you."

"He saw me at Angela's room that time…"

"Forty years ago!"

And maybe in the basement… It was still forty years ago.

It had been stalking around in the back of my mind: my worst fear. Now it reared its ugly head, baring long, sharp teeth. I wanted to reach through the phone, hug her, make her safe. I tried to reassure her, though I was just reassuring myself. "You're not one of the Four Brothers. And up to now…shit. He's crazy. There's no telling what he'll do. You need to leave your office right now, but don't go home. Drive someplace, and don't even tell me where."

"Really?"

"Really."

"I'm just finishing the footnotes on that paper. As soon as I…"

"Fuck the paper! Get out of there. I'm getting on the plane now, but you need to call me as soon as you go, leave me a message saying you've left. You still have that burner phone?"

"Yes."

"Use that and leave it on. If I call you it will be on that. And don't tell me where you are."

"OK. Lighten up."

She hung up. She didn't sound entirely convinced, but what could I do? Maybe I'd pushed too hard.

The flight was boarding in fifteen minutes. That worst fear hadn't left— that Wheezer was going to get to Sharon. And connected with it was the knowledge that I was missing something. Something essential.

28.

Airports are a circle of hell where the sins of seeking greener grass—or being in the wrong job—are punished by soul-crippling anxiety. I'm usually immune to it, but as I sat in the departure lounge my fellow travelers seemed positively serene compared to me. I racked my brains trying to find what I was missing, my body jangling with agitation. I was practicing sixteenth-note runs on my thighs. I didn't care if it looked weird. Finally, it was too much and I got up and paced. Eldridge in her Sherpa pack had been quiet up to now but must have sensed my agitation, because she whined. I sat back down and put a hand on her through the bag and she calmed down.

My mind, honed by years of discipline to a fine problem-solving tool, had devolved into chaos, like someone had taken all the dramatic events of the past weeks and chucked them in a mental Cuisinart, chopping George, Wheezer, Angela, Waldo, Buzzy, Rick, Sharon, and the rest into chunks which randomly spun around in my head.

I boarded. I let Eldridge out of the bag, and she crawled under the seat in front of me and went right to sleep. Oh, to be a dog.

I considered getting a drink—or three. No. I needed to be clear for what was coming. And I needed to find the missing thing. It was like when you lose your keys and you look over and over in the same places, knowing they won't magically appear. The missing thing was someplace I hadn't looked yet.

I thumbed through the in-flight magazine. Sunny resorts, interviews with over-the-hill TV stars, a tour of churches in France...

Religion. What I was missing had something to do with religion. Wheezer's enacting Biblical punishments made a kind of crazy sense, but why had he stolen the nuns' gravestones? He said it was sacrilege. If I could figure that piece out… I worked at it on and off throughout the rest of the flight but got nowhere. Maybe Ray could figure it out.

The plane landed around nine. It was dark out. As it taxied to the gate my phone chimed as it regained service. But there was no message from Sharon. I called her, and it went right to voice mail. "I just got in. Call me as soon as you get this."

Right to voice mail. Had she turned her phone off? I'd told her to keep it on. Was she out of batteries or out of range? But then why didn't she leave me a message?

I slouched against a pillar next to the pickup lane with Eldridge on a leash. Five minutes later, Ray pulled up in his old Volvo. Eldridge growled and a dog leapt up in the backseat and started howling. Mingus!

I usually find his howl quite annoying. Now it sounded like a choir of angels. It was great to see Ray, too. But he was frowning at me. I opened the passenger door, and Mingus scrambled to the front seat. I reached in to hug him, but Eldridge was climbing in the car. Mingus retreated to the backseat with a whimper.

"Bodine?"

"None other." I was wearing baggy pants and a plaid shirt I'd borrowed from Spider's closet, and the fedora Ray had worn when we went to the Fairmont.

"Up to this moment I'd say that's a getup you wouldn't be caught dead in."

"That's the idea. It's my disguise."

"You had me fooled."

"Good."

I got in the car.

I said, "You saved my dog."

"And you stole my hat. I went downstairs to get in my car when I heard a whine from the front door… He was just sitting there patiently on my stoop."

"What? He's only been there once or twice." He was a smart dog. But he was scared right now.

A cop gave Ray a nasty look, so he pulled away. I turned to the back and said to Mingus, "She's half your size."

He glared at me. Eldridge crawled in back with Mingus and there was a flurry of scrambling and claws as they tried to sniff butts in cramped quarters. After a noisy minute they got it sorted out and lay down. If only people were so easy.

Ray glanced in the rearview. "Hey, that looks a lot like…"

"Jeannie's dog. It is."

Ray laughed. "That's why you stayed! Not that I'm surprised. She was…nice." He cranked the AC. In the time I'd stood outside waiting, I'd already worked up a sweat.

"The weather still hasn't let up."

"This is the worst it's been. But I hear there are thunderstorms coming. I never knew you had this talent for disguise. First the short hair wig, now this. You shaved your head! That some kind of homage to your friend Buzzy?"

"No. This woman down in Chinatown got a little carried away."

"So what's the deal?"

"I figured with reports of me being dead I might get by in Hudson for a bit without Wheezer catching on."

"You can stay at my place."

"Thanks." I glanced in back.

"Your dogs, too. I snuck by the smoldering ruins of your place."

I sighed. "I told you not to."

"Just on the off chance that your organ and my guitar survived. But no such luck. The whole front of the building collapsed. I got inside the back. Your museum is just ashes and bits of melted glass. It must have been two thousand degrees in there. How did Wheezer know to come east?"

"Easy. The car you took to the airport still had that tracker on it. We thought he was dead, so we forgot about it. He got on his computer and saw the car going to the airport. He didn't know it was just you. Christ, he could have killed you!"

"But he didn't. It must be tough. Coming home to…"

"Nothing." No home. I had the laptop, but with my main computers fried, no way to do serious work. And… "I don't care."

"You don't care about your organ? Your *museum*?"

"Hey, at least I don't have to get a new air conditioner now. Like the man said, 'When you got nothing…'"

"You got nothing to lose."

"It's just *stuff*. It's almost a relief having it just burn up like that. It's like it's made an opening."

"To what?"

It was a good question. I glanced in the backseat at the pile of snoozing fur. "I've got my dog. *Two* dogs, and a backpack full of dirty clothes." And Ray. Who'd saved my life. Were the Chinese right? Did I owe him my life now?

Oh, and Sharon. The fear stormed back. "I'm worried about Sharon."

"You're afraid Wheezer…."

"I can't imagine why or how he could get to her. We emailed, but one thing I know is that no one has hacked my account. So Wheezer can't know that I know her. He might have seen us down in the basement of the Four Brothers house, but that was a million years ago. How could he connect her then with now? I told her to leave her office and stay away from her house, but she insisted on finishing this fucking paper first. I told her to call me when she left and leave a message, but she didn't. And she's not answering."

"Try her again."

I did. "Damn. There are no bars."

"Maybe she just forgot to call. It sounds like she was busy."

"I wasn't getting through to her in that last call. What she was worried about was that paper." And maybe she hadn't gotten in her car, was right now in her office, after hours, the only light lit in the building…

I said, "We're going to Middleburg."

"Got it." He sped up.

The worry was stitching into my gut. I got bars on the phone and tried Sharon again. "She's still not answering."

"She finished the paper, was tired and went to bed early?" He didn't sound convinced.

"Ever since the airport in San Fran I've had this feeling, like I'm missing a crucial piece of this thing. It's something to do with Wheezer and religion. And *Sharon.* I can't put my fucking finger on it."

"When it comes to Wheezer and religion, we've got a lot to work with."

"Too much. The damned Internet out there crapped out on me while that surveillance video was playing of my theater on fire. I want to see the missing part. Or maybe your eye will catch something mine didn't."

We were on the Taconic Parkway. Ray pulled onto the narrow side of the road.

I showed Ray the video on my phone. It was small, but clear: there was my collection and the sound of distant barking coming closer. Just as the figure had started down the stairs, the video had frozen. It played past that point.

Ray said, "Christ, it's old Nosferatu, back from the dead."

Wheezer flew down the steps, wearing the bodysuit, with a rock in his hand. He saw the collection and stopped cold. He approached the first row and studied it with the curiosity of an avid museumgoer. He picked up a stack of long-abandoned manuscripts in his gloved hands, recoiled, and dropped them on the floor.

Ray said, "The smell must have gotten to him."

The upper half of the theater was filled with smoke, but the ceiling was high enough that it didn't bother Wheezer. He got to the neat array of abandoned prosthetics, lifted a leg, and threw it on the floor. He trashed the opera score and parts, flung the pages in the air.

Ray asked, "Why didn't he appear earlier, if he came in the back door? There isn't another door."

"No. He must have gotten in another way...through the basement. There's an old bulkhead, which I was going to replace, but I didn't have time. And I keep a can of gas down there. He breaks in, comes upstairs to get me. When I'm not there he gets the gas and sets it on fire. Meanwhile Mingus is barking up a storm."

"Why isn't he all over Wheezer? He isn't making a sound."

"He must have hit him with that rock. The one he was going to kill me with."

He mustn't have hit him too hard, because here came furious barking, followed by the dog leaping down the stairs. He launched himself onto Wheezer's back, knocked him down. Wheezer got up, grabbed an antique microscope, and flung it at Mingus. Mingus dodged and howled. The video stopped. I'd lost the bars on the phone. But I'd seen what I needed.

I said, "One thing in my collection he wasn't fucking with in that video was the nuns' gravestones."

"Because he stole them before."

"I obsessed about them for half the plane ride, thinking they were the key."

"Nuns. Sharon's a Christian?"

"No. She's a *Buddhist*. That's how she knew Buzzy."

"Wheezer knows that?"

"No. Oh shit. Yes. His *blog*. The last article, 'Worshipping False Gods,' only with a lot of *z*'s. Which is why I gave up on it. I was all *z*'ed out."

"False gods. That would include the Buddha. As far as Wheezer was concerned, Buzzy had *two* strikes against him. He was gay…"

"And he didn't worship Wheezer's god. I was right to focus on the nuns' gravestones. Only it isn't about them, but Wheezer's reaction to them. He called it 'sacrilege.' That's the key."

"I still don't see how he got to Sharon from there."

Two bars on my phone, but a second later they were gone. "I need to get on the Internet, and stay there, and this shitty service isn't going to cut it."

"There's a rest stop in ten miles. Maybe they have Wi-Fi."

They were ten very long miles. The inside of the convenience store seemed too brightly lit, aisles of junk food screaming in garish colors. But the Wi-Fi worked.

We stood at a narrow shelf next to a coffee machine and shared my laptop.

I went to Wheezer's blog, to "Worzhipping Falze Godz." I scrolled down past where I'd read before, to photos of religious art. Ganesh. Shiva. A stone Buddha. And a Tibetan thangka painting.

Ray said, "I saw that at Buzzy's house. Wheezer was *there*. Before he killed Buzzy, or after?"

"It doesn't matter." I got into Buzzy's email. It was sad that it was still there, with him gone. But there was no time for that.

Buzzy to Sharon: "See you Tuesday night?" Sharon, getting into a little philosophy. "I'm still struggling with this 'no self' concept. If I don't have a self, then…"

Ray said, "So if Wheezer saw this…"

"That's how he knows Sharon's a Buddhist." I looked through Buzzy's emails. "He emailed other members of his sitting group."

"Why would Wheezer zero in on her?"

"No reason." A rush of relief came. A moment later it crumbled. "Oh, no."

The missing piece hit me like a hollow-point bullet, punching like a tiny fist, then exploding inside. "Wheezer got into Sharon's email from Buzzy's. And there's one from her to me…" Making very explicit the nature of our relationship. Then and now.

And when we'd been lolling in her bed with that cabernet, she'd told me her email password, saying, "You're the expert. Is it strong enough?"

"Not if you go telling it to everybody you meet."

"You're no everybody, but maybe I should change it…"

Had she? No. As her account was loading, I heard a ping.

Ray asked, "What's that?"

"She just got an email… No. There's nothing new here. That was *my* email." I switched accounts. "There's no subject, but it's from Sharon." I felt a burst of enormous relief and clicked… It read:

WHERE ANGELZ FLY, THE WHORE ZHALL DIE

By the second z I knew. Ray looked at me. I froze, body rigid, diaphragm locked up. My mind shut down. Forced a breath and my worst fear found words. "This is Wheezer. He's hacked into Sharon's email. Or else…he's got her computer."

"Oh, man."

ZHE NEVER LEARNZ. ZO ZHE MUZT BURN

I ZHALL MEET YOU IN HELL

```
      4              4            4            4
     4z4            4z4          4z4          4z4
    4z4            4z4          4z4          4z4
   4z4            4z4          4z4          4z4
  4z4            4z4          4z4          4z4
 4zzz4          4zzz4        4zzz4        4zzz4
4zzzzzz4       4zzzzzz4     4zzzzzz4     4zzzzzz4
4zzzzzzzzz4    4zzzzzzzzz4  4zzzzzzzzz4  4zzzzzzzzz4
4zzzzzzzzzzzzz4 4zzzzzzzzzzzzz4 4zzzzzzzzzzzzz4 4zzzzzzzzzzzzz4
4zzzzzzzzzzzzzzz4 4zzzzzzzzzzzzzzz4 4zzzzzzzzzzzzzzz4 4zzzzzzzzzzzzzzz4
```

Ray was reading over my shoulder. He asked, "Is he trying to draw waves?"

Waldo in the ocean. "No. Flames."

Ray took over the keyboard. A minute later, he said, "I thought there was something funny about the fire in your theater. Here's a commentary on Leviticus. Stoning is the required punishment for most sins. But there are two exceptions. The creep who bangs a mother and her daughter. And priests' daughters who become prostitutes. They get burned to death."

"Sweet. I haven't exactly lived the pure life, but a mom and her kid? And that other thing…I guess it's stoning for me. What a crazy fuck!"

"But what 'whore' is he referring to in this 'poem'?"

"Angela. An angel who 'flew' off a cliff. Remember, she teased him the night of the storm, pretending to come on to him. Which made her a whore in his eyes."

"But she fell a long, long time ago. Why, then, does she have to burn? Why is he writing in the present tense? Is that part of his 'poetry'?"

My account pinged with another email from Sharon's account.

I've got your whore.

"Fuck. It isn't just her email account. He's got *her.*"

Ray said, "She's no whore."

"To Wheezer all women are whores." And the email she'd sent me wasn't exactly G-rated.

I closed the laptop and ran for the door, Ray behind me.

As we headed to the car, Ray said, "He's taking her to Garnet Hill."

"How do you know?"

"'Where angels fly.' He's talking about where Angela flew through the air. Where she fell."

"Then he's setting her on fire."

"I'm afraid so. If he doesn't push her or stone her. Great choices." Ray handed me the keys. "You're driving. I'm calling 911."

"And telling them what?"

"Get in."

I got on the highway and headed north. Flashes of light appeared over the hills to the west, followed by distant thunder. A storm coming.

Ray said, "Finally. Maybe it'll cool things down."

I got off the Taconic and headed east toward Middleburg. As we drove, I counted seconds between lightning and thunder. They weren't changing. "That fucking storm is following us."

"West to east, that's how they roll. I'm telling the cops to go to the place where Buzzy fell. That his killer's there, and he's got another victim."

"And they'll start asking you all these questions, which will take half the night to explain. Even if they believe you, what's to stop them from stomping up there like a herd of elephants? Plus, with all the sirens… Wheezer will have done what he's doing before they get there."

"And he won't hear *us*? What if he's armed with more than a rock?" He got out his phone. "Fuck! No bars."

"You should have some by now. We're close to town. Maybe these thunderstorms took a tower down." I was relieved.

I parked and we got out. The atmosphere was impossibly close. We huffed up the path, sweating like pigs in a sauna. And like a wounded animal, I felt the coming storm at the sore back of my head.

Halfway up, I said, "Now we need to be quiet."

We crept up the last stretch.

We reached the top. We were alone. It was exactly as it was the last time I saw it. I pictured Buzzy's body up here on a tarp, Angela and George... I felt the edge pulling at me, like a magnet. I took a step back and leaned against the tree.

I whispered. "Why aren't they here?"

A flash of lightning illuminated an angry cloud bleeding diagonal sheets of rain, followed by a sharp crack of thunder. It wasn't much longer than a second between them.

Ray said, "If he's thinking of setting her on fire, he'll have a tough time when that rain hits. It would be easier to drown her. Should we wait?"

"No. You're right. He's not bringing her up here in the rain."

"You know where her house is?"

"I do."

We ran down the hill, jumped in the car, and headed for the other side of campus.

Ray had his phone out again. "Still no service."

"What was Wheezer's poem again?"

"'Where angels fly, the whore must die.'"

"No, the last part."

"'I'll meet you in hell.'"

"Hell. *The basement.* The scene of the crime."

"What crime?"

I said, "Free love in the Rabbit Hole, on that couch. The origin of Wheezer's roots of evil. *That's* where he has her. That's where her office is, where she was working on that paper when I called to warn her. 'Where angels fly'—Not Angela falling off the cliff, but where I last saw her, at the Four Brothers house, flying on acid, like the rest of us."

"I'm confused. Is she supposed to be an angel, or a whore?"

"She's both. Think of his mom. *She* had to be both to him. You can't help loving your mother even if she's sexually abusing you. And she was probably the only female to ever touch him. Despite the horror of it, his body probably *enjoyed* it. That's what's so awful about that stuff. The night of the storm he's riding this Promethean dose of psychedelics when Angela pretends to come on to him. And he sees her as his mother. An angel."

"You're starting to sound like me."

"The clincher is that the email Sharon sent me referred to a night when I was with her down there in the basement."

"I knew there was a vibe when I saw you two together. You were on that couch."

"And I don't know how I know, but I'm sure now Wheezer was watching."

The thunder was getting louder. Even so, the dogs didn't stir from their pile in the backseat. They'd sleep through the apocalypse.

Ray said, "That's crazy. Maybe too crazy. What if he has her at her house?"

"Fine. Drop me at the Four Brothers house and you go there. If they're not there, you meet me. If they are there, you come get me before you do anything." I gave him directions to her house.

As I got out, Mingus sensed it and sprung into the front seat. I held him and said, "It's all right. I'll be right back. Promise." He didn't look convinced.

29.

I ran up to the front door of the old Four Brothers house. The wind was gusting madly and the air was thick with the smell of ozone. The storm was almost here. The door was locked, as it should be. There were floodlights on the corners of the house, as elsewhere on campus. One light was on in an upstairs office. I tried to remember the complicated interior layout of the house. It could be hers.

I charged at the door and hit with my shoulder. It hurt like hell but didn't budge. I struck the knob with my foot like I'd seen in some movie. Damned if the door didn't fly open and I fell on my ass.

I got up and listened. There was only the faint ticking of a clock. The place felt empty. Maybe Ray was right.

Still, I crept silently upstairs and felt my way down the hall toward the light. It came from Sharon's open office door.

I peered around the edge of it...no one. There was also no sign of a struggle. That was good news. Maybe he just had her email. Except that a desktop computer was on, the screen filled with text. She'd been working here.

I went out into the hall. The other offices were dark. She wouldn't just leave without turning out the lights.

Where angels fly.... The last time I'd seen Angela was downstairs in what had been the living room. I crept down and through a maze of halls. What had been the living room was now a dark library behind a wide interior window.

But I'd seen Wheezer in the *kitchen* that night…I walked faster to where it had been. There was no kitchen. Just a silent hall with office doors. They were all locked.

The basement.

Ray was right. I needed to get the cops. I checked my phone. There were still no bars, but I could walk to the police station in ten minutes. Easier, use the secretary's phone in the front hall.

No. I'd been right at Garnet Hill. Unless Middleburg had started hiring geniuses, they'd come stomping into the basement again, like that night. And get Sharon killed.

I ran to the steel door that led to the basement. It was locked. I knew where the key was, in that coat closet the girl had gotten it from. But Wheezer had a rock, gasoline, for all I knew the sword of God's vengeance. It would be a tough door to open without noise. I had the light on my phone, but it was bright.

I needed to sneak in so he couldn't see or hear.

I ran to the front door and out into the night. A blast of cold rain lashed at my arm. The lightning was coming a couple of flashes a second, and the thunder was almost continuous.

I pounded down the street until I was even with the backyard of the building. It gleamed with floodlights. I squeezed through a slot in a hedge and across a secluded lawn.

How had Wheezer snuck into the basement that winter?

I saw a steel bulkhead like the one I was going to install at home. A replacement for the one he'd snuck in? In that case, I was screwed, because this one had a big, shiny lock. I tried to remember the back of the house then. Nothing came. Had I even come back here?

Past the bulkhead was a low, rusted iron door. A coal chute. It looked too narrow for anyone but a kid.

I ran to the other side of the building and turned the corner. There was a garden shed. With a door to the inside?

An earsplitting crash and I jumped. The sky opened up and I was instantly soaked to the skin. The torrent felt solid as a waterfall. It was crazy, but I put my head down, like I might drown.

Rain hammered on the shed's tin roof. A spout overhead burst to life and gushed onto my head. I reached for the doorknob, hesitating at the sound it might make. It wouldn't be a problem with the storm.

Inside, I got out my cell phone and trained the light on a lawnmower, leaf blower, and garden tools neatly hung on a wall. At the far end of the shed, behind a wheelbarrow, crouched an old, wooden bulkhead. It wasn't locked. Was it where he'd gotten in back then? It didn't matter. It was how I was going in now.

I oriented myself. I was on a side of the building near the back of the basement. The three rooms were to the front, maybe a hundred feet away.

The storm raged outside, but it was much quieter in the shed. I hauled the wheelbarrow to the side, then yanked open the bulkhead. Hinges screamed. I stood still and listened.

A faint sound came from below. I turned off my light and crept down a half flight of steps into the black opening. The sound was louder down here: scraping alternating with clattering. The storm was barely audible. It was an old building with thick walls.

I turned on the light on my phone, training it against my leg so little of it leaked into the room. I had no memory of ever being in this part of the basement. Was there a door connecting it with the three rooms making up our part? There had to be in order to access the furnace, but which of the three rooms was it in? I didn't remember any door.

I pointed the light at the floor and had a bad moment. There were stacks of old stuff lined up in neat rows, just like in my museum, like this was some crazy wing I'd never seen before...

I was in Middleburg, not back in Hudson. There were suitcases and floor lamps. Dusty furniture and ancient football helmets. Old wooden boxes with items sticking from the top. This was what students left at the end of the year, accumulated over decades. Some students came back for it, many didn't. And the collection grew. Like mine. This collection had been here *in 1969*, because it was storage for students before the year the Four Brothers had "liberated" the old frat house.

Had I come in this part of the basement that year and seen this? Had that been the seed of my museum? How much of life had roots buried in the past?

Wheezer had been interested in my stuff in that video. Did it remind him of this place?

I yanked my consciousness back to the present. The scraping and clattering continued. I cupped the phone with the light and gingerly trained it in front of me and to the sides. Why? I didn't want him to see it. But there was a solid wall between the three rooms and here, wasn't there? Never mind.

The rows of stuff were perpendicular to that wall. I couldn't see the extent of the room without flashing the light around but could sense that it was huge.

I tiptoed down an aisle between two rows of the junk. The piles grew. Now the stuff was on shelves. A little further in, I had to step around items that had fallen into the aisle.

I trained my light toward the left wall and saw the cause—the side of the hill had collapsed into the basement. As the collection approached the three rooms on this side of the basement, it degenerated into a tangled pile: rugs and furniture, a bed frame and hockey sticks. A cloth with giant lettering, a banner from some long-forgotten sports rally.

I climbed over the stuff toward the sounds. The raging storm was just background accompaniment to the scraping and clattering. Which was what? A shovel. And stones? Hitting something. I shuddered. *Wheezer on the cliff with his rock...*

The Rabbit Hole was on the left behind the wall past the pile of junk, about ten feet away. That's where the sounds seemed to be coming from. They stopped and I froze.

After a moment's silence came Wheezer's croak. "'The nakedness of thy father, or the nakedness of thy mother, shalt thou not uncover: she is thy mother; thou shalt not uncover her nakedness.'"

He seemed to be getting right down to the primal trauma. He'd stopped what he was doing and was reading his Bible. I entertained the faintest hope that he was reading it to himself. That Sharon was out driving in her car, halfway across the state.

I crept forward on hands and knees over the junk and smelled gasoline. Shit.

I clicked off the flash. A flickering pinprick of light pierced the darkness. I moved closer. The light came from a hole, as big around as a middle finger, at about eye level. I moved forward and peered into it.

The Rabbit Hole was lit by candlelight, as it had been the night of the snowstorm. *And it's storming again...* These candles were the same kind as then, fat Christmas jobs that stood by themselves without candlesticks. There'd been one then, but now there were four, lined up before the Free Love Couch like it was an altar.

I looked up and hope collapsed. Sharon sat on the couch, hands, feet, and mouth mummified in yards of duct tape. Could she breathe? Wheezer sat next to her cradling his Bible, reading aloud. The ruins of the Free Love mural looked down on them.

My gaze was drawn by the color red to a can of gas on the floor to one side of the couch. The gas smell was strong now that my nose was near the hole. Had he doused Sharon in it?

This is where Wheezer had watched from when I was with that anonymous girl the night of the storm. And he'd been here another night, watching Sharon and me.

Our roles were reversed. The thought, along with that ragged voice droning, slipped a gear in my mind. As if we'd actually switched places, and I was him. I felt his insanity, sensed this great magnet of irrationality pulling at me, channeling that speed freak from long ago, telling me, *It's all connected, man! It all has meaning!*

And damned if Wheezer wasn't reading about the Tree of Life, and the Tree of Knowledge, and the forbidden fruit. *Trees with roots. The roots of evil...*

I wrestled my mind back from the nonsense.

There was just an old basement and a lunatic with...Sharon. All I could see of her face were her eyes. They were wide with fear, naturally. But she was one tough woman. And I was going to get her out of this.

How?

How had Wheezer gotten her down here? With a knife? A gun? All I saw was the can of gas. Which he was going to use to set her on fire. *You can't count, asshole? You should have* five *candles. Four for the brothers, and one for...her.*

A flame flared behind the gas can. The fifth candle was hiding there, waiting to do its job with the gas. Sharon's candle.

A pile of fist-sized stones sat next to the couch on the side opposite the gas, along with a shovel next to the part of the stone floor he'd been digging up to get them.

That explained the scraping and clattering.

I was confused. Was he going to stone her first, then burn her?

At the thought, my grip on my mind faltered and again I felt a part of me switching with Wheezer. Wheezer had added Sharon to his list of "evil roots." She was going to burn. But first her purpose had been to lure me here. Which had worked. The stones weren't for Sharon, but *me*. Stones, and then perhaps a shallow grave, down in the earth from which the roots had first sprung in his mind.

Four had become five. Four Brothers and a Sister.

I swung the flash to my right. There *was* a door into this part of the basement, about eight feet away, mostly concealed by the pile of junk, which rose in places to within two feet of the ceiling. Did it lead to the Rabbit Hole or Music Room? And did it open in or out?

In either case, I needed to get through it. Something was stopping me.

Wheezer read, "'If she profanes herself by harlotry, she profanes her father; she shall be burned with fire.'"

He was working himself up to act. But how? If he set her on fire, the whole house was going to go up. Then he wouldn't get to stone me.

What was stopping me from racing in there was my knowledge of just what a tough woman Sharon was. She hadn't come down here willingly. She would have fought like a tiger, unless he had a knife or gun to force her down the stairs and as he taped her up. I didn't see any weapons, aside from the shovel. Maybe he'd used that?

There was something scarier than going up against him unarmed—

crashing in there and triggering him to light her on fire.

But Wheezer didn't pick up a candle. Instead he got off the couch and crouched on the floor in front of the candles, fussing with something brown I'd overlooked. It was an old leather suitcase. He pulled out some clothes, held up an item, and Sharon's eyes glinted in the candlelight as they focused on it. His other hand appeared, and the light gleamed on the blade of a big knife.

Shit.

He said, "I am going to cut the tape on your feet and hands, and you are going to put this on." He walked over and lifted the can of gas, spraying her front with it. The smell got stronger.

"Don't try to escape. If you do…" He nodded toward the nearest candle. He put the gas down. And picked up…oh, God. A peasant skirt. Just like the one that had turned Waldo's jeans into bell-bottoms.

On his blog, Wheezer had described how George had ordered him to pack Angela's clothes in a suitcase so people would think she'd just left college, instead of being murdered. Wheezer was familiar with this part of the basement, had drilled this hole in the wall. What better place to hide a suitcase than in all that junk? There had to be fifty suitcases there already.

"Before you receive your punishment, I will dress you as an angel. Perhaps it will go better for you in the eternal flames." He was going to dress her in Angela's clothes.

I needed to draw his attention away from Sharon. And…It came in a flash. *And lure him in here with me.* So she could escape.

Wheezer used the knife to free her feet, then her hands. He left the tape over her mouth.

He said, "Stand and take off your clothes."

She stood and began unbuttoning her shirt. She was taking her time.

"Hurry up."

I suppressed the urge to scream. I needed to get him in here *now*.

I flicked on the light on my phone and looked around.

I surveyed the junk. A pile of books and an alarm clock. I needed something heavier. There was an ancient transistor radio with a metal casing.

I took a last look in the peephole. Sharon had her shirt unbuttoned. It was time.

I hoped to launch my missile to the far end of the room. He'd head there and I could get in front of him and get to Sharon.

I'd never been a ball player, but I whipped the radio over my shoulder as hard as I could. It hit something far short of the other side of the room and clattered to the floor.

I looked through the hole. Wheezer stood, not moving. The knife clanged to the floor and an instant later he dropped the candle...*the gas!* But it rolled away toward the door and went out.

He grabbed a roll of duct tape from the floor and ran to Sharon. She backed up and fell onto the couch. He leaned over her and taped her wrists. She struggled. He bound her legs. He threw the tape away and raced for the door. There was loud thumping as he struggled to get it open. It opened into this room and was obstructed by junk.

I scrambled across the pile away from the door and rolled behind a large bureau and crouched, peering around the side. I clicked the light on my phone off again.

There was a crash as the door splintered and candlelight spilled in from the other room. He'd broken off the top half of the door and was climbing in. A bright light played over the piles of crap. He had a flashlight. The top of his head appeared, and I ducked down.

Throwing the radio hadn't fooled him. He was headed right for the peephole. When he didn't find me, he turned and headed away into the right side of the room. Away from me. If he kept going in that direction, I could maybe rush to the door...

I was headed there when a shot rang out. It was deafening, yet strangely flat, its echo sucked into the piles of stuff. I froze. Had he seen me and missed? Or was he trying to get me to break cover? I crouched, holding my knees, trying to get as small as I could, like prey.

A second shot. It seemed to hit closer. I scurried back behind the bureau.

I'd figured he had to have a knife or gun to get Sharon down here. I hadn't figured on both.

I'd only remain hidden here until he found me. Then, bang.

His light flickered on the ceiling, maybe fifteen feet away. He was crawling over the stuff, coming toward me. His light reflected off the ceiling, making me feel terribly exposed even though I was behind the bureau. But it also illuminated a pile of books. I grabbed one and flung it across the room. It was a better pitch than the last.

Wheezer stopped for a moment. When he started moving again his light pointed away. He fired again.

"Hutchinson, come out of your hole, or I'm going to burn you both." Without thinking, I picked up the alarm clock. It was heavier than it looked. It must be solid brass, from before things were made of plastic. *A weapon.*

His breathing became audible, with a new whistling tone. His asthma. How could I exploit it? By getting him upset. That had worked up on the rock. But if I yelled something taunting now, he'd locate me and shoot.

Would physical exertion do the trick? Before I could second guess, I grabbed the alarm clock and dashed from behind the bureau and over the junk to one of the aisles then down it. I sidestepped through a gap and into another aisle. His gun boomed, but I was a fast-moving target. And he couldn't see me.

He was scrambling, then running, and the whistling got louder. I was panting myself. I raced down the last aisle to the right. Another shot. How many rounds did he have?

What I needed to do was *get behind him.* His light was brighter than mine, and he'd naturally look to where he pointed it. He wouldn't see mine unless he was looking right at it. I clicked it on, cupping it in my hand. I saw a bookcase on my left. It was large, deep, and empty. The bottom shelf must be for oversized books, because it was just high enough for me to fit. I fell to my knees and slowly crawled on my belly into the shelf. I pushed past the shelf into a hollow, a cave whose walls were the bookcase and a couple of armchairs, with a mattress draped over as a roof. A foot-wide gap opened on the next aisle. I clicked the light off and lay still.

I was trapped. If he found me, I didn't have a prayer.

His breathing got farther away. Was he heading back for Sharon? A flicker of his light and the sound got louder. He was coming back this way. Slowly. I heard him digging in the stuff, throwing things, like he was trying to unearth some vermin. A cat after a mouse.

I sensed him very close and stopped breathing. I glimpsed a leg, not six inches from my face and sucked in an involuntary breath. It was not as loud as his, though. I let him pass, then barreled out of my mouse hole. He was in front of me with his back turned. I launched myself at him and grabbed both his legs. He fell on his face and struggled to get up.

I was back where I'd been on top of that cliff. It was kill or be killed, and I could not kill. Except a new variable had altered the equation.

Sharon.

I dove onto his body and smashed the clock on the back of his head. And again. And...

I stopped. He was still wheezing, but otherwise unmoving. Blood oozed into his graying, wispy hair. The arm with the clock was raised and set to smash down like it was on a spring. I held it back as my thoughts raced forward.

Kill him. Get Sharon and use Wheezer's gas to torch the house. Get away before the fire department and the cops. Avoid messy explanations.

No. There was a middle way. I got up, freely using my flash. I scurried down the row. There was a neat coil of hemp rope. Rotten? I snagged it and ran to the body on the floor, working the end loose as I went.

I'd never been a Boy Scout or a sailor but I knew knots from camping in the Adirondacks. I knew how to secure a bunch of gear on top of my car.

I trussed him up like a turkey and scrambled to the Rabbit Hole. "Sharon!"

She didn't answer. Had she escaped?

I crawled through the top of the door and climbed down into candlelight.

She wasn't there. I headed for the door to the Music Room and stopped at a sound. What? From where?

Humming, from behind the couch. I walked over.

Sharon was huddled there between the wall and the couch, still taped, hugging the back of it, her eyes tightly shut. The humming was her voice from behind the tape.

"Sharon. Sharon." I said her name, gently, almost at a whisper as I eased the couch away from the wall.

She opened her eyes and they darted frantically around until she saw me. She locked her gaze on mine, sending an electric thrill from head to toe. I pointed to the tape on her mouth. "You want me to get that off?"

She nodded. I ripped it off without pulling her hair too badly.

"Where is he?"

"I took care of him."

"Put out those fucking candles! All I've been able to think about is that I'm about to catch fire." She stank of gasoline.

I snuffed them and came back to her, the phone with its light in my teeth. I knelt and got her hands and legs loose. I pulled her up to sitting and we hugged. I melted into her until there was nothing but the warm sensation of two bodies breathing. It was impossible to know just where one started and the other one stopped. But at least one of them experienced this extraordinary bursting in the chest.

I said, "Let's get out of here."

"Let's. But you need to help me up. That gasoline's got my head spinning. Worst fucking high in my life."

I helped her up, but she collapsed into me. I got her to the couch and sat next to her. "I'm too dizzy. I need a minute." As I got a good look at her face, my feeling sunk. She looked like someone who'd been in a war. What if Wheezer got loose? I'd hear him coming over all that junk.

She said, "You saved my life."

"Yeah, after putting it at risk by getting you into this mess."

"You don't need to go there." She hugged me.

She said, "I wish I could get out of these filthy clothes." She eyed Angela's suitcase and laughed. "There's always her dress. I don't imagine it...fits me."

"Nope. And that's a good thing." I held her tighter. "Still dizzy?"

"A little better. Well, you and I finally made it back here, to this couch."

"Yeah." I stood. "And now it's time to..."

"Just stop. I know you. I know what you're thinking. Run away, pretend none of this happened. Make an anonymous call to the police."

She was getting very good at reading my mind. "And what's wrong with that?"

"I work here in this building. There's probably evidence in my office, and I don't want to answer any more questions than I have to. But it's not just you potentially dumping it in my lap. I know you're Mr. Do-It-Yourself. And you don't like the police. But Wheezer isn't your business. He's *theirs.*"

Fuck. All the evidence I had I'd hacked or snuck. It was all illegal. Except she was right. As right as I'd been when I restrained my hand and didn't crush Wheezer's skull.

I punched 911 in my phone but there were still no bars. "I think the storm took out a tower."

Sharon nodded. "How did you kill him?"

I took a deep breath. "I didn't."

"Where the hell is he?"

I pointed. "He's in there tied up in a mile of rope. He makes a move we'll hear him."

She wasn't buying it. She struggled to stand, and I helped her up. She leaned on me as we stepped toward the door to the Music Room. We passed the door to the rest of basement. There wasn't a sound.

She said, "Fuck. I feel like an invalid."

Those stairs were going to be a trick. But first things first. We made it to Dope Central.

She said, "I need to rest for a moment." We sat against the wall like the Four Brothers had back in the day.

She said, "You didn't kill him. And you could have."

"I suppose so."

Her voice broke. "I was wrong, getting all shrinky, saying your nonviolence was a way of avoiding feeling back with Angela. You're the real deal. Not a killer. I'm glad."

She was making me squirm.

Muffled sounds came from above.

She clutched my arm. "What's that?"

"It must be Ray."

It couldn't be. It was more like a thundering herd, pounding at the door. Shouting, "Police!" The Middleburg Police. For an instant I fell back in time, to the night of the storm, to the bust.

But I wasn't tripping now. And It was raining out there, not snowing. Those weren't the same cops pounding down the stairs. And I wasn't the same Bodine.

Keep reading for an excerpt from the next book in the Ray of Darkness series, *The Girl in the Game.*

PART ONE

1.

The door is stuck half open. I slip in and sweep my flashlight down the left tier of lockers. They're stacked double, 101 on top of 103, 105 over 107. Rust nibbles at the edges of the gunmetal gray doors. One-oh-seven is mottled with orange, like a nasty skin rash, which spreads onto the next units, growing until the last, 129, is engulfed. It's like the progression of a fatal disease, ventilation slats exhaling dying breaths.

Even lockers face the odds, a low wooden bench between them dividing the floor into two narrow paths. The right is buried under a jumble of collapsed ceiling panels. So I squeeze down the left side, ducking a florescent fixture dangling from ganglia of wires. Most doors gape a few inches. One-fifteen is wide open, a once-white towel hanging inside, furred with mildew and streaked with an inky glistening substance. The straps of a woman's one-piece bathing suit spill from the bottom, moist and brown, like rotten leaves in a gutter. Perhaps it's the source of the sick-bed smell. The floor is strewn with relics: a wooden hairbrush, tangled with black hair. Maroon plastic barrettes.

The room dead-ends at a cinderblock wall with passages to either side. To the right are communal showers, two cycles of drips echoing from beige tiles, like windshield wipers out of sync—the only sound aside from my socks scuffing the floor. To the left stand another set of lockers. These are full height. More expensive. They're all closed. The last three on the left appear to have something growing in them. It's bright orange, squeezing from the ventilation slats. Not my favorite color, and a butt-ugly shade of it. Call it "screaming orange." At a glance it's just more fungus. And who's going to come in here, anyway? I can imagine a million better spots for a lover's den.

Despite precautions, the contents of the three lockers are getting ripe, stronger than that sick-bed smell.

I turn and get down on all fours. It's tight, but I can crawl. I leave the way I came, brushing away the faint prints of stockinged feet with my gloves. Through the lower-class section, past that smelly one-piece to the entrance. I stand and squeeze out.

There's no hint out here of that stink. Just normal decay. Do smells move, flow like water? If so, it'll take time.

No one will ever find them in those lockers.

2.

Ray opened the door to Jo's Joe and inhaled the warm atmosphere of his friend's restaurant. The bite of espresso, tang of burnt sugar on freshly baked muffins, the sweetness of sourdough. Smells of life.

The deep, narrow room was almost full, but even now it only hummed pleasantly, because Jo kept the music practically inaudible and didn't have a liquor license. Ray headed to the back and passed Jo as she emerged from the kitchen, effortlessly balancing lunches for a table of four. She caught his eye and cocked her head toward his table—take it before I have to give it to someone else. She mouthed the words, "The usual?" He nodded and sat.

Jo delivered the food to a couple and their two kids and headed into the kitchen to place his order—the same thing he'd been eating for a year. Pastrami and Swiss on sourdough, extra Dijon and extra pickles. He loved mustard and pickles. Liz hated them.

Ray looked around at the other customers and sank into his chair, doing his best to let go of a frustrating morning of work.

Jo delivered his lunch, along with her smile. She was always smiling. Like the sun–if the sun had the virtuosity to convey twenty-seven different moods, from excitement to skepticism, even sorrow. He thought he'd seen all her smiles in the years he'd known her. Not this one. It was too bright. And a little…crooked.

He was about to say something, but she was off, serving other customers. He studied her movements out of the corner of his eye as he ate. It didn't matter if every table in the place was full. Jo was always steady and deliberate.

Except today. She was rushed. Distracted, like she wanted to be someplace else.

When she brought his check he asked, "What's up with you?"

She sighed. "I'll tell you later. You going to be around?" She nodded toward his house across the street.

"Sure."

"I've got someone who wants to meet you."

As Ray was heading out, Jo went behind the counter and pulled a fat éclair out from under the glass. "On the house. Hundred percent white flour, white sugar."

"Don't know what I'd do without you to take care of me."

He hit the sidewalk, wrestling Jo's gift from its wrapper. He took a big bite. Almost as sweet as its seller. If only things were as simple with Liz. He walked across Warren Street to his tall, thin Victorian house and entered the gallery on the first floor.

Someone wants to meet you. Who? It wasn't like Jo to be mysterious. That was more his friend Bodine's thing.

***

He sat at his desk in front of his laptop and attempted to get back to the book he was writing. The only thing keeping him awake was trying to figure out what to do about the display window. He stared out at the backwards letters, in Gothic script: "Ray of Darkness." He'd repainted them last year after someone tossed a brick through the glass. It had been early spring, and apparently too cold to paint, because the bottom of the "y" was already peeling. He should fix it before winter. Not that there were enough customers to—

The discordant bells jangled. The door opened and Jo entered, followed by a strange woman. She looked to be in her early thirties. Her straight auburn hair was held up in back by a big green comb, long tendrils loose at the sides, framing her face. Which was nice as far as it went. Because she wore a vague smile, like most of her hadn't arrived yet.

Jeans, a plaid shirt, funky jacket with shiny buttons. Black boots. A hipsterish look.

Jo said to Ray, "This is my niece." She introduced them to each other, "Faye, Ray."

Ray and Jo laughed. Jo said, "Sorry."

Faye looked mystified.

Jo said, "Fay Wray was an actress, in King Kong…way before your time."

Faye rolled her eyes.

Jo said, "I told her about the great talent living right across the street and she had to meet you. She works in design. She's…an artist, too."

It almost sounded like a question.

Jo nodded across the street. "Must get back to work." She hugged Faye and left.

Faye glanced at the sculptures. Her gaze locked on Ray's for a second and that smile slipped and something leaked out. His face got hot. She looked away and the vague smile returned. But some animal instinct in him had sprung alive to her presence. It tracked her as she glided into the gallery, pausing methodically at each piece, assessing, like dealers he'd seen. Like a pro. Now he followed her physically. He said, "What kind of art do you do?"

"Drawing, computer stuff. I've made a few sculptures."

"You have photos of your work?"

"Unh-uh. It's nothing like this."

"Not as dark."

She shrugged. "Mm. You play games?"

"Video games?"

She nodded.

Ray said, "Not in a while. I've played a couple of dungeon crawlers."

"No casual games?"

"Huh?"

"You know, for smart phones and tablets."

"Games on a phone?" He frowned. He couldn't see it. "I don't have a tablet. My…wife Liz has an iPad. I think she plays, what is it? The candy one."

"Candy Crush. That's fun. But there are others. Games are the new art."

"Really. What others?"

But they'd reached the back of the gallery, and she was distracted. Ray had staged the sculptures so that the deeper you got into the room, the darker the work. There was a fine edge between keeping to the Ray of Darkness style and offending customers. Hiding in the shadows of a corner was his buddy Maurice's latest. His "Psycho Ax-Murder Baby" had languished here for months, but after it finally sold, Maurice showed up with the first of what he deemed his "Religious period": a sculpture of a tonsured priest bowing in his confessional, a plastic monster hand snaking from the curtains to grope the faceless child on the other side.

She was staring at the sculpture, and he could feel the power of her concentration prickling the back of his neck. She reached out and feathered the priest's cheeks with fingertips. She patted the bald crown with her palm as if offering absolution.

Her fingernails were blue. Huh. She jerked her hand away. "Sorry."

Ray took in a quick breath. "Uh, no, it's OK." It would be nicer if you touched *my* head. At least I've got some hair. He winced guiltily at the thought.

She said, "Is this your work?"

"No, I um…"

"I know, Jo told me you're retired. Any of this yours?"

"My last piece sold over the summer." Except for the bathroom installation. Which was right behind the wall. "But—" He was about to point to it when the bells jangled up front. Liz bustled in, a shopping bag in one hand and her purse in the other. Ray and Faye walked toward her. Liz smiled at Ray. She looked at Faye and frowned.

Ray said, "Liz, this is Jo's niece, Faye."

Faye pointed to the iPad peeking from the top of Liz's purse. "You play Candy Crush?"

Liz glanced away. "Uh, yeah."

"What level are you on?"

She shrugged. "I don't count. It's actually a little embarrassing."

Faye said, "Not at all. They've done studies. Casual games are good for your health."

"Really?"

"But some casual games aren't so casual. There's this new one you should check out."

Liz asked, "What?" She was obviously losing interest.

"Core Quest."

As they spoke, Ray's hands clenched. He wished Liz would go upstairs and that Faye was still talking to him. Because as she'd talked games her foggy smile had melted and she'd beamed at Liz. She had a talent for smiles, like her aunt. But Jo's were warm. What he sensed coming from her was *fire*.

She was passionate about games. Trying to warm Liz to them, but Liz didn't care.

He said, "Core Quest? What's that about? Search for the perfect abs? Journey to the core curriculum?"

Faye's eyes blazed and he shrunk back. She closed them, opened them, shook her head, and choked out a laugh. "Don't knock it if you haven't tried it."

Ray's eyes darted to the iPad.

Liz said, "Nuh-uh." Liz hugged the tablet and said, "He sure isn't using mine!" She glared theatrically at him. "I don't like him messing with my stuff."

The terrible thing was she was only half joking. Liz was proprietary about her possessions, especially the electronic ones. If he were her, he'd dream up some dark psychological explanation for it.

Faye said to Liz, "But you don't mind if I do?"

Liz laughed. "Of course not." She pulled the tablet from her purse and handed it to Faye.

Faye tapped at the thing. "Hey, there's a special promotion on Core Quest this week—it's free. I'll download it for you. It'll just take a minute."

"That's really sweet of you, but I don't think I have time to play right now."

Faye ignored her. She swiped and tapped at the tablet. "Easy peasy, huh? Let's set up your character."

Ray moved closer, looked over one shoulder as Liz looked over the other, pretending interest, her eyes glazed.

Faye said, "You're a girl, of course. You have the choice of Warrior, Mage, and Priest."

Liz perked up. "I'm a warrior. Duh."

Ray said, "Actually, Liz has always wished she was a shrink. She likes to say shrinks are the new priests... Let her dream."

Faye said, "Priestess it is. Here's your hair color—auburn."

Liz said, "And here I was thinking it was just reddish-brown."

"What about this stole?"

Liz was doing a bad job of pretending to get into it. "Ooh. Do I get to wield that scepter?" She sounded snippy, but Faye ignored it.

"Soon as you earn it."

A synthesized trumpet fanfare theme blasted from the tablet. Faye said, "You're ready to go."

Liz glanced away as she took the iPad back. "Well, lovely meeting you. But I've got work to do." She gave Faye a quick hug and went upstairs.

Faye said, "You're a lucky man." That vague smile again. But now he sensed what was behind it. A low hum, like a furnace on standby. When the thermostat clicked on, the fire roared to life.

"Uh-huh."

She started toward the door, and he felt her leaving in his body, and it felt bad.

He said, "Uh, I was about to say when Liz came in, I do have one piece of mine, if you want to see it."

"Maybe some other time."

She gave a tiny nod of her head then left.

He turned the sign in the door to "closed" and headed upstairs.

Liz was sitting at the kitchen table going through mail. He sat with her. She asked, "What do you think of this Faye?"

He paused, felt his face flush. "Faye's...intense."

"You think she's cute."

"Liz, she's practically half my age."

She frowned at him then laughed. "Intense? She was....something. Unusual?"

"So—you going to try that game?"

She snorted. "When exactly will I find the time?"

"You had time for Candy Crush."

"A temporary lapse. That was odd, downloading that thing for someone she just met."

"You saw—she's really into games. Maybe it's one of those multiplayer ones."

"Well, she's going to have to find someone else to play with. Too bad you don't have an iPad. You could play with her."

"I have enough trouble getting any work done."

"Those zombies eating you alive? Isn't that their job?"

"I'm just not feeling it."

She said hopefully, "At least zombie books sell."

"So does kiddie porn."

"Zombie apocalypse wasn't built in a day. You remember how it was with your art? You had doubts all the time."

"This is…different. There's doubt. And then there's knowing for sure something's no good. And it's no good because my heart isn't in it."

"I'm sure it's fine."

"Really? Then why don't you read some of it?"

Her silence answered his question, but then she went on. "I told you, I don't know anything about those kind of books. If you insist."

"Insist? When I was making art, I had to fight you off from coming in my studio to see things before they were done. You pored over every crummy sketch. You loved my art."

"I'm sorry. I'll read it."

"No, you won't. Because I don't want to make you lie. You're going to hate it, because it sucks."

3.

Liz went out. Ray headed for the bedroom with his laptop and lay down. You didn't want to make napping a habit. And it wasn't. Just five, six afternoons a week. And this wasn't really going to be a nap. He'd just read the newspaper online and space out. If he dozed? Let the nap police come.

He got comfortable beneath the spread and turned to a favorite news blog. Glanced over toward Liz's side of the bed. She'd left her iPad home, on the bedside stand.

He'd long ago learned not to mess with her towel in the bathroom, even though they slept and made love in the same bed. He wouldn't think of opening her laptop with its case files.

But this was only an iPad. More a toy than a tool. And what was the harm? She'd never find out.

He scooched over toward her bedside stand. He pictured Faye after she'd dropped that faint smile. His face got warm. He just wanted a peek at that game. He reached over and plucked the tablet from the stand with his fingertips, like he might get prints on it.

He punched the thing awake and swiped to the last page. The icon of Core Quest was a translucent globe. He tapped on it, then drummed his fingers on his knees as the game loaded. Faye had saved him the trouble of setting up a character.

Ha! Cross-dressing as a priestess. Not a particular kink of his, but hey.

He stands, gazing down at tall black suede boots. Looks up to a perfectly round room with a slightly concave ceiling, like the interior of a woman's

compact. The space is the definition of well appointed. Luxuriant and dimly lit. A polished parquet floor gleams in light softly spilling from wall sconces. Fine paintings line the walls. The couch, with matching teak side tables, exudes comfort. The colors are warm browns and ochres. There's not a straight line in sight, everything fashioned in the organic curves of Art Deco.

He glances at a tall gilt-framed mirror and is startled to see himself. A priestess. A woman. Faint ambient music with soothing chords cushion tinkling bits of ear candy, like jewels in velvet.

Brakes screeched, a car horn blasted from the street below, and Ray surfaced, as from a spell. A memory came, from long ago: lying on the back seat of his parent's Chevy on the way home from Thanksgiving dinner with friends of his parents. His belly is stuffed long before the threat of heartburn. He's warm and safe from the cold and boundless night outside the window, in the sweet spot between waking and sleep. The pleasure is deep, and so is the wish for it to last forever.

He wakes to a blast of frigid air and his mother's tired face. "Get up, sleepyhead. We're home. You'll be in bed in a jiffy."

And he was, but it wasn't the same. His bed didn't move through the night, and his parents weren't up front.

He knew *longing*. He rode in the back seat again, even lay down to try to repeat the experience, but the feeling had never come back.

Until a moment ago. In the game. Warm, cocooned. And that screech of brakes had evoked the second part of the old experience, the shock of it being over. He dove back in. But now with that feeling of longing.

He has to move. But how? He taps at the virtual controller, slides fingers over its surface. And he's moving! He hears faint scuffling as his boots glide across the lustrous floor toward the door.

Locked.

The longing grows. He's gotta find the key. He searches under the couch, barely aware that his character can crouch. He squeezes behind a bookcase, with its fine leather volumes. Scours the shadowy corners.

Ray looked up from the tablet. In no time he'd gone from bliss to major irritation. A moment later, guilt. What had possessed him to mess with Liz's iPad? This wasn't like him. When Liz didn't want him doing something, he just didn't do it. Until now. What if she decided to play? She'd know from his progress that somebody had been playing. Who else but him? He could delete his game—if that was even possible— but then he'd have to start from the beginning. How was he going to progress, then?

He lunged over and slapped the iPad onto her bed stand. Exactly where had she left it? He inched it over to where he remembered it being. Or had it been closer to the lamp?

He wasn't the least bit sleepy. He got up and headed downstairs to write.

But he couldn't let the game go. He couldn't remember the last one he'd played, but this was a thousand generations ahead on the evolutionary scale: the sumptuous colors, the visual detail.

And what they'd evoked. He'd spent what, a half hour playing that game? In that time, he'd felt many things. That delicious sense of safe pleasure. The longing its interruption caused. Terrible frustration.

Faye had said games were the new art. Maybe she was onto something.

Art. For the first time in a couple of years, he felt the impulse in his hands. The desire to grip a tool, run fingers along a freshly sanded surface. But what was he thinking?

His eyes focused on the laptop keys, black on silver. Like it or not, this was his tool. He ground out a whole page, but with only half a brain. The other half churned on, trying to digest his experience with the game.

He wasn't making video games. But what about art? A few years ago, he and his muse had suffered a messy break up, what he'd been sure was divorce.

In recent months he'd seen signs that she might be back in town. His eyes were studying shapes, colors, and textures again. His fingers itched for something more satisfying than clacking on keys. He remembered that art show at the old perfume factory and smiled. He checked the time. It should be open for another hour. A little research always beat arguing with yourself.

He walked across town to the building. There wasn't a hint of perfume in the place until he got to the gallery on the top floor and passed an aging art patron wearing oversized glasses. And, to his relief, there wasn't a hint of his brand of art. He cast a baleful eye on bland watercolors, pretty photos of landscapes, and a semi-quirky sculpture. There was nothing barking up the tangled tree of his art, or even a hundred miles from the dark forest it grew in.

He left with a smile. A block from the factory, and he lost the smile. Just because there was a niche in the market for his stuff—at least in Hudson—didn't mean he was ready to make up with his muse. It was a matter of love. It wasn't enough to know you could create art like no one else. Your eyes, your soul needed to *hunger* for that missing thing. When you got to starving, the art came.

He wasn't there. He was stuck. Trapped in an artless project trying to bring life into the merciless undead. That was why that old prick tease of a muse was hanging around.

He pictured that round room in the game, and his fingers were moving. He rushed back home, up to the bedroom, and fired up the tablet.

There must be thousands of people playing this game right now, just feet from where he stands. Maybe right where he's standing. But there's no trace of them, just this calming music, the sconces casting a soothing twilight over the scene.

The key. He scurries around, searching the same places as last time he played. It was as maddening as looking for lost keys in your real house.

About to give up, he thinks to jimmy with the virtual controls. Ah. You can look at your hands. And there's the key, in the right one, where it had been all along. Ha!

He slots it in the keyhole and with a most satisfying snick, it turns! He pushes the door and it opens with a creak. He steps across the threshold and into history, and out-and-out luxury: a grand foyer resplendent with baroque tracery and red and gold velvet draperies, illuminated by an enormous glittering chandelier. Twin staircases wind their way upstairs in a series of almost musical curves. Between them, a few steps disappear down into a shadowed nook.

He ignores it and heads up. And up.

Exploring. Like in Italy that time with Liz. Discovering one wonderful little hill town after another. You never knew what was around the next bend in the road, except after a while you were sure it would look, smell, and taste unfamiliar and great.

He enters a dining room hung with glowing tapestries, three chandeliers illuminating lavish table settings for fifty. Ten pieces of silverware and four glittering goblets surround each Limoges plate. At the far end of the table, opposite where he came in, is an intricately carved Baroque door. The clock face above it reads ten-thirty.

The music stops. He moves to skirt the table when a hollowness in his footsteps has him looking down. The table and chairs float above blackness. An abyss, and he's almost fallen into it. Not that it matters. It's just a game. Still, he scurries back from the edge.

He's got to get across this room, through that door. Will the game let him climb onto the table? There's one way to find out. He messes with the controls and finds the finger gesture for lifting his legs. He gets one up onto the table, then the other and tiptoes between urns of steaming soup, bottles of burgundy, and orchid arrangements. Something tells him not to touch anything with his feet, so he moves at a crawl.

He's halfway across when the bell tolls, deep and sad. He looks up. Midnight. The screen goes black for a moment, then he's back at the beginning of the room. It's ten-thirty again.

He tries again, faster. He strikes a glass with his foot. It pings and the clock begins to tick loudly. The minute hand is now moving. He brushes against a serving dish. It barely makes a sound, but the ticking speeds up, and the minute hand spins.

Twenty tries at crossing the table later, and his palms are so slick he can barely control his movements. He's made it three-quarters of the way across.

And then, in some leap of both his feet and eye-hand coordination, he's there, at the door. To his relief, he's standing on a solid floor.

The door is locked.

Where the fuck is the key? He's standing at the threshold, tapping a finger on the touch screen, which makes his character jump, when he suddenly jumps...higher. And he gets it. If you tap twice in just the right rhythm, you do a double jump. Like mastering a difficult guitar chord.

So what? He crosses the table using the high jumps, and his head crashes into the chandelier at the mid-point. He hears the tinkling of a hundred crystal shards as they rain on the table, along with a click. He looks down. Broken glass. And something poking from behind a soup tureen.

The key.

With effort, he tore his eyes from the screen and closed the tablet. He placed it back on the stand and walked upstairs to his couch behind the round window, his favorite place to think.

That game was a drug. It had his heart racing and flooded his brain with chemicals. Stuff that made him feel smart and athletic. Super competent. Getting through that door had been hard. But he did it.

It took a few minutes for the buzz to wear off, for the challenges of his real life to seep back in, souring his stomach, furrowing his brow. Him and Liz. Him and deadbeat zombies. It was a nice house he was living in, but there was no peace in it.

But the house in the game? He wanted to live there.

Speaking of feeling smart: what about the people who made this thing? They *knew* he'd walk too slow, then too fast. Knew he'd figure out how to jump, and that he'd hit that chandelier. And knew the whole process would make him feel great.

What if... He let out a groan as the longing seized his chest, twisting like a fist. The feeling raced down his arms, streaming into his fingers. This was the same mad excitement as the first time he heard the Beatles. It had made him run out and get a guitar. Compelled him to become a musician.

Later he got the same feeling seeing Joseph Cornell's spooky little boxes in a museum. Soon he was drawing, sculpting. Becoming an artist.

What if...he could blow people's minds, like this game did? What if he could be one of the people that make them?

He was half off the couch. A moment later he collapsed, and his fingers dug into his palms. He sure wasn't going to be blowing any minds writing the zombie book. Because it was all work and no play. To create something fun you needed to get some of that buzz making it. Whoever made this game must be having a blast.

Lurking in the back of his mind was the thought, *You're hiding the game from Liz.* And he should feel bad about it, but his emotions only had so much bandwidth, and right now it was maxed out.

4.

Ray was sitting in the gallery the next morning around eleven, the laptop closed, staring out the window wondering what would happen to his digestion if he lunched at Jo's this early, when the bells jangled. Faye edged past the door, dressed in the same pants and jacket, but a different plaid shirt. His pulse ticked in his temples.

She stood by the door and looked at him with that vague smile.

"I hope I'm not interrupting."

"Just writing."

"Oh, right. Jo said you did that. What about?"

"Zombies."

He expected a raised eyebrow or perhaps more—*Zombies are so cool!* But she seemed bored, as if he'd said he was writing about the national debt. Maybe his boredom was contagious.

She said, "I looked at your website."

He drummed his fingers on the desk. "And?"

A teeny nod of her head. "I'd like to see more. You referred to an installation, something to do with a bathroom. You've got some decent reviews."

Decent? The *New York Times!* And Liz called it his "masterpiece." Liz might have been flattering him—did barely known artists make masterpieces? But he was proud of it. Now he said, "I know it's weird, making art out of a bathroom."

"Not so weird. I made a sculpture in high school with a bathtub in it. Why no photos of it on your website?"

"Because it's not for sale. And...I don't think pictures do it justice."

He led her to the back of the gallery. She stepped into the 12 x12 room, and he stood at the door behind her, willing his hands not to fist, forcing the breaths as he awaited her verdict. Her hair flipped from side to side as she inspected the installation, with that professional assurance she'd shown when she first came to the gallery. He couldn't see her face, but the walls seemed to shiver, to glow under her gaze.

He'd rounded the edges, turning the space into a mahogany cocoon with a silky skin of resin, a surface that invited touch, until you noticed that what floated below the surface, just visible, were bone fragments. Faye ran fingers over the wall and said, "Lacquer on resin. Nice." She turned to the centerpiece, the medicine cabinet with a miniature plastic skeleton behind glass.

He said, "That was an old toy, the Visible Man model. My younger self and future self. A kind of—"

"Memento Mori."

"Yes! You get it."

She turned, looked him straight in the eye, and took his upper arm with those blue-nailed fingers. He sensed the warmth of her hand through his shirt.

She said, "It's you." She turned a big smile on him, and the heat rolled off her in waves.

Her words and the smile fell on him like rain on desert hardpan. His artist's craving for praise arose from deep in his brain, the primordial place from which he craved booze and chocolate. Sex. A hunger for adulation that hadn't been so much as tickled in the years since he stopped making art. The sensation was delicious as her voice reached down into his brain and *squeezed* that tender spot. His eyelids drooped, like she was swinging a shining object before them, hypnotizing him.

He was not much of a smiler, but now one escaped. She left the bathroom, and he followed her to the front of the gallery.

She gripped the door knob, and the bells gave a discordant shiver. She stopped with her hand on the knob. "Weird bells you've got."

He pointed to the gothic letters in the window—*Ray of Darkness*. "They're to give fair warning."

Again, she was silent. It was a disconcerting habit. But she also didn't leave. She seemed to be deciding something. He gazed at her fingernails. She noticed and extended a hand toward him so he could see better. Blue polish. Not polish. More like paint, because there were miniature scenes on each.

He couldn't help himself, clasping her hand, lifting it and staring. He said, "I'm sorry, I just—"

"Don't be." She held both hands up to his face. The detail on the nails was amazing, like jade carvings in geometric semi-abstract patterns.

He said, "Damn. These are amazing. Who painted them?"

"Me."

He looked at her, and she gazed back, and he could feel a circle close around them. I showed you mine. Now I've seen yours. Members of an elite club. Artists.

She said, "I've got to go."

She left.

He stood for several minutes, not moving, skin tingling, his pulse hammering at his temples. What was this?

Desire. For Faye? Of course, only he wasn't going there. Not with his new bride Liz with the proverbial Calphalon pan. Not with her so much younger.

But there was another part of the desire: the impulse to make art again. Just yesterday at the perfume factory it had been missing. Or disembodied, just curiosity at the tips of his senses. This felt like a rubber band in his gut, taut, trembling. The sight of his installation had sparked something in Faye and the spark had leapt into him.

But what form would it take? Did he still have the talent? And hadn't he been certain it was over, that his muse was never coming back? Like an answer to a prayer, the bells jangled and Faye was back.

She came in. "I made a phone call. My boss wants to meet you."

"What boss? Where do you work?"

"It's a secret. You like secrets?"

Good ones. "Sure."

"When?"

"Now, if you have a few hours."

363

He glanced around the gallery, which hadn't seen a customer in days. He nodded.

She pointed back toward the bathroom. "You have any photos?"

"On my computer."

"You said they didn't do it justice."

"You judge."

He opened the laptop, scrolled through pictures of the installation as she looked over his shoulder. She started choosing, making little appreciative noises at the ones she liked. She plucked a thumb drive from a pocket. "Okay to put them on this?"

"Sure. We can take my car."

She nodded toward the bathroom. "Uh, does that actually work?"

"The toilet? Sure."

"I'll just be a minute."

He drove his ancient Volvo wagon out of town and they talked art.

She said, "I really like late Bonnard."

"The bath pictures. That makes two of us. Did they inspire your bath sculpture?"

She made an unintelligible sound, and they lapsed into silence. She directed him south out of town, across the Rip Van Winkle Bridge, then south toward the Catskills.

Ray was sensitive. Permeable to everything around him. The crisp blue sky, brilliant leaves, the dilapidated repair shop they passed, all triggered different micro moods in him. People's states were always leaking into him, drowning him in feelings. He sometimes suspected he felt their feelings more keenly than they did.

Not so with Faye. Whatever was inside her remained shrouded in fog. Closed up with her, he sensed that mist seeping into the car, blurring his thoughts, bringing on a kind of intoxication. The only way to tell there was anything inside her was from the puffs of heat that occasionally escaped. But maybe that was just him, projecting his own heat. His...desire.

The silence got to be too much. He said, "Who is this boss? And what..."

She set fingertips to his lips, sending shivers down his spine. "Soon."

Her boss. At a gallery? Or some rich art lover. Who wanted to *buy* his masterpiece. *A museum.* A retrospective— Ray of Darkness, the bone period. He laughed.

She asked, "What?"

"Nothing."

This was a young man's pipe dreams. And he wasn't young. How could you move that bathroom, anyway? There were no museums down this way. What was? Old resorts. He'd never played at any, but musician friends had. But that was a long time ago.

He was heading past the town of Catskill when she said, "Is Liz playing that game I downloaded for her?"

"Uh...the iPad one?"

"Core Quest."

"Right. I don't know. I guess." He should own up. And why not? It was *Liz* he was hiding it from. But somehow the words just didn't find their way out of his mouth.

As they approached Kingston, she said, "Turn off here." They headed south on a secondary road, and he took in the scenery.

The flawed gem of Hudson was set in the vast blight of upstate New York. It was like New York City had sucked the juice from the rest of the state, leaving behind husks: shabby towns and broken-down farms. The Ray of Darkness part of him *enjoyed* it.

So he was disappointed to find them cruising down a pleasant valley between rolling hills, past neat stone houses with echoes of old bourgeois Holland. It was boring. There was obviously money here, though he couldn't imagine where it came from, with no visible industry and not even many farms.

As they reached the bottom of Ulster County, a ten-foot gnome statue signaled a turn down-market. Single trailers and compounds with plain white-washed cabins followed. Some of the latter were clearly abandoned, roofs stove in and walls leaking windblown trash. Others were almost as derelict, yet bore signs in Hebrew. He'd heard of these Orthodox Jewish summer camps but thought they were extinct. Apparently not.

They came on a sign, "Grandview Hotel," but the only view from the car was of an expanse of chain-link fence guarding a vast wall of empty windows. One of the old resorts?

They crossed the county line and things went to total shit. Over half of the houses had for sale signs or were plain tumbling down. All the billboards were empty except for barely visible phone numbers, with the desperate legend, "Put your business here!" *I'll get right on that.*

They wound around a curve into the hamlet of Burnwood, overlooked by a steep hill crowned by the razor wire of a prison. It made Hudson's medium security facility look like a country club. The single block of the main street itself looked indictable, every business except two boarded up. The prison was the only sign of life in this ghost town.

The City may have drained the energy from upstate, but this devastation spoke of a more local and lethal malignancy. Was the prison cause or effect? It made him only slightly guilty that the worse things looked, the better they made Ray of Darkness feel. And the anticipation, the mystery of where they were headed was icing on the cake.

They passed through another town, a step above Burnwood, though still clinging to life support. They rounded a bend and an anomaly loomed on the right: a massive office building. They'd passed nothing remotely like it. It was a '60s-era Brutalist box, but in better shape than anything he'd seen in miles. It gleamed with fresh paint.

Faye's voice startled him, "Turn right past this building." The windows were tinted. And, oddly, there was no sign out front with a corporate logo. What business would be out here, anyway? He scrambled to imagine a graphic design shop or museum in the place. Neither fit.

He turned, came around the building, and entered the parking lot in back. There were at least fifty spaces, most filled. This must be a museum. But he would have heard about it. He looked over at Faye. Her smile was a brick wall.

He followed her around the side of the structure and up to the front door. It had hidden in the shadows of a modern portcullis as they drove up. Now that it was visible, it didn't fit the building any more than the building fit the neighborhood.

It was oversized, its oak panels ornately carved and polished to a gleam, with a fat brass knob. It would have been elegant if it wasn't so…exaggerated.

Faye placed a keycard in a reader. A tiny click and she pushed the door open.

He followed her in and stopped cold.

He stood in a round room with a concave ceiling. Gentle light seeped from wall sconces, and there was a comfortable looking couch with teak side tables.

It was an exact replica of the entrance room from the game. The same soothing ambient music played from hidden speakers.

He was not soothed. The muted pastels glared like neon. The music screamed, distorted, like it came through a fuzz box. The floor under his feet was solid oak, but he felt like he'd slipped through a crack in reality and was tumbling head over heels into Crazyville. He grasped for some simple explanation. But that would require a working brain.

A Word from John

Thank you for reading *If I Fell!* And I want to thank everyone who's contributed to its coming into the world: my wife and sons, and all the friends who read the manuscript in various stages of development. Oh, and my dogs.

I'd love it if you could take a moment to write a short review and post it on **Amazon** and/or Goodreads. Reviews help others to discover my series.

Visit www.johnkmanchester.com/free/ to sign up for my newsletter and receive an exclusive FREE Prequel Novella to the Ray of Darkness Series.

Also in the Ray of Darkness Series: *Never Speak*

John Manchester was born in Baltimore, which perhaps explains his early fascination with the works of Edgar Allan Poe. His passion for music led him to a performing career starting at age thirteen in a Beatles imitation band, where he posed as John Lennon in a wig. He later played guitar in a group that toured opening for Linda Ronstadt and Fleetwood Mac. He taught himself to compose and soon made a living at it. His compositions are heard worldwide on TV, radio, and the internet. They were popular for the happy, hopeful feelings they evoked. Wishing to indulge his darker impulses, he taught himself to write. His pieces about the arts, life, and growing up with his late father, the historian William Manchester have been published at Salon.com, Medium.com and on his blog. He's haunted by memories of strange, terrible, and even miraculous things. And so, he transforms them into fiction in the Ray of Darkness series of Deep Psychological Thrillers. After decades in New England, he moved to California with his family. He misses the seasons but not digging his car out of the snow. Sign up for his newsletter or visit his website at www.johnkmanchester.com.

www.ingramcontent.com/pod-product-compliance
Lightning Source LLC
Chambersburg PA
CBHW021434240626
47153CB00001B/142